Between The Darkness And The Light

Chronicles of the Night Book Two

G L Houser

This is a work of fiction. All characters, events, and settings in this book are purely the products of the author's imagination or are used fictitiously. Any resemblance to actual persons, living or dead, is entirely coincidental.

Between the Darkness and the Light, Chronicles of the Night Book Two

Copyright © 2024 by G L Houser

All rights reserved. No part of this publication may be reproduced, distributed, or transmitted in any form or by any means, including photocopying, recording, or other electronic or mechanical methods, without the prior written permission of the publisher or author, except in the case of brief quotations embodied in critical reviews and certain other noncommercial uses permitted by copyright law.

Published by G L Houser

Dedication

"I dedicate this book to all who have supported and believed in me. To my family who have loved, endured, and encouraged me."

The Blackened

The Twisted

Cave
Smoking plains

Forge Warth M
Torn Flowage
The Steps Of Glass

The Vale Lan

Black Sto
Riffs Crossing

Leaf Waters

The Light Land

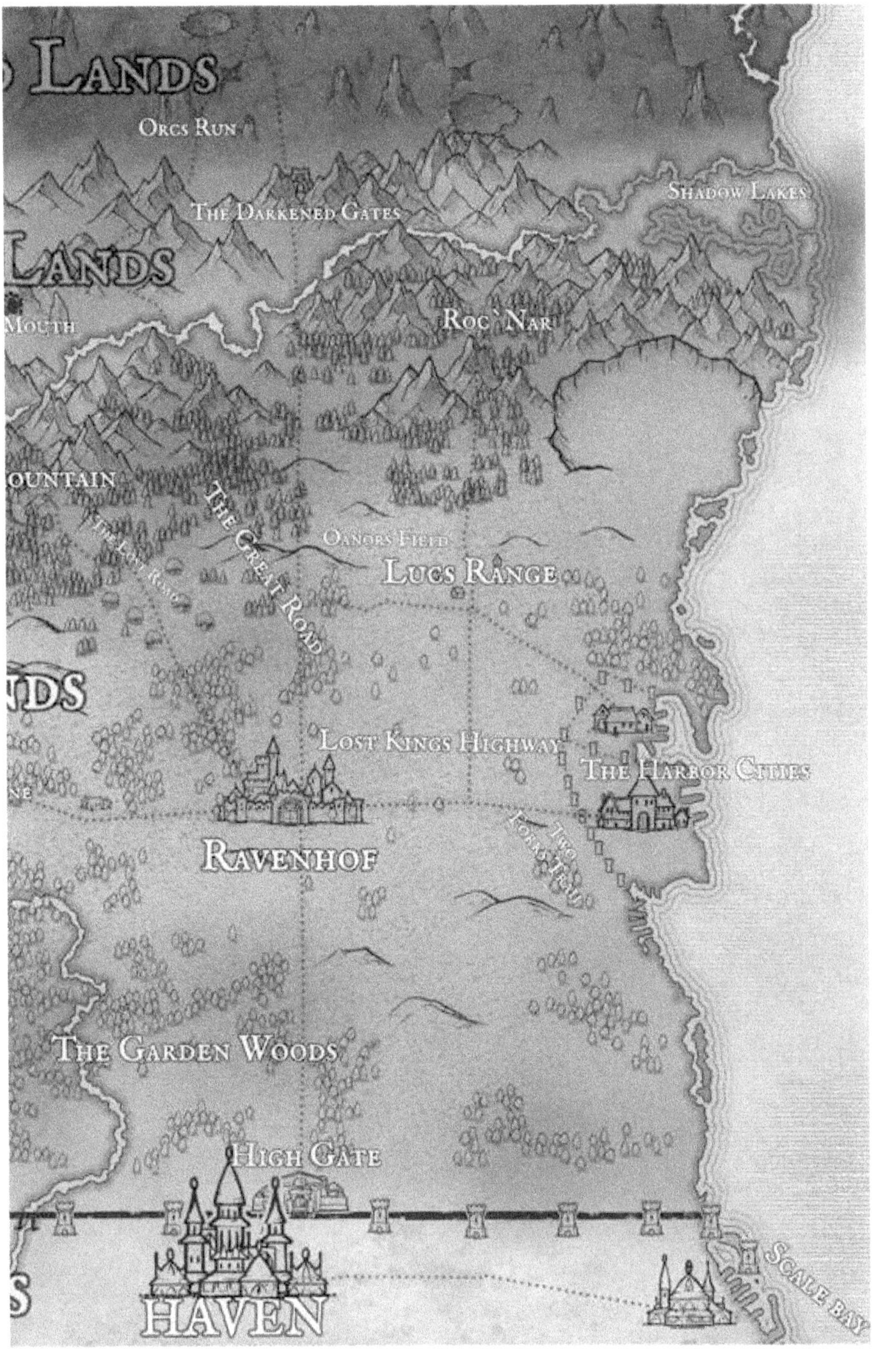
Lands
Orcs Run
The Darkened Gates
Shadow Lakes
Lands
Mouth
Roc`Nar
The Great Road
Lucs Range
Lost Kings Highway
The Harbor Cities
Ravenhof
The Garden Woods
High Gate
Haven
Scale Bay

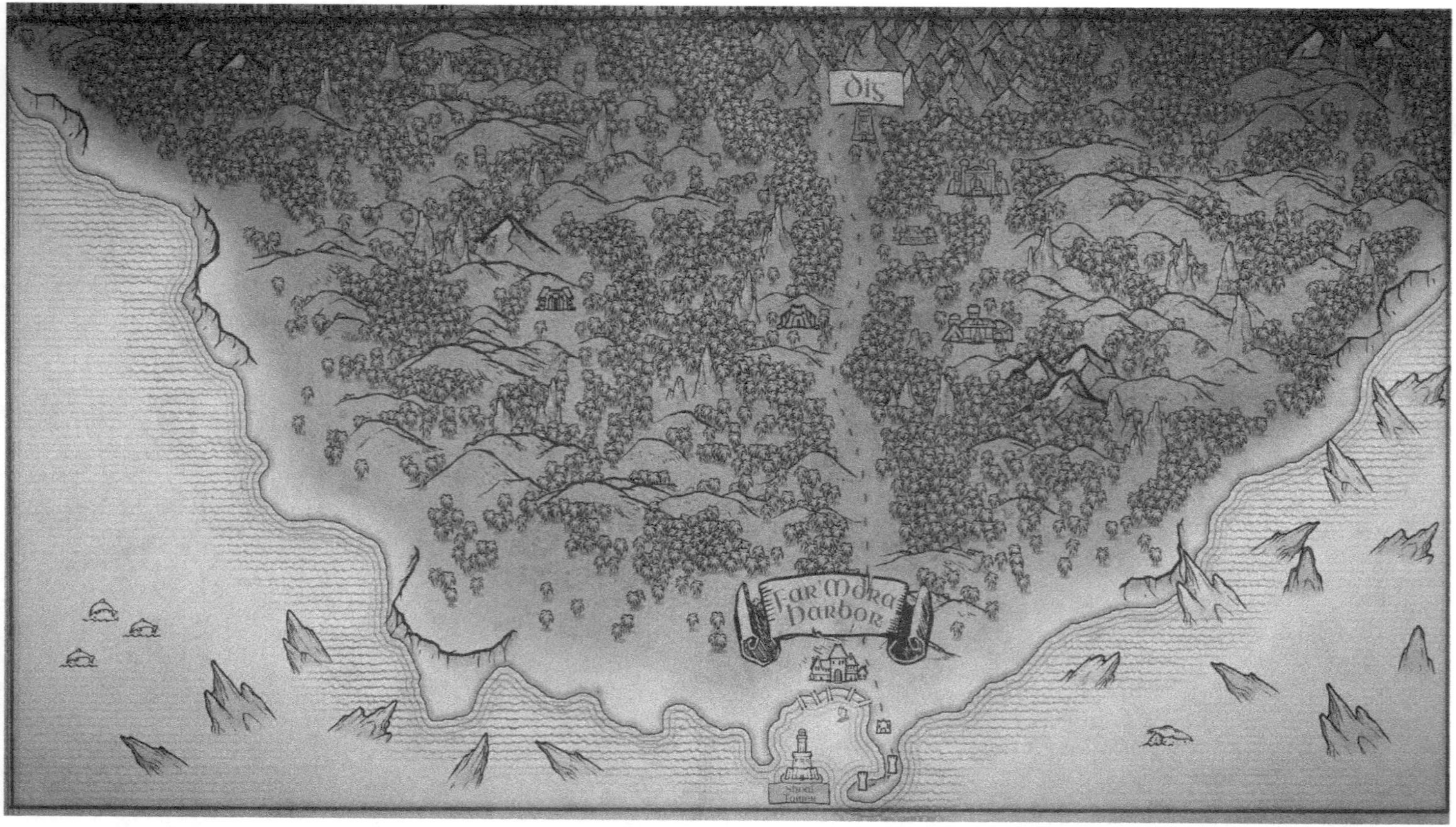
Dis
Far'Mdra
Harbor
Shoal
Tower

Contents

Preface	1
Prologue	3
Chapter 1 Paradise Of Lies	7
Chapter 2 Mistaken Light	17
Chapter 3 Treatise Of Maids	28
Chapter 4 Hath No Fury	41
Chapter 5 Stir Of Shadows	52
Chapter 6 State Of Peace	64
Chapter 7 Whims And Prayers	75
Chapter 8 Veil Asunder	84
Chapter 9 Haven By Knight	95
Chapter 10 Blade And Bone	103
Chapter 11 God Fire	115
Chapter 12 Divided Light	124
Chapter 13 Day Break	131
Chapter 14 Devotions Upended	137

Chapter 15 Darkness Rising	146
Chapter 16 Sea Of Fear	156
Chapter 17 Heart Darkened	166
Chapter 18 Daylight Memory	176
Chapter 19 The Calling	186
Chapter 20 Kings Of Light	194
Chapter 21 Affairs Of Fate	207
Chapter 22 Sea Or Dirt	218
Chapter 23 Maids And Lords	230
Chapter 24 Blood And Blades	239
Chapter 25 Discovery	246
Chapter 26 Overpriced Package	251
Chapter 27 Wraith Walk	261
Chapter 28 Bed Of Stone	269
Chapter 29 Seat Of Pride	276
Chapter 30 Beneath Rocky Dirt	284
Chapter 31 Fearful Visions	291
Chapter 32 Pearls In Shells	300
Chapter 33 Fallen To Sea	307
Chapter 34 Dance Of Shadows	315
Chapter 35 Traps Of Time	325
Chapter 36 God Storm	332
Chapter 37 Holes Beneath	338
Chapter 38 Lost Sister	346
Chapter 39 Gods Enamored	352

Chapter 40 Blood and Sisters	358
Chapter 41 Blood For Blood	364
Chapter 42 Lies Between Sisters	372
Chapter 43 Weary Trumpet's Call	380
Chapter 44 Fealty Or Murder	386
Chapter 45 Feast For Gods	394
Epilogue	399
Afterword	400

Preface

Mission Log: Captain Mark Adams is in command. USS Titan remains in orbit around the smallest planet of the Alpha Centauri system, located 4.3 light-years from Earth. Our quest to decipher the chronicle led us to a cave overlooking a valley, harboring a perplexing anomaly. Neither our scientific knowledge nor our advanced artificial general intelligence (AGI) has unraveled its mysteries. Time's flow appears compressed within this space, and upon entering, we found ourselves in what resembles a lengthy corridor. The potential effects on the human body remain unknown without further investigation. The energy demands to uphold this quantum structure defy comprehension. I am transmitting the complete records of our studies up to this point. USS Titan, out.

Note: Because of the challenges of translating the text, the computer replaces less defined text with human words believed to approximate the meaning, ensuring better understanding on our part. Capitalization of some words is to infer greater meaning, which goes beyond the confines of human language and understanding.

Artificial General Intelligence Interpretation Date: 08/12/2089

The world was in chaos as mortal beings waged war with ancient Powers, disrupting the delicate fabric of creation and pushing it into disharmony. Amidst this turmoil, birth, life, and destruction unfolded. The Mages, wielding the

Powers of Darkness and Light, strained the fabric of creation and shattered the balance.

Driven by greed, the Mages sought to create their own utopia by eliminating the opposing faction and tipping the balance. The fabric of creation couldn't recover faster than the war brought changes, resulting in fractures at the focal point of our reality, tearing it in two.

The mortals on our planet soon discovered the devastating cost of their reckless pursuit of Power. Gods emerged, turning our planet into the primary battleground in their struggle between Darkness and Light.

Our planet became divided into two fronts, with the forces of Darkness and Light clashing on either side, leaving the Grey Area as a purgatory-like demilitarized zone in the middle. The aftermath of this shattered balance left our planet in ruins, with civilization crumbling under its weight. Those who used the arcane Power at the time of the rupture perished.

Among the survivors, those with the talent to wield this Power now sought to restore balance. The Order of the Light aimed to restore the previous equilibrium, while the Order of Darkness sought to overcome the Light entirely and establish a new balance. These two factions conspired against each other, manipulating their followers as pawns in a grand scheme for domination fueled by greed.

The gods influenced the intelligent races of the world, who unleashed horrors with increasing ferocity. Mortals harnessed this Power to create new breeds of beings and adapted existing races, perpetuating an endless struggle. There was no turning back. Ages came and went, civilizations rebuilt on both sides of the conflict, and in the middle between Darkness and Light, people lived, died, and prayed for the balance to be restored.

This passage is a fragment from the lost author's Third Chronicle of the Shattered Age.

Prologue

It was only a dream. We were never in control. Thinking of ourselves as wise, we became fools. Darkness can dwell in the heart, that deep well of rejoicing or despair. Sometimes, we call what is in our heart our world. Darkness entered our world, and we were too blind to see it. Some could see it but had mistaken it for the Light and they fell from the Light. If you mistake Darkness for Light, how great is that Darkness?

A wind rose in the Lands of Light, sweeping across Haven's pristine white walls, cascading into the Garden Wood. The towering trees exhaled, leaves dancing in a frenzied rush. Little Sister, the second sun, ascended above the horizon, painting the treetops from red to pink, then rising into the deep blue of a cloudless spring sky.

Nature's symphony sang, its wonders unfurling as Leatherwings darted among the treetops, their scales catching the light. Hungry chirping calls echoed from the forest as mothers calmed a famished brood hidden amongst the branches. Life's eternal rhythm unfolds. Its majestic dance continues, whether we witness it, or not.

Hammers and saws echoed from RavenHof, their sounds reverberating through the ancient woods. Local men and women worked to rebuild their world, shattered by the Dark Order's attack. The city, with its densely packed buildings of stone and brick capped with tiles, slate, and thatch, bore the scars of devastation—a path of ruin from the broken gate to the shadowed, gothic remnants. Yet, as always, the resilient people of the Gray Area rose, rebuilding upon the old city's foundations. Around them, the remains of Coth'Venter, an ancient ruin encircling RavenHof, stood as a solemn gray reminder of a civilization long gone and the world's former grandeur before the Breaking of the Balance.

Deep within the decaying remnants of Coth'Venter, life breathed again. A Cathedral of Light, once abandoned and foreboding, now nourished hope. From its central square rose a three-tiered fountain with a solitary mounted figure, a Priest Knight, chiseled from the same gray stone. His sword raised high in one hand, and in the other, he held a banner emblazoned with the binary suns. Ram'Del, the long-dead Hero of the Light, still silently gave hope to everyone who passed by. The symbol of Light stood lonely, a defiant beacon against an encroaching Darkness.

To the left of the Cathedral of Light, a cobbled road ran to the rear, leading down below the foundation and opening into the stable yard. A stable of the same architecture rang with a blacksmith's hammer from the open double doors, where a man toiled at the forge and anvil. A large Stinger warhorse stomped impatiently as the smithy fitted it with a steel-clawed shoe.

Above the stable, the silhouette of battlements and two broken towers, wounded relics of ancient conflicts, cut sharply against the sky. Patrols moved with vigilance along the ramparts, where a white-and-gold banner snapped in the breeze. Its emblem is of two dragons, one black and one white, facing a hand holding two lightning bolts. Beyond the wall, waist-high yellow grass rippled with the wind in Dan'Nor's Field flowing out to a thicket bordering the road.

The grand entrance of the cathedral rose dramatically, a cascade of thirty stone steps sweeping upward. From a balcony high above, a young woman's laughter drifted down to the cobblestone square below. Tara danced with Edward, wearing a light blue spring dress that came to her knee and black flats. Her movements were graceful, her head barely reaching Edward's chin. She smiled at him, gazing into Edward's brooding face trimmed in short blonde hair and sea-green eyes. Dressed in black leather britches and a white shirt with puffy sleeves, Edward struggled with the broadsword at his waist, as much as he did with his own feet.

"Pay attention, Edward. I will hum the music, and you lead as I showed you. I can't lead you when we dance for real, you know?" As Tara resumed humming the song, he exhaled slowly. He would do anything to hear her laugh and see her smile. Tara was Edward's world. He smiled down at her, taking the lead as she hummed again. Her dark hair framed a pretty face, white bangs cascading around her shoulders. Tara bore arcane markings that shifted and moved while she used her Power. Others would see the delicate tangle of swirling, deep grey lines etched from the corners of her eyebrows to the peaks of her cheeks, as they vanished down the graceful curves of her neck. The markings were unsettling to look at, scaring the seven hells out of any man who dared.

"I am trying, Tara," Edward's voice cracked, tinged with frustration yet determined. His gaze, vulnerable and intense, held hers—a silent plea for understanding.

She laughed at him again. "You are doing better." He held one of her hands in his and placed his other hand on her waist as they danced, to Tara's delight. There was something else, too.

Tara was a storm, seeing images that others, lacking her talent, could not. Seeing only pale and washed-out visages of true reality. In this world, an eternal war raged between good and evil, between the forces of Light and Darkness. They were opposite poles, forever in battle, each fighting for an advantage while struggling to restore a lost balance. Tara stood amidst this torrent of Power, even as it sought to consume her. Before, she barely held against the Power that tried to absorb her essence. But now, having melded her essence with the dragons, they served as her anchor and as vast reservoirs—one for Light, the other for Darkness. Edward knew about the storm that raged in the woman he loved, the one to whom he would soon give his life's vow. She belonged to him, just as he belonged to her; and for them, nothing else mattered.

On the gray marble balcony, their feet moved in perfect rhythm. Edward had mastered the steps, no longer tripping over his sword. In the past he might have simply removed it, one less obstacle to deal with, but not anymore. Not since the attack by the Dark Order. They had tried to take Tara from him, and that was simply out of the question.

Chapter 1 Paradise Of Lies

"Hope—It is not merely the beginning of a plan. It does not wait when there is need. Hope reaches for suffering now and knows that a future exists where evil deeds are set right, and their damage undone. Hope calls forth heroes, demands truth, and bravely embraces change. In the deepest of oppression, when lost in shadow, we share hope, as whispers from one frail soul to another. Spoken as the first trickle, then a stream, gathering strength until it becomes a mighty river. And when hope swells, it gives birth to a cause. Its judgment flows swiftly, sweeping away greed and Darkness. Ending them, in one last thunderous fall."

Surfaces can often betray appearances, like gift wrapping that falls short of what lies beneath; when opened, it rarely matches our expectations. Lord Lars, atop his white stallion, surveyed Haven, his gold-plated armor etched with silver tracery, a testament to his noble lineage. Under blond-gray hair, his sea-green eyes gleamed with authority and secrets, the lines along his jaw attesting to a life seasoned by experience.

Beneath his imposing exterior lay a secret: a parasitic entity, inhabiting Lars' body, manipulated his identity for its own ends. Though the truth painted a far darker portrait. His true identity was Dem'Endas, a being from the very depths of the Dark Well. The Dark Well was an eternal abyss of gloom and isolation. Within, voices echoed like a tempest of senseless ravings and the screams of the damned. An unending torrent of hopeless pleas cried out for release, sending a shiver through him as the remnants of those memories continued to haunt his mind.

For Dem'Endas, this vessel was his first taste of life, a stark contrast to his desolate existence in the Dark Well. At first, he had feared being discovered by the Order of Light, but that worry had since waned. The religious and militant cult had unraveled itself through the insidious grip of greed. As the ruler of Haven, Lars enjoyed privileges beyond the reach of most in the Order. For countless days and nights, he delved into ancient tomes, each laden with millennia-old records, each page bearing the weight of epochs. Forgotten histories had transformed into legends and myths, and therein lay the crucial truth.

Gods, beings of immense Power, shaped reality with sheer will and vast imagination. Despite their immortality, these beings weren't exempt from the complexities of morality and conflicting ethical perspectives. Just like mortals, they grappled with internal struggles. Their desires, hopes, and fears wove into the fabric of reality, continually reshaping time and creation. Mortals who aligned themselves with these gods reaped Power, driven by the desire to mold reality as they pleased, obliterating the old order.

This relentless war for control eventually ruptured the delicate balance. The Power of creation tore the fabric asunder. Choosing to withdraw, the gods entered a deep slumber, refraining from direct interference. They sought to restore balance while subtly influencing the world through their loyal servants. Divided into Darkness and Light, the gods allowed talented mortals to choose sides, while the rest of mortality prayed for balance to be restored.

The problem lay with the greedy beings within the Order of the Light, who sought to seize the Power of a dormant god. She abandoned them to their Darkness. Within the records, Dem'Endas recalled her last message, word for word:

"What shall I say to you? How can I say it? Shall I recount the frigid ages of my solace? That you shattered a heart of gold, yet not a single tear stained your cheeks. I shall have none of you. Until the day you turn and declare your allegiance to the Maid of Light. My silence shall remain unbroken. Your cries shall echo through the desolate halls of the Darkness that consumed you. But if you turn toward me and acknowledge my presence, I shall turn towards you. Yes, even I, the Maid of Light, shall turn toward you and answer your call. Let all the heavens tremble and

the foundations of El'idar roar, and may the Darkness flee from your sight, for the radiant glory of the Light shall burst forth in a Priest Knight once more!" And there was the issue: The Maid of Light had found that Priest Knight in Antoff Grant.

Dem'Endas found himself entangled in the whole mess. He had framed his host's son, Edward, for murder and banished him. Planning to use the young man's body next—as he had the proper lineage to inherit the throne. Despite ensuring he had enough coin to indulge himself, the lad still joined forces with an ex-Priest Knight named Antoff Grant. The Light's own bishopric excommunicated Grant for claiming to serve the Maid of Light. After stealing her Power, they tried to erase all memory of who the Maid of Light was, and if Grant was openly proclaiming himself for her, it would create problems.

Yet hope still kindled, fueled by the prospect that Dem'Endas might persuade the bishopric to hand over his son, thus buying time for the possession. Yes, there would be a matter of clearing the boy's name, but he had the means to find a '*volunteer*' to take the blame and clean it up for the young Lord to assume the throne. Yet if all failed, he could sire another heir. The time it would take to raise him would be unfortunate; his host was feeling the stress of sharing his life force. With the proper incentive, they could overcome even that, and there was always someone willing to share their life's sweet energy for the right price.

Compelled to serve the Dark Order he despised, Dem'Endas cleaved to this mortal vessel. He was firm in his decision, confidently declaring to himself, *I will keep this vessel*. The bishopric had issued an order for the capture of the heretic Antoff Grant, to be brought before them in chains, along with any others who refused to repent. Dem'Endas desired to expedite this task as soon as possible.

The rhythmic sound of hoofbeats heralded an approaching messenger. Dem'Endas leaned closer in his saddle, turning his gaze toward the page who rode beside him. "Yes, what is it?" he inquired. The page, intimidated by Lord Lars Haven's distinguished features—gray-blonde hair tied back with a red ribbon and the rugged contours of his face already revealing stubble—seemed hesitant to share the news. Impatient, Dem'Endas urged the lad to speak. "Well? Out with it!"

After a moment's stammering, the page relayed the information coherently. "A force attacked RavenHof, my Lord, at least fifteen hundred minions from the Dark Order. The city is in flames! This message comes from the City Master two days ago. The Priest Knights and Clerics of the Light fought valiantly, their

Powers shining like the gods. Two dragons engaged the horde in battle, my Lord! The City Master sent me to request aid."

"What nonsense is this?" A cleric riding next to him exclaimed, his voice filled with disbelief.

Taking a deep breath, the page continued with his account. "It is true, my Lord. I witnessed it myself—the sky turned blood-red, and powerful energy surged down from above, striking the attackers. Dragons unleashed their fiery breath upon those attempting to breach the city walls. Zoruks caused significant destruction in RavenHof, my Lord."

A skeptical scoff escaped the cleric's lips, but Dem'Endas silenced him with a swift, upraised hand. "Ride back to RavenHof and inform the City Master that we are already en route and will arrive soon." The page swiftly turned his horse and galloped back towards RavenHof.

"Fanciful exaggerations and ridiculous tales!" the cleric scoffed. "Every time something occurs in the Gray Area, the stories become more extravagant. It's fortunate that we were already on our way to apprehend the heretic."

Dem'Endas let out a sigh, indulging in a moment of ironic appreciation. "Yes. How fortunate." With a nod to the cleric, Dem'Endas spurred his horse forward, his mind already racing with plans for RavenHof.

As the song wove its way toward its last notes, Antoff Grant took center stage in his battered armor of a Priest Knight of the Light. His solid build, piercing ice-blue eyes, and chestnut brown hair tied in a leather knot at his neck all spoke of his seasoned experience as a Warrior of the Light. The assembly's attention shifted to him, eagerly awaiting his words. Before him stood the grand Gothic temple, its gray stone and dark marble evoking awe and inspiration. The air was cool and damp after the rain, adding to the solemn atmosphere within the vast temple hall. The icy air sharpened his mind, deepening his sense of devotion.

The nave stretched out before him, its vaulted ceiling disappearing into darkness high above. Slender columns rose from the floor, adorned with intricate carvings and reaching upward to the arches above. Fluted columns beautifully contrasted with the dark marble floor, creating a feeling of depth reflecting the eternal.

Sunlight streamed through the windows, casting vibrant hues and dancing colors on the dark marble floor. Delicate patterns, depicting scenes of heroic battles and mercy, gilded the windows, adding depth to the feeling of religious devotion.

Antoff's gaze followed the delicate carvings up to where an elaborate network of overlapping arches defined the cathedral's majestic height. They adorned the vaults with delicate arrangements carved into the stone, symbolizing sacrifice and redemption.

Statues and reliefs decorated the temple walls, depicting clerics, Priest Knights , and EL'ALue—the god of Light. Their stone forms came alive in the shifting light, expressions ranging from serene to righteous rage, evoking emotions within even the most stalwart observer.

The hall filled with uplifted voices, echoing against the stone. The sound reverberated through the grand hall, adding to the gravity of the space.

Ending in a chant, the song leaving only a ringing silence. Antoff began, "We engaged the forces of the Dark Order here, outside of this very Cathedral of Light. You have seen things that have not been reported for generations of our order."

"How can this be? Truth. The Light is truth and love. The Light compels me to explain it to you simply. Our clergy has misled us, those with access to the truth. Content to indulge in wealth and opulence, considered sinful for anyone who does not hold their rank or privilege. And in all this excess, the one thing you do not see is the gifts that come from humble service. The gifts that come from truly knowing a god of Light—the gifts you felt in the charge before a vast host when your blinding Light threw them back."

Al'len sat spellbound. Her long blonde hair flashed the color of hay in the daylight streaming in from the windows. She wore light tan leather from head to toe, a white cloak trimmed in gold and a beautiful long sword belted on her hip held in place by a buckle bearing a white dragon. Watching Antoff, absorbed by his Power with simple words. She loved him; everyone knew that. The clerics and Priest Knights gave up on the idea that she was just a ranch hand here to care for the beasts the first time they caught sight of her defending the top of the battlements. She was more than that, and they knew it. They did not know how much more.

Antoff continued, "They taught you EL'ALue is neutral in gender, save for male in battle." The female Priest Knights shifted uncomfortably during that part, as they always did. "They taught you that females can hold the rank of Priest Knight and no higher, denying access to the canonical text to everyone below the station of Diocesan. Indeed, until you reach the rank of bishop, access to our complete history is forbidden. Why? The lack of transparency tells the truth. Something is hidden.

"We are of the Order of the Light. Light does not hide, it does not cower in the truth, and cannot be diminished by Darkness. It is a revealing force."

Murmurs ran through the companions seated on the stone benches. "Antoff, what are you saying?" Mel'Anor, a large cleric, yelled from the rear so all could hear. Others took up the call demanding to know.

EL'ALue the goddess listened in her slumber.

Antoff called back to him, his voice thundered with divine Power, "Mel'Anor, you said in the days of old, the entities that had hidden in vessels would flee at your sight!" Then he whispered and yet still carried throughout the hall. "But you got weaker, and they are stronger. How can this be Mel'Anor? Either the Light has grown weaker, which I will not believe, or you have grown weaker in the Light. We all have become weaker in the Light because we lack one thing: the truth about the Light we serve."

Antoff pointed up toward the vaulted ceiling. "Every morning, the suns come up and shed Light upon our world, and we do not question if these will rise the next day. For each day they rise, and we trust in them to shine. But if those suns do not rise, how can we look toward morning? How can we trust in their Light?"

Antoff pointed at Tes'sus, a young female Priest Knight, who stood to be recognized. You asked, concerning Tara, "If this girl is neither chosen to serve the Light nor Darkness, why should we intervene in the outcome? Will fate not choose the course?" And yet you knew the Light must confront the Darkness. So, you are here. All of you came here. The Light dispels the Darkness. We have all basked in that Light, which until now, was but a myth and legend. It is because of whom we serve. This is the truth. The one that will have you flogged, at the very least, or hung if you are unwilling to deny it.

Antoff's voice, a blend of conviction and vulnerability, filled the grand hall. His ice-blue eyes, usually steadfast, now bore a hint of righteous rage. "EL'ALue is neither neutral nor male. EL'ALue is the Maid of Light," he declared, his gaze sweeping across the assembly. He paused, feeling the weight of their gazes upon him, the weight of his truth.

Al'len met his eyes, her expression a mixture of pride and concern. The clerics and knights were all on their feet arguing with each other, yelling at Antoff, but his voice thundered. Antoff reached towards them, his hand sweeping the length of the stone benches. "If you could believe me. Can you not also believe the ones that you know were there?"

That question brought silence, except for the sound of footfalls echoing down the hall. Her beauty was a bewitching fusion of shadowy allure and unrivaled elegance, a presence that left onlookers breathless in her wake. A cloak of midnight black, form-fitting silk cascaded around her form, accentuating every graceful curve. She is not proud, but humble. She came and stood next to Antoff. "You all know who I am: De'Nidra, the Daughter of Shadows. I would have destroyed any of you, all of you, to save Tem'Aldar." All the companions sat again, all but one. He stood to be recognized. De'Nidra continued. "It was me. I destroyed Ram'Del, the Hero of the Light, long before any of you were born."

She looked at Al'len, hesitating until Al'len inclined her head. And then it came like a flood. "I served the Order of Darkness, and they commanded me to destroy him by withholding his lieutenant an extra day so the reinforcements he needed to fight a battle did not arrive in time to save Ram'Del or the Army of the Light." She pointed, "Tem'Aldar is that lieutenant." The knights and clerics yelled at Tem'Aldar, 'Speak!' and he did.

"I am Lieutenant Tem'Aldar of the First Order of the Light. I served under Captain Ram'Del, whom you call the Hero of the Light," he pointed toward the front of the cathedral, his voice broke, "whose likeness haunts me from this very square. My oath was to EL'ALue, the Maid of Light, whom I have beheld with my own eyes." However, those eyes never left Al'len.

Antoff intoned, "You have spoken the truth. Please, take a seat." He motioned to them with a sweeping gesture, and De'Nidra settled beside Tem'Aldar. "Now we have that out of the way and can choose to believe it or not. There is more. I have not said everything. The Order of the Light became desperate before the Breaking of the Balance, using both the Power of Light and Darkness to create new beings. Later, they stole children from the Under City." He pointed downward. "Here below. Vam'Phire, you think them evil because our clergy says to destroy them; they are malevolent and dwell in Darkness. It was our science in a time of madness that made them so. Destroying them was to cover up our shame. They were mortal, like us, before we corrupted their lineage. Then we sought to use them to mix their essence with other things of dark lineages, evils pulled from other realms. We used our creations as vessels, injecting the souls of our fallen heroes. Then sent them to infiltrate the Dark Order and destroy them from within. You have met Ivan, a Half-Dead, a construct of our Orders creation. These creations failed and were consumed by the evil of the Dark lineage of their host. All but Ivan. He is a dead hero brought back, and he does not know his real name or history. We should honor him and not reject him."

"Finally, now that we've addressed this history and you have the choice to believe it or not, there's more I need to reveal. If you want to, you can return to Haven, go back to your units, and for those of you who are already retired, your rectory. You can deny what I have told you here, and you can be safe living in this world of lies. Or you can be what I am: a heretic for the sake of the truth. A heretic who is to be hanged when they find out what I have told you here today. I swear to you by EL'ALue, the Maid of Light, that my witness is true. And I thank you for hearing my confession before the Light, in Truth, and Love." He made the sign for the Light with his fingers and an up-raised gauntleted right hand. Antoff had left them stunned.

With that, Antoff and Al'len left the dais, leaving the assembly in a buzz of murmurs. Al'len exchanged knowing glances with a few Priest Knights as they walked out, while others shot skeptical looks at their companions. The murmurs grew louder, and the hall was alive with a mixture of disbelief and curiosity.

Mist emerged gracefully from the shadows, her petite form gliding through the darkness of the hall. Behind her trailed the remnants of smoky spiderwebs, tethering her to the pooling blackness. Extending her bat-like wings, she stretched her weary muscles before elegantly folding them against her back, creating the illusion of a deep brown cloak. As she descended through the lower halls, she navigated the inner radius of a spiral staircase, her fingers clutching the rusty metal rail, guiding her descent of ten floors. While a simpler route to the lower portal room existed, this one wouldn't accommodate her master's Dominion form. Yet, her curiosity burned like a relentless flame, a hunger to unravel the mysteries hidden within the portal's depths. This fervor only intensified after her audacious theft of the key and the book from Ivan's grasp in the Cathedral of Light.

Trapped in this old Bastion of Light since before the tearing, her master was eager for the portal to operate. Ever since the Torrent opened the small compression portal, any being of a certain size could come and go freely, as long as they were not undead. However, the Dominion was far too large to fit through. Her clawed feet made a clicking as they touched the stone tiles of the main portal room, where a colossal double arch sat within a round depression, ten spans wide. The arch seemed to rest on a ball embedded in the metal floor of the device, and a thin line separated the top of the sphere from the depression's metal, barely visible to the naked eye. Directly across from the portal, there was a rectangular area filled with fine black sand, level with the floor tiles.

With slender fingers, Mist retrieved and opened the book, her gaze fixed on its single, thick page adorned with arcane symbols. Her brow furrowed in concentration as she puzzled over the cryptic script. The page had a metallic texture, and its contents seemed to shift and scroll, although she couldn't comprehend the language. It was unmistakably an instruction book, accompanied by images depicting the sandbox and the arches. She reached for a necklace featuring a tear-drop crystal, which emitted a flickering light. A realization dawned on her: the book required magic to function.

Footsteps crunching on the tiles echoed through the main hall connected to the portal room. Mist's instinct was to flee. However, she decided instead to kneel and await her master's arrival.

From the shadows emerged the menacing Dominion, its enormous wings stretching wide as it advanced. Mist's heart raced as she watched the colossal figure move closer, her fingers trembling around the book and amulet she held. With an air of command, the Dominion reached out its massive hand for Mist to speak. The stone tile splintered beneath the Dominion's weight, and Mist's gaze flickered between the items and the creature before her. Her mind raced with curiosity and uncertainty. Its eyes glowed with a demonic red hue, radiating intellect. Seeing she was hiding something. The Dominion's voice reverberated with command, a guttural and demonic tone. "Speak!"

Mist replied in the same language. "My master, I have retrieved the items you requested."

She unfolded her hands to reveal the dark metal book and amulet, all while keeping her gaze fixed on the floor. The Dominion moved to her and extended its colossal hand, prompting Mist to respond in kind. "Rise."

Reluctantly, Mist handed over the items, placing them in the Dominion's hand. The palm was the size of a saddle with long thick fingers ending in dagger-like pointed nails. "You have done well. I shall consider an appropriate reward. You may leave." She yearned to stay and observe what he would do with the items and how the portal would function. But she knew he lacked the magic. However, with his abundance of gold and gems, all he needed was a single powerful and greedy mage.

Chapter 2 Mistaken Light

"Search everything, except nothing, discover motives. Your interests, tests, or critical review do not disturb the truth. This is the act of shining the Light, the separation of lies. Darkness is the deception that obscures, divides, and tries to hide all that should be in plain sight."

It was early morning and Tara's footsteps echoed through the dormitory, a stark contrast to the quiet, hollow emptiness that clung to the halls. From a distance, the rhythmic hammering of a smithy shaping a horseshoe broke the silence. The coolness of the stone permeated the air, drifting through the stillness like tendrils. Skin prickled, forming fear bumps as much from the cold as excitement for the upcoming ceremony. She wore a blue spring dress and black flats. Her onyx hair tumbled down her back, spilling over her shoulders. Thoughtlessly, she brushed away the white bangs that had fallen into steel-grey eyes.

Tara called out, hope in her voice. "Cur'Ra?"

"I am here, child," a voice replied, filled with warmth and maternal care.

Tara walked down the hall past two sleeping cells next to Cur'Ra's. A mature female Elp'har, in the prime of her beauty, smelled of rosewood and lavender. Her hair appeared dark and wet from washing and her skin tanned, kissed by the sun. She wore britches, and a blouse made of earth tones. Her green eyes took Tara in.

There was deep and old wisdom there, but also the intuition of a motherly type weighing a child with interest.

Tara exhaled a breath she hadn't realized she'd been holding, her chest tightening. "Edward and I are giving our life vows soon, and normally I would ask my mother and father to give me to him, but Antoff is giving the vows, and Al'len, I ask to witness. I saved the place of the mother for the person who I know has loved me in that way. I wanted to ask you to give me to Edward, as you are the only one who can." Her eyes blinked away tears that trailed down her cheeks.

Cur'Ra shook her head, touched by Tara's sincerity. "You should know there was never any question. Of course, I am giving you to Edward," she chirped, opening her arms. Tara reached and Cur'Ra enfolded her. "It won't get you out of your lessons, at least not for more than a day."

Tara sniffed at that, still enfolded in Cur'Ra's warmth, and then laughed. It came out in a rush and the tightness in her chest was gone.

"Learning to heal goes beyond merely mending a broken body, don't you think?" Cur'Ra said with an expectant smile. Her green eyes held a spark of mystery and a touch of mischief.

"What do you mean?" Tara breathed, stepping back, interested in new knowledge.

"Healing brings more than physical recovery; it fosters a complete state of being. You and Edward are exchanging life vows. The process will merge you into one soul forever. Wholeness. The lessons I taught you give you access to the flows of life," Cur'Ra explained. She hesitated before adding, "And those threads of life will let you sense his emotions and his heart's deepest desires."

Tara thought about it for a moment, then raised an eyebrow. "Won't he mind?"

"No, child, he won't," Cur'Ra laughed.

Tara thought about the advantages of knowing Edward's emotions and his most intimate desires. Understanding dawned on Tara's face. She blushed, resisting the urge to cover her mouth and laugh. "Oh... I see! I will make sure I attend my lessons, Mother."

"I thought you might, child." Cur'Ra's eyes held a twinkle and a curl of amusement, touching the corners of her lips.

Rising defiantly from the heart of desolation, the fortress of Are'Amadon stood as a testament to the enduring might of Darkness. It stood solitary amidst the vast expanse of blackened earth, its shadow casting a foreboding presence across leagues of murky soil. Below, the Zoruks toiled like a menacing swarm in the vast fields, where meager crops struggled to grow. Wind-blown banners, once symbols of the Zoruks tribes, now hung tattered and shredded, marking the boundaries of a wicked, barbaric, and territorial society.

Great Lord Amorath's withered hand gripped a twisted staff. Weariness had settled into his bones. His right hip bore the burden of a painful limp. The staff, once a cherished artifact of mages, now bore the scars of its malevolent purpose, its once-proud form twisted and blackened. A single large crystal embedded within it flickered with Power. These arcane devices were designed to store and unleash energy, amplifying the abilities of a Mage beyond their natural limits. But today, it served a different purpose—for Amorath to use as a walking stick. His undead form walked slowly, draped in a black silk robe and a leather overcoat etched with intricate arcane symbols in gold—markings of his sinister craft. His shriveled, gray legs displayed telltale signs of necrotizing degeneration, with the flesh slowly flaking away in grotesque decay. Amorath gazed at his deteriorating limbs, a twisted smile crawling across his gray, lifeless face.

Someone waited and listened, but Amorath dismissed their presence as insignificant. "It may be time to pay a visit to the slave quarter again," he murmured, his voice a chilling whisper. "Yes, long overdue. The spectacle of witnessing life's energy being drained from someone in their lowly station inspires fear and compels others to toil harder." He waved his hand as if answering an unvoiced question. "Ah yes, the tedium of protocol. I shall, of course, make a proper show of it. I will speak to the Task Master, allowing him to point out one or two individuals for my pleasure. The prospect of being chosen can be a potent motivator." Amorath's lips curled into a bitter smile. "How pitiful that lifespan conversion has plummeted so drastically. In the days before the Shattering, a slave with thirty years remaining could sustain me for at least half that time. But now," he breathed out a long sigh, "I am fortunate to extract a single year from every five."

He exhaled. It was more of a dry wheeze, really. Nothing could bring Amorath pleasure any longer. His chambers, a blend of dark opulence and decay, exuded an unsettling aura of malevolence and impending death. The rough-hewn volcanic stone walls adorned with tapestries depicting forgotten battles, and the oversized fireplace emitted an unnaturally comforting light. Its raised hearth seemed to mock the warmth he once felt. Dark drapery adorned the windows and balcony door, suffocating the feeble traces of light that dared to intrude.

"Great Lord?" A voice bid admittance to his thoughts.

Amorath turned, and in his view was the person of the rank of middle mage. "Rem'Mel." He said his name as if it tasted rotten. His eyes brushing the form of the middle mage with disgust—figure neither completely useless nor truly powerful. The red robe he wore, expensive and ostentatious, far exceeded his worth, while the arcane symbols etched upon his shaved head resembled the crude scribblings of a child attempting magic before the Breaking of the Balance. "Speak!" Amorath snapped, his patience waning as quickly as his decaying form.

"Great Lord, the child has embraced Darkness as his chosen discipline and is swiftly gaining Power." The middle mage informed, his voice trembling with a mix of fear and reverence.

Amorath's dead eyes sparkled with anticipation. The child would need to grow immensely powerful before becoming a vessel for Amorath's essence, enabling him to transcend his decaying form. "Very good, Rem'Mel," Amorath crooned, his voice laced with cruel satisfaction. "You may go." He waved him away dismissively with a graying hand.

Lord Modred, '*The Great Black Demon of Legend,*' stood beside a black high-backed chair festooned with intricately carved demon-headed armrests. The chair's wings spread wide, extending beyond his head's height. Normally, a blazing fire illuminated the room from a hearth crafted from black volcanic stone. However, today, the over-hot atmosphere left only a single lamp to cast shadows on the gray stone walls. Heat radiated from the open balcony, and on the gray marble mantle above the fireplace, he displayed his prized possessions—bonded leather books with arcane markings. Before them lay an ancient book, aged and darkened, open on a large slate map table. Using forms of Power, the table constructed a three-dimensional landscape made of fine black sand, forming a map of Coth'Venter. The Cathedral of Light rose molded of the black sand in every detail, and on it, a glyph blinked mockingly at him.

Lord Modred strode toward the large open door, revealing a balcony overlooking the heart of the Blackened Land. From the tallest tower of his sprawling fortress, he placed his hands on the sun's hot rail. His fingers stroked its surface, weathered smoothly, after ages of blowing sand. He surveyed the leagues beyond. Tents and banners bearing Zoruk's tribal symbols fluttered in the breeze, scattered across the black and red soil of the plains below. The sight resembled thousands of insects toiling. He twisted his mouth in disgust.

How was he supposed to locate the treacherous rats who had infiltrated the Dark Order? De'Nidra, the Daughter of Shadows, had held a position on the Dark Council, yet she had betrayed them all. Word had already reached him. She had joined forces with the Torrent, the same group that had eluded him during his attack on the Cathedral of Light. That failure had nearly cost him his life. If it had not been for De'Nidra's exposure as the traitor she was, he would be nothing more than a lifeless husk, withering away beneath the tower. Now, he had to uncover De'Nidra's spy network, untangle her intricate web of plans, and identify her agents.

Results needed to come swiftly now; otherwise, Great Lord Amorath would drain him dry and leave his desiccated remains hanging, frowning from the tower. The first step was to have Ja'eam, the tradesman, interrogate the City Master of RavenHof to gather information. He harbored a fervent desire to eliminate the Daughter of Shadows for her involvement in his past failures, in which he was certain she had a hand. However, the time for vengeance had not yet arrived. If he could only infiltrate her ranks and keep a watchful eye on her, she could lead him straight to her accomplices. But he could not employ a possessed individual for this task. Priest Knights and Clerics of the Light had revived an ancient source of Power from a god of Light. The infiltrator would have to be someone truly loyal to the Dark Order. The question remained: who would that person be?

Great Lord Amorath had gained something from the witch before she abandoned the Dark Order. Lord Lars Haven and his escort of Priest Knights should quickly deal with all of them. They should be safely back within the walls of Haven, with his prisoners heading for the gallows before a five day was out. One good turn from the Daughter of Shadows before her departure.

Perhaps Be'elota has a solution. He thought. Lord Modred spread his massive bat-like wings, stretched his corded muscles, and leaped from the balcony. He slowly spun the circumference of the lofty tower, letting the winds beat at him on the way down, and landed inside the sunbaked square surrounded by soaring battlements and towers made of the same volcanic stone. He passed through a weathered blackwood gate reinforced with dark, ancient metal, then turned left into a tower descending into the dungeon's depths. This was the place where Master Tormenter Be'elota worked. The lies he told were truly a work of art, a thing of legend, as he twisted tales of freedom to the souls of the broken, wretched, and damned. Fools who struck a deal with this fabled master of torture would provide a home for entities of Darkness.

The sweet screams of his interests cried out for mercy in an unending wash of misery. "Epic work, Be'elota!" Lord Modred exclaimed as he caught sight of Master Tormenter Be'elota's tall, twisted form. Be'elota held a hook in his overly elongated fingers, his thin arm reaching toward his work. "This poor fool of a Priest Knight chained to the floor is thinking himself brave," Lord Modred mused.

Be'elota's voice became deep and menacing. "Lord Modred, to what do I owe the privilege of the company of The Great Black Demon of Legend?" he cackled wildly, removing any doubt that he had lost his mind long ago. If he had ever had it.

"I hope you can help with some people associated with the Priests of the Light. Be'elota, this has to be done delicately and without the benefit of possession. I hope you understand," Lord Modred said.

Be'elota's laughter echoed once more, a chilling sound that underlined his madness. "Without the benefit of possession, my Lord?"

Lord Modred interjected. "Yes, no possession," he confirmed. "Priest Knights with Antoff Grant and the Torrent have regained much of their order's old potency. I am sorry to report, and so possession, regrettably, is out of the question," Lord Modred explained.

"Pity," Be'elota smiled down at the Priest Knight, who was squatting over a pot on the floor where he was chained. "I will keep you informed of my progress, Lord Modred. I believe we will have to move this one's lessons up a notch to get the cooperation you are looking for," Be'elota said. He tossed his hook into a brazier of sizzling coals and pulled from it a long red-hot needle that smoked under his examination. Horror filled the captive's face. Lord Modred left to the sounds of rapturous screams.

The Cathedral of Light was alive with activity. Edward trained Tara's volunteer guards in the square, rallying them at the familiar mustering point beside Ram'Del's statue. Arrows whistled and thumped into burlap targets backed by wooden tripods. And the clacks of men and women in mock combat using wooden swords resounded around the cobblestone square. These people represented both family and friends. They were a people drawn from the ranks of the hopeful poor.

Fifty light cavalry maneuvered in complex formations, their broad spears aligning at the same angle and round shields at the ready, as they practiced quick reformations before a charge.

Edward, clad in smoked plate mail, trained the cavalry. Meanwhile, Lieutenant Tem'Aldar demonstrated sword forms with the guards, showcasing techniques to shoulder under blows and move past a line of attackers. There were two hundred training on the cobblestone and an additional thirty on watch on the cathedral grounds.

Tara leaned over the balcony high above the square, her gaze fixed on the training below. With a sigh, she glanced at Mic'Ieal, the First of Her Guard, who stood in the background, ever vigilant. Sandy hair framed his face, and a thumbprint-sized glyph, symbolizing Light, adorned his forehead. His lanky frame clad in simple attire—a gray shirt and brown britches, accented by a light gray cloak trimmed with silver dragons. Two large daggers hung from his hips. Tara turned her attention to him, resting her elbows on the balcony rail as she spoke. "Mic'Ieal, you don't have to be by my side constantly. If you have other duties, I understand." She hoped her words conveyed her desire to be alone with her thoughts of Edward, rather than feigning interest in troop training—Which she had to do so long as he was there.

Mic'Ieal smiled indulgently, "My Lady Tara, you know I cannot."

She breathed out a long sigh. "I was afraid you were going to say that."

Below in the cathedral, the Clerics and Priest Knights of the Lights armed and armored in silvery plate mail. These were not monks or elevated clergy, these were Warriors of the Light, both old and young. Of the original fifty-five that had ridden out from Haven with Antoff Grant, there were fifty-three. Two lost in the battle, but more saved. Some of the heavy horse riders that had been part of the attack were formerly Priest Knights taken during the campaigns. They had been tortured and then possessed. Used as vessels of dark entities to fight against the Order of the Light. Seven of these men and women were recovered including Tem'Aldar, bringing their number to sixty, with Antoff Grant. None had left following Antoff's confession, and none would. They had taken each other's council and understood the price of their choice. How could they deny the Power of his confession? The Power of EL'ALue, the Maid of Light, had surrounded them. Now they, like Antoff, were all heretics in the eyes of the church.

Ja'eam harbored a secret, one even his wife and children were unaware of. Almost a month ago, he set out on a journey to the Harbor Cities, but he never reached his destination. Instead, he was captured by an agent of the Dark Order. Under the custody of the capable Master Tormenter Be'elota, Ja'eam found himself sharing his body with a resident named Sam'Ieal, who was determined to maintain control and preserve his newfound host.

The unsettling reality of this arrangement manifested itself through seemingly trivial observations. Sam'Ieal noticed peculiar behaviors, such as his foot tapping to a melody or whistling while walking. These actions, though innocuous to most, troubled Sam'Ieal because they were not his own. The fact he was not entirely in control of his own body signaled a problem. Unbeknownst to Ja'eam, he was subconsciously exerting influence over the vessel that was meant solely for Sam'Ieal.

According to Be'elota, the agreement stipulated Sam'Ieal had to provide Ja'eam with unhindered time with his family, while refraining from any actions that would cause them harm. However, the challenge lay in the fact Ja'eam, the host, had the authority to interpret what constituted harm, rather than Sam'Ieal. Consequently, minor issues began to interfere with Sam'Ieal's ability to fulfill the tasks assigned by his Dark Order handler. One such task involved infiltrating the ranks of the disadvantaged individuals seeking refuge with Lady Tara's service. Unfortunately, since being absent from home within the agreed-upon period would violate the agreement, Sam'Ieal could not carry out his mission.

Be'elota claimed problems could arise when he didn't have sufficient time to prepare the host. Sam'Ieal believed this was precisely the issue with Ja'eam's case. However, mentioning this difficulty to his handler would result in his host being taken away, and Sam'Ieal being replaced by a 'stronger personality'. Meaning they would banish him, sending him back to the hellhole known as the Dark Well. *Okay, I am not going back there again. That will not happen! You can believe that!* He told himself, the fear of the memories crawling within like worms.

Struggling for control, he kept an eye on the Torrent as often as he could. Sam'Ieal had taken on tasks such as arranging for his wagon to be used for grain deliveries to the ancient Cathedral of Light. He also engaged in trading and repair work, but struggled to go beyond the confines of a normal day's work due to his circumstances. He had even haunted the local inn and watched Tara, but that was about all he could do.

Today, he received a new assignment and walked there. The City Master had been an asset of De'Nidra, the Daughter of Shadows, and a high-powered Lord of the Dark Order was trying to determine whether the City Master had a larger role in De'Nidra's schemes or knew to a greater degree the other contacts involved in her plans. In short, the Dark Order tasked Sam'Ieal with making contact and convincing this asset to work for them. Their goal was to uncover all the hidden leaks within the organization. It all sounded easy enough when you said it that way, but Sam'Ieal thought that the possibility of meeting this legendary spinner of webs, De'Nidra, the Daughter of Shadows, was going to result in his host's demise. That was a big problem. If his host died, he would only have minutes to find a new temporary host, or it would be his end as well. Normally, you could find someone sick or mentally unstable who could not resist. Absent that, your choices became bleak.

First, you were weak after an emergency transfer, and if the only host you found was a rat, you would not survive long because they neither had the life energy to feed on to regain your strength nor sufficient energy to allow you to transfer again. More than that, De'Nidra, the Daughter of Shadows, had already seen him and was likely aware he had possessed this vessel when he was at the Rusty Bucket watching Tara. A sense of dread coiled in Sam'Ieal's gut. *This is getting sticky, and I have not even started yet.*

By the time he reached the City Master's home, Sam'Ieal was muttering to himself. The gray stone manor was a relic of the ages, a refurbished building from the old metropolis with a lovely iron gate and a cobbled circular private road, leading to the main entryway with large, elegant columns rising above to a balcony overlooking the drive. *How rich.* He entered the gate and climbed the steps to the door. Used the massive brass knocker and waited. A man opened the door. A lanky fellow with a fancy black coat had his nose in the air before he could even speak. "May I help you?"

Sam'Ieal detected disdain for the working class in the man's tone. "Yes, you can. I am Ja'eam, and I am here on personal business to see the City Master."

The secretary or butler or whatever he was, looked Ja'eam up and down. "I see," the butler droned, "however, he is not receiving visitors today. I am sorry."

Sam'Ieal casually reached behind his back, fingers brushing against the cold steel handle of his knife. "Do you want to tell him I am here, or is he out?"

The lanky bastard lifted his nose in the air. "Oh, he is here. He simply does not wish to waste his time on someone like you. So, move along."

"Oh, I see," Sam'Ieal said as he drew his knife from its sheath, causing the butler to stumble backward, flailing his hands defensively. Sam'Ieal swiftly advanced and stabbed him in the heart, watching him fall with a satisfying thud. "Don't trouble yourself, butler. I can find my way." Sam'Ieal ascended the stairs with a smile, not particularly concerned about being quiet. He ran his hands along a rich wood banister.

A voice emanated from the room above. "Did you get rid of him? I didn't see him leave," a voice called from behind the door.

Pushing the door open, he walked in. The balding, portly City Master was wearing the velvet red robes of office and was peering through a curtain at the balcony window. Still clutching the bloody blade, He replied, "Oh, I took care of him alright."

The chubby man spun around, wide-eyed, realizing the visitor was not his butler.

With a subtle click, Sam'Ieal shut the door behind him and casually settled into the plush chair behind the ornate desk. "I represent an organization concerned about your loyalty to De'Nidra, the Daughter of Shadows," he stated calmly.

Ja'Rid scanned the room as if someone invisible stood before him. "I have been loyal!" the City Master demanded.

"Then why don't you start by explaining what you have been doing for her and who else is involved?"

The City Master became suspicious. "If you were an agent of De'Nidra, the Daughter of Shadows, you would already know why you are here and what I am supposed to tell you. Since you don't know those things, and I have no idea what you are talking about, it is safe to assume you are not an agent of De'Nidra, the Daughter of Shadows." A small curl of satisfaction touched his lips.

Sighing in frustration, Sam'Ieal absentmindedly picked at his fingernails with the bloody knife. "I do not work for De'Nidra. I work for the people De'Nidra used to serve before betraying them. Do you comprehend our predicament now? Allow me to clarify. She was part of the council." Sam'Ieal glanced at the City Master, awaiting agreement.

His head bobbed in ascent.

"She betrayed my employer and joined the opposition. Did you know that?"

The City Master shook his head. Beads of sweat formed on his brow.

"If you are not working for my employer, you will work for no one. Do you understand?"

The City Master nodded.

"Good. If she returns and issues instructions, you must comply. But first, you will inform me of your actions. In addition, you will furnish the names and whereabouts of anyone you are directed to collaborate with in the future. Failure to comply with these straightforward instructions will lead to the termination of your employment, and we both know what that means, don't we?"

The City Master swallowed, sweat trailing down pudgy cheeks.

Sam'Ieal grinned and slapped his knee as he stood, causing Ja'Rid to startle. "Excellent. I'll await the information, ensuring you won't have any more unfortunate incidents with snooty butlers. Do we understand each other?"

The City Master nodded vigorously.

"You have a pleasant day." Sam'Ieal departed with a final, menacing grin.

Chapter 3 Treatise Of Maids

"Each day, as I stand on death's doorstep, I survey life's fragility. It encompasses our final breath and our tenderest kisses, the embrace of passion, and the unspoken words that should have long been said. Within time, my currency is the sand slipping away, and I choose to spend it in fervent love, as the first to forgive. Each day becomes a new chance, my last day to truly live."

Al'len stood in the stable, brushing the dirt from a powerful stinger warhorse. Dust particles floated like motes in sunlight streaming through a cracked board of a covered window. She hummed the melody from her first dance with Antoff. The only dance she had had in a thousand years. The line between herself and EL'ALue was blurring, more and more each day. She daydreamed and drifted in slumber. EL'ALue the Maid of Light—high above the valley, amidst the mountains called the Steps of Glass. Her gaze swept over cloud covered glassy peaks and down into the charred fields. The land stretched out before her, scarred by a devastation the world had forgotten. Without monuments to honor him, for them, he no longer existed.

Time unraveled before her, an embroidery of memories woven from a thousand years, yet as vivid as the dawn of yesterday. There, amidst the echoes of eternity, stood Ram'Del. His armor, burnished to a radiant sheen, caught the nascent glow of the first sun, casting aureate reflections that danced like torchflies. The dawn's red light, spilling over the horizon, bathed the clouds above the Steps in a crimson tone, a spectacle of light and shadow. His voice was low, and it called to her. It took all she had to resist his draw.

Ram'Del's gaze, intense and blue, pierced her very essence, edging her toward a shiver at the very edge of her control. "You are the blade that has cut me deep, a wound that only you can heal EL'Alue."

She shook her head, struggling for words that refused to come. EL'Alue, the woman, wanted to reach for him, wanted to say *yes to all those hidden questions. Yes! to his secret love.* But EL'Alue, the Maid of Light, stomped that down. "You stand before me, yet you must also stand with them—Lead them. Every word, a reminder of what I must deny. Not because I wish it, Ram'Del, but because fate demands it. My heart yearns to say yes, yet duty binds it to silence. You are everything, yet I can offer nothing more than I have already given. I will remain EL'Alue, the Maid of Light, and nothing else."

Ram'Del reached for her. "EL'Alue, goddess or woman, I'll be the one who loves you. Let me be the one?"

She turned her back on him. "I cannot give you what you want, Ram'Del. But know this, if I could, you would be the one. Return to your army, Lord Captain Ram'Del. Sound the march."

Ram'Del bowed and placed his fist over his heart. "EL'Alue, it is as you command. For you and never another." He turned and left her. She wanted to run to him, to take him into her arms and never let go. If he had not left there and then, she would have. He had won this battle for her heart. But he would not get the chance to know.

Astride his white dragon-horse, the revered Defender Ram'Del led his valiant Army of the Light, a beacon against the encroaching Darkness. Their golden-trimmed white banners, emblazoned with binary suns, whipped in the wind as Ram'Del thundered with divine Power, fueled by his love for a goddess and his desire for the woman who refused to confide in him fully.

Suddenly, the Torn Flowage erupted with a horde of nightmare creatures, pouring onto the battlefield like black oil spilled on the ground. Their howls for blood echoed across the land as they charged forward, driven by their relentless savagery and thirst for violence.

Ram'Del raised his banner, rallying his troops for the fight ahead. "Rise up! This day we fight! Whether we survive or die, we will never be forgotten! We are fighting for the truth! We are fighting for the love of all we dare not lose! The time has come for us to rise up! For this day, whether we live or die, all we love will be preserved! Henceforth, no one will forget we gave our all, for the Light and for Love!"

The call rose like a wave from the Army of the Light. "For Light and Love!" they shouted, charging forward to meet the black mass in one last glorious flash of Light upon the field. Ram'Del, thoughtless of himself, bravely rode, dirt spraying up around him. He gave himself one last longing look toward EL'ALue, the Maid of Light, before dying. He could not see her, but he knew she was there.

EL'ALue the woman, not the goddess, reached out in her pain and regret. She struck with all her fury and love. The field exploded in a blinding flash of Light and flooded that Vale Lands, accompanied by a blast leveling the outskirts of Coth'Venter. A cloud rolled upwards brightly toward the suns, climbing high into the atmosphere, consuming the clouds, and leaving circular rings in the strata of the heavens' rose-colored sky.

Al'len's hand halted mid-stroke, trembling as tears carved paths down her cheeks. *Never again! This one will know I love him. He will know I am a woman first, above all else.* She told herself.

De'Nidra's perfume, mingling memories with expectation, wafted through the air. Al'len persisted in her grooming, each stroke a deliberate delay to facing the inevitable conversation. "De'Nidra, do you need something?" she asked.

"No, my Lady. Your grief has permeated our bond until now." Sliding open the stall door, De'Nidra walked behind Al'len. She turned, her cheeks stained with tears. De'Nidra embraced her. "Forgive me, my Lady. Thank you for restoring Tem'Aldar to me, despite all I have done to you and the one you loved."

Al'len backed away. EL'ALue the woman still struggled with the loss, and this was the woman who had killed Ram'Del. Fortunately for De'Nidra, the Maid of Light stamped that down. "De'Nidra, you acted out of love for Tem'Aldar. I have already forgiven you and accepted your service. That is enough. Now, we must face what lies ahead. You know the Dark Order will attempt to kill you, seeing this as your ultimate betrayal. Let it mark the beginning of our victory over the madness that has plagued our world for far too long."

De'Nidra stepped back further under Al'len's gaze. "Yes, my Lady but there is more to be revealed. Before you rescued me from the Darkness, they forced me to manipulate the greedy bishopric in Haven. I used a witness who overheard Antoff proclaiming himself for EL'ALue, the Maid of Light. Their anger is without restraint, and they are dispatching Priest Knights to capture him and bind him in chains. My Lady, I am sorry."

Al'len's fierce smile emerged through her tears as she wiped one away. "Thank you, De'Nidra, but it is they who are in chains. I intend to set them free."

Beneath the ancient ruins of Coth'Venter, the Under Cities sprawled with passages that stretched for leagues. Dark halls, enveloped in an oppressive atmosphere, whispered secrets of forgotten ages. At first, Ivan found the air stifling, but it grew more tolerable with each passing moment he spent below. The inhabitants, with their deliberate footfalls, echoed through the corridors. A practiced form of politeness rather than necessity. In this well-orchestrated society, transparency and deliberate actions took precedence over the elusive behavior common in the sunlit world above. Vam'Phire could hide and elude, when necessary, as shadows answered their call, yet their ways were softer. They reached out gently to one another, leaving traces behind like signatures on parchment. Their touches served as meaningful interludes, sharing experiences that transcended mere civility. Politeness simply scratched the surface of the profound depth of the intimacy they possessed.

Wisdom, cultivated through years of existence, passed from one Vam'Phire to another in silent appraisals, unheard by any mortal race. Minds opened and closed to each other without hindrance. Deep knowledge and understanding flowed at the speed of thought, yet the silence remained unbroken, undisturbed by errant voices. At least, that had been the case until Ivan arrived below. Vam'Phire continued their existence for as long as they desired, if they could glean knowledge. However, if interest waned, a silent repose would soon follow.

In a vast chamber, Ivan sat on a stone bench near a bridge that spanned a rift created by the Shattering of the Balance within the foundation stone. Known only as Ivan, he embraced this moniker as his entire identity. His eyes, a striking blend of gray and marbled gold, gave mortals an unsettling feeling of being intensely scrutinized, a reminder of their own mortality. Ivan's raven-black hair cascaded down to his shoulders, framing a strong jawline and a prominent brow. He wore a black shirt, tan britches, and matching boots, while a long-handled sword hung from his waist, its hilt adorned with a pulsating blood gem radiating a red, insatiable glow.

The rift emitted relentless heat. Its sheer walls descended leagues below to meet bubbling liquid stone, casting a bright orange glow. Chiseled gray stone shelves lined the chamber walls, stacked high with books and tomes. The unending cascade of knowledge filled the hall, occasionally interrupted by the line of stone benches. There, amidst the sea of knowledge, sat Ivan, accompanied by a black dire wolf the size of a warhorse. The wolf slept with deep growl-filled snores and the occasional dream-induced whimpering, while its claws twitched and kicked at imaginary foes.

Ivan delved into many tomes written in a language no longer used or understood by most—a language of science. Numeric descriptions and equations filled the pages, depicting the intricate complexities and interworkings of archaic concepts. As he navigated the deep halls, he marveled at the array of machines collected by the Vam'Phire, a testament to their insatiable thirst for understanding. When necessary, these creatures possessed the capacity for ferocity, but their preference was to share knowledge and even humor. Ivan often encountered lyrical conundrums that took him hours to unravel, but once deciphered, they flooded him with a wave of amusement, leaving him in a state of humorous malaise. Each time he crossed paths with the Vam'Phire, a suitable curl would grace his lips.

Lord Ivan? echoed the voice of Chronicler Da'Vain in his mind telepathically. *My Lord, Prince, your people grow jealous of these books.* Da'Vain's tone remained inwardly calm and perpetually polite, laced with a hint of mirth.

Ivan acknowledged the truth, responding, *I know, Da'Vain. They are curious about everything I have witnessed outside, seeking my perceptions and experiences like this dire wolf chasing a rabbit. Difficult to shake off and rarely eluded.*

Da'Vain savored the taste of Ivan's wit, reveling in his humor as he retaliated with a tale of his own—a vivid vision of Ivan surrounded and ensnared by Vam'Phire, both young and old, vying for a place within an untamed mind.

My Lord, if it pleases you to spend a period with one individual at a time, perchance you could delegate the ceaseless questing to another, thereby, limiting your conversations to a single person. This would grant you more time to delve into your weathered tomes with a knowledgeable companion who can assist you in comprehending their contents. While simultaneously satisfying the cravings of the ravenous hordes. Amusement rippled through their conversation.

"So, I am to be chained, then?" Ivan mused.

However, it was a woman's voice that responded from the doorway. "Nay, my Lord Prince. I seek only to serve you with truth and honor." With a deep curtsy, she placed her right hand over her heart.

Ivan rose and reciprocated the gesture with an equally profound bow. "Truth and honor, my Lady."

The room remained shrouded in Darkness, with only her outline visible, intentionally veiling her in mystery. She purposefully kept him waiting, heightening the intrigue.

Ivan held a lamp, its feeble light casting a faint glow around him, binding his dark vision. "Forgive me, my Lady, for my words. I have offended you."

Her thoughts brightened only slightly, not enough for him to discern, but enough to sense her curiosity. "I am not offended by you, my Lord Prince. May I have your permission to attend you?"

Ivan bowed once more. "That would please me."

Her emotions deepened, revealing her own pleasure. She stepped forward into the pool of light, captivating Ivan's gaze with her creamy complexion. His eyes drank in the sight of her, noting the small indents on her pink, plump lips where her fangs lightly pressed against them. Swirling with shades of gold and silver, her eyes held a mesmerizing allure. Clinging to her curves like a warm breath, she wore a garment woven from the silk thread of the Ruespider, and her rich dark locks cascaded in long, luxurious ringlets down to her waist. Radiating beauty, Ivan's gaze shifted from her appearance to the depths of her mind, eager to explore her inner world.

If it were possible to witness her interest shift, it was like a blush. The subtle brush of her thoughts that conveyed it to him. They delved deep within and measured his substance.

Clearing his throat, Ivan spoke, his voice tinged with a hint of apology. His voice softened, a trace of genuine remorse threading through his words. "Forgive me, my Lady. It seems I've stumbled once more, lost in your presence. You are not a side-of-beast to be hungered over. Nor are you a bottle of wine for tasting."

In response, she smiled at him like a teacher amused by a child's innocence, yet with a hint of curiosity and a desire to further manipulate his strings. Her thoughts brightened faintly. "You have not offended me, my Lord. Allow me to assure you of that."

Glancing around the hall, Ivan sought Da'Vain the Chronicler, but found him absent. He realized he was now alone with her, captivated by her presence. She was mesmerizing, and it was taking all his concentration to stave off instincts he had not even recognized he had.

"I am called Lil for short, my Lord," she revealed. "My name is not…," she paused with a smile, "it is incomprehensible in the tongue of mortals. I am not used to such a bright source of light." She said as she picked up Ivan's book titled, Particle Entanglement.

He placed the lamp on the floor, suddenly aware he had been holding it up to her as if examining a bottle of fine wine in a cellar. He sighed deeply, "It appears I am seeking your unending pardons," Ivan confessed, feeling the weight of his past mistakes. "My mind is untrained and everything within just seems to leak out in your presence. You have reduced me to a clumsy oaf, and you, Lil, are—perfect."

Lil smiled, her mind opening further as she responded, and now her voice flowed into him like warm milk and honey. *Then you shall have an unending supply. Shall I dim the light a little so we can begin?*

Ivan's instinctive mind responded, *No. I will see you with my eyes and my mind. I will not miss a single note of your complexity.*

Her mind sent him a mental blush, and Lil's smile deepened in response. *It is an unfortunate side-effect of our species, my Lord. Females give off pheromones. Believe me when I tell you, I have no wish to befuddle your thoughts.* Frustration laced her inner voice. *I need to exert tighter control; or it gets away as it has now.* Lil's eyes met his. *It happens when I hunt or when—I have interest.*

He wondered which one it was now. Was she hunting him or was she attracted to him? Whichever it was, he intended to find out. Ivan's thoughts whirled, overwhelmed by the openness of her mind. He knew her loneliness as a scholar, and she was hiding from something. He reached for it and she allowed him in. *Lil, you are hiding from the judgment and hate of the masses that dwell above. Enduring the stigmatization of your very existence. They hate you for what you are. They do not perceive your delicate grace, nor do they witness the profound transformation of being in your speech.* Ivan's thoughts turned inward. *I wish mortals could see you as I do. See the picture that is forming in my mind? Anything I shared would be only a shallow interpretation. How could I possibly capture your essence on a page? Your mind Lil. It is so vivid. I would paint you in a world of light. Yet in all its beautiful colors, it would not define you. How can I pour out upon a page the fruit of your being, one so hated and unembraced?*

Her hand instinctively went to her heart, listening intently as his thoughts intertwined with hers, unlocking a hidden secret: a poet. His charms called to her. Lil devoured his words.

❧

It was midday, and the largest sun, known as the Elder Brother, had already passed overhead, slowly making its way toward the horizon. The smaller sun, the Little Sister, stood directly above Tara, De'Nidra, and Va'Yone as they sat in the grass beneath the ancient thicket that bordered the field known as Dan'Nor. Twisted branches cast intricate patterns of light, shifting, playing shadows upon them. Edward lay resting in the tall grass.

Va'Yone, a diminutive figure with a dark complexion and wild, nearly black hair, peered curiously at Tara. A mischievous smile playing on his lips. Despite being a grown man, Va'Yone's size resembled that of a twelve-year-old child. Like Ivan, a construct of mages, part of his material drawn from the same sources.

De'Nidra cleared her throat, capturing their attention. Her voice carried a hint of excitement as she explained, "Light is energy, and there is a force behind its movement, akin to the wind that rustles the grass. Most people envision arcane Light as a sphere, but it is more like a ribbon fluttering in the wind." With a graceful gesture, she held out her hands, and a long beam of shimmering Light materialized between her palms, resembling a swaying ribbon. "See? You can shape and mold it, transforming the fabric of creation to accommodate our desires." De'Nidra deftly manipulated the Light, forming intricate patterns that mesmerized her companions.

Va'Yone's eyes widened with understanding as he spoke up. "I've always thought of Light as a sphere, as I want it to provide its basic utility. I never thought of it as anything else. If you think hard enough, everything has other uses."

De'Nidra nodded approvingly, while Tara, raising an eyebrow at Va'Yone's playful remark, couldn't help but smile. They had always shared a bond akin to siblings.

Va'Yone's dark gray eyes sparkled with insight as he continued, "But you're right, it's more like a ribbon."

De'Nidra's smile deepened. "Exactly, Va'Yone. And with skill and ingenuity, we can even bend the edges into a radius." She winked playfully at him, knowing his penchant for clever tricks. The beam of Light transformed, growing in circumference until it formed a seamless, cylindrical shape. "This is a higher level of control, surpassing the sphere," De'Nidra explained, her voice brimming with confidence. "You can shape it into any form your imagination conceives. Moreover, observe closely when the Light passes through itself; you can catch glimpses of what lies on the other side. It's like having the ability to move in and out of view, although true invisibility is a different lesson altogether."

Tara's curiosity flared as she listened intently. She closed her eyes, her mind entwined with the dragons she had melded with. With the dragons as her anchors, she could navigate the storm within her, harnessing its Power without being consumed. Opening her eyes, Tara raised her hands, and a radiant ribbon of Light burst forth, cutting through the air with a mesmerizing glow. It undulated and transformed, manifesting her vision of reality. It billowed like a banner, then straightened like a sheet of paper.

Tara's focus sharpened, twisting the ribbon of Light into a radiant, flat plane. Finally, she deftly fused the ends, creating a perfect loop. Her eyes sparkled with pride as she gazed at her creation.

De'Nidra's voice resonated with awe. "Tara, that is a remarkable display of magic for the first time, manipulating a wave of Light. I have never seen someone catch the concept so quickly in all my years."

Edward reclined in the lush grass; his gaze fixed upon the heavens as two magnificent dragons glided through the sky above. "But what about time? If it flows like the wind, it must surely require time to reach its destination. So, time becomes a significant factor. How does it all work?"

De'Nidra arched an eyebrow at Tara. "This one is astute; he will certainly prove to be a challenge. Time is expansive, Edward, and puzzling. It's about the interplay of our thoughts and energy within creation's fabric, shaping our reality—a concept most find elusive."

Edward grumbled, "Tara attempted to enlighten me on the subject the other day, but I'm still perplexed."

De'Nidra exchanged a questioning glance with Tara, a glimmer of curiosity in her eyes. "Well, Tara, care to try?"

Tara met De'Nidra's gaze with unease. "I can attempt, though my magic works differently from yours. You store it, employing it for specific spells or images like a purpose-built tool. For me, it doesn't work that way. I wield it as I create the image, shaping the pattern of reality's flow. Magic brings the most solid reality into being, a dance of perception, matter and energy manipulation."

De'Nidra raised an eyebrow once more. Having a Torrent explain her magic to her was an invaluable gift, and she found herself captivated by the prospect.

"Come now, Tara," Edward chuckled. "Stop stalling."

Tara let out a deep sigh, her eyes filled with wisdom. "Very well Edward, listen carefully. Time is a fundamental aspect of our existence, intricately interwoven with reality and space, forming an interconnected dimensional framework we refer to as time. Within this framework, objects and energy create curves and distortions, challenging our understanding. It's akin to a fabric that stretches out, and when energy patterns manifest as matter, they generate depressions or distortions in the fabric of reality. Our perception of time is contingent upon our position within this fabric."

De'Nidra's eyes widened, fixated on Tara's every word.

Edward furrowed his brow, lost in contemplation. "How does your magic operate within this framework?" He inquired, his smile leading her on.

Tara's smile radiated, and her eyes gleamed with arcane knowledge. "Edward, everything is perception. The reality that possesses the greatest solidity is the one that manifests. Magic, at its core, is the art of perceiving and manipulating these underlying realities. Through our connection to the fabric of space-time and the energies coursing through creation, we harness what people perceive as magical abilities. However, the Breaking disrupted the equilibrium of this fabric, tearing it asunder into two warring halves. Our reality's fabric is not fully solidified. Not as it should be. Broken into two parts and they war for control."

Edward chewed on a piece of long grass and pondered her words for a moment, his eyes brimming with fascination. "I must confess, I do not fully grasp it all, but hearing the sound of your voice gives me immense joy."

Tara glanced back at Edward. She squinted at him. "Sometimes, Edward, your behavior leaves me with a desire to thump you!" *This man can be infuriating. Making me explain all that just to hear the sound of my voice.*

He huffed, "What did I do?" But his roguish smile betrayed him.

De'Nidra found herself engulfed in the concepts Tara had unleashed—a deluge of information that even the grand mages of her era could not have comprehended entirely. "How do you possess this knowledge, Tara?"

Tara's eyes filled with the unseen images of reality that surrounded her. "It's where I live, De'Nidra—both the lesser and greater realities. My heart, my loved ones, they anchor me to these planes, allowing me to exist concurrently in both."

Tara smiled petulantly at Edward. "Let's talk about something else," she said, giving Edward a wicked smile.

Edward knew he was going to get it later, of that, he could be sure.

A black and white dragon gracefully glided above, their forms circling in the sky. Their translucent wings, both powerful and ethereal, kept them aloft, riding the updrafts rising from the Spring Tide Valley and the City of Coth'Venter. Below, they drank in the vibrant landscape, teeming with abundant life. Amidst it all stood Tara, their bondholder, her body radiating heat like forged iron against the backdrop of the terrain. Buffeted by gusts of wind, the dragons glided through the icy curtain of the world.

The white dragon's gaze brushed westward along the Great Road, and a fiery glow illuminated its eyes. Focusing intently, it blinked, and a second lens slid into place. Its fiery gold iris constricted and its vision magnified. First, its gaze streamed to the black dragon, then shifted to Tara. The black dragon banked hard, soaring towards Tara and the meadow, before tucking its wings tightly and plummeting from the sky like a dart. The white dragon, maintaining its westward trajectory, kept its vision focused so Tara could see what it saw.

Tara concentrated on the mental images flooding her mind—an intoxicating blend of scorching heat and cool vaporous forms. She could feel the chill of the wind against her skin, the uplifting force beneath her wings, the thunderous roar assaulting her ears, and the exhilarating rush filling her lungs. The images overwhelmed her; the dragons engaged in a dynamic aerial ballet, churning her stomach. "They are coming from the west," she echoed the white dragon's thoughts, speaking with her own voice.

Edward, observed Tara struggling to remain steady, leapt to his feet and reached out, catching her before she could stumble. "Who are they, Tara?" Edward's voice was urgent, his eyes searching hers for an answer.

"Soldiers and Priest Knights from Haven," she replied, her descent rushing rapidly toward the meadow. In her black dragon's mind, Tara spread her wings. They snapped open with a resounding pop, like the release of a sail catching the wind.

The black dragon skimmed the treetops, wings unfurled, sending a shockwave through the leaves. With a trio of mighty flaps, it veered west, ascending past the Cathedral's gothic spires. Startled by its warning roar, bloodbats erupted from the towers.

In the Cathedral of Light, a monstrous sound shook, alerting its inhabitance to danger. The stable yard and square burst forth in motion, horses being saddled, soldiers of Tara's house guard forming up, and the drums of war beat once more. You did not need to hear them, yet in every heart, they thundered like the dragon's roar.

Chapter 4 Hath No Fury

"Some dust never settles from your soul's sight, an imagery of your most arrogant failure forever haunting your mind. Liquid fire roars from the heights, pouring down like molten rain. We, who bore witness to her vengeance and her pain, never fully recovered. We bathed in her fire, and in her fury, she reforged us anew."

Lord Lars Haven led the procession, followed by Priest Knights and Clerics in silver plate armor. A mighty roar reverberated through the air, causing the horses to tremble and leap, torn between their instinct to charge down the Great Road or flee in fear. Amidst the chaos, Lord Lars' warhorse danced, yet maintained composure.

Meanwhile, wagons on the road swerved erratically. Items tumbled from their beds as drivers desperately tried to escape the unsettling sight. RavenHof, consumed by the clutches of Coth'Venter, loomed ahead, shrouded in a dreadful gray mass of gothic decay. Above the city, a massive avian creature ascended into the sky, soaring over a towering gothic cathedral.

Lord Lars turned to the cleric beside him, whose face was a blend of awe and terror. Struggling to rein in his uneasy warhorse, the cleric's voice trembled. "By the gods!"

Lars savored the raw terror plain in the cleric's eyes. "What say you now, Cleric, Warrior of the Light? Does the message brought by our page ring true?" Lord

Lars' tone dripped with cruel sarcasm as his eyes absorbed the spectacle of horses frantically turning in dismay.

Lars pursued. "No, it would appear that we will fill our hands with swords before the day is out. He knows we are here, and I do not believe this exiled knight will come quietly, nor quickly, to your chains."

Armed, Antoff and Al'len clattered down the two long flights of stairs at the back of the cathedral's rectory, overlooking the stable yard below. The gate, patinated bronze, stood ajar. Tara, Edward, De'Nidra, and Va'Yone ran through the waving grass towards the yard. Warhorses and common alike were being led one by one out of the stable.

Behind them, the shouts of Priest Knights and Clerics urged them forward. "For the love of the Light, Captain Antoff, please move your ass!" Antoff's head whipped towards the sound and Al'len shot him a quick smile. As soon as Antoff's feet touched the yard's cobblestone, Warriors of the Light streamed past him. Some ran into the stable to help with the saddling, while others mounted their warhorses, which pranced with anticipation.

It took half an hour to gather everyone in the main square. The Warriors of the Light, in a formation of ten across, mounted six rows deep, stood before the fountain. In gray stone, Ram'Del, the Hero of the Light, sword and banner raised high, waited for the charge. Antoff was at the center with Al'len next to him and Tem'Aldar to her right. To the left, formed up Edward and his light cavalry. They stood back from the main road that entered the square, horse bows in hand and round metal strapped wooden shields slid to their backs. A long wicked looking boar spear sat propped against shoulders with its butt in a stirrup cup on the right side. Only a single banner rippled in the wind, adorned with a black and white dragons facing a fist holding lightning bolts.

The air was still, and the sky turned red as twilight approached. High above, on the balcony of the Cathedral of Light, Tara, De'Nidra, and Va'Yone, armed with bows, stood with house guards overseeing the square. Mic'Ieal, the First of Her Guard, awaited commands in the background. Cur'Ra and her triage team stayed in the cathedral above the grand flight of stairs to care for the injured. When the battle began, her time would come. She was prepared, her people bearing bags of medical supplies and backboards. In silence, they awaited the screams, the fire, and mercy call. The stillness, a deafening herald of woe.

The dark spires of Coth'Venter, gray stone towers resembling broken skeletal hands, rose ominously from the ancient metropolis, casting somber shadows behind the city of RavenHof. As the Haven procession rolled through the broken gates that lay open to the smaller city, they were met with the charred remnants of two- and three-story buildings lining the cobblestone road leading to the main thorofare. Some sections showed signs of new construction, while other storefronts stood gutted, with only their supports and salvaged floors remaining. Piles of river rock and recovered stone from the fires lined the street. As they rode toward the abandoned city of Coth'Venter, it was revealed that the Dark Order had selectively targeted the structures in their path, leaving the rest of the small city untouched. The recent encounter had left its mark on the strained faces of the city's inhabitants.

The absence of the City Master to greet them showed his preoccupation with the pressing matters of the city, and news of their arrival had not yet reached him. *No matter*, thought Dem'Endas, clearly disdainful of the City Master. *I had no desire to endure his incessant complaints, anyway.*

The procession of three hundred Haven warriors trotted through the broad and desolate streets of the abandoned gray-stone city, their determined pass leading them toward the aged Cathedral of Light. Above them, two creatures circled high in the reddening sky, observing the trail of heat generated by the advancing warriors, drawing closer to the motionless figures standing in the square below.

There are moments when one must question whether appearances deceive. A mere glance offers little insight into the true nature of a situation. Making fatal mistakes in ignorance haunts us for the rest of our days. The Haven Knights of the Light reached the broad main street that led to the cathedral. Facing their adversaries. They stopped and waited.

A cleric, dressed in gleaming silver plate armor, rode to Lord Haven's right and approached the middle ground between the two forces. Antoff, witnessing this, advanced as well, accompanied by another companion. "Wait here, Al'len. I shall return shortly," he said, kicking his horse into motion.

Al'len trotted alongside him. Teasingly she said, "Not tonight, Priest. If you are kind to me and we survive, perhaps I'll let you command me later." Al'len in a matching set of tan leather, with a sword belted at her waist, secured by a belt adorned with a white dragon on the buckle. She also wore a white cloak trimmed in gold, bearing a matching dragon emblem. Completing her ensemble was her knight's shield with the same design, laying crossed her animal's flanks.

Antoff grunted in response, continuing his forward ride. The Lord of Haven, observing the two figures approaching instead of one, spurred his mount to a trot.

Edward saw his father's advance. He commanded his line to remain still before urging his steed forward. His warhorse, sensing his tension, cantered with a spirited prance. Simultaneously, a third figure approached the line, prompting another Priest Knight of Haven to ride toward the group, evening the odds in preparation for a potential confrontation.

Given Antoff Grant's legendary status from recent campaigns, the concern for numerical balance was justified. A three-on-three confrontation would suffice until the main bodies of both sides clashed. Moreover, additional witnesses to the impending trial were undoubtedly necessary. Regardless of any clergy's opinion, Antoff, being a Priest Knight, would receive every opportunity to prove himself. However, there was another witness—the Maid of Light, EL'ALue—watching the events unfold in her slumber.

The Haven cleric was the first to reach the middle ground of the cobblestone square, followed by Antoff and Al'len. Unrolling a writ of arrest for Antoff, adorned with the Seal of the Light and bearing the signature of the High Bishop of Haven, the cleric declared, "You are hereby, ordered by the Light to surrender your weapons so that you may stand trial for the charges brought against you. Specifically, the defamation of EL'ALue, the god of Light. For the crime of heresy, you're stripped of your rank and title of Priest Knight until you're vindicated or sentenced to death by hanging."

As the last words hung in the air, the others reached the middle ground as well. Antoff responded with a flat tone, "Your orders are clear, and you are determined to carry them out?"

Edward spoke up, "Father, you won't take him without a fight."

Dem'Endas looked at the son of Lord Lars of Haven, piercing him with his eyes, and replied, "He will not be the only one going. You are coming as well. You have spent enough time in this place," he added, disdain apparent in his voice, "and with these people." His eyes drifted across Edward's companions, eyeing each one with disgust.

Al'len gazed past the shell of Lord Lars, seeing Dem'Endas within him. "Well, what do we have here?" She winked at him. "How are you two doing in there?"

Fear coursed through Dem'Endas' veins for the first time since he had assumed this vessel. This woman had recognized him. "Silence, woman!" His voice broke, betraying a mix of desperation and a faltering grip on control. His gaze darted frantically, reflecting the turmoil within. "Do you have any idea who you're addressing?"

Al'len offered him a knowing smile, a smile that spoke of shared secrets and understanding. Without another word, she turned her gaze back to the statue. "Mel'Anor, you must come and see," she called out.

Mel'Anor, the aging but towering cleric, sat atop his gray warhorse. "Of course, my Lady," he declared, his voice resounding. Urging his horse into a canter. The opposite side sent another cleric, resulting in a four-on-four.

Mel'Anor was not alone. As his horse's hooves thundered against the stone, resonating like a hammer striking an anvil, a radiant glow emanated from him, creating a horrifying spectacle for Dem'Endas to witness. Clad in gleaming silver armor that shone with blinding intensity, Mel'Anor resembled a god. Justus, one of the divine Lights, was about to reveal himself upon his arrival.

Filled with fear, Dem'Endas swiftly turned his warhorse and retreated toward the Haven lines, seeking refuge among his own forces. "They are using witchery! Prepare to charge!" Dem'Endas commanded, drawing his sword.

Mel'Anor's voice reverberated, "Lord Haven is possessed!" The two groups in the middle briefly eyed each other before galloping back to their respective positions in the battle lines.

The cleric rode swiftly to join Dem'Endas. "My Lord, you stand accused of possession!" Accusation drenched his voice.

Dem'Endas retorted, "I, the Lord of Haven, am accused by heretics of possession, you idiot! You witness witchcraft and yet arrogantly believe that you know better than the bishopric—the order that sent you here to apprehend these apostates? If you take the word of a man who defames EL'ALue, the god of Light, over the righteous court that has dispatched you, then you are a fool! Whom do you truly serve? Now, fulfill your duty or step aside!" Spittle flew from his mouth, rage and fear overtaking his senses.

Antoff spun his Stinger. "Listen to me." His voice resonated with divine Power. "We should not be fighting amongst ourselves. We are all Warriors of the Light!"

Dem'Endas bellowed in response, "And we outnumber you five to one. No! These," his arms gestured across his ranks, "These are the true Warriors of the Light. You are heretics, commanded by your own High Bishop to lay down your arms and face a fair trial. You have chosen death."

Antoff's jaw clenched, his eyes ablaze with resolve. "So be it!" He said, his voice a booming growl, laden with the weight of his decision. The ranks of warriors behind him ignited like a blazing Light launching forward in a charge.

Tara and her companions watched, horrified, from the cathedral balcony above the square. Antoff, Al'len, Edward, and Mel'Anor, clad in gleaming silver plate, moved forward like unwavering knights, their resolve shining as bright as their armor. Mel'Anor followed Al'len's lead. Each time one of Antoff's companions emerged, an opponent appeared in response. The Lord of Haven wheeled his horse and galloped towards his army, drawing a sword. The others hesitated before galloping back to their own lines. Antoff's powerful voice boomed, "So be it!"

That moment just hung in the air like a held breath. Frantically, Tara's mind searched for some thread of reality she could use to halt this madness. Normally, she had the control, and could change reality. This was an unstoppable flood, surging toward Antoff and Al'len—a torrent of reality she could neither halt nor bend. It was the will of someone more powerful, more determined. The overwhelming flow of Power solidified, engulfing Antoff, Al'len, and everything around them. EL'ALue, the Maid of Light, refused to be detoured.

"No! Stop!" Tara cried out. Her hand reached helplessly toward her loved ones.

In her panic, De'Nidra spoke to her, urging her to calm down. "You cannot fight against the will of the Maid of Light, Tara, but you can aid her." Tara locked eyes with De'Nidra, and her hope ignited. Hope that she could do something. Hope to save the ones she loved.

In the higher reality, the fiery essence of EL'ALue, the god of Light, engulfed the square. Tara reached for the storm and EL'Alue granted admittance. Willing it into a protective envelope of reality within her own mind. Her dragons felt their bondholder pull on the stores of Power. They roared and swooped through the air, then their wings folded as they plummeted towards the square. Tara understood she was not fighting against the Maid of Light. Not taking over, but standing as her counterbalance—an anvil to her hammer working metal, a shield against the blow, should something try to overwhelm her. Tara screamed in anguish, and creation shuttered, rippling outward, like a stone thrown into a pond, causing time to nearly freeze.

Time echoed, and a divine voice declared, 'So be it!' Dem'Endas froze in terror as the opposing force transformed into living legends, an inferno of Light. Dragons soared through the skies, their roars amplifying the chaos. He found himself thrust into the forefront of the charge, carried by the knights behind him. Suddenly, existence shook and the Cathedral of Light rippled outward, enveloping him in a wave, and time slowed to a near halt.

Dem'Endas grew frantic, his vessel barely responding to his commands, no matter how desperately he tried. The sky above turned a deep, bloody hue as it surged like a living liquid. Power crackled, made manifest by a lattice of lightning ripping open the sky. Arrow-shaped projectiles descended leisurely upon the rear ranks of his troops. A glow emanated from the warriors advancing ahead, inched closer, and both intrigued and terrified him. They took the form of angels of death, a haunting aspect that both fascinated and horrified him. Time stuttered and threatened to shatter, then rebounded and resumed its natural pace.

As if rung like a bell, time quivered before regaining its normal rhythm. The billowing clouds appeared as if the world had held its breath in a collective bloody sigh. The Little Sister struggled to descend below the horizon, while light erupted in cascading ribbons of flashes, igniting the clouds like furious orbs in a blinding radiance. Thunder resounded, echoing the answer to each ethereal burst, as Tara and a sleeping god played the song together that shook the world. Its atmosphere thrumming with Power, threatening to break loose.

The clash of warriors echoed loudly. The Haven frontline secured the street, allowing Antoff and his comrades to hold their ground. Edward's cavalry fired a barrage of arrows at the Haven's rear lines. Despite his concern for his father, Edward refused to waver. "Ready," the arrows poised, taut. "Steady," they drew back, firmly planted against cheeks throughout the ranks. "Fire!" The broad-headed shafts soared through the air in a graceful arc, before descending with anguished screams.

The dragons plummeted toward the living glow of life, leaving visions trailing before Tara's eyes. She chose the rear of the enemy lines as her destination. The wind prickled against Tara's skin, a sharp reminder of her connection to the dragons. She could sense their deep, voracious breaths, their gas-filled bladders with putrid substances ready to be expelled. As the city approached, the dragons extended their wings with a resonating pop. Exhaling the volatile gases from their lungs, they roared, causing sparks to ignite within the strikers of their throats. Fire rained down in two fluid streams of scorching chaos. Her dragons, like shades from hell, passed overhead, leaving a writhing mass of the living and smoke from burning dead.

Tara let loose, and fire fell from the sky on the rear of the Haven line. Forking lightning struck in long, twisting ropes of liquid Power, disintegrating whatever they touched in flashing wisps of smoke and dust. The energy explosive discharge fell mortal and beast alike in waves. The residual Power left the living, a writhing mass, like fish out of water laying on a dry beach.

Blinded by his radiance, he engaged them in battle, Antoff pierced a brother of his order with a blade. His divine cries resonated, echoing the anguish and remorse that consumed him as he slew the men he had once called comrades and friends.

Al'len fought valiantly alongside Antoff and Tem'Aldar. She glimpsed Lars of Haven, positioned behind the fray, desperately parrying the incoming blows with his sword. Launching herself from her saddle, Al'len propelled headlong into the heart of the conflict. Her sword, fueled by fury and love, moved in an indiscernible blur. The cleric, entrusted with the arrest warrant, spotted her and attempted to strike her down with a crushing mace blow. Al'len deftly evaded the attack, using her momentum to slide beneath, disemboweling the cleric's horse in a single devastating arc. The cleric fell. Antoff's sword followed him down and snuffed out his spark.

Seizing the opportunity, Antoff and Tem'Aldar surged forward into the gap made by Al'len guarding her flanks. Al'len blazed like a divine inferno as she closed in on Lars. He bellowed, and pointed his sword, "Kill that maid, kill that Maid of Light!" Yet, Lars's warriors moved like molasses, while Al'len was already upon him, severing his saddle girth and a substantial portion of his steed with the swiftness of a striking serpent. Lars tumbled face-first onto the street. However, as he descended, a hand reached out, gripping his mail-clad form and lifting him, as though he were a child. Al'len pressed her sword against his throat, unleashing a scream of righteous fury.

The Haven warriors, witnessing Lord Lars of Haven's imminent demise, bellowed, "Wait!"

Al'len commanded, "Stand back!"

Both factions obeyed. "Haven't enough of your comrades already fallen?" Her voice echoed, thrumming within them like a thunderclap.

With a swift, fluid motion, Al'len expertly kicked Lars' blade from his grasp, causing it to clatter to the ground. She forcefully drove him to the earth, leaving Dem'Endas gasping for breath as the air escaped his lungs. Struggling to regain composure, he watched as Al'len placed her left thumb against Lars's forehead, her words escaping through clenched teeth, and a smile danced across her lips as her ice-blue eyes chilled his soul. "I see you," she whispered. A surge of light engulfed Lars, and he vomited Dem'Endas. In a long mixture of smoky tendrils and inky oil intertwined, he fell away to the cobblestone, and Dem'Endas was no more.

"Lord Lars Haven is unharmed," She declared, stepping back to let him lie there. Al'len stood and swept her blade in an arc, gesturing toward the assembled warriors. "What are you thinking?" she bellowed at them, her voice resonating with righteous fury. "Do you realize how far you have fallen? Once, you were Paragons of Light. You were the hope of our world. They needed you and you abandoned them. Now, I must forge your metal again. Kneel and declare your allegiance to the Maid of Light, or remove yourselves from my sight!" Her words surged with an unyielding intensity. One by one, dismounting from their horses, they bowed before her. Each individual knelt, affirming their loyalty to EL'ALue, the Maid of Light.

Tem'Aldar pointed directly at Al'len. "There, Antoff, stands your Maid of Light!"

Antoff fell to his knees. He had been such a fool. This was EL'ALue, the Maid of Light. A goddess. What would she need him for beyond his service as a Priest Knight? His brain couldn't comprehend that his Al'len, his beautiful Al'len, reflected the essence of the Maid of Light. There was a sinking feeling in his chest. He was unworthy of her.

He saw her feet coming towards him. Soft hands, the hands of the woman he loved, touched his chin, traced his jaw and then gently prompted him to look up and he found her blue eyes, filled with so much love. "Antoff Grant, you are mine and I am yours." She kissed him, right there, in front of every Priest Knight that was present, declaring herself in front of them. "Antoff, I'm here for you. Do you comprehend? The only thing left for us to do is give our life's vows." He felt his heart ready to burst. "Until the end of time." She whispered.

"Until the end of time." Antoff murmured back and kissed her forehead. He had gone from stricken with loss to the heights of the heavens in one breath. His mind still reeled with the realization. *EL'ALue, the Maid of Light, loves me of all the mortals in the world. She loves me.* Though his heart knew it for true, before she had spoken it. "I thought I was supposed to be the one to ask?"

Al'len's face lit in a smile that was only for him. "Perhaps, later, and if you are nice, I will let you ask, and we will pretend you asked first." She tapped his nose with a fingertip.

They called for the healers, and Cur'Ra arrived with her team, doing what they could for the wounded. However, for those unfortunate enough to be caught in the path of the dragons, there was no hope. One hundred and eighteen warriors were dead from steel, dragons, and the fire from above.

***

They gathered and placed the dead in repose. Al'len delivered the Warriors' Eulogy in the temple hall. "This," Al'len pointed to the dead, "is the cost of following the greedy and those who have forsaken the Light. These honorable clerics and knights, so misled, failed to question and failed to correct what was said. They believed those they thought their betters, wise and true. Yet, they too went astray when they disregarded the obvious teaching of truth and love. When women and men of good conscience fail to speak or question, greed and lies are free to replace truth and love. The Light reveals and banishes the Darkness. This is the lesson that these dead cry out, a lesson we must never forget: if you forsake truth and love, even while breathing, you are already dead."

"Stand and address the injustices, demand the truth, and if your leaders fail to do what is right, remove them and choose new leaders from among yourselves. From this day forth, you will know when your leadership is evil. They will declare it loudly to you when they are afraid to speak the truth and no longer cherish order. When a law that applies to everyone else no longer holds true for their elevated station. Leadership is neither high nor mighty. It should be humble, accepting correction, and serving for the sake of service, embracing the Light, truth, and love as their compass."

"So, as the funeral pyres burn and these souls relinquish their last Light, let us remember their sacrifice and our failures. Let these dead forever burn in our memories that we will choose next time to speak and to fight." Along with all the grief-struck warriors mourning lost friends, Al'len wept with them. For those that could not yet, she wept for them.

Chapter 5 Stir Of Shadows

"There is a depth of Darkness that drives you so deep, you lose sight of the truth. You cannot hear its voice. Your heart is stone and nothing can move you. Darkness has become your truth. Hiding in an illusion of lies, within shame so heavy, it becomes too deep to move."

In the chamber's heart, the archway activated, slowly rotating, accelerating, driven by an orb embedded below. War mage Mel'Temdel channeled arcane energy into the mechanism with a precise movement of his staff. The portal's rotation quickened, blurring its form until a vibrant core of pulsating light burst forth, signaling the awakening of ancient magic. "Okay!" Mel'Temdel exclaimed, raising his staff before letting it drop to his side. The archway gradually slowed down, and the illumination faded.

Mist's voice trembled with anticipation. "Did it work?" Her eyes were wide, reflecting her hope.

Mel'Temdel turned to reply, "We're closer, but not there yet. I've powered the device, but determining the destination is a unique challenge," he explained, waving his hand dismissively. He chuckled to himself, knowing the little demon girl wouldn't catch the pun.

Clearing his throat, he continued, "Do we have any more of that lovely wine?" Mist fetched him a bejeweled goblet and poured the wine into it. "Thank you, my dear," he said, gulping the wine and returning the empty cup. After a moment to catch his breath, he carried on. "You see, my dear, it's about time, space, and specific details of where and when."

Mist gave the old mage a sly smile. "Well, whatever it is or isn't, you won't be paid until it works. That much is certain," she giggled, though her dark humor didn't seem to dampen his spirits.

"Of course, my dear," he replied, walking to where Mist stood. Looking down, he saw what looked like a sandbox embedded in the floor in front of the archway. He observed the box, its interior filled with fine black sand that intriguingly never seemed to blow away. If one spilled some of it on the floor, strangely, it moved as if drawn back into the box, under its own Power. Mel'Temdel retrieved a little book, and through his long, bushy eyebrows, stared at its single thick metal page. Hanging from a chain around his neck was the key—a quartz crystal in the shape of a teardrop—which he used to scroll through the book's information. "Aha, hum, yes, yes, I see," Mel'Temdel muttered.

"What were you trying to see?" Mist asked, her head craning, attempting to get a look.

The mage let out a huff. "My dear girl, you are quite the inquisitive one, aren't you?" He turned the book towards Mist, revealing a picture.

"Aha, I see," Mist said. "The picture shows a world floating in the sandbox."

Mel'Temdel smiled and playfully pinched her cheek. "Are you sure you don't have a little magic in there? All right, so the image in the sandbox," he chuckled and cleared his throat, "is not floating, but made from the sand. The necklace, or more precisely, the crystal," he winked at her, "the key is the focus." Mel'Temdel held the crystal in his hand and positioned it in front of the box of sand on the floor.

The crystal's light brightened, and the sand shifted into the form of a creature, starting with hooves and ending with a tail. "There, you see? It takes images from your mind and projects them there," Mel'Temdel explained.

It captivated Mist. "Okay, so if you know what the place looks like and where it is, you should be able to go there, right?" she asked, spreading her hands questioningly.

Mel'Temdel's laughter continued, fueled by Mist's curiosity and joy. "Well, there is indeed more to it than that," he admitted. "Still," he continued, "it's important to note it's a one-way trip unless there is another portal arch nearby.

What's more, you must be certain of the existence of the place or you could end up somewhere with no way back, if you take my meaning. The one using the key would have to know exactly where they were sending someone in every detail. Alternatively, if you knew where a portal was and hypothetically, if it was exactly the same, it would simplify the process immensely."

Mist tapped her chin thoughtfully. "So, we have to locate an external portal to bring the master back in?"

Mel'Temdel thought, tapping his chin, mimicking her act. "Normally, my dear, that is how it works. Until we open it and he steps through, there is no way to give a definitive answer. It may be possible to bring him back if it is bidirectional..." He spread his hands, trailing off.

In the vastness of space, planet El'idar drifted, caught in the gravitational dance of its dual suns, Little Sister and Elder Brother. Its slow, elongated orbit cloaked the planet in layers of mystery and wonder.

Amidst this cosmic ballet, Mali'Gorthos, dubbed "The Corrupter" by El'idar's inhabitants, remained in stasis. His title, a testament to his ominous sway, was not of his own choosing. Frost veiled the chamber's window, offering mere glimpses of his dark form within.

Inside his icy chamber, Mali'Gorthos mind wandered free of his frozen form. The ancient being navigated El'idar's gravitational embrace. Detached from his body, his consciousness hovered at existence's edge, trapped by his own deeds. His quest to harness the inhabitants' genetic marvels had led to this self-inflicted exile. He sought their extraordinary gifts, only to find himself ensnared in endless slumber.

El'idar's inhabitants shared a unique bond, their collective consciousness a force that could mold reality. To outsiders, such Power might seem mythic, yet El'idar thrived, its wonders transcending the commonplace of other worlds.

Mali'Gorthos traced the legacy of the Tec'tons, ancients who chronicled galaxies. Their heritage, unearthed in archaeological digs, revealed a network of inert nanites. These pioneers, armed with technology to mimic and enhance life, aimed to archive and uplift civilizations. Their quest for perfection, powered by vast computational might, could reset worlds to rectify their course.

The massive, automated ship sent to El'idar, intended to record and learn from life, became an unwitting agent of destruction. The violent eruptions and flares of the suns damaged the delicate system during genesis, forcing it to repair itself with limited data. However, during the process, part of El'idar's World Print was lost, leading to the extrapolated distorted planetary creation below.

Centuries after post-calamity, Mali'Gorthos stumbled upon the crippled world surveyor, a find unparalleled in his race's annals. Moon-sized and hollow, its core brimmed with the machinery of creation, capable of cataloging and reshaping entire worlds.

Mali'Gorthos delved into the relic's mysteries, uncovering its relentless trials on a beleaguered world. Each failure to meet its exacting standards led to a reset, erasing and restarting civilizations. El'idar, once lush, bore scars of these trials, its survivors wielding mind-bending powers. In their struggle for mastery, they mirrored gods at war, a testament to the surveyor's unintended legacy.

Within the weave of their myths, Mali'Gorthos cast himself as a deity, his technologies so advanced they merged seamlessly with the realm of magic. Donning the mantle of a shadowy god, he shared mere whispers of his knowledge, a guarded strategy to keep them dormant. His arrogance, aiming to blend his genetics with theirs for their might, led to his downfall. Now, trapped in stasis, he pondered the folly of overreaching, a common downfall across the cosmos. His story, a caution against hubris, underscored a universal truth: wisdom must temper ambition.

From his ship, Mali'Gorthos played the part of a god, his technological marvels crafting miracles for the awestruck below. He unleashed fire from the heavens, a testament to his 'divinity,' all while secretly yearning for salvation from his self-wrought chains. Great Lord Amorath and others, who saw him as a deity, unaware of the desperation cloaked beneath his divine performance, embraced this delicate charade as his only hope.

The sound of metal ringing in the square does not resemble the rhythm found in the Smithy. Instead, of a series of taps—tap, tap, tap—the sounds of a hammer shaping a shoe. This song is the flow that arises from battle when two warriors test the strength of their practice blades against each other's skillful strikes. It embodies a true rhythm, a beat born from the symbols of war. Today, it became a family affair—a father assessing his son's growth, evaluating the balance between boyhood and manhood. Perhaps it was a negotiation between father and son, but if that were the case, victory wouldn't come easily for either of them.

Edward stood shirtless, as did his father, Lars. Both men shared the same height and appearance—sea-green eyes, strong jawlines, and blonde hair, although Lars had a touch more gray. Lars, the older man, possessed strength, though not equal to his son's.

"Edward, time to head home," Lars said, swishing his sword to feel its balance. "I'll do whatever I can to make things right."

Edward stretched and warned, "You better be careful. They assigned you to bring us back to Haven in chains to face judgment. Dad, not only did that not happen, but all the knights and clerics you brought along are choosing to stay here."

Lars lunged, and Edward blocked the attack, countered with a string of forceful blows that pushed him back. "I think you should stay with us because it won't be safe for you. That corpulent bishop will be most furious."

Lars lunged again, this time launching a relentless attack of five blows and a slashing strike that nearly hit its mark. Edward easily repelled all the blows, except for the last one that caught him off guard. His father switched styles mid-swing, trying to throw him off balance.

"You're coming with me, Edward," Lars declared, his tone final.

Edward begun a series of aggressive attacks that forced Lars to retreat. Although his father recovered his ground, it was a narrow escape. "No, I don't believe I am, Dad. First, you banished me, and then the Order of the Light did the same, issuing an arrest warrant. I am devoted to Tara, and I am going to exchange life vows with her later. So, my answer is a resounding no, without meaning to offend you."

Lars swung his sword, and Edward successfully blocked it, but his father followed through with a powerful shoulder check that knocked him back. As Edward beat back his downward stroke, Lars said, "Son, you're destined to be the ruler of Haven, and your wife must come from a proper noble family. This girl, no matter how much you care for her, cannot be your partner. They won't accept her in Haven. You know that."

Edward's strikes grew forceful, bringing Lars to one knee, each swing punctuating his resolve. "You can either accept her or forget about your throne. Do you get it?"

Edward threw his practice sword down at his father's feet. "I love her, and I have pledged myself as her protector. I won't go to Haven or anywhere else unless she wishes to accompany me. So, if we ever come to Haven one day, and if you want grandchildren, those grandchildren will come from her. Do you understand?"

Lars stood up and smiled at his son. "Yes, I understand. I just wanted to make sure. I'll be there at your vow ceremony if you'll have me, son?"

Edward extended his hand, and Lars took it. "If we have your blessings, you can come."

Lars pulled him into a hug. "You have my blessings. Gods help us. You do."

It was bright and warm. A day that was perfect for shopping. Tara and Cur'Ra strolled along the porches lining RavenHof's main road to reach the seamstress. The emblem of the Silk and Needle resembled the name with a bright red bolt of silk and cream-colored bobbins and needle on a sign that hung beneath the walks covered roof. Tara had ordered a dress after a tiring, uncomfortable long fitting with so many selections of fabric patterns and cloth types. In the end, she had settled for a white splashed-in rose.

Cur'Ra felt it was a mature and reasonable choice for a gown, given the conservative opinions of her ladies and men, who gave her loyalty. Not to mention the endless gossip and prattling her announcement of Edward and her giving vows had made. The bell above the door rang as they entered, and Fer'win was fitting an older woman for a cloak. "I will be with you in a moment, young lady. Your gown is complete. All we need to do is check the fit and you can take it home."

The seamstress completed her customs and went to the rear past a curtain and bustled back in, carrying Tara's gown. "Here we are, young miss. Your choice was fantastic, and the dress turned out to be just beautiful. You can wear it for future events as well. I have the matching shoes from the cobbler, and I paid his bill." Tara was nervous, but when she looked at the dress, her heart stopped. It was perfect, and Edward had no idea she had gotten it. Antoff gave her the coin without grumbling for a change and more besides for the meal that would come after. "Well, young woman, put it on so we can have a look."

Tara took the gown and Cur'Ra carried the shoes to the dressing rooms behind the curtain. Tara changed and Cur'Ra buttoned up the back and led her to the mirror in the front. The white gown and hints of rose reflected back at her. Tara felt… beautiful. It was not that she was an unattractive girl, but all her life, dresses, shoes and now, *life vows,* they were never something that she paid much mind to. But now, looking at herself in the mirror, she could imagine her hair pinned up with a few strands let down, a rosy blush adorning her cheeks and a subtle pink tint on her lips, standing in front of Edward and declaring their love.

She heard Cur'Ra gasp behind her, and when she turned around, her eyes were holding back tears. "You're more than beautiful, daughter. You're radiant."

Tara, gave a tear filled laugh, "I hope Edward thinks so."

Late, the main temple of the Cathedral of Light lay vacant except for Edward. He sat on one of the many gray stone benches that lined the nave. The ceiling traveled upward and then was lost in the emptiness of shadow. It reflected his mood; he was lost as well. Everything was trying to destroy Tara. At every turn, something or someone was intent on removing her from existence, and he just could not figure out how to stop it. On the eve of the upcoming ceremony, the reality of losing her was crushing. His world was Tara, and he wanted more than anything else to keep her safe. *I swear I will keep you safe, Tara. I don't care what it costs me. If there is a price, I will pay it.*

Absorbed in thought, he did not hear Tara until her shadow, cast by the lamp, spilled through the open doors, and fell upon him. She sat next to him. His eyes were ablaze as he knelt before her, clutching her hands as if they were his anchor in a boundless ocean.

Edward's eyes found hers. "If anything ever happens to you, Tara, I will die. I will simply cease to exist. When I found you, it was by accident—an invitation that got me out of town, away from all of my selfishness. You saved my life and gave me a place in yours. Tara, you are my world. Your love is priceless to me."

Tara's eyes were wet when they met his. "When I was a girl, I dreamed of a small house in the Garden Wood. I had chosen a place near a pond where the spring flowers and lilies grew. I would have a garden there, and a man would love me. We would have children and be happy. The world took it all away, Edward. It took every dream I ever had. Until you said you love me, and all those other childish dreams fell away." Tara wept, "I won't let anyone steal a single moment from us, Edward. I promise, not one day."

He kissed her, and it was with true abandon. The abandonment of a man holding his whole life and world in his arms. A world that he vowed he would not lose.

Sand and grit slid relentlessly over the cracked, red, and brown soil of the Blackened Lands, as the scorching suns hung mercilessly overhead. Behind a seated child loomed the imposing fortress of Are'Amadon. Great Lord Amorath observed from a dimly lit room in one of the lower towers, finding pleasure in the discomforting light that failed to dampen his enjoyment.

Moros, a sixteen-year-old child, engaged in imaginary charges against a line of soldiers, his weathered wooden horse serving as his trusted companion. Nork, his Zoruks guard, stood watchful nearby. In Nork's eyes, the child was feeble, an unworthy descendant of the Lightlanders who unjustly inhabited lands that rightfully belonged to the Zoruks. If it were up to Nork, he would let the child burn under the scorching midday suns. But alas, the decision did not rest with him. The Great Lord had decreed that he pamper the little one, and so Nork had no choice but to fulfill his duty. With a sense of obligation, Nork decided it was time to escort the child indoors, away from the punishing heat.

"Soft Light, it is time to go inside before your tender skin suffers the wrath of the suns." The child's raw, dark skin had already begun turning a painful shade of red.

"No. Let me be!" Moros spun around and flung a clod of red dirt at Nork, his laughter echoing in the arid air.

"Nork decides, not you. Now, come."

"No. You go. Leave me be." Moros pounded his fist against the ground, shattering the wooden horse. Rising to his feet, he confronted Nork, pointing accusingly. "You did this!" he declared, clutching the broken toy. "You!"

With a swift throw, the child struck Nork beneath the eye, leaving a scratch. It was a mere scratch, Nork reassured himself, touching the spot with his hand, but dark green blood stained his fingers. The child pointed and taunted, igniting Nork's anger. "I will teach you a lesson, you rotten little shit!" he seethed, advancing toward the child.

Moros, standing his ground, faced the imposing Zoruks. As enraged as Nork was, he failed to perceive the hidden Power the child possessed. The world roared around Moros; the Light assailed him, yet Darkness held it at bay. From a higher reality, a figure advanced, reaching out for him. The Darkness coursed through his veins, scalding like oil.

The Zoruk seized Moros' arm, lifting him from the ground. Nork shrieked as his fingers and hand turned as black as night. Losing his grip, the child plummeted, and his brown eyes transformed into deep pools of Darkness. Wisps of life, infused with a sweet essence, drawn into a smoky energy, like a writhing tether connecting them. The Zoruk wailed in agony, as blackness of decay crept up his arm. Corruption spread swiftly, consuming Nork's shoulders, head, waist, and limbs, until it reached his feet. Nork struggled in vain as his organs withered and blackened, crumbling into dusty particles. The child turned and resumed playing. The pain vanished, replaced by an eerie calm. Nork, the Zoruk, was gone, his life extinguished to relieve a burned Soft Light's skin.

Great Lord Amorath emitted a dry, rusty giggle. "Rem'Mel, acquire another Zoruk for the boy. It seems he has lost his toy."

The sound of expensive fabric rustled faintly, unfailing with the presence of a middle mage. "My purpose is to serve Great Lord Amorath," Rem'Mel replied.

His Lord dismissed him with a wave of his gray, decaying hand. "Yes, for now, you may continue to do so. Now go."

It was evening. The dying rays of sunlight streamed through the chapel's windows, casting vibrant shafts of pink, blue, and purple onto the gilded flecks of the dark marble floor. The delicate patterns inscribed in the windows depicted scenes of heroic battles and acts of mercy. Within the gray stone nave, slender columns rose from the floor, decorated with intricate carvings, reaching upward to the vaulted ceiling disappearing high above into the darkness.

Lining the walls were statues and reliefs depicting clerics, Priest Knights, and El'Alue, the god of light. As the shifting light breathed life into the stone forms, their expressions ranged from serene to righteous rage, eliciting a range of emotions from those who beheld them.

Antoff and Al'len stood absorbed in the atmosphere of the chapel, waiting. Mel'Anor's deep and somber song of love reverberated throughout the hall. Soon, his brothers and sisters joined in, harmonizing in a sweet melody that stirred the depths of the soul. Their voices symbolized the union of two individuals forever becoming one.

The grand doors swung open, and Tara, dressed in a stunning white gown splashed with rose, glided down the aisle. With her left hand, she gracefully lifted the hem to avoid it trailing on the ground. Her black hair, accentuated by white bangs, cascaded around her shoulders, capturing the last rays of the setting sun and turning her necklace and earrings into fiery drops. Tara's stomach was full of Hornbees buzzing nervously. Walking beside her on her right was Cur'Ra, proud and reflective, and Tara held her hand, led toward the unknown. Behind them, Edward and his father, Lars, wore joyful smiles.

Bees fluttered in Edward's stomach, a tangle of anticipation and fear. His commitment to Tara was unwavering, yet standing before her in that gown, he saw not just her outward beauty but their shared future. In the past, his gaze had drifted among many, seeking a connection no single soul could offer. But Tara—she captivated him entirely, securing his heart and gaze in a way no one else ever could. As he stepped towards this pivotal moment, he realized the truth: no one could ever replace her. Her elegance might capture the room, but it was her spirit that ensnared him, guiding him towards a destiny intertwined, their souls uniting in a dance. Their vows were not just words but the very strokes of an artist, painting their future, each step closer, a lash of that brush.

As the sun dipped below the horizon, the lamps bathed the scene in a warm, golden glow. The hallway outside was now packed with everyone who called the cathedral their home. Silently, they filed in and seated themselves on the stone benches. Ivan, with milky white Lil on his arm, entered last, taking a place near the rear to avoid causing a stir. Lil looked radiant in a deep cream dress that complemented Tara without overshadowing her. Cur'Ra and Lars led Tara and Edward before Antoff and Al'len, turning to face each other. Cur'Ra placed Tara's hands in Edward's, and as she kissed Tara's cheek, Lars offered his arm to Cur'Ra and escorted her to the front bench.

Antoff's voice filled the sacred space, "I see before me two souls who shall become one, bearing witness to their sacred calling."

Stepping forward, Al'len held out a golden cord ablaze like a living fire, declared, "I, Al'len, bear witness. I make this call in the sight of El'Alue, the Maid of Light." Handing the cord to Antoff, she watched as he held it, shimmering, before both of them.

Antoff's gaze met Edward and Tara's, and he spoke with solemnity, "Edward and Tara, have you willingly come before El'Alue, the Maid of Light, seeking this union with full knowledge and intent?"

Edward, holding Tara's hands, looked into her eyes. "Tara, right now at this moment, you have my heart. But I am incomplete, a man torn in two. I see you and feel the love you give from the outside. I am but a beggar staring in a window. Let me in, Tara. Let me join with you and be whole. I do not want to be separated from you. I ask you to join with me and be one soul always."

Tara smiled up at him. "I will be one in all ways with you, Edward. Our souls bound forever, not two, just one."

Antoff wrapped the golden cord around both of their arms to their wrists. Al'len walked to the other side, so she was facing Antoff, and placed her hand on the cord.

Antoff placed his right hand on hers. "Who here besides these two claims a right?" Antoff looked over at the crowd sitting on the benches. He whispered, "Last chance, children. Has either of you changed your mind?"

Edward and Tara smiled at each other. Edward answered no, and Tara shook her head.

"So be it!" Antoff's voice rebounded from the walls like divine thunder, startling onlookers. Antoff and Al'len lifted their left thumbs. Antoff placed his on Tara's forehead, and Al'len pressed hers to Edward's, and they spoke in one voice, thundering, "I name you as one and mark your souls in the sight of El'Alue, the Maid of Light. You are now made forever one." Their thumbs glowed brightly as the Power of a god threaded through their bodies, intertwining their souls.

There was a long moment of silence. Tara could feel Edward; his eyes were alight and filled with love. It poured through like a gush. They were one. They kissed, and everyone stood, cheered, and clapped. It was done.

As the crowd began dispersing, a hush fell over the Nave. As soon as the doors were shut, Mel'Anor and Tes'sus, dressed in shimmering silver plate armor, emerged from the back of the chapel.

Antoff shared a knowing smile with Al'len, Mel'Anor approached Antoff, and a golden cord passed between them, gleaming with an otherworldly brilliance. With a sense of purpose, Mel'Anor raised his voice, his words commanding. "I see before me two more who shall be one. Who bears witness to their call?"

A Priest Knight. A young woman, "I, Tes'sus, bear witness. I make this call in the sight of El'Alue, the Maid of Light."

Mel'Anor asked, "Antoff and Al'len, you have both come of your own free will to submit yourselves before El'Alue, the Maid of Light, and you knowingly ask for this union?" Antoff, holding Al'len's hands, looked into her eyes. "Al'len, you are my joy and I would be with you always as one, not just in my heart, but as one in every way. I ask you to join with me and be one soul always."

Al'len's blue eyes held him for a moment before she answered, "I have never wanted to be the center of so many. I always wanted to be loved by just one man. Fate chooses many things for us and we do not have control over it. But this I can choose. You, Antoff, are that man. I will be one in all ways. Our souls are bound forever, not two, just one."

Mel'Anor and Tes'sus lifted their left thumbs. Mel'Anor placed his on Al'len's forehead, and Tes'sus pressed hers to Antoff's, and they spoke as one voice, "I name you as one and mark your souls in the sight of El'Alue, the Maid of Light. You are now made forever one." Their thumbs glowed brightly, and the Power of a god threaded through their bodies, passing from one to the other, intertwining their souls. Antoff felt El'Alue, the Maid of Light. They ended with smiles and kissed.

When they finished, Mel'Anor asked, "Antoff, for the love of the gods, are we done?"

Antoff and Al'len laughed. "Yes, we are done."

"Good, let's eat," Mel'Anor said. "I'm starving."

Chapter 6 State Of Peace

"Love is always breaking your heart. It whispers in the ache of waiting for a beloved's return, empathizes in witnessing the struggles and growth of those we love, and trembles with bittersweet pride as our children find their own paths. Yet, within the breaking, our hearts burst with joy, painting our world in the warmth of pure delight. Love, a mysterious masterpiece of emotions, shapes us, reminds us, and finally, our breaking hearts define us."

Lamps, candles, and crackling hearth fires illuminated the dining hall, revealing rows of stone tables set to host hundreds in shifts. Crackling fires set in hearths burned on each end, casting a warm glow throughout the hall. On one side, a double door led to a small balcony with delicately carved stone rails and balusters, offering a view of the Field of Dan'Nor beyond the battlements, where a banner audibly flapped in the wind. The breeze filtered in slowly, bringing a cool air, while the moons rose above the mountaintops, their golden light gently kissing the trees that bordered the meadow.

Tara's kitchen staff, a team of dedicated young people, prepared a splendid meal, arranging tables with an array of plates, meats, vegetables, and wine, ready for the bustling crowd. As the doors swung open, the crowded hall flooded in, creating a wash of sound and voices.

De'Nidra hired Mrs. Devens from the Inn of the Old Rusty Bucket to provide entertainment. Musicians dressed in white livery hurriedly set up on the open balcony, tuning their harps and lutes. They began to play a joyous and moving song with a lively beat, perfect for dancing and smiling. It was a beat that invited people to rejoice and momentarily forget life's struggles, a beat for reminiscing and love.

People found their seats, and some took to the dance floor. A young blonde woman in a violet spring dress with plumb scrollwork on the sleeves sang a song. It was about a single flower and how it opens to the rising suns, like a young couple awaiting their lover's embrace—a song that evoked memories of firsts. The first love, the first dance. That breathless first kiss. The first moment when you knew you loved someone and experienced your first heartbreak. A night unfolded, rich with firsts and cherished memories.

Tara and Edward entered the hall, and applause erupted. Following closely were Al'len and Antoff, who received enthusiastic claps and hoots from the warriors. Ivan followed, with Lil on his arm, and then De'Nidra and Tem'Aldar. The dance floor cleared for them. Edward, visibly nervous, led Tara to the floor, smiling down at her with the familiarity of two people who had become one. It was apparent he had practiced. He took her hand and placed his other hand on her waist as they glided across the floor. Tara smiled up at him with pride.

Antoff led Al'len to the dance floor, bowing in the traditional manner. He took her hand in his, and he placed one on her waist. They danced, lost in each other. The newness and unity of their love, a singularity.

Ivan insisted that Lil join him, even though she was shy. He persisted until she took his hand. She danced with grace, and when a smile lit her face, it warmed the entire room. Everyone applauded for them.

The last to enter the room were Lars and Cur'Ra. He led her reluctantly to the floor, wearing a wide, indulgent smile. He took her hand guiding her in the dance. De'Nidra and Tem'Aldar received applause as they spun around, bringing a blush to her cheeks and a smile to her face. Everyone wanted to join them, and the dance floor became packed with songs, laughter, and joyous dancing. It carried on, and when the music changed, the men sat down. However, there was always another man waiting in line to ask a lady for a dance.

Al'len felt like she had danced with everyone in the room. After only dancing with Antoff before, her only two dances in a thousand years, it was a little overwhelming to be surrounded by so many people and their hopes. Stepping from the floor, she almost ran into a tall, dark man with a lovely woman on his arm. He was tall and handsome.

Her breath caught—De'rious. The recognition was instantaneous. He bowed in the old form and gave a knowing, quizzical smile, a smile that held questions but no threat. Al'len curtsied deeply, placing her hand on her heart. He took her hand, and she allowed herself to be led to the floor. He looked at the musicians, and they began to play an ancient song, one from the courts of old that evoked a flutter, because it was one they could not know.

Gliding in De'rious hands, Al'len felt a dip as the music softened. When she was on her feet again, he whispered to her. His voice was low and secretive, like a man who knew things about her that no one else could see. "A joyous occasion, this El'Alue. It hurt when you failed to invite me. So much so that we came on our own, seeing how we are such old friends. Hil'Di and I were sure it was a mistake, hmm?" He dipped El'Alue deeply again and smiled at her.

Al'len smiled back at the dip, "Had I knew you were about, I would have."

De'rious grinned indulgently, like you do when a naughty child is caught in a lie. "You press the boundaries of the agreement, El'Alue. I wanted to tell you that others are now using these same new rules in the game. The new rules you made when you created Al'len. We all have one now, and it is refreshing for Hil'Di and I to walk together as we did in the old days. I'm sure, since you were the first to do it, you remember. I wanted to warn you that every time you step outside our little box, you are changing the rules for everyone."

The dance ended, and De'rious gave a generous and grateful bow to Al'len. Inclining her head, feeling butterflies bouncing in her stomach, she took a bench in the open space next to Antoff.

The musicians played a local piece, a joyous melody with a fast tempo. De'rious and Hil'Di, a smoldering dark-haired girl with large oval brown eyes, looked longingly toward the dance floor. De'rious laughed and led her to the floor. They danced like the young, set free to explore a new life beyond the scope of a sheltered existence.

Al'len decided there and then that Antoff would only receive the Power due to him as a Priest Knight and not a drop more. Fortunately, that included the Power she had given to Ram'Del, Defender of the Light. As for the things that passed between them in the lazy hours of the night notwithstanding, trying to deny her, that would cause a fight.

Antoff looked at her with his ice-blue eyes, the ones that made her shiver. "Al'len, when you were dancing with that man just now, I felt a stab of fear. Are you okay? It seemed like you knew him and that lovely woman on his arm." There was a seriousness in Antoff's voice, the seriousness of a Priest Knight that could burst into a violent, well-drilled soldier if necessary.

Al'len replied, "It's fine. He just surprised me—an old friend turning up out of nowhere and asking for a dance." She gave Antoff a look, suggesting he inquire later when they were in a less public setting.

"I see." He said. Letting it go for now.

A lively crowd of mortals filled tables, surrounding Lil and Ivan with the pulse of life. Eager to acquaint themselves with her, some mortals approached Lil for a dance, their thoughts veering into realms of desire. They found her captivating beauty and mysterious aura irresistible. On her plate, untouched food sat as she absently pushed it around with a fork. Ivan discreetly helped himself to some, creating the illusion that she had partaken in the meal. Although repulsed by the thought of consuming dead animals, Lil forgave him for not comprehending the weight of her closeness to vibrant life and the overwhelming pressures it imposed on her.

Amidst the bustling atmosphere, Lil couldn't help but tremble within, bombarded by an avalanche of sensations. Life surged and enticed from every corner, its attractive charm making her hold on to Ivan's arm like an anchor in a tempest. Lil, who had only interacted with mortals out of necessity for survival, found the experience intoxicating. Ivan remained oblivious to their means of survival in this shattered world after the change. While he understood the need for life energy to sustain oneself, his essence, partly drawn from mortals, allowed him to stave off its effects through conventional sustenance. Although it would only provide a temporary reprieve, it offered him more time—a luxury Lil did not have.

"Lil, are you all right?" Ivan asked, sensing her inner struggle.

"I am fine, my Lord. It's overwhelming to be so close," she hesitated, "to so many people." She projected an image to him, revealing the seductive pulsation of life surrounding her.

Do we need to leave? He responded through their mental connection, curiosity filling his query. "My Lady, would you care to step outside and enjoy the night air?"

Lil smiled, appreciating his wit and concern. "If it pleases you, my Lord, I would relish that."

Ivan rose, extending his arm to her. "I believe I shall take this enchanting lady for an evening stroll in Dan'Nor." He nodded politely to Antoff, excusing them from the crowded table.

Ivan placed her arm in his. They walked out through the rectory's rear entrance, descending the imposing steps and crossing the stable yard. Ivan opened the creaking gate made of heavy bronze. The Field of Dan'Nor unfolded before them. Ivan led Lil through the tall grass, guided by the golden brushstrokes of moonlight painting the swaying blades. Life teemed, chirping, shimmering, and exhaling in every direction. They reached the trees, an oasis of vibrancy, where creatures took refuge in branches like suspended lights, and life fluttered and crawled ceaselessly.

"Lil," Ivan whispered, drawing her hands against his chest, "do you hold affection for me?" His emotions resonated powerfully and securely within her mind.

"I do, my Lord. I have sensed the pleasure you derive from my company," she paused, her voice tender.

Ivan's smile acknowledged the unspoken attraction he shared with her. "I had hoped you, too, felt similarly towards me. I do not want to overwhelm you if you would rather wait to speak of these things in a more subdued setting."

Lil's blush gently brushed against his thoughts, a testament to her reciprocated desire. "I have found our time together exceedingly gratifying, and I wished to avoid overwhelming you with our unfamiliar ways. I fear taking advantage of an uninitiated mind."

In that moment, something clicked within Ivan, and a floodgate of emotion burst. Not just his, but hers as well. They kissed, a kiss filled with hunger and vitality. The mortal part of Ivan was a fire that called to her. Lil responded, returning his kiss in a manner familiar to mortals. It was an experience both new and extraordinary, as his hunger satiated her own.

She was breathless. "My Lord, you don't comprehend the implications of your request. The workings of my existence differ from those of a mortal woman," Lil interjected, her voice tinged with caution.

Ivan burned with desire, completely captivated. "If knowing you fully, Lil, comes at a cost, I shall gladly pay it for the privilege of understanding you."

Lil smiled, savoring his hunger and his yearning for her. She pondered for a moment before responding, cherishing the intimacy they shared. "There is a price to pay, my Lord, in such a bond. We would share what sustains us, and since you carry the essence of life within you, I cannot predict its effect on your longevity. I would not willingly diminish what is so precious."

Without hesitation, he kissed her once more, warmth and vitality emanating from their embrace. "Is a life without fulfillment truly living, Lil? I think not. Is an eternity spent yearning for unattainable desires worth living? It is not, Lil. I have witnessed the consequences when your pursuit of riddles reaches its end. It extinguishes your essence, for existence loses all meaning. You are an essential part of that meaning and existence for me."

Returning his gaze, Lil's eyes locked with his, the swirls of gold and silver dancing with traces of her blood. "I accept you, Ivan. You have my permission to court me. I shall endeavor not to hurt you beyond," she hesitated,—"repair." Her mind delved deeper, knocking at the door of his soul, which he opened slowly, unexplored territory revealing itself. Their thoughts intertwined in ways his body could only strive to emulate. Lil kissed him gently, her voice laced with promise. "As for the other aspects, my Lord, it shall have to wait."

Hours later, Antoff and Al'len escorted Ivan and Lil through the dimly lit corridors of the sparsely inhabited section of the cathedral. Edward and Tara followed closely behind, their footsteps hurried.

"I couldn't let you leave without saying goodbye, Lil," Tara said, breathless. "You're a wonderful person. Please visit us whenever you can. I am so glad in the last hours we have had the chance to get to know you. I want to know you better."

Lil reached out and took Tara's hands in her own. "I'll try, Tara. I promise. And maybe, eventually, you can come and visit our city too."

Tara raised an eyebrow in surprise. "Really? I'd love to see the city below, and once I learn the way, I can visit whenever you want."

This time, it was Al'len who raised an eyebrow and asked, "Is that so, Tara? How does that work?"

Tara, visibly excited to share her newfound knowledge, replied, "I've been studying a book that Da'Vain gave Va'Yone, and together we discovered how to create a Mage Gate. I've only managed to create a small one so far, but the principles remain the same."

Al'len muttered something under her breath about children playing with fire.

However, Lil spoke up eagerly, "I've read that book, and I understand it, but we don't possess the talent to use it. Are you certain you can?" Obvious excitement in her voice.

Tara's eyes sparkled with confidence. "Yes, I'm sure. I just need to know both locations, and once I do, I believe I can travel between them easily."

Lil looked at Tara with a questioning expression. "If I took you to our city, could you open a Gate there for others to pass through?" Tara nodded.

Tara turned to Antoff, hope shining in her eyes. "Can we, Antoff?"

He grunted and asked seriously, "Is it safe, Lil?"

Lil replied, her voice steady, "It's risky to bring her to the Under City using shadows, but as long as she is with me, it will be safe for you to move about within the area once there. However, I can't guarantee Tara's safe return. I don't fully comprehend how the Torrent uses Power, which may not be enough to ease your concerns."

Tara glanced at Al'len, silently seeking her support.

Al'len smiled at her and said, "I've witnessed her achieve remarkable feats when she puts her mind to it, Antoff. Haven't you?"

Antoff sighed. "Ivan, it seems I'm once again outnumbered."

A wide smile grew on his face. "One should consider themselves fortunate to have such excitement from two lovely ladies, my friend. Denying them would be a substantial loss." Al'len playfully glanced at him. He could feel her certainty through their bond.

"Very well, Tara. If you're certain, we'll wait here. I've been curious about what Master Duncan had been talking about for so many years."

Lil moved closer, but not before Edward expressed his concern, "Tara, please be careful."

Tara reassured him, "Yes, Edward. You're as protective as Antoff." *Maybe worse.* She thought.

Lil whispered, "You need to keep your mind open, Tara. I'll create the image in your mind so you can see it and know its exact position in space. Let's try that first. It's risky to carry someone through the shadows who doesn't possess the talent."

Tara held Lil's hands, finding comfort in the connection. She closed her eyes as Lil did. Lil's mind was overwhelmed by the images of Darkness and Light locked in a struggle for dominance. It was almost too much to bear. If Lil hadn't been holding her hands, she might have fled in fear. Tara tightened her grip, feeling Lil's fear coming through the connection. An image materialized in her mind—a bridge suspended over a rift in the foundation stone of the world below. Its position in space became clear.

"I see it, Lil," Tara said.

Lil reached for Ivan, who embraced her. She fled the connection, still shaken by Tara's mind. *She is like two beings. The one we see before us and another, limitless, floating in a void. The greater mind is like a universe.* Her mind whispered to him.

Tara took a step back, perceiving the Mage Gate as a ribbon of pulsating energy surrounded by a shimmering halo of strange matter. The ribbon flexed and bent like a living entity, connecting distant places by stretching through the fabric of reality. Tara channeled raw Power into the strange matter halo, positioning one gate at her feet and aligning the other with the image Lil had provided. She stabilized the fragile structure of the gate, preventing its collapse. She poured the Power of Darkness and Light into it until the image solidified in her mind. Maintaining a passage that allowed mortals to traverse instantaneously required an immense amount of Power.

A ribbon of light sliced through the air, towering over a man's height and twice as wide. It shimmered, on the verge of collapsing, before bursting into a purple globe in the center—a liquid pool reflecting the image of the rift. The breach emitted intense heat through the gate, its sheer walls descending to meet bubbling molten rock leagues below, casting a vivid orange glow on a stone platform just before a bridge spanning across a massive tear in the stone. "There it is, just as you showed me, Lil." Tara stepped through to the other side.

Ivan and Lil allowed the shadow to reach and envelop them within its embrace. They emerged from the shadows, landing near a wall close to the bridge, wisps of smoky spiderweb dissipating around them.

Antoff eyed Al'len suspiciously, but she raised her hands, assuring him, "That was all her doing, Antoff. Shall we go?" Edward was the next to cross, and Al'len led Antoff by the hand. They passed through the barrier, and a chilling cold washed over them like ice water. They had arrived.

"Exceptional work, Tara!" Al'len exclaimed, her approval unmistakable in her voice. "The larger and more distant the Gate, the greater the cost." Tara nodded.

Mist stepped from the shadows, her slight form still cloaked in the dim light of the hall strobing in purple nimbus. The Mage Gate pulsed with Power, a Power she would kill to possess. Peering through the barrier of the liquid pool, she watched them cross the bridge that spanned the rift in the massive stone chamber. Once Ivan and his companions had crossed, she fixed the location in her mind. Although it was still risky to use the shadow without physically being there, Mist decided, "I'll risk it, but I will use the gate!" she whispered to herself. Mist stepped through the event horizon of the gate, its cold liquid caused a shudder as she passed through. Immediately, she sprinted towards the shadows, which enveloped her as she reached the edge of their darkness.

Tara turned, sensing a pull on her Power as if someone had come through, but the Gate was empty; no one was there. Letting the Mage Gate collapse, she turned back and continued.

Ivan led them to the Repository of Knowledge. A dark room that echoed with their footsteps. Ivan lit his lamp. The light pooled around it like an oasis. He handed the lamp to Tara, who lifted it high as she stepped around a line of stone benches. The light illuminated a wall with gray stone shelves stacked with tomes and books.

Tara's breath caught. "It's full! This room is filled with knowledge!" She was almost running, sweating from the heat radiating from the rift. Moving along each shelf, she saw titles of every type, grouped by disciplines. "It would take a lifetime, a lifetime!" Tara was in awe.

Lil caught up to her and said, "By yourself, it would take many lifetimes. However, if you had a friend who had read most of it, we could prioritize your interests and significantly reduce the time."

Tara's eyes sparkled. "Really? You would teach me?"

Lil smiled at Tara's hunger for knowledge and replied, "I will."

Tara threw herself at Lil with a hug, and Lil embraced her warmly. Tara was heat and life.

"It would require great effort on your part. This environment is, well," she paused, "unhealthy for mortals. Therefore, we would have to select a subject for you to study. You would take a book, learn the language of math and equations used in some texts, and we would come together here when needed and discuss it further in the world above. You will not initially understand the languages in which some of these works are written, but you will have to learn this language to comprehend much of the content."

Tara gasped. "You're going to be my teacher?"

Lil laughed warmly. "No, I'm going to be your friend." She released Tara from the embrace and added, "Now, pick something before you melt."

Sib'Bal, the Veil of Darkness, gazed into the full-length mirror attached to the wall of her lavish dressing room. Her eyes, a mesmerizing blend of brown streaked with warm gold, captured her reflection, drawing attention to the delicate curve of her lips. Painted a deep shade of crimson, her lips held a seductive draw, adding to the enchanting aura that surrounded her. They curved into a knowing smile, hinting at secrets and promises, while remaining as mysterious as the rest. Her carefully nurtured ebony skin possessed a radiant glow that accentuated her voluptuous curves. Dressed in black and gray silks that bordered on translucency, she revealed just enough to tantalize while keeping her secrets intact. Despite the passage of time, she appeared ageless, defying any notion of being a day over twenty-five. With gentle hands, she delicately plucked the locks of her hair, braided with silver and seashell beads, cascading over her shoulders in a meticulously arranged manner. Sib'Bal was a master at presenting the image she desired others to see.

The reflection of her dressing room mirror showcased opulent surroundings, with warm, brightly colored wood paneling in hues of syrupy sunlight. white silver stone floor tile enhanced the dark furnishings, filling the room with an air of luxury and richness. The faint scent of the briny sea mingled with the fragrant blossoms from her carefully tended garden, extended through the breezeway and offered a breathtaking vista overlooking the harbor.

The Harbor Cities within the Gray area provided a perfect backdrop to her grandeur. Her mansion, perched high upon the steep hills, commanded an unrivaled view of the bustling streams of ships, loading and unloading cargo. Dockworkers skillfully maneuvered waggoners amidst the flow of goods. This seat of Power that she had manifested for herself mattered more than the reality it had overwritten. The oblivious mortals had no inkling of the transformation; it was as though a mere hiccup had occurred, and all she had envisioned within herself had seamlessly replaced whatever had existed before. She was the center of her world and everything else in it was just part of the play.

Chapter 7 Whims And Prayers

"Tread cautiously within the realm of prayer, for words aren't just sounds; they are vessels of Power, shaped by the breath on our tongue and spoken with passion. Handle With care the elements birthed of things that dwell within. Once loose, they touch worlds and evolve. They grow, and then they return. Having concluded their work, the outcome and everything attached, laid before the doorstep of your home."

EL'Keet entered the onyx-carved portal, his gaze capturing the ornate archway's intricate patterns and ancient scripts. As he entered, a chill like ice water washed over him. An oppressive gloom pushed back against his lamp's light. Eerie shadows played on the wall cut smooth. The stone resembled glass, adding depth to the hollow hall. The compression portal was a marvel of time and distance manipulation. Its design held ancient science of space-time, a secret long forgotten for ages.

Gripping a gentleman's cane in his left hand, EL'Keet tapped it incessantly, breaking the heavy silence with an unsettling intrusion. Yet, he preferred to continue tapping away, if for no other reason than to appear unruffled. The journey was tedious despite each step, propelling him through hundreds of feet with each stride. At either end of the hall, a guard stood with a crossbow that could easily kill him. The compression portal left a deep effect on the talented, nullifying their connection to Power within the dead zone.

Concealed within the cane's handle, a slender, razor-sharp dagger awaited need. Perhaps it offered little practicality, but it provided comfort. An appointment to the Dark Council was indeed an honor, but it also carried the peril of a death sentence, given the treacherous nature of its members. It was a lifetime appointment. The only question was, how long would that life be?

The focus of today's meeting revolved around De'Nidra's impending doom. A consequence of leaving the Council of the Dark Order. No one had ever successfully escaped its clutches. De'Nidra, like him, found herself trapped. Despite his warnings about the dangers of rebellion, she had chosen her path. In the end, she had selected a brief life over an eternity of living in Darkness. He never truly believed she was evil. She was just another talented individual caught up in cataclysmic events ensnared by greed.

The bronze doors swung wide. Two of the Dark Guard escorted EL'Keet into the open expanse. A chill ran down his flesh as he left the hidden hall. Using an instrument—a rod—it could be relocated anywhere within a hundred leagues of the Dark Order's meeting place and still provide access.

EL'Keet's boots crunched through the brown grass and stony soil. He muttered his disdain for the desolate terrain. A veil of inverted light hid the entrance, visible only to the talented. Crossing this barrier allowed connection to his Power.

"Gods of darkness, deliver me from this desolation," he murmured, his chestnut eyes absorbing the barrenness of the jagged mountain peaks that rose into the sky before him.

The air crackled with a hiss as a ribbon of light transformed into a pulsating purple globe. The portal revealed a breathtaking garden overlooking the sea. EL'Keet trembled in awe of the energy emanating from the orb, a Gate not of his creation.

From within the globe, a woman's voice, silky and tempting. "Will you just stand there, or shall I answer your prayers?"

As he emerged on the other side, a woman awaited him, bathed in the soft glow of the garden's sunlight. Her golden-brown eyes held a magnetic charm, and her presence was as enchanting as it was commanding. Clad in a mix of gray and black silk, the fabric clung to her shapely curves, accentuated by the sunlight's caress.

She gave EL'Keet a teasing smile. "Will you keep staring all day, or kneel, Great Lord EL'Keet?" Her voice shifted from amusement to a commanding tone.

Obliging, he knelt on one knee, placing his right hand over his heart, and declared, "It is my honor to serve, my Lady."

Sib'Bal tasted his choice in words. "*My Lady.*" She shook her head, and the beads clicked as her lips slid into a disappointed frown. "I am Sib'Bal, the Veil of Darkness, and let me assure you, I am no myth."

Thunder rumbled above, and darkness rolled in from the sea as she rejected the title. "Either you serve me, or you won't be serving anyone at all." Before he could respond, lightning flashed and thunder echoed, demanding his silence. Sib'Bal circled him, her electrifying touch tracing his cheek, evaluating him with her eyes. Her fingers explored the ornate cut of his coat, lingering on his arm with a squeeze. "Finally, I will see your teeth."

Great Lord EL'Keet, proud and defiant, refused to be treated as mere flesh for the amusement of a goddess. Sib'Bal's finger traced his chin, sensing his resentment and relishing the crushing of his pride. Lifting his chin and grabbing it roughly, she commanded him, "Now, show me those teeth." Lightning punctuated her order, and thunder intensified the fear welling within him. Struggling to please a woman as beautiful as she is formidable, EL'Keet forced the best smile he could muster.

She seemed pleased with his effort, "well-brushed teeth and fragrant breath. As for your service, we shall see." She traced his high cheekbones and asked herself a question. "Shall I assess your situation further and evaluate your worth?" Sib'Bal smiled and the Mage Gate collapsed behind him. "Yes, I believe I will. What, surprised, EL'Keet? Did you think to court the Veil of Darkness and then bend me to your will?"

Tara and Edward stood in the Field of Dan'Nor. Its long grass swayed gently in the wind. The midday sun cast a warm glow while its companion followed it lazily across the sky, painting the cloudy canvas with hues of red and pink. Tara held Edward's hand, and shielded her eyes with the other, anticipating the presence of dragons drawing near. Edward felt a strange sensation, a side-effect of their bond and new singularity. It both intrigued and frightened him. Witnessing Tara using her powers differed greatly from feeling her immense strength through their connection.

Tara pointed toward two figures high above, resembling birds—one radiating a shining black hue, and the other emanating an angelic white glow. Edward could see them but also sensed their presence, much to Tara's puzzlement. She questioned how this was possible, suggesting that he must be perceiving them through their connection. Dressed in black leather thief's armor, she had daggers stashed in strategic places and silver-inlaid short swords hanging from her hips.

Edward, on the other hand, donned a simple black leather outfit that felt inadequate compared to Tara's, equipped only with a broadsword and a fine dagger. Antoff had warned him about Tara's growing skill.

The White dragon descended first, its wings drawn tight, resembling a lance of radiant light. Its scales shone as he fell. The Black dragon followed suit, rolling and retracting its wings while pursuing its brother toward the ground. Visions flooded Tara's mind, molten heat emanating from their bodies, visible in the field below. Vapors shimmered upward, casting a luminous glow over the entire landscape. The White dragon spread its wings with a sound of a sail catching a strong wind, while the Black dragon circled overhead in a graceful arc, gradually slowing down before landing. As they entered the field, their massive wings beat the air, creating a hurricane effect with their impressive fifteen-meter span. The words *beautiful* and *powerful* fell short of describing the awe-inspiring presence of these intelligent creatures. Muscles rippled beneath their scales, adorned with overlapping plates—white-edged in gold for one, and black-edged in gold for the other. The gold originated from their mother, Al'amire, the Golden Shadow.

"Tara, why don't they have names?" Edward asked.

The Black dragon nuzzled Tara, and she wrapped her arms around his neck. "I missed you both," she expressed. "The dragons earn their names and decide whether to accept them." Dragons glanced back at her, their horned heads swaying, but they also observed Edward in a manner unlike before. The White dragon moved closer to Edward, baring its dagger-like teeth, and sniffed him. Tara giggled, but Edward felt a tinge of fear. "The White believes he can detect your presence within me, and he claims that he could find you anywhere because of it," she clarified.

Edward swallowed hard. "Tara, that sounded like a threat."

She smiled, assuring him, "No, well, yes. They're still adapting to our connection. They think I'm your bondholder." She snickered.

"Sometimes Tara, I feel that way too," he confessed, a smile gracing his face.

"Edward, do you know you say things that make me want to thump you?" The White dragon playfully nudged him with its nose, almost knocking him over.

"All right, let's see that sword style Antoff was talking about," Edward suggested.

She slid off the Black dragon's neck, standing beside Edward, affectionately patted the White dragon's head. The dragons moved away and settled in the grass, their immense bodies reaching twice the height of a warhorse.

With a flourish, Tara unsheathed her short swords and spun them skillfully. "This is called At'Aelcontoe, Edward," she announced.

He laughed. "Whatever it's called, be careful. Those blades look sharp. Shouldn't we train with wooden ones first?"

She arched an eyebrow at him. He drew his broadsword and loosened his arm. "Edward, you can stop stalling." Engaging in a whirling form, Tara's blades sliced through the air as she approached him, a smile on her lovely face. She struck at him repeatedly, and he parried her blows.

"You're dropping your left shoulder, my dear," he remarked.

Her smile wavered, but she intensified her assault. Gracefully flowing through her forms, she deflected his strikes and skillfully evaded his attacks. Her style differed from his own, which relied on aggression and force, taught to warriors from a young age. She effortlessly redirected his Power rather than confronting it head-on. He pressed harder, pushing her faster. She deflected his strike with her left blade and tapped his side lightly with the flat of her right.

He checked for blood but found none. *Well, it stung as if she had.* "Take it easy," he exclaimed.

She laughed sweetly; the smirk returning to her face. "I've been practicing with Al'len every day, Edward," she said with a playful grin. "Besides, I don't recall you ever saying, 'take it easy' before."

He grunted. "Before?"

She raised an eyebrow.

"That's it!" Edward yelled, tossing his sword aside and giving chase. Tara ran, laughing. She slowed so he could catch her. They tumbled into the grass.

Mist drifted through the dark halls, concealed by enveloping shadows. The inhabitants of this place possessed keen intellect and perceptiveness, fully attuned to their surroundings. Although she could see clearly in the Darkness, she hesitated to venture beyond its confines. These shadows occupied the space where Light and Darkness intertwined, pulsating with the conflict between the two realms. Most beings used them solely for travel, never daring to step onto the boundary that represented a partial merging of fixed elements from both realms—a kind of enduring crossroads. Mountains, cities, and oceans—accepted constructs in both realms—existed here as a hazy interpretation of acknowledged truths. To interact with the world, Mist had to step out, but whenever she did, their minds fixated on her, questioning and probing.

Ivan and the milky woman devoted an inordinate amount of time to what Mist regarded as the library. She needed time to search it herself, but someone was always engrossed in reading, which infuriated her. In its place, she chose instead to explore the distant lower halls of the Under City first. Swift travel required knowledge of both the current location and the destination; otherwise, aimless wandering could consume precious time. Exiting the current location was possible, but being lost meant finding a familiar place from memory before visualizing the desired destination. And that was her current predicament—she was lost. Nothing within this foggy existence seemed familiar.

The corridor Mist traversed was long, leading to a spacious, round room. In its center stood a massive double arch, nestled in a depression in the floor, surrounded by the top of a giant metal sphere, barely separated from the stone floor. She recognized it—it was even larger than the one in her master's bastion beneath the twisted lands.

I will risk it! She thought, emerging from the shadows. Thin wisps, resembling smoky spiderwebs, clung to her and slowly dissipated, connecting her to the blackness of the portal room. As her eyes acclimated, the remarkable features of the place gradually revealed themselves.

Glowing symbols and diagrams covered the ceiling and walls crawling across them, creating an ever-changing scene. It resembled the small book she had taken from Ivan, but on an enormous scale. The sprawling script mirrored the language within the book, but its meaning eluded her, offering only fragments of understanding. The pictures depicted spheres—planets—and lists of locations within each one. Hundreds and thousands of them moved across every surface of the room. Scattered stacks of parchments held drawings and copies of magical Scripts, all incomprehensible.

Hurry! She urged herself, sifting through the piles of parchments that were arranged neatly, maintaining focus to avoid detection. She gathered anything with scripted names resembling her master's tongue and folded them into a pouch. Some pictures contained a script that closely resembled her master's language, but certainty eluded her. *Hurry!* Then a powerful mind found hers and probed, sending chills down her spine. Terrified, she fled back into the shadows.

Lord Ivan, an issue requires your immediate attention. Da'Vain, the Chronicler's voice, reached him. There was no trace of mirth as was usual; only information conveyed, removing anything that could cause confusion.

"Tell me," Lil questioned. She looked up from the translation Ivan had attempted. It was poor, but he was learning quickly.

"Da'Vain conveyed reports of a presence in the lower portal chamber; he's en route as we speak. He is heading there now. Are you aware of it? I have never learned of it until now."

Lil stepped closer and took his hand. He closed his eyes and let Lil project the image that flowed into his mind. The shadows reached for them, and they were there. Da'Vain stood next to a double archway in a depression, sifting through scattered materials on the floor, which lacked the usual neatness characteristic of their species.

"What is this place, Da'Vain?" Ivan asked.

"It is a room that has been our salvation for a long time. An enigma we have not completely solved, nor had the talent to use it fully," Lil continued to hold his hand. "It looks like someone has ransacked this place. What is missing?" She inquired.

Da'Vain placed a handful of papers back on the stack to which they belonged. "Some locations of the De'Moggda Lucida."

Ivan was confused. "De'Moggda what?"

Da'Vain pointed at some glowing script crawling across the wall. "De'Moggda Lucida, Ivan. *'The Clarity of Dimensions'* or *'The Illuminated Realms'* is a translation of the images and script you see displayed on the walls and ceiling. The language is one of math and equations, similar to what you are learning from Lil now." He smiled. "Or at the very least, some things you have been learning from her, anyway." That last part contained mirth, and Lil sent him a blush that entered his mind. *Was that embarrassment?*

"I have seen a smaller version of this when we found one of your lost ones. The book and crystal stolen from Me had similar uses. There was also a large portal there, buried in a collapse. What is the importance of the De'Moggda Lucida, and what did they take?" Ivan inquired.

"The De'Moggda Lucida, a mystical artifact, unveils the coordinates of hidden portals across time and space. In the hands of the talented, it opens doors to distant realms and safe returns," Da'Vain explained. "That is as much as we understand of it."

Lil was fearful, and Ivan felt that fear seeping into him. *Why are you afraid, Lil?* He questioned it in his mind and waited for an answer.

"My Lord, this is a tragedy. Some of us have long argued for sharing this information with those who possess the talent to use it, but there was no one we could trust. The fear was that if an evil mage with the talent gained access, it could lead to more destruction, and the Power it grants, limitless travel would be devastating in the wrong hands."

Ivan contemplated the information swirling in his mind. "Can you retranslate those sections and prepare new copies?" he asked.

"Yes, it would take some time, but since the work has already been done, it should not be difficult to replicate," Da'Vain replied.

"And how many of those locations did they take?" Ivan asked.

"Seven." He said.

Ivan wrestled with his options, but the urgency of the situation left him no choice but to act.

The nest was stirring, as Da'Vain interpreted his request for translation as a command. The work was about to begin.

"It is likely that someone from the Bastion of Light in the Twisted Lands was here, ransacking the place. The Dominion that lived there wanted to escape, and unearthing the portal would have been its way out. Some of my essences came from that creature, and we encountered it there. The Dominion asked Tara to help it escape. She damaged it and left it banished, unwilling to release it upon the world. If anyone was likely to have sent a spy, it would be that creature. Pulled from another realm before the breaking, possibly one of your De'Moggda Lucida."

"Sending it back does not concern me. If it escaped, it can return, and it was angry about our world disrupting its rule. Vengeance was clearly part of its plan. While I am not as skilled at reading people as you are, that much was clear in our encounter with it. Once the translations are complete and copies have been made. I want Tara to be trained on the translations and familiarized with this room. Antoff and Al'len need to be told about the breach and fully briefed on what we have uncovered during your epoch of study. I will head up and talk to Antoff and I expect he will have questions. I want to have the answers quickly."

Now there was no question, those were commands. Da'Vain bowed formally and Lil curtsied deeply as pools of Darkness slid over him and enveloped Ivan in shadow.

Chapter 8 Veil Asunder

"Ignorance is like a veil: not completely blind, but it obscures clarity. Knowledge is a fundamental catalyst for change and preserves a person's unobscured conjecture. By imparting wisdom, you bring Light, we equip minds to perceive truth and wonders with certainty. The future stands to benefit from clearer sight and perpetual curiosity."

Al'len and Antoff sat opposite De'Nidra in the dining hall. The Elder Brother descended toward the horizon, casting a warm afternoon glow through windows. The balcony stood open, allowing the light to spill forth, accompanied by a fresh breeze. Spring neared its end, and the imminent arrival of summer was palpable.

De'Nidra shared what she knew about Haven. "Wards are behind the gate and spread throughout the city, making it difficult for you to enter unnoticed. While passage through the gate is not impossible, it would undoubtedly lead to discovery afterward. Concerns about assassins employed by both sides have persisted since the Breaking. Assassins orchestrated the Bishopric's removal of Master Duncan."

Antoff's eyes went icy, "What did you say about Duncan?" His jaw clenched.

Al'len sensed Antoff's simmering anger, ready to erupt. "De'Nidra, we need the full story about Duncan."

"I assumed everyone was aware of what happened, or I would have revealed it earlier. Master Duncan had been delving into the hidden truths behind the Breaking long before his retirement. For years, they attempted to dissuade him from pursuing that path, fearing the exposure of the stolen Power. Duncan drew close to uncovering the truth, prompting his assignment to the campaigns in the Gray Area and Twisted Lands. He remained there until his retirement. Upon his return, the High Bishop denied him a promotion to Diocesan, implying suspicions of Duncan's perusal of heretical texts during his studies. Duncan departed for the Gray Area, choosing to live in RavenHof and continue his work. Fate intervened, leading Tara to him. When the High Bishop discovered his departure and years of ongoing research, they dispatched an assassin to poison him."

Antoff pounded his fist on the table, then rose and leaned against the balcony rail. He wanted to scream, but younglings in the stable yard played with hoops and balls. He refused to introduce fear into children's lives already upended.

His voice emerged subdued and seething. "We didn't know. Had I known, I would have personally killed that imposter myself." He gazed out upon the Field of Dan'Nor, where dragons reclined in the grass and Edward chased Tara in the meadow. Her laughter filled the air, her happiness a vision. Now he would have to inform her and mar what had been a wondrous day—the first full day with the man who had captured her heart and shared her love completely. That pained Antoff. Tara sought justice, and he would make sure she got it. He called out into the field, waving for Tara and Edward to join him.

"Oh boy, Tara, do you think he saw us?" Tara had long yellow grass sticking out of her hair, and her armor was undone.

"Edward, we have said our vows! We are not children." She bit her lip. "Still, don't bring it up unless he says something first. You are always telling on yourself."

"Am not," Edward smiled at her indignantly. "That, Tara, was uncalled for. I do not tell on myself."

Tara put her hands on her hips. Edward found the display cute in her disheveled state. "Edward, you can't act like that anymore. I can tell the difference."

He laughed, picking up his sword and sheathing it. "Because you're my bondholder?"

A smile slid from her face. She chased after him. They ran toward the cathedral, Edward trying to evade her playful swipes.

As Tara and Edward entered the dining hall, their appearance in disarray, they nearly collided with Ivan. He raised an eyebrow, a smirk playing on his lips. "Have we been frolicking in hay storms?"

Tara's cheeks turned the color of ripe peaches, a silent testament to their earlier escapades, while Edward's smile held the shadow of their shared secrets, "Yes, a very exciting hay storm," Edward said.

Tara's blush could not possibly get any deeper. Edward smiled at Tara, and she gave him the going to get it later look. It also passed through their bond. "We are heading to the dining hall. Antoff called us in."

"That's good." Ivan said. "I need to speak with him as well." *Tara, I am going to act as if I can't hear your thoughts.* He sent.

She nearly stumbled. Tara could feel the heat creeping into her cheeks. She was going as red as a bloodbat. She had been thinking about Edward and that stupid field. *Damn it Edward!* She wanted to scream.

They entered the dining hall, following Ivan. Antoff and Al'len sat together, while De'Nidra took the seat across from them. Al'len appeared troubled, and Antoff was angry. Something boiled beneath his surface.

"Ivan, I'm glad you're here. We have a big problem," Antoff said.

"Well, as bad as you may think it is, my friend, it is far worse than you know," Ivan replied, sitting next to Antoff, leaving the spot next to De'Nidra for Tara and Edward.

"What do you mean, Ivan?" Al'len asked, allowing Antoff time to collect his thoughts.

"In the Under City, we had a breach today. I believe the Dominion sent someone to infiltrate the portal room," Ivan explained. His statement grabbed everyone's attention, and a flurry of questions ensued.

"What are you saying?" Tara asked. "Why would the Dominion do that?"

"I didn't find out until it happened. Something gained access to the portal room and stole some research, a part of the De'Moggda Lucida. *'The Clarity of Dimensions'* or *'The Illuminated Realms,'* he translated. "It's a massive room with script crawling across the walls and ceiling and a large arch in the center. I recognized the portal because there's a similar one in the old bastion where we defeated Lord De'von. That's why they desired the book and crystal. It's likely the same thief took them from me."

Al'len tapped her chin in thought. "If they find someone to decipher those fragments of De'Moggda Lucida, they could use it to escape and travel to another world. We can't allow that to happen, Antoff. If they can leave, they can also return."

Tara's voice held fear. "That's what the Dominion wanted, and if he escapes, I don't know what he'll do."

"He seemed furious when you spoke. He wanted out. You made it clear that he couldn't leave, using a bolt of lightning that nearly killed him," Edward recounted.

Tara asked. "Did he understand?" She raised a questioning eyebrow.

"Yes, he did." Edward answered. "What I'm saying is, by refusing him, you've likely earned his enmity."

"Tara, if you wouldn't mind, I'd like you to work with Lil on the translations," Ivan suggested.

"Sure, I'd love to help Lil. I can learn the language in the process." Tara agreed.

"Hold on, Ivan," Antoff interjected. "There's another issue. Tara, when I tell you this, you must remain composed, okay? We have children and families here, and we don't want to frighten them unnecessarily. Understand?"

"Just tell me," Tara urged. She clutched Edward's hand under the table.

"Tara, the Dark Order didn't kill Master Duncan. The High Bishop in the Haven Cathedral of Light had him murdered," Antoff revealed.

"What?" Tara exclaimed. "Why?"

"Because he was going to expose the Bishopric's blatant misuse of EL'ALue, the Maid of Light and the Under City. They were using the Power of Darkness, all of it, Tara. He intended to bring their entire operation into the Light," Antoff explained.

Ivan's eyes flicked between them. "Well, my friend, we need to figure out what to do."

Al'len chimed in, "We can't make any progress until the Order of the Light is restored. If we get attacked and the Order of the Light is not whole, it would be devastating. One of the few things that maintains a type of balance is our ability to resist sufficiently to hold back the tide but not overcome it. A fictitious balance, but it is all we have for now. At least until we can get out there and figure it out. There's no guarantee the other gods would intervene. We need to devise a plan."

"De'rious danced with me during last night's dinner." The statement caused everyone to pause. "He warned me about pushing the boundaries too far, emphasizing that each of them now possessed their own version of an 'Al'len.' He conveyed that constantly testing the limits of our agreement would entangle the other gods in the reality of the world," Al'len said.

"Last night, there were so many strangers; I couldn't recognize most of them," Tara said. "But De'rious, the God of Dismay and Sorrow, truly scares me. I did not even feel him there."

Al'len clarified, "If I meddle with the course of fate, they will do the same, potentially leading to war. Truth is, he is right. My presence has already affected reality, although you all might not see it."

Antoff stroked a lowered brow. "Al'len, What are you saying?"

Al'len shook her head. "I mean, I wanted to be with you, Antoff, and I'm happy that we've exchanged vows. But it's not just us. Everyone else is trying to do the same. My desires are affecting everything around us. Desire has an impact, and Tara, you have to be careful too, because Edward will influence your desires and will. Do you understand?"

"Yes, I think so. Since I can overwrite it, and I'm always connected to a higher reality. If I'm not mindful, I can change things from the way they are to the way I want them," Tara replied.

"That's right, and Edward can also influence that because he is connected to you. He is one with you. The same goes for us, Antoff. All of you need to be careful. It will be up to you to strategize and devise a plan to get Lars and the two hundred and forty-two Warriors of the Light into Haven without being noticed. My role will be limited to providing physical support," Al'len declared firmly.

"As long as the result is me wrapping my hands around that fat bishop's neck, it's a good plan. It will take a few days to put this together, so let's get to work," Antoff added.

As early summer arrived, the winds grew stronger in the Blackened Lands. Beyond the fortress of Are'Amadon in the desolate lands, huge dust storms swirled, lifting black and red soil into the air. Amorath paid little attention to the tribes enduring the relentless winds beyond the fortress walls. From the highest tower's balcony, he overlooked the vast expanse of land, though he rarely bothered to gaze upon it. Withdrawing his aging hands from the balcony rail, he entered the chamber to await Lord Modred.

Inside, the map table focused on Coth'Venter. Constructed from black sand, it mirrored every detail of the city, particularly the Cathedral of Light, where a blinking glyph pulsated rhythmically.

Lord Modred maneuvered his flight path wide of the tower, buffeted by the gusts from all directions. His wings flared wide as he touched down on the stone floor. Upon arriving from the twisted lands, he wasted no time and sought his reports. Acquiring them proved challenging, as the Dragon Hounds had nested with a large gold dragon somewhere north of the Steps of Glass. Folding his bat-like wings behind him, he transformed them into a black, leathery cloak and entered Modred's chambers.

"Modred, why am I waiting in your room for my report instead of you waiting in my hall?" Modred dropped to one knee. His surprise was unmistakable.

How does he do that? Modred let out a half drawn breath. *Popping up like that. I nearly fill my armor every time he does it.* "Forgive me, Great Lord. I was—detained." He dared not lift his gaze from the floor, aware of the strained relationship he had with Amorath since his failure to secure the Torrent and the subsequent loss of most of his troops.

"Well, Modred, I am waiting. You can give your report now."

Modred stuttered, "My Lord, the City Master is under our control, and I have received word that De'Nidra will make contact soon. Additionally, Be'elota is completing the reeducation of a captured Priest Knight who will infiltrate the traitor's ranks and maintain surveillance until you order her death."

The black sand on the map table jittered, causing the three-dimensional model to flatten and spread out. Amorath questioned, "What is this?"

"I do not know, my Lord," came the reply.

"Stand up and see for yourself," Amorath commanded.

"This has never happened before, my Lord." Modred retrieved a teardrop-shaped quartz crystal from around his neck and concentrated, causing a faint light to dance within. "Nothing."

Once more, the sand shifted, gradually forming a figure Amorath hadn't seen in ages. Amorath snapped, "Mali'Gorthos, kneel, you fool." Modred was the first to kneel, and Amorath bowed deeply. Amorath then rose as a new glyph blinked. "How may I serve you, master?"

Mali'Gorthos' voice, a gentle whisper as dry as sand. "Tell me the latitude I have granted you have not been wasted. Tell me you have secured a vessel for us to share and that your attempt to recover the technologies for our ascension has not failed."

Modred sensed that somehow he might be blamed for any forthcoming failure, causing his hackles to raise.

Amorath answered, "Mali'Gorthos, I have found a Torrent, and his training is progressing rapidly. In a few years…"

"Silence!" Mali'Gorthos said as two red beams of light struck the battlements below the tower, engulfing the area in billowing dust.

"You do not have years. I grant you one. Any further failures, and a new Lord shall reign over this keep. Do you test my patience, Amorath?"

"No, Great Lord, of course not. I will redouble my efforts, and within the year, all will be ready." The black sand collapsed back onto the table, and Coth'Venter took shape once more.

A red flash streaked through dusty air and the ground shook the fortress of Are'Amadon. Dust billowed into a large round room that served as Moros's quarters. Rem'Mel, the Middle Mage, hurried toward the child playing among his toys in a sunken central octagon, five steps below the ground floor. Moros cried out in fear, and Rem'Mel quickly covered him with his crimson-colored robes.

"Hush now, little one. Nothing will harm you while I watch over you," Rem'Mel reassured the child. Moros cries subsided, and he clung to the Middle Mage, finding solace amid the rustling fabric that surrounded them.

"What was it?" Moros asked.

"I don't know, Moros, but when unexpected events occur, it's natural to feel panicked and want to run. Safety must always come first," Rem'Mel explained, gently pulling the clinging teen away from his robe. He held him at arm's length. "But once we are safe, we can explore, learn, and grow. Everything in the world holds knowledge for an attentive mind. Although your gifts surpass my own, we can still learn from each other."

"Can we go see it?" Moros whispered, extending his hand. Against his better judgment, Rem'Mel felt a fondness for this child. Great Lord Amorath had forbidden kindness and connections, but this child represented a future for him, as much as his Lord did. Rem'Mel took the child's hand and led him to an open hall exposed to the air. Two span-wide holes had punched through the battlement walls, causing a small outbuilding to collapse. Rubble cluttered the yard, as the wind rose above the walls carrying away dust. It had been perilously close to the child's quarters.

"You see? Now, what do you observe?" Moros shielded his eyes from the suns, looking out at the wreckage.

"The holes are round and come from above, but not straight up. It's more like this." Moros aligned his hand to demonstrate the trajectory of the holes. Rem'Mel followed the boy's presumed angle.

"Yes, just so. Now we know that it was from above and at that angle," the Middle Mage said, squatting down and pulling the child with him. He traced on the dusty stone floor, first a circle and then lines radiating from the center. "These markings are degrees. The circle starts at zero degrees and goes around in a full circle of three hundred and sixty degrees. To simplify, we divide it into quarters and ninetieths. Do you see?"

Moros nodded.

"Tell me, child, which line is closest to the path you showed me with your hand?"

Moros pointed to the line numbered sixty.

"Okay, and how many lines would you add to match it exactly?" Rem'Mel inquired. Moros drew three tiny lines with his finger.

"Good, Moros. So tell me, how many degrees of angle are there?" The child studied the drawing in the dirt.

"Sixty-three?" Moros ventured.

Rem'Mel nodded. "Yes, that's correct. Now let's expand our thinking a little more, shall we?" The boy showed interest. "Just as there is a circle that goes this way, there is also a circle that goes the other way." The Middle Mage drew in the dirt with his finger. "This creates a sphere with degrees that encircle it. You can determine the angle from the horizontal, which represents the land's horizon, or ninety degrees straight up for the vertical." Their eyes followed the path upward into the cloudless, dusty sky.

A ribbon of light split the air next to the destroyed building. It wavered and blossomed into a purple orb larger than a man. In its center, a pool floated like water, revealing a dim room. Lord Modred, a great black demon, knelt within. "I will not fail you, my master." The image of Amorath's withered form stepped before the pool, leaning on his aged staff, its gem strobing an amber light in the darkness. He limped out and stepped onto the dusty cobblestones of the open courtyard square. "See that you don't!" the Mage Gate winked out.

"Ah, boy, I see you there. We have a lot of work to do. Your training is being intensified," Amorath said, pulling the silk hood over his gray, shriveled head. Taking the boy's hand from Rem'Mel, he led Moros toward his room, with the Middle Mage following behind. Suddenly, his master turned. "No, not you," he said, waving a gray, flaky hand. "Make sure this mess gets cleaned up. The knowledge I will impart to the boy exceeds your capabilities. Perhaps if the child progresses as I approve, I might reconsider." He gave Rem'Mel a wicked smile and gestured for him to attend to the still-smoking wreckage. Heavy, age-blackened doors closed behind them with a wooden thump.

Rem'Mel walked toward the slave quarters, sweat forming on his brow in the searing heat, his burning desire to learn the secrets granted to the boy. "The only way that old crone will teach me anything is if I can learn from him through the boy." Great Lord Amorath never shared actual Power with anyone, especially if they lacked a talent he could exploit for his own gain.

I will bide my time. Patiently, wait and gather whatever I can.

Tara surveyed the dimly lit room, her eyes settling on Lil, who stood among candles and lamps, fully absorbed in deciphering the writings on the wall with a writing board.

"I've been thinking about how the arch stays suspended on that metal ball inside the ring," Tara began. "The key is polarity," she continued.

"Indeed, polarity," Lil agreed.

"Exactly. The arch must float within an interconnected space-time, held in place by the ring without any physical connection. This isolation allows the arch to exist in its own separate realm. When the two locations align, the arches merge, regardless of their size. The anchor points are predetermined. So if you, Lil, possessed a Power source, you could activate it and travel through with no need for an inherent talent," Tara explained.

Lil raised an eyebrow, clearly perplexed. "What do you mean?" she asked.

Approaching the ring's depression, Tara asked, "Remember the field theory book?" she inquired, and Lil nodded in response. "Well, this ring acts as a superconductor, requiring the lower ball to remain suspended. Polarity serves as a repelling force, keeping the arches levitating. Observe." Tara approached the nearest arch, being careful not to cross the ring, and gently applied pressure with her finger, causing it to move effortlessly. "As you can see, there's almost no resistance. By controlling the Power flow to the ring, forming a vortex, and spinning the arches on the ball, when the 'resonance frequency' aligns with the desired frequency on the other side, the Gate opens. So, Lil, you don't need complex equations like a Mage Gate. Just the resonance frequency and the corresponding Power that generates it."

"Let me clarify, based on the texts we have studied. They could employ a resonance frequency and Power as a speculative device to stabilize and maintain a wormhole. The resonance frequency could establish and align the properties of the wormhole with the desired target location in space-time. By carefully adjusting the frequency, it is possible to create a stable connection between the two points. Power, in this scenario, would be essential to generate the energy to sustain the wormhole. They could derive it from exotic matter or advanced energy sources, possibly involving quantum fields or other theoretical constructs."

Lil watched the equations swirling within Tara's mind, awe-inspired by the Power fueling her intellect. Despite her immense strength, Tara remained humble and loving. Yes, Lil concluded, Tara was a treasure, and Lil loved her. *It was as if she pulled knowledge out of nowhere that would take lifetimes to accumulate.*

"There must be an instrument here somewhere that can Power it, Lil. We just need to find it," Tara said, determined. "I can activate it without the instrument, but you'll require one. Look here." Tara pointed to the ring, revealing metallic holes on each side. "Lil, you'll need two instruments that match the circumference of these holes. It's only a guess, but by adjusting the polarity and Power using a crystal similar to the one we had for the book, made from the same materials as these walls, you can attune the device through thought. The crystal serves as an excellent medium for transferring the imagery on the wall. The pictures represent a place within your mind. By observing them, you align your consciousness with that place, making it real. Do you understand?"

Lil watched as Tara explained something that had puzzled them for an eternity because they believed it required the talent to Power it. "You can stand near the wall, look at the image, and the frequency and Power requirements will transfer to the device through the crystal. You don't need to understand them," Lil said.

Tara and Lil burst into laughter, embracing each other tightly. *Anyone can use it!*

Chapter 9 Haven By Knight

"Having a title does not make you right."

It was the evening of the third day, and the meal had concluded. The night grew late as Mel'Anor ushered the remaining people from the dining hall and closed the doors. Antoff, Al'len, De'Nidra, and Lars sat on one side of the large gray stone table, while Tara, Edward, Ivan, and Lil sat on the other side. The Dire Wolf, lit by moonlight, lay near the open balcony doors, letting the cool breeze wash over him as he chewed on a beast bone. Satisfied crunching emanated from the corner as he remained blissfully aloof.

Antoff briefly entertained the idea of taking the bone for some quiet, but ultimately decided against it. Taking a bone from a wolf the size of a warhorse would likely cause a ruckus.

Ivan and Lil exchanged a smiling glance. "You're wise, my friend," Ivan remarked. "You don't want to get on his bad side,"

Antoff spread his hands, "It was just a passing thought."

Ivan and Lil meant no offense. Ivan had been receiving training, and his mind was becoming perceptive. In Vam'Phire society, they valued openness, their thoughts shared freely, aligning with Antoff's beliefs in honesty and Light, though he was still adjusting.

"Okay, let's get started," Antoff said. "Tara and Lil, you have been working on the portal?"

Tara began, "Yes, we have. I believe we can use it if we have a specific location." Tara handed the conversation over to Lil smoothly.

"Indeed, Captain Antoff. Tara's been helpful in solving many issues related to the portal's use. It appears with all the required instruments, anyone could use it, even without the talent to create a Mage Gate. Da'Vain is currently leading the search for those items. He believes he knows what to look for, although we can't be certain if the instruments are in our city," Lil concluded.

"Don't be so formal, Lil," Antoff answered, his mind conveying his care and acceptance as he spoke. Lil smiled at him, her expression shifting from outsider to more like a daughter when she sensed genuine care. Antoff thought of her as a good friend to Tara, and he trusted her.

"Edward, how are the preparations going?"

Edward exchanged glances with his father before responding, "Everything is prepared, Antoff. I've been working with Mel'Anor to determine the positioning of the Mage Gate. Tara is confident that she can open it there with sufficient size to accommodate two riders abreast. The entire house guard will be on duty, and the light cavalry will patrol the inner cordon. Ivan has enlisted the help of our friends from the Under City to watch over us during the vulnerable evenings. The Priest Knights have taken over guard training, and Mic'Ieal will be in command while we carry out the operation."

Antoff nodded, satisfied.

Al'len took over. "We had initially planned to use disguises to enter the gate, but I'm still working out the details with De'Nidra. She needs to leave for the Harbor Cities to fulfill her guild duties. It would be best not to deprive her of the intelligence network she has developed over lifetimes. Since she can use a Mage Gate, applying disguises won't be difficult, and Tem'Aldar will accompany her as added security. Mortals won't recognize him, of course. I'll have a more subdued role to avoid potential backlash."

Lil spoke, "If it pleases you, Ivan and I have a plan to get you in unnoticed."

Antoff, intrigued, responded, "Really?"

Lil hesitated for a moment, then smiled at him. "Antoff, we believe we can use the shadow safely moving Tara past Haven's walls at night. We can then take her to a secure location where a small group can use the Gate."

He concurred, "I can draw you a map; I know the city well. Some buildings are unused in the evening and could serve as entry points for a small group."

"Just remember, Tara, not to take unnecessary risks, okay?" Antoff asked.

Tara nodded in agreement.

Lars had been listening attentively, his demeanor reserved. "The High Bishop will probably decide to seal the city because of our delay. He will suspect that something is wrong and likely doubled the guard. They will be patrolling the streets in force. I believe entities of the Dark Order have compromised some of my staff and house guards. Since those memories belonged to my former occupant, I don't know what we may encounter. I just hope they can't discern the change in my situation, or things could escalate quickly, which we don't need. So the sooner Tara can get Antoff, Al'len, and myself inside the castle, the better. Once we secure that location. We can use it as a safe point to bring in the Warriors of the Light, and if necessary, it will be a good place to retreat."

Antoff fixed his gaze on Lars, his voice cold. "Lars, there will be no retreat."

The portal gradually increased in speed, strobing faster and faster until it transformed into a singular bright sphere, blurring before Mel'Temdel, the High Mage. He concentrated on the paper he held, and within the black sand, a glyph rose, taking shape on the surface of the world with intricate details. The arches had transformed into a powerful globe. Mel'Temdel pushed his concentration to the edge, pouring his last effort and imagination into the image through a teardrop crystal. With one final glorious flash, the portal burst into an event horizon, and a shimmering pool stood, reflecting a copy of the room they were in.

The Dominion hesitated only briefly. His red eyes glistened with alien intelligence. He spoke in the demonic tongue. But Mel'Temdel did not understand it.

The High Mage, at his absolute limit, did not respond. The hulking form of the demon walked through, instantly clearing the portal on the other side. Mist was going to burst as the event unfolded before her, a mix of wonder and complete fear of the unknown. Relieved that her master did not ask her to go through the portal.

"He said one week!" Her master's voice cut through the sound of the spinning globe of energy, interrupted by a rippling pool reflecting the room they stood in.

"One week!" Mist's master shouted again and threw a gold coin back through the pool. It landed and rolled into the mage's room. The sand planet fell into the rectangular box, and the Gate collapsed as the old mage lowered his staff to the floor, supporting his weight. He was on the verge of collapse. Sweat ran down his brow and he puffed, trying to catch his breath.

Mist trotted to Mel'Temdel, providing support, stuttering as she tried to speak. "That... was amazing!"

"Water, my girl," he replied. She handed him an open skin, trembling, while the other hand had a white-knuckled grip on his metal staff, the only thing keeping him upright. He drank greedily, water spilling down his chin. He returned the skin to Mist. "I was pushing myself to the very limit, girl. The process of forming the image and connecting it to the portal consumed a great deal of Power. It should take less time, but I will need a week to recover. Bidirectional, remember? That's what you wanted to know. The coin proved it."

Mist's heart continued to pound in her chest as she nodded in agreement, her reply ragged and breathless. "But will you have the Power in a week?" she asked.

"If I do nothing else, yes. Had I told your master it would take less time, he would have demanded it sooner. He's not a patient creature, your master. Now, my girl, my staff is drained, and I need help to get to my blankets. Rest is what I require now. Food and rest."

Al'len's hair shimmered, catching the streaming rays of light from the room's doors. She and Antoff melted together, enveloped by the soft glow of the Little Sister. Sunlight traced her hair, carrying scents of lavender and rosewood. Antoff gently brushed aside a fallen lock of hair, relishing its silkiness. Her deep blue eyes fluttered open, captivating him.

"You're awake. I thought you'd sleep for a week," he remarked, a smile playing on his lips.

Al'len stretched and met his gaze. "You're growing younger every day, Antoff," she observed.

He tenderly kissed her. "It's our love, without limits, no matter how deep I delve," he whispered.

She kissed him back passionately, filling his very core. "Then you'll have to keep digging," she playfully tapped his nose and traced his chin with her finger.

Al'len sat up, revealing her flawless form decorated with a few battle scars. With an indulgent smile, she asked, "Do you like the view, soldier?"

"I do," he replied, his gaze appreciative.

Gracefully, Al'len rose and began her morning routine. She poured water into the washbasin, brushed her teeth, and donned a tan outfit. Securing her sword belt around her waist, she nonchalantly draped her white dragon cloak over her back, its fabric falling over the hilt of her blade. She playfully tossed her travel mirror to Antoff. "Complements of the house," she said, flashing a mischievous grin. Strolling towards the door, she opened it. Arching an eyebrow at him, she teased, "You should put on some clothes." Al'len shut the door as she left.

Antoff sat up, his bare feet touching the cold, smooth gray stone. He felt restored and fulfilled, unlike anything he had experienced before. The stone sent a chill through him, contrasting with the warm sunlight that bathed the room. Was Al'len doing all this out of love? Trying to make their shared experience as real as possible? No, it was for both of them, ensuring their journey together was complete. She dared to be here with him, embodying fire and sunlight—the entirety of his world.

Opening the mirror, Antoff prepared to shave. Examining the blade's edge, he confirmed its sharpness and placed it carefully on the table. Lathering his face, he stole glances at his reflection. His hand froze just short of touching. It was his, but young. Memories of Al'len's grin and the immense joy flooded his mind. *Complements of the house.* Her words echoed. He appeared to be in his early thirties, a stark contrast to his previous age. He had lost twenty years. Joy pulsed through the bond. She knew he had just found out.

After shaving, Antoff dressed. He put on his underclothes, followed by loose-fitting boiled leather and chainmail. He donned his greaves, sabatons, and cuisses over heavy leather boots. "Mel'Anor will never let me live this down," he muttered, securing his sword belt around his waist and fastening the black hawk-shaped buckle. Throwing on his cloak and pushing back the hood, he prepared to face a day filled with curious glances and inevitable questions. Exhaling deeply, he grabbed his gauntlets and strode out to embrace the day.

"Lord Captain?" Intoned knights, clerics, and the people. He nodded, heading for the stable yard. He was trying hard to avoid the questions on their faces.

Mel'Anor's deep voice rang out. "Mother's milk in a bucket! What happened to you?"

"I don't know, Mel'Anor, but I won't ask for a refund, if you get me!" he laughed.

"I should say not, my boy." Mel'Anor playfully slapped him on the back. "You look about the same age as our Maid of Light," he grinned. "No question, she's doing you good, and you're not doing her any harm. She's been full of smiles and well-wishing. You'd think we're going to a dance rather than war."

"War is almost her favorite dance, Mel'Anor. Almost."

If we could assign a sound to war when in the presence of the Maid of Light, it was the absurdity of silence. There was no wavering or fluttering of nerves. She was cool and had a smile of warm fire like a promise when she sent Tara, Ivan, and Lil on their way. Chirping insects filled the air that stirred in the moonlight that flooded the square. Ram'Del, the Hero of the Light, stood mounted on his dragon Horse. Alone atop the dry fountain, holding back the night.

Tara concentrated; she knew the Garden Wood well. A strip of light split the air with a hiss. It writhed in place on the verge of collapse before blossoming into a ball twice the height of a man, awash in a purple glow of strobing light that shimmered across the cobble of the square. The pool in the center held a view of the deep forest and endless trees. "That puts us about three leagues from the wall and one from the road," Tara said.

Edward stepped next to her. She could feel him there. "Be careful Tara; I am going to be waiting for you right here. You get into trouble, you open a Gate and I will step through." He kissed her. It was a kiss that came with a promise he intended to keep.

She kissed him back, ending with a smile. "Edward, every moment, not one day, I promised." She stepped through, Ivan and Lil right behind her. The Dire Wolf darted past, nearly bowling him over and the gate winked out.

The Warriors of the Light were making ready to ride and Edward leaned against the fountain, his smoked armor plate clanked as he leaned his shield against the stone. He was going to wait right here.

Purple light flickered through the lush forest, and the grass softly crunched under her knee-high boots. The cool air wafted beneath the canopy, smelled of pine, with branches stretching high overhead. Ivan and Lil followed closely behind. Before Tara could close the Mage Gate, the Dire Wolf bounded through and nearly knocked Ivan down. The Gate immediately winked out.

"I guess that's him not taking 'no' for an answer," Ivan said.

"He loves being with you, Ivan. He can't help himself," Lil replied.

Both Ivan and Lil wore black leather-scaled mail. Ivan carried a wicked sword with a pulsing gem, while Lil had a thin, curved longsword. Tara adjusted her twin swords and a bone-colored short bow. Her quiver packed full of feathered arrows over her cloak. Silently, they moved through the trees. The Dire Wolf ranged ahead of them, stopping just before the tree line near the road. A league away, the white walls of Haven rose, gleaming under the moonlight. The leaves rustled as moons cast patches of light and shadow that danced on the grassy forest floor.

Above the cloud-covered sky, two dragons glided through the curtain of the night. The warm glow of life spilled from the land like embers. Soldiers walked along the tops of walls and battlements, while Priest Knights patrolled the cobblestone streets in units of tens throughout the city. The images from the dragons streamed through Tara's head. Lil and Ivan exchanged a look, stealing only glimpses, as they could barely handle the glimpse of the storm of reality within Tara's mind.

Ivan turned to the Dire Wolf and pointed at the ground. It was a comical sight considering the wolf's size compared to the towering man, who appeared like a child next to the enormous wolf.

"Okay, Tara," Lil took her hand. Ivan towered over her, placing his hand on her shoulder. "Just stay with us and don't stray, no matter what."

Shadows swirled like mist as they moved toward the road's faint outline, transitioning from the world of ghosts to reality. Passing through gates and porticos, misty figures of warriors patrolled half-seen in the evening fog. Inside the gates, torches and lamps lit up the night.

Ivan and Lil guided Tara along the wall, where shadows still clung as pools. They crossed the misty road's threshold, entering a dark alleyway that felt oddly comforting amidst the well-lit city. At the alley's end, they emerged into a cobbled street. The fog dissipated, revealing a normal night under the moonlight, with lingering shadows pooling in dark corners.

"Tara, we're here," Lil whispered in her ear.

They crept through dark alleys, and backstreets as a few raindrops threatened to fall. The atmosphere held its breath before an imminent downpour. The light pitter-patter of rain was comforting and masked their sounds, not obscuring like a downpour, but a gentle mist that softened the edges of buildings and physical forms. Thunder rumbled after a flash, and the rain began in earnest.

The sound of steel ringing on stone bounced off buildings as mounted Priest Knights of the Light approached along the road. Beyond the alleyway, a broad street stretched deep into the inner city, rising toward a hilltop adorned with walls and battlements surrounding Haven Castle, where Edward had grown up. Tara was completely soaked, her heavy woodland green cloak dragging, running with rainwater. Ivan pointed toward the castle gate, which stood closed, with torchlight flickering in the murder holes, casting long, shifting shafts as figures moved inside. They positioned themselves under the arc of rainwater sheeting from the roof, waiting for the knights to pass.

"Lil and I will get you inside, and then we'll find a quiet place where you can open a gate to bring the others through," Ivan said. Shadow enveloped them the moment Ivan and Lil touched Tara. The foggy rain nearly blinded them as they crossed the street and walked alongside the houses. The square before the battlements was wide and open, and beyond it, the thick block walls topped a mound that descended into a pit with a lowered, barred gate at its center, leading to the massive double doors standing open.

Chapter 10 Blade And Bone

"For some mortals, it is blood and bone that decide their way. They take life and property, believing that to steal from our world and its people is the only way. Stepping upon the corpses of the fallen, they walk through our world like a plague. Should they not be removed? Have they not lost their way?"

Ethereal silhouettes patrolled across the drawbridge and misty porticos with an otherworldly presence. The rain veiled the inner court, obscuring the view and revealing only faint outlines of outbuildings and the castle itself. Ivan guided Tara, keeping a firm hand on her, while Lil clenched her other hand tightly. Next to them stood a stable housing a smithy and two barns. Ivan chose the stable, its heavy wooden door slightly ajar, revealed the forge beyond. As the fog cleared, the wall's outline came into view. Wisps of smoky spider threads floated in, clinging momentarily to their bodies before vanishing. The only sources of light were the faint glow seeping from under the door and the smoldering coals within the open forge.

Tara whispered urgently, her grip on Ivan's arm tightening. "Wait!"

"If anything happens, Lil can help you escape."

"Wait, Ivan!" Tara pleaded.

He shook his head and pressed a finger to his lips, signaling her not to open the portal until he instructed. He quietly stepped out.

Shadows reached around Ivan, enfolding him as the sparse light momentarily dimmed.

"He has been here, Tara. He won't have any difficulty getting back quickly," Lil whispered, answering the unspoken question in Tara's mind.

The darkness was quiet, except for the rain on the tiled roof. Tools hung neatly on pegs on the wall, and before the forge sat an anvil, a hammer, and tongs. Quench barrels, filled with dark liquids, sat on one side. The room smelled of oil, coal, horses, and sweat. Lightning flickered and thunder responded, flooding the bottom of the door with fitful flashes.

The stable door creaked open, revealing an orange glow that sent flickering warnings across the space. Footfalls approached, with the clank of steel armor and thud of a shield echoing, as doors were checked and secured. Tara gripped her short swords and exchanged a knowing glance with Lil. Without words, they communicated their plan. *I'll take the soldier if he enters,* Tara thought, and Lil nodded in understanding.

Metal-clad boots clanked, echoing in the stable. The door creaked open before swinging shut once more. Tara's heart raced, her body coiled as she dropped to one knee, her short swords gleaming in her grip. She pressed herself into the shadows, the walls cold stone rough against her back. Tara waited to spring into action at the first sign of the soldier's presence. The handle lifted, and the door pushed in. In an instant, the Darkness enveloped Lil, and she disappeared. The armored guard cried out in surprise, and Tara launched herself. The well-trained guard raised his shield, sparks flying across it in the dim light as Tara's blades struck. He stepped back, dropping his torch and drawing his sword, but Tara pressed forward, her blades spinning.

"To arms, to arms!" the guard bellowed.

Lil emerged from the shadow, her eyes filled with angry light. Gold swirled in silver, edged in blood. Tara witnessed the horrifying sight of a monster spat from Darkness as if born from the womb of night. Horses screamed in panic as she moved with supernatural speed. With a swift motion, Lil grabbed the guard's shoulders and yanked him off his feet. Her eyes, now right above his shoulder, she bit deep. The soldier's body went rigid, and his sword fell to the floor. Tara ran for the front door of the stable. Torches glowed and flickered in the hands of soldiers running, approaching their door. "Lil, they are coming!" Tara heard dragging feet behind her. She must be concealing the kill.

Tendrils clung to Ivan as the dire wolf emerged with him from the shadow. "Get the Gate open, now Tara," he said, pushing open the door and stepping out. His hand rested on his sword hilt, feeling the bloodstone pulse in time with his heartbeat. Guards with shields and drawn swords ran toward the stables. Ivan's breathing slowed, and he unsheathed his blade. His knee bent, the blade spinning inverted with its tip towards the ground. His eyes closed, and everything slowed down. Rain dripped down his scaled armor like the skin of a wet snake. The first guard closed in as Ivan opened his eyes, their unnatural light swirling gold and blood red. He moved with supernatural speed, stepping under the blow and slicing just below the man's arm. As he stepped back slowly, three more guards rushed in. One held a long spear, and two more wielded swords. The wounded man held his side and fell to one knee. In the rain, his blood trailed on the stone.

"Just put it down now. We outnumber you three to one and more will come," the spearman said.

"Three to one," Ivan's voice whispered with a rasp. "Hard odds, but I'm not alone."

A black mass the size of a warhorse leapt through the door. His eyes reflected the torch's orange glow as he took in the sight of the guards. The dire wolf's head lowered, its fur bristling and lips peeling back to expose dagger-like teeth. A low, deep, predatory growl escaped his open jaws.

Ivan smiled. "It's good that more are coming, because you are going to need them." The dire broke into a trot, flanking to the left, and the spearman backed up, raising his spear. Fear filled their eyes as the nightmare took shape.

Lil stepped from the door, blade in hand, her eyes filled with hunger. "I apologize, my love. I have not introduced you," Ivan said. "This is Lil, soon to be my wife."

At that, she stumbled a bit. Her eyes flicked to Ivans. A menacing smile touched her lips and Lil raised her blade.

Light and darkness engaged in a fierce battle as Tara's ribbon of light sliced through the air, undulating before erupting into a vibrant purple sphere. The Mage Gate shimmered, revealing Edward and the fountain on the other side.

Edward was the first to step through, followed by Antoff, Lars, and Al'len. Outside in the square, the clash of steel resounded.

Lars hurriedly dashed from the smithy, through the stable, and burst through the door, only to find chaos in the yard. Three guards were locked in combat with Ivan and Lil. The dire wolf dragged a man by his bleeding leg, filling the air with his piercing screams. "What in the name of the gods of Light is happening here?" Lars bellowed, causing the guards to back off.

"My Lord, are you with them?" the spearman questioned.

"No, I am the ruler of Haven, you idiot! They are with me, and you are attacking my guests," Lars responded firmly.

A female guard challenged him, "I did not see you enter the gate, my Lord."

Lars furrowed his brow, fixing her with a stern gaze. "Put away your weapons, tend to the wounded, and find me the captain of the guard. Ivan, have the wolf release the soldier," he ordered.

Ivan gave the dire wolf a commanding look, pointing to the cobblestone. Reluctantly, the wolf let go of the soldier, as if releasing its favorite toy.

"My Lord, there is one more inside. He is asleep and pale, but still alive," Lil reported.

"Of course, my lady. Soldiers, once you've attended to the injured, gather all the troops in the square," Lars commanded. The soldiers offered curt bows and led the wounded away.

Antoff and Al'len emerged from the chaos. "Let's head to the square. Once the captain arrives and the troops assemble, we'll secure the keep, allowing no one to leave," Antoff suggested.

The rain had subsided, with only occasional drops falling. Cobblestone shone slick, and the air carried a cool, damp feel. The troops had already started mustering, and the aged captain was making his way toward Lars. Tara and Edward had their cloaks drawn up, concealing their faces. Edward's cloak, like Tara's, was drenched. He had obviously waited by the fountain through the storm for her to open the Gate.

Lars addressed the captain upon his arrival. Al'len stepped forward, looking into the captain's eyes, and nodding at Lars.

"He is clean," Al'len confirmed.

Lars returned the nod. "Captain Tem'Ral, order the roundup of everyone in the keep and bring them to the square. Seal the keep using the soldiers I've cleared for you after reviewing their credentials," Lars instructed.

The captain bowed, said, "As you command, my Lord."

The castle, crafted from white stone resembling the city walls, reflected meager moonlight even amid the overcast clouds. As the soldiers mustered, Lars, Antoff, Al'len, and Captain Tem'Ral walked along the line. One by one, Al'len or Antoff nodded, signaling the selected soldiers to be pulled from the line and positioned ten paces away from the other guards, forming a separate unit. They chose and dispatched one hundred soldiers to seal the keep. The next one hundred gathered everyone from their duties or beds and held them near the square, including Edward's mother. The scene became a spectacle of complaints from courtiers, secretaries, dandies, and hangers-on, all held neatly under guard. This left seventy-three soldiers from the original line, significantly outnumbered by the newly selected ranks, with a ratio of five to one.

Lars spoke softly to Captain Tem'Ral, who then yelled, "Remain in formation. I repeat, do not move."

Tara watched the theater unfolding before her. The remaining soldiers in the original formation, now reduced to a small unit, were restless but maintained their discipline.

Antoff turned toward Tara and shouted, "Okay, Tara."

She focused her concentration, knowing that it would be a significant Mage Gate. She envisioned the Mage Gate as a pulsating ribbon of energy surrounded by a shimmering halo of strange matter. The ribbon flexed and contorted like a living snake, bridging vast distances by stretching through the fabric of reality. Tara channeled raw Power into the halo of strange matter, positioning one end of the Gate in front of her and aligning the other with the chosen location just beside the fountain with Ram'Del. She stabilized the delicate structure of the Gate, preventing its collapse, and poured the Power of Darkness and Light into it until the image solidified in her mind. Maintaining a passage that allowed horses and riders to traverse instantaneously required an immense amount of Power. A wiggling strand of Light sliced through the air with a hiss. A woman from the court screamed as she fainted and tumbled to the cobblestone. The Gate shimmered, on the brink of collapsing, before exploding into a purple globe at its center—a liquid pool reflecting the image of the rift. It stood four times the height of a warhorse and was wide enough for four abreast. Mel'Anor led the charge of two hundred and forty-two Warriors of the Light pouring forth from the Gate like a flood. He organized them and trotted towards Antoff. Tara allowed the Gate to collapse.

Antoff shouted, "Dismount!" The Priest Knights and Clerics promptly dismounted on the cobblestone. "Mel'Anor, pick a warrior for each of those soldiers standing over there and make sure they are aware of the entities infesting them."

Mel'Anor saluted, "As you command Lord Captain!" He led his horse toward his troops without sign of anything untoward. He whispered orders as he walked down the line and the warriors passed the orders back in connecting files. Seventy-five Warriors of the Light fell in on him. He guided them in a line towards the original soldiers, who remained standing where they had been paraded.

The parasitic entities looked out through their host's eyes. There hadn't been a reason to worry before. It was quite safe that the greed of the bishops had ruined the militant order and besides, Lars, or rather Dem'Endas, was in charge. There had been rumors, of course, but there always were. No Priest or Cleric of the Light had a trickle of the Power needed to cast them out. The warriors took a place and stood five paces across from each of them, what was more, half of them were female. "Oh, this is going to be good, the entity thought smugly."

"*An absurdity. They are smiling. Wait, something's wrong.* A light shone in the eyes of each Warrior of the Light."

The big old cleric yelled, "Advance!" The warriors stepped up eye to eye, laid hands on his shoulders, holding them in place. A glow grew within the eyes of the Coth'Ventor knights until the ember that was inward ignited outwardly engulfing the possessed. Some soldiers tried to fight, and some dropped to the ground in a violent fit. But one thing was certain: they all spewed an inky black oily snake that slithered into the cracks in cobblestone.

Ivan, Lil, and the dire wolf approached Tara. "Let Antoff know that we have departed. I believe our presence is no longer required, and we will make the mortals nervous."

Tara inclined her head. "Thank you. I will see you soon."

They walked back to the stables, closed the door, and were gone.

De'Nidra's brownstone manor, known as the House of Deepwater, held a historic legacy spanning six centuries. Inherited from previous owners, the ancient family name carried a significant reputation as merchants. Over sixty years, De'Nidra honed her skill in capturing the likeness of Lady Ka'ron Deepwater to a point where she could effortlessly recreate her image, even in her sleep.

Seated at her study desk, meticulously crafted from exquisite dark wood, De'Nidra poised her quill, ready for the next round of dipping and scratching. Antiques of rich, dark wood radiated warm light in the sun-filled study. The floor of the study displayed a lovely artful fresco, providing a glimpse into the past of Harbor Cities when the manor was built. The paneling was dark and rich, and the ceilings adorned with moldings etched in gold gilding, tracing embossed flower petals, and raised scrollwork. She loved the house library and the view of the gardens, which is why she had made it her study. Her secretary, a diligent individual with ink-stained fingers and a mountain of paperwork, handled each purchase order and parchment containing instructions and negotiation details.

"This one is for the purchase of the warehouse at Waterside, closest to the docks," Lady Ka'ron Deepwater declared as she scratched her signature. With flawless precision, the secretary folded the document and sealed it with red wax, letting it drip just right before marking it with a wax seal.

"And this one is for the acquisition of wagon masters." De'Nidra meticulously replicated Lady Ka'ron Deepwater's signature.

"All right, Libby, you've been driving me like a Dark Order taskmaster for two hours now," she admonished with patience. "Thank you, Libby. We shall continue tomorrow."

Libby, a middle-aged woman, curtsied. "Of course, your ladyship. It's just that you've been spending less and less time in the city, and the requests keep piling up."

Lady Ka'ron rewarded her with a warm smile. "Very well, Libby. I have prepared some documents and a letter of credit that must be taken to the attorney immediately."

Libby curtsied again. "First thing, my lady." She hurried from the room.

With Libby's departure, the weight of the office lifted slightly, though it still lingered in the back of De'Nidra's mind. Rubbing her temples, she felt the pulsating ache in her head return. It had started the moment she had entered the Gate and had only subsided when she focused on blocking it out. Leaving her chair, she opened a window and the garden's paneled door, inviting the warm sunlight, the fragrant scent of blooming trees and plants, and the salty breeze to wash over her. Tem'Aldar, dressed ostentatiously like a plaything of an old woman, sat at a table, relishing his favorite Corel'lean Coffee from the southern islands—a highly prized drink among the city's overachievers and late-night workers. A young woman fluttered around him, tending to his every need and seeking his attention. Fortunately for him, he remained oblivious.

De'Nidra Approached the small table and liberated the decanter and tray. "That will be all, Mar'garete," she said, and the girl curtsied with a pouty smile.

"Yes, my Lady," she replied, swaying seductively as she exited the room. Tem'Aldar didn't even glance up from his daily paper.

"What a performance," De'Nidra remarked dryly.

He raised an eyebrow and then snapped his paper. "What do you mean?" Tem'Aldar inquired.

"The girl is doing everything but revealing her true intentions, and yet you remain oblivious." She positioned herself next to him and executed an exaggerated curtsey, leaning forward to expose more cleavage than would be appropriate for a servant, all while refilling his cup and capturing his gaze.

"Ah, I see," he finally comprehended, taking the tray from her hands and placing it, along with the paper, on the table. He motioned her to sit on his lap.

"Oh, your Lordship," De'Nidra pretended to blush as she took her seat.

"You know, you needn't worry. I hardly noticed her presence."

De'Nidra wrapped her arms around his neck. "That's a good thing because otherwise, I might have had to disguise you as Nor'Ray, the reliable old stable hand, for the rest of our journey. He possesses a uniquely vintage ugliness, and he sleeps in the stable rather than in my bed."

He kissed her, a slow and deep kiss that dissolved any lingering doubts, and if he wasn't careful, everything else she was wearing. "Well, I wouldn't want that," he replied, grinning mischievously. "So, my love, now that you've chased everyone away, what shall we do?"

She returned his smile. "Control yourself, trooper. We have work to do." His smile wavered, but she wasn't going to let him distract her today. "Because we need to conduct a reconnaissance operation, and then we're going to purchase a substantial ship so we can afford all that Corel'lean Coffee you've been indulging in."

Tem'Aldar, the dashing fop, released a long, indulgent breath. "All right, what's the plan?"

She pointed toward the garden, up to a colossal marble mansion perched atop a steep hill.

"Wow, it would take a team of horses to carry your team of horses up there," he whistled.

De'Nidra, embodying the appearance of an old, petulant woman, nodded. "It wasn't there a month ago."

He winked at her. "I see. And since the only beings capable of what you're suggesting are those we can't confront alone, why don't we just report it to EL'ALue and let her handle it?"

She raised a finger. "Firstly, because she'll ask who's behind it, and secondly," she raised another finger, "because I need to find out."

"Shall I call the coach, your Ladyship?"

De'Nidra shook her head. "I have no interest in tipping off an elder god that I am spying on them. That would bring the kind of notice that could turn deadly. This god is not playing by the rules the rest are, and while the manifestation of this reality was deftly done and the effects of the overwritten history are giving me a splitting headache, I won't allow it to overwrite my perception of the past. Had I not recognized it for what it was, I might have just accepted the new reality entirely and allowed it to replace my memory. That is the danger of what this god is doing and why the others agreed to sleep. It disrupts the very fabric of creation and overwrites the natural course of existence and history."

Tem'Aldar let her settle closer. While it may look like an old lady, it was all De'Nidra. "I certainly did not see any change in reality, and this city was full of mud huts and fisheries when last I saw it."

"If you had not seen the history overwritten, you would not notice at all. The mind just accepts what it sees and moves on. No, we will need to set up a viewing, and that has to be intricately done to avoid notice," De'Nidra said.

"My love, let's go down for lunch first, shall we? Then we can do our best not to upset our neighbor."

She smiled at him. "You soldiers are all the same. If you can't get one thing you want, you try to satisfy the next—your stomach."

He kissed her again. "What do you say we stay right here and handle both?" She felt him undo a button on her dress.

The docks jutted from the land like fingers into the sea. Ships laden with cargo were being unloaded by heavy wooden cranes, filling the steady stream of large merchant wagons pulled by ten-draft animal strings. De'Nidra and Tem'Aldar arrived in a black lacquered coach, the late afternoon sun glinting off its mirror-waxed surface. The scent of the salty sea, intermingled with the fishy aroma of the bustling vessels, lingered around the docks, particularly oppressive on sweltering days. This had become an exceptionally hot day in the afternoon, and De'Nidra intended to purchase the ship and get it out of the way as quickly as possible. Being assailed by the heat and unpleasant smells after such a lovely afternoon was difficult, and besides, her stomach had easily been upset every morning for the past week, and now she could feel another bout coming on.

The coachman opened the door and offered her a hand as she stepped out. She had changed into a lighter green dress, and since Tem'Aldar had already helped her out of it, it seemed like a prudent choice. He stepped out behind her and offered her his arm. He wore a wickedly out-of-place broadsword belted at his waist over his foppish uniform as a house guard. The green outfit had a double line of golden buttons traced in silver embroidery, bearing the marks of command within the merchant rank. He looked dashing.

The new acquisition was a heavy Corsair design, rigged fore and aft with sail, named for its cutting lines and rakes. While it was, in fact, more of a frigate with its three masts and deep hull, there was little question that she was fast. Tem'Aldar led De'Nidra down the length of the ship before going aboard so she could have a look, then up the wide gangplank that was crosshatched by wooden strips to provide sure footing. Had she not been wearing heels, that is.

The two of them stepped onto the deck, built of a light-colored wood from the islands. This wood, a species of poplar, was hard as iron and would not rot, not even in a salty sea. Along the deck were twenty ballista on each side, meant to dissuade pirates from helping themselves. The shipbuilder had had it delivered by a hired crew and waited at the rail to welcome them aboard.

"A fine ship," De'Nidra said.

"She is yours, your Ladyship, if you will have her. There remains the particulars of signing a note of purchase so I can make the withdrawal, and your acquisition of the Neal 'Lance' is complete. Let me take you below to the patrons' quarters to see that all is as you described it, and if acceptable, we can conclude, and I will be on my way home," he said.

Below the wheelhouse were big twin doors of the same wood that led below. The hall was well-lit with new brass lamps, the kind that had an automatic stopper to plug the oil if it fell or turned to the side, preventing accidents. Safety on a ship was paramount, as a fire at sea meant death. A rail ran the length of the hall to provide stability in rough seas, and cabins lined each side. At the end were the captain's quarters on one side, the first mate's on the other, and a spacious cabin for the patron when she traveled. De'Nidra meticulously opened each cabin and looked inside. Her room was beautifully done, opening onto a balcony that wrapped around the ship's aft, shared by the captain and first mate. It was a narrow balcony, but serviceable for a chair and table to enjoy meals in the fresh sea air. Inside, there was a large four-poster bed that was attached to the ceiling and floor.

Tem'Aldar pulled the curtain and gave the firm mattress a push, accompanied by a roguish smile—quite unbecoming of a merchant guard of his station. The floor had a red woven carpet that covered the planking, depicting a scene of many island ports of call in map-like surroundings. On top of it was a table with six chairs, holding the sale documents. Against the wall were cabinets for clothing and storage for longer journeys, and at the foot of the bed, there was an impressive trunk with a lock.

"It's perfect, just as I ordered her." De'Nidra sat down in a chair and picked up the quill. She dipped it into the inkwell and signed. "You may collect the money when you present the bill of sale. Wish your master shipbuilder well and tell her I am very satisfied with her beautiful work. I have included a tip for her to share with the builders. Inform your master that I want to order five more."

He bowed deeply. "She will be pleased, my Lady. I look forward to seeing you upon my return." Then he departed.

"This ship? What will we use it for?" Tem'Aldar asked.

"We will use it for our trips to buy goods, spying, and other purposes," she said elusively. "The other five ships I have ordered are to protect the merchant fleets while carrying a reasonable cargo sufficient to cover the cost of the extra protection. I want to hire a skilled crew. You could help me with that. You are much better than I am at judging scoundrels and rogues." She winked at him.

Chapter 11 God Fire

"I wish my dreams did not always end in fire. Dreams and existence are indistinguishable when you can so readily replace one with the other. Life should flow within the stream of time. We gods and our existence are an accidental perversion of truth. It can only end in one conclusion. The ending of our world."

Steam billowed from the furnaces below, heating the water and sending droplets into the air. It was a marvel of engineering, a bath as vast as a small building, nestled within white marble steps that shimmered below warm liquid. Colonnades and columns supported the ceiling, exquisitely etched and decoratively fluted. High Bishop Er'laya of the Order of the Light reclined as a monk offered to soap his brush.

Diocesan On'omus stood by, examining the treasury's records, noting the declining tithes. "My Lord High Bishop, the plate has seen a decrease in offerings lately."

Er'laya's ponderous expression deepened. "It displeases us. Perhaps it's time for a sermon on generosity and clergy visits to local homes. They pay for that privilege regardless of their desires."

Diocesan On'omus quickly agreed, "Of course, my Lord."

"An excellent plan, Diocesan On'omus. Act on it immediately." Er'laya signaled for him to proceed, waving him away.

On'omus took a single step, but then raised a finger, turning back to face the bishop. "Just one more thing, my Lord. We haven't had word about the return of our noble clerics and knights, but rumors abound regarding a battle in dreary Coth'Venter. Keep in mind, these are mere rumors. However, each passing day without their return fuels more whispers among the populace. They say that EL'ALue, the Maid of Light, has vanquished our order's soldiers and conscripted them as her own."

Swallowing hard, the High Bishop asked, "What heresy is this? Are people openly speaking of it?"

Diocesan On'omus shook his head. "Not at all, my Lord, but it's whispered among them."

Er'laya huffed. "Then I shall decree that anyone repeating such filth will publicly be whipped in the square. That will put an end to this matter. Besides, when the Warriors of the Light return, we shall hold a trial and finish this whole bloody thing."

Diocesan On'omus bowed. "Yes, of course, Your Excellency."

The brush-soaping monk tried to hand him the brush, but Er'laya grabbed it roughly and threw it into the pool. "Leave me. I need to be alone!" The monk bowed and left. *If EL'ALue, the Maid of Light, has done that, it will be the end of me!*

Dark as it may be, nature never sleeps. The Night Bane, a flying lizard, flitted around the walls, stealing eggs from nesting birds in the inaccessible corners of the white towers and battlements of Haven Castle. Summer had come early, bringing hot days followed by deluges of rain. In the lands along the border of the Gray Area, the midpoint between the Lands of Light and Darkness, shifts were sudden, where reality was always in flux.

The Coth'Venter Clerics and Priest Knights yearned to rid their order of the infection that plagued it. Lord Lars, now comfortably back on his throne, desired to wait just one more day and night before launching the next phase of the attack. Al'len and Antoff begrudgingly accepted the delay to gather intelligence on patrol timings and guard changes. They also decided that when the early morning shift change occurred, they might slip out and join the returning patrols, potentially making their way outside Haven Cathedral Square undetected, if all went well. From a distance, they would be indistinguishable from any other priest or cleric. The armor, mounts, and even the tack worn by the animals would be the same. However, the problem lay in the instituted passwords, which they did not have, and which would change with every guard shift.

"That's the thing about plans, Al'len, as I'm sure you're aware. The best-laid plans are worth little once that gate opens. Everything becomes a suggestion, and our mission becomes simply getting there," Antoff said. They sat together on a stone bench in a small park within the castle grounds.

The air was uncomfortably humid after the rains, and Al'len's shirt clung to her. "Morning will come, and the battle will take shape. But we have the advantage, and they don't know we're coming. You're right though, even the most skillful plan is only good for wiping when the first arrow flies. Let's ensure we're the ones deciding when and where that arrow is loosed."

Edward lay in bed, praying for a cool breeze to enter through the open doors and windows. Tara lay beside him, one leg crossed over his, and one hand with intertwined fingers. In her petite elfin frame, Tara concealed a reservoir of strength that often eluded casual observers. He recalled a vivid image of her perched atop a towering battlement, a lone sentinel against a relentless horde of fifteen hundred darkness-infested minions. But as he gazed upon her in this moment, with her serene beauty and tranquil demeanor, it concealed the tempest raging within her, a storm imperceptible to those who merely skimmed the surface.

She stirred and stretched. "Edward, why are you still awake?"

He smiled at her and played with her hair. "I'm not tired, Tara. This wet heat is bothersome, and I'm worried about tomorrow. I don't want you to get hurt."

She nestled against his chest. "Hmm, not tired, you say? How shall we remedy this situation?" She climbed until her steel-gray eyes smiled into his. "I will hum the dance tonight, Edward, and you will follow my lead."

***

Coth'Venter, in the depths of the night, stood in slow decay. Like a forest shedding its leaves in fall, but spring brought new life and removed decline. Such was the case here as well. New faces filled with hope for the future. The Cathedral of Light had already become a place of safety and a comforting home. In the city, small lights burned where work had begun. People and families moved in, slowly breathing new life into what was a decaying place.

Cur'Ra stood on the open balcony that overlooked the square. Cavalry patrolled below, while Ram'Del stood above the central fountain in the cobblestone square. The stone railing felt rough and warm, matching the night's temperature. Torchflies clung around every lantern, creating a soft illumination. Bloodbats swooped down, devouring the mouthfuls of insects that gathered in the pools of light.

Above, a flock of large flying creatures, neither lizards nor birds, soared high in the sky, engaged in their instinctual hunt. Coth'Venter was now within Narean's reach, its Cathedral's lamplight shining brightly against the subdued gray. The air hung heavy with wet, sticky heat, clinging to every surface like a damp towel. The red-scaled armor covering Narean's scaly skin felt stifling compared to the dusty air of the Blackened Lands. Flapping his wings rhythmically brought some relief, blowing air across his body. However, the humidity prevented the sweat from evaporating.

"Lieutenant Narean," Lord Modred had demanded, "we need to apply pressure to Antoff Grant and his troop." Narean and five of his brothers volunteered for the task. According to reports, the location was lightly guarded. In retribution for De'Nidra, the Daughter of Shadow's betrayal, they planned a small raid. Killing her was not the objective; they sought her agents who infested their order. Since she had refused to contact anyone. They would provoke her and await her response. Tonight, the opportunity presented itself. Whether it was Tara, the Torrent or the woman she referred to as mother standing on that balcony above the square, Narean didn't care.

As he dove, Narean drew his wicked blade, its blood gem pulsing red. His brothers followed suit, descending with him on a single mission: to tear her apart before she could unleash her magic.

Cur'Ra glanced upward, noticing the birds had grown larger. Recognizing them, she pulled out her dagger and screamed, "To arms!" The creature, its scales the color of blood, crashed into her as she attempted to retreat, driving its blade deep into her middle. They slid across the floor, and Cur'Ra retaliated, stabbing with her dagger, driving it deep into the creature's neck and shoulder. It bellowed in pain, draining the last drops of her life through her own spreading pool of blood.

Lamplight spilled through the open door and windows of the study, casting a warm blush into the garden. De'Nidra carried a gilded brass lamp and placed it on the table beside a large clay bowl. Tem'Aldar brought two large pitchers of water and set them next to the bowl. The sea air had blown some of the heat away and smelled of the gardens, flowers and blossoming trees. The moons stood high, casting golden light dancing shadows as shafts passed through the reaching limbs above.

"De'Nidra, what are we doing?" She grabbed the pitcher and poured water into the bowl.

"We are starting a viewing. The water acts as a simple medium found in any house. When linked, its vibrations can transfer sound from a room where the water is linked to this bowl. With the enhancement, we can hear what is being said. Since the owner likely has water in most rooms, we might get lucky and overhear conversations. Once we locate the voice, we bind it and try to use the reflection to identify the speaker."

Tem'Aldar gave her a sidelong look. "Remind me not to get on your bad side. How lucky do we have to be, and what are the risks?"

De'Nidra added another splash of water for good measure. "Well, since it is obviously an old god," she gave him a serious look, "and they bend the world to their whims. It is a considerable risk if this god has set anything up. Other gods don't need to resort to these tricks to check up on each other if they know their whereabouts and whom they are dealing with."

That brought a concerning crinkle across his brow. "So if the god discovers this little trick of yours, how much time do we have before we need to run?"

De'Nidra laughed and patted his cheek. "You're so cute, Tem'Aldar. If this god discovers us, there won't be much time to run. That's why I'm going to open a Mage Gate back to Coth'Venter cathedral square just inside the library, so we can escape before we get disintegrated."

Tem'Aldar, who normally wore a smile, lost it at the mention of getting disintegrated. "Well, there are worse ways to go, not that one comes to mind right now."

"Oh, it gets better. Let's say, for example, that this god finds us and decides to keep us alive as playthings for a while. See my point?" De'Nidra asked.

He swallowed hard. "My love, you certainly know how to inspire with these wonderfully motivating outcomes. Is this the best way?"

"Hmm, let's see. Would you rather go knock on the door?"

He shook his head. "No, rather not."

"Then yes, this is the best way. I am only going to use a trickle and do a sending with water. It won't disturb her reality or change anything."

De'Nidra hushed him and closed her eyes. She tapped the water, and the bowl rang like a chime, rippling outward. The sound seemed to come from everywhere. She moved her finger from the center across the top of the water toward the manor on the hill. The reflection of the passing houses appeared within the water. In the library behind them, a thread of light split the air and blossomed into a Gate.

Tem'Aldar let out an audible sigh.

"Shush, I didn't forget."

The image formed just above the first room, near the grand approach to the entry door. The exterior, adorned by white marble, gold columns, and a silver door with golden hardware. Perfectly placed shrubbery served as a waist-high border, adding a decorative touch.

As the first sound passed through, they listened.

"It's the staff." De'Nidra said.

The image moved to the garden, and a problem arose. Great Lord EL'Keet sat before a ravishing girl with flawless skin, entranced by her every word and revealing every secret he had. And then he said it, "Sib'Bal."

De'Nidra ended the viewing.

"What's wrong, De'Nidra?" Tem'Aldar asked, concern etched on his face as he grabbed her hand.

She squeezed his hand tightly as they ran for the portal. It closed behind them as their feet touched the cobblestone square. De'Nidra was an emotional mess. "What is wrong? Tell me, De'Nidra," he pleaded.

"Sib'Bal, the Veil of Darkness is real, and she is not sleeping. EL'Keet is her servant, bound to her as I am to the Maid of Light. I have to tell her tonight." De'Nidra dropped their disguises.

"The Veil of Who?" Tem'Aldar asked.

"Sib'Bal, the Veil of Darkness, is the oldest and the first of the gods to ascend. No one believed her to be real. She never communicated with the other gods, and neither historians nor the old gods confirmed her existence. Never withdrawing from the world, she is still changing reality, even with the balance being torn in two. She does not care whether it does damage or may be to blame for extending the time needed to seal this broken reality."

One of Tara's house guards came running toward them from the main stair. "For the love of the gods of light, come quickly!"

De'Nidra and Tem'Aldar rushed to the stairs. "Tell me," De'Nidra demanded, "what is it, woman?"

Shaken, the guard struggled to compose herself. "Cur'Ra is dead. She was attacked on the balcony. Her knife was covered in black blood. Whatever attacked her cut her straight through." The guard wept.

"Take us to her." De'Nidra commanded.

The guard led them to the chapel. The entire Elp'har troop was around Cur'Ra. Ivan and Lil stood to one side. Lil was weeping. Ivan looked ready to kill. The Elp'har were praying and singing a lament, hammering sadness at their hearts. They held hands as they sang, encircling her. Voices so filled with life and loss, it crushed the soul. "They wait for Tara. They need her to lay Cur'Ra to rest," Lil said.

Ivan answered as soon as they approached. He whispered. "It was the Dark Order that sent demons to kill Tara. We felt the disturbance, but Cur'Ra was gone before we could help her. Lil and I do not yet have the words to tell Tara. It will hurt her too deeply. Cur'Ra is the closest thing that she had to a mother."

It was early, just before the first sun rose. The faint light of false dawn painted the horizon in pale red, replacing the moon's silvery glow. The rain combined with the relentless heat had produced a balmy fabric-clinging morning that stirring air refused to blow away. Tara, Edward, Antoff, and Al'len stood together in a circle. They would soon be moving through the streets, trying to blend in with the rest of the Priest Knights and Clerics, who were changing the guard. To avoid detection, they organized the Coth'Venter Priest Knights and Clerics into groups of sixty and separated them into four lances.

However, this division was still risky, as city patrols rode in smaller units of twelve to fifteen. Despite the danger, Antoff believed that having larger lances would allow them to reinforce and overcome the smaller patrolling units if they made contact at the vanguard or rear. Stretching mounted units from Haven Castle to Cathedral Square seemed like a recipe for disaster.

"We can't allow ourselves to be more than a short gallop from each other. If something happens, stay with your lances and hold your ground until the closest lance comes to support you," Antoff advised. "I will go out first. Once the lance in front of you crosses the square and turns down the street, you follow. Let that be the distance you maintain until we all meet in the square."

Tara looked at Edward and then back at Antoff. "You can't hope to make it all the way to the square. The change of patrols isn't going to be completely timed. Some guards will wait until a replacement comes. Some will be early and some late." She said.

Edward nodded reassuringly, "Tara, it is going to be Okay. We are not so close to the main gate. We have already seen the last replacements head for the gate. Soon, the previous shift will ride by."

High on the gate tower, a sentry signaled the last of the guards were making their way down the main street toward Haven's Cathedral of Light. Antoff gave a wave, and the portico's gate raised while the drawbridge lowered, allowing the first lance to ride out. Once Antoff's lance turned and trotted down the main street, Al'len led her lance forward. Tara followed with her assigned lance. The crowds of city folk bustled about and surrounded them as they trotted out across the cobblestone square and onto the main thoroughfare.

As soon as Tara's lance made it, the guard waved Edward's lance forward, and they crossed the square, the sound of their mount's steel shoes echoing off the walls. In Edward's opinion, the whole endeavor was so suicidal that it was only a matter of time until it failed. *I am not telling Tara that. I will just watch close and when she needs me, I will be there.*

The streets and alleyways intersected with the main thoroughfare, and merchant wagons moved in and out, loading and unloading at the rear of the stores. Edward could just see Tara's lance ahead. He could reach her in less than a minute at a gallop. "Let's increase the pace slightly and close the gap. We shouldn't allow ourselves to spread out any further," he suggested. The Priest Knight nodded, and they cantered slowly, closing the distance. Just as they passed the next alley, a patrol of ten city guards almost collided with them as they rounded the corner. However, Edward had two disadvantages: first, he was the son of Lord Lars Haven, and secondly, he was a wanted man. Recognizing one of the city guards changing at the same time they were passing, he tried to ride hidden within the lance.

Unfortunately, they noticed. A guard who had been up all night and wore a judgmental smile said, "My Lord, is that truly you?"

Edward nodded. "Yes, they caught me, and I am being transported to the High Bishop."

Mel'Anor signaled the lance forward. "Clear a path; we're escorting him to the square." The city guard stepped aside but trailed behind them. Mel'Anor whispered to Edward, "This is a problem."

"We'll handle it before the attack." Edward said out of the side of his mouth.

Chapter 12 Divided Light

"You must discern the difference between desire and reality. What you wish for is not the same as telling the truth. It steals choices and we become as robbers, trading our lies for their truths—and there is a price to be paid. The bill comes due at the end of our subterfuge."

Morning sunlight painted the rooftops with a warm, golden glow, casting a radiant aura upon the cobblestone streets. The air hummed with the frenetic energy of merchants and traders bustling about. The city came alive as deliveries arrived, with carts and wagons gracefully navigating the labyrinth of alleyways behind bustling storefronts.

From her elevated vantage point, Tara's senses flooded with the city's heat patterns. Her dragon's thoughts in her mind supplemented her perception with thermal images. Well-formed lances, positioned at perfect distances from one another, and smaller patrols weaved through the streets and alleys. Occasional commercial wagons pulled by teams of beasts moved along the street—a stark contrast to the sheer number of patrols.

Tara's instincts flared as trouble loomed. She wrestled with a torrent of conflicting emotions. The Power seethed within her, yet she knew that acting prematurely could draw unwanted attention and jeopardize their carefully planned assault. The Power within her was a molten fire coursing through her veins, a tempest urging release. Yet, wisdom prevailed over impulse; she clamped down on this inferno, wary of the attention premature action might invite. Al'len's Lance could bridge the gap between them. That was possible, but such a maneuver might lead to Antoff's vulnerability should the alarm sound—a certainty at this point.

She would bide her time, just as she knew Edward was doing. Anything she did now would only compound the problem. *I should have told Edward I love him again before we left. But he worries about me so. No reason to make it worse. Filling his head with my insecurities. The gods know he has his own.*

Antoff's Lance entered the square deliberately, passing a patrol of Priest Knights from the cathedral's stable yard. As he was well-known and his burnished plate mail remained stored at the rectory temple across the square, it was plain that he was being escorted. The twelve Priest Knights, between the changing of the guard, hadn't fully donned their armor as the first rays of the Little Sister painted the rooftops golden, illuminating the square.

An older Haven Priest Knight challenged, "Hold! Is that you, Antoff Grant?"

"It is," Antoff said.

"You are supposed to be brought in chains by order of the High Bishop Er'laya. Why do you still bear arms?"

Recognition dawned on Antoff as he faced Kel'Dor, a knight who had fought by his side in campaigns nearly six years ago. "Kel'Dor, please. I have everything under control, and I will meet the High Bishop in due time."

Kel'Dor shook his head and pulled line restraints they all carried on patrol for just this type of situation. "I'm afraid not Antoff. You know the procedure as well as anyone. The law is the law. Only the bishop himself can rescind the order once written, and I know it wasn't, as I have just left the posts. The order stands, and it reads *in chains*. I hope you understand. Now let's get you disarmed and in a cell before the rest of you get strapped for insubordination."

"Please, Kel'Dor," Antoff's voice cracked, a blend of desperation and resolve. "Just walk away. You don't know what's at stake."

"No can do, my friend. You know that better than most." With that, the Haven Knights drew steel. The Coth'Venter knights and clerics did the same.

From the edge of the square, Al'len could see combat erupt between Antoff's Lance and the Haven Knights. She broke into a gallop toward him. Her lance rode behind her, keeping stride—just as the alarm went up. The cathedral bells rang out the warning of attack to muster the troops.

The Alarm sounded from the square ahead. Edward pulled his broadsword and attacked. His lance, easily outnumbering the city guards, drew their weapons and brutally crushed the smaller unit, But the clash of steel and the alarm drew soldiers from everywhere like Hornbees to fresh flowers. Disabling his attackers, Edward charged his troop toward Tara, but drew up short as they encountered more soldiers coming from a side street, cutting the way between them.

Tara struggled with the dilemma, whether to aid Edward or rally her troops to Antoff. She yelled while wheeling her Stinger around and pulling one of her short swords free, "The first thirty to the square and the rest of you with me!" The dispatch of these warriors thundered a charge to aid Antoff and Al'len, who were being pressed on all sides by ever-increasing numbers of troops, both knights and city guard. She led the charge toward Edward's Priest Knights and Clerics of the Light as they ignited in a divine blaze.

Divine Power was coursing through Antoff. His lance of Warriors of the Light glowing with the strength of EL'ALue, the Maid of Light, as they attacked the small force. Swift as a striking serpent, Kel'Dor's sword leaped into his hand, and he closed in on Antoff, slashing with precise, skillful strokes. Knights and guards were pouring into the street, some only wearing britches or just in their shirt sleeves. He aggressively pressed his attack against Kel'Dor while parrying his initial blows. He saw the strain on the other knight's face, almost blinded by the light.

Antoff took the next blow on his shield and then slapped the back of Kel'Dor's helm with the flat of his blade. Then shield bashed him from his warhorse with a backhanded blow.

***

Amidst the opulent confines of gilded chambers, High Bishop Er'laya's plump frame trembled with the alarm's ringing. His body quivered with anxiety of the imminent attack, while the cathedral's bells reverberated the warning throughout the halls. One thought echoed through his mind—his worst nightmare was about to materialize. With urgency, he called out to the attending monk, "Summon everyone!" The young monk ran out calling to arms!

Er'laya fervently prayed for the downfall of the Maid of Light, but not all prayers were answered by the Light; in fact, some were heeded by Sib'Bal, the Veil of Darkness.

As the last words of his prayer escaped his lips, a ribbon of light tore through the air, unfolding into a Mage Gate the size of a man. Diocesan On'omus rushed into the room just as a breathtakingly beautiful girl emerged from the gate. Translucent black and gray silks flickering with the purple light showing the outline of elegant curves, revealing just enough to leave them breathless. Despite her youthful appearance, her knowing smile hinted at hidden secrets. With delicate hands, she adjusted the cascading silver and seashell beads gracing her shoulders.

"Well, well," she said, eying High Bishop Er'laya with an air of disdain. "It seems you have summoned my help amidst your troubles. Unless I'm mistaken, EL'ALue, the Maid of Light, prepares to put an end to both of you."

Er'laya and On'omus pleaded before her shimmering translucent silks. "Please, Goddess of Light, save us," he begged.

"Well, not exactly a goddess of Light, my dear High Bishop, but a goddess, even so. Do you still desire my help? It will come at a cost."

On'omus glanced at the High Bishop, then whispered, "My Lord, she is no goddess of Light."

Sib'Bal smiled ominously. "No, you are correct. I am a goddess of the Night, and we are deliberating whether to leave you in the hands of a very aggrieved goddess—namely, EL'ALue, the Maid of Light. We both know how that will turn out, don't we? Now, a choice! Do you want my help, or shall I depart and leave you to her?" She turned toward the flickering Gate and stepped back through.

Their hands reached desperately. "Wait!" Er'laya and On'omus called out in unison.

Sib'Bal's silky voice carried back into the room just as a group of Priest Knights arrived to escort him to safety. "If you wish to serve Sib'Bal, the Veil of Darkness, you better make your minds up swiftly. I am growing tired of your wavering faith."

Er'laya and On'omus lunged for the Gate just as the Priest Knights rushed forward to grab them, but it closed with a flash before they could reach it.

Sib'Bal would grant them an escape route from the Maid of Light, who would now, according to plan, discover the High Bishop's allegiance to the ancient god Sib'Bal, the Veil of Darkness, who had yet to slumber. This revelation would grant El'Alue the authority to respond directly.

The Mage Gate sealed behind them, and they found themselves in a garden permeated by the lingering scent of the sea. The Little Sister cast a vibrant nimbus of light through the swaying trees. Sib'Bal asked. "Should I aid the Maid of Light in capturing you, or can you be of greater use to me?"

Amidst the clamor of battle, steel blades clashed and horses cried out. Al'len's stinger danced beneath her as she guided him solely with the pressure of her knees, one with the rhythm of combat. She raised her knights shield, blocking a bashing blow from a mace that sent vibrations from her arm deep into her core. The attacking cleric, large and powerful, strain clear on his face, squinted as the godly light from her companions flooded the square. The cleric struck again and again, and Al'len countered the blows. Killing was an inevitable part of the battle, one she desperately tried to avoid. Whether they knew it or not, the Priest Knights and Clerics of Haven belonged to her, and she was determined to save as many of them as possible.

The cleric closed in, raining hammering blows upon her shield and sword arm. With each strike, her arms grew numb, the vibrations resonating rhythmically through muscle memory alone. Al'len gazed into his squinting eyes and found the answer—how this cleric could continue with such Power. Deep within the brown irises of his eyes, she could see the telltale signs of a construct infused with another god's Power.

Let's see how much skill this god possesses beyond the brute force poured into this constructed being, Al'len thought. She summoned every ounce of concentration she could muster, teetering on the edge of awakening from sleep. Her glow intensified, and her blade ignited. Her strokes grew faster and faster, the shield blocking and deflecting blows. She positioned herself next to him, under his strikes. With a gentle nudge, she urged her warhorse to kick, catching the cleric's mount in the ribs. The animal faltered, and Al'len's mounts steel-clawed shoe gouged a deep cut in the cleric's steed. At that moment, Al'len's sword spun, and its pommel struck the cleric squarely in the snout. His eyes rolled up as the injured mount spun away, and the godly constructed cleric crashed to the ground, melting away.

Sib'Bal stood by a marble birdbath in her elevated garden, overlooking both the sea and the harbor below. The battle raging outside the Haven Cathedral of Light in the square painted vivid images on the shimmering water. Sib'Bal watched with nail-biting interest as her construct clashed with the Maid of Light's image. Her construct faltered when the Maid's warhorse wounded his mount. Sib'Bal observed her carefully crafted work of art tumble from the fleeing horse. "You bitch! El'Alue," she uttered her name with a hiss. "You will pay for that!" Sib'Bal disassembled her construct, and it faded away.

High Bishop Er'laya and Diocesan On'omus knelt beside a table in the center of the garden. Their gazes shifted to each other, apprehensive about drawing Sib'Bal's wrath. However, she turned to face them with anger and said, "I have a job for you two little mice. You are going to the main Cathedral of Light in the capital city of Alum'Tai to explain how you lost your posts, your troops, and if you do not lie well, your lives!"

A ribbon of light sliced through the air, blooming into a purple sphere that opened onto the capital's bustling square, startling pedestrians and guards alike. "Now, you little mice, go prepare brilliant cheese for my trap. Remember, I can always choose to leave you at their mercy. As clergymen, I'm certain you remember how well that will work," Sib'Bal said.

Er'laya and On'omus exchanged glances. The pudgy High Bishop turned red, and Diocesan On'omus swallowed. They departed, relieved to still have their lives, however short-lived that might be.

Chapter 13 Day Break

"In the overture to sunrise, where shadows dance with fate, champions are made in the crucible of choices, their souls alight with the undying flames of love, sacrifice, and an unwavering resolve to confront the encroaching Darkness."

De'Nidra guided Tem'Aldar through the dimly lit halls of the temple. "I will send you back to Harbor Cities while I inform Tara about Cur'Ra's fall," she said, her voice steady but tinged with urgency.

Tem'Aldar's brow furrowed, and his hands clenched at his sides as if grasping for something just out of reach. "But if you send me away, De'Nidra," his voice trembled slightly, betraying his attempt at steadiness, "I won't be able to protect you. What about Sib'Bal, the Veil of Darkness? Won't she be lying in wait?"

With a reassuring shake of her head, De'Nidra sought to calm his fears. "No, she won't. If she had been aware of the viewing, she would have surely reacted when I performed the sounding. We wouldn't have had time to enter the Gate. Your task is to gather a crew and provisions for the ship in the Harbor Cities. Sib'Bal can't attack a moving target with the Mage Gate, so it may be our only means of escape and our best chance of eluding her grasp."

Tem'Aldar's arguments welled up, but a gentle touch of her finger to his lips silenced him.

Her eyes met his, filled with understanding. "Trust me, my love. I have navigated this world, its gods, and their machinations for far longer than you. This ship may be our only sanctuary when the other gods discover that Sib'Bal, the Veil of Darkness, has awakened, or worse, that she has never slumbered. She may have deliberately prolonged the Mending of the Balance to further her plan."

Reluctantly, Tem'Aldar conceded, his voice laced with resignation, "Very well, De'Nidra, but I don't like it."

Leaning closer, De'Nidra's lips met his in a tender, fleeting embrace. Pulling back just enough to whisper against his mouth, she murmured, "You don't have to like it; you just have to do it," her breath mingled with his, her loving concern softening the resolve of the command.

A ribbon of light cleaved the dimness, opening into a Mage Gate. He offered a last look, brimming with hope, but with a gentle head shake, she urged him onward. As he stepped through, his Gate dropped, while another luminescent thread split the air, birthing a pulsating sphere of amethyst, large as a man. An event horizon formed, revealing a dusty storeroom. She inverted the light surrounding her. Disappearing, she stepped through the Mage Gate, allowing it to vanish.

She arrived to the sound of bells ringing, summoning soldiers to arms. "*Oh, this just keeps getting better and better,*" De'Nidra muttered to herself. She sensed Al'len's presence toward the square. Pushing open a wooden door, its strap hinges creaked as it swung wide. Although anyone passing by might not have been able to see her, they certainly could have heard that sound. De'Nidra paused, her ears straining for any sound beyond the ringing bell. Satisfied that it masked any noise, she silently closed the door and stepped out of the rectory's stable storage.

Tara desired to summon her dragons, but if she did, they would respond, and these buildings would erupt like a Redleaf tree in a brushfire. She galloped towards Edward, accompanied by her thirty Warriors of the Light. The cobblestones echoed under the thundering hooves as horses charged, lances poised. Edward faced a larger number of soldiers attacking him, some on horseback, and others on foot. In short order, he found himself encircled, impeding their progress towards the square. Raising her short sword, Tara loosed a battle cry, charging forward to lead her warriors into the fray. The clash of steel and the thundering hooves of warhorses echoed through the street.

Edward fought with two soldiers: one mounted, armed with a sword and shield, and the other wielding a spear. He deftly maneuvered his opponent's horse, shielding him from the spearman.

Tara's voice echoed from all directions, "In'Sindra, Um'Freeha." The spearman and the mounted attackers shrieked as their armor ignited, radiating a searing heat akin to forge fire. Their once silver armor transformed into a blazing red hue as they fell, thrashing and writhing, and then it shifted to a blue glow. Ice formed and quenched the molten metal, hissing steam billowing up from the street's center. When Tara glanced up, the remaining assailants had already met their demise. The Coth'Venter Priest Knights and Clerics had executed their lethal duties.

Tara rode alongside. "Edward, are you all right?"

"Yes, yes, I'm fine. Are you okay? Tara." Edward asked urgently, his eyes scanning her, looking for any injuries. When he found none, his shoulders relaxed a fraction. "We must help Antoff and Al'len in the square. More knights and troops will undoubtedly flood the area. Form up!" Edward bellowed. The lance and a half promptly aligned as one, and Tara and Edward charged toward the square, striving to outpace the impending deluge of guards.

The hammering of clawed shoes rivaled the alarm bells, a deafening race to the square. They could see the fight. Antoff and Al'len were surrounded as their front rank of lances tipped down.

"Look right!" Edward shouted, but it was too late. A lance from a Haven Priest Knight slammed into the front of their line. The shaft just missed Tara's head as it passed her. All her mind could see was Edward unhorsed, tumbling to the cobble street. His eyes were closed, and his face was bloody as he dropped his sword and rag dolled to the stone of the square, sliding with the momentum of his Stinger. He lay motionless.

"No! Edward!" She felt the blow tear away his spark, then the loss, and the need to reach him. *You cannot die Edward!* It was her worst nightmare come to life. That was all the time she had; before the battle engulfed her. Edward was still alive. She felt him within their unity, but he was fading fast. She had to act. A Knight swung a blade from the side to finish her, but out of sheer muscle memory, she deflected the blow with the left short sword. The higher reality raged around her. The Darkness beat at the Light, the heat of the suns trying to swallow the night. Everything slowed around her, but this time she controlled it. Time shuttered in a wash that only covered this part of the battle.

The Priest Knight that had attacked spoke in a slow drawl. She could not understand the drawn-out words. The clang of an errant sword crashing against steel sounded like a reverberating gong. To anyone else's eyes, Tara would have moved with blinding speed. Throwing herself from a galloping horse, Tara's feet slid as she touched down, but she did not slow. Edward was slipping away, and Tara's soul was slowly being torn in two.

She broke through, dodging the slow forms of warriors battling each other, and saw Edward's dying form. The Priest Knight that had unhorsed him was circling for a merciful kill. Tara watched in horror as the lance descended toward Edward. With a burst of speed, she reached him and summoned a swirling orb of Power, a turbulent clash of Darkness and Light, above her hand. Lightning of the blackest hate and the brightest stars crawled its surface. It writhed, trying to find an advantage. Tara pushed it toward the descending lance. As the tip met, the lance burst into flames, quickly reducing it to an ashy dust that dissolved into the air. The fire ran up the lance, turning each sluggish inch to ashy dust that slowly drifted away as it consumed it.

Reflexively, Tara moved a shaking left hand to Edward's face as she fell to her knees next to him, still keeping the small liquid ball between Edward and the knights. The lance slowly disintegrated. She felt through their bond and used what her mother had taught her to delve into his flesh. His heart was a slowing thud. "No, Edward, you cannot slip away. I will not allow you to go. I need you. There is no world for me without you in it." She whispered. Her left hand burned blue-green as she tried to coax and fan the spark of his life. His body arched slowly, but it was going out. "No,!" she wailed. "You made me promise. Not one moment, Edward, not one single day!"

The Priest Knight's face wore a surprised look as he passed by, releasing the remnant of his lance. It fell slowly away. She watched him slide by, and there was desperation and animal anger inside her that threatened to boil over. The futility of all these mortals fighting each other that were supposed to be aligned. They were of the Order of the Light, and it was the evil of greed that had brought them to this. Edward would not pay for their choices, and while she may very well have promised Cur'Ra that she would not take the spark from herself, neither would she allow him to die without trying something, anything first. *He is the love of my life, and I refused to just let him slip away!*

Rage flared within and she closed her eyes and drew. Then she cried out, her scream visceral echoed in the vastness of reality, "Not one moment, Edward, not one single day!" She knew it was dark. Tara did not care. She did it anyway. Her eyes closed. It filled her with regret. When Tara's eyes opened again, they were all black. Tentacles of greasy smoke burst from her chest and back. One struck the Priest Knight, his face slowly filled with realization and horror. The other found a different guard attacker. The black coil struck the knight's chest, lifting him from the saddle and suspending him in mid-air.

Tara could feel both mortals and every cell in their bodies that held life. She drew from every smallest bit. The Torrent markings that marred her lovely, twisted face transformed into the burning color of hot coal as it pulsed in time with the energetic tentacles' pull. Life was pulled from the mortal forms raised above. It pulsed down the greasy, writhing smoke to Edward, the one she loved. The green-blue of her hand went alight, and the mortals' life drained from them. They aged, and their skin grew gray and wrinkled like a fruit left in the sun. The exchange was not right. It was as if five years of each man's life had become one. Edward's heart became a stable rhythmic thud as the desiccated knight and the other mortal fell away. Edward opened eyes to her black eyed fiery face, and she whispered to him, "Not one moment Edward. Not one single day." Time shuddered to a normal pace. The smoky blackness of Tara's eyes faded to steel-grey.

Al'len spurred her Stinger, colliding with the guard attacking Antoff from behind, swiftly incapacitating him with a bash to his head that sent his helm flying and his body tumbling to the cobble below.

The alarm bell ceased its clamor, replaced by the blare of a horn, signaling the city to stand down. Moments later, a Priest Knight, clad in polished plate armor adorned with a captain's golden cord, emerged from the stable yard behind the cathedral. Although the warriors lowered their weapons, they maintained their tactical positions. Without escorts, the captain rode into the square. As he approached Antoff, he drew his blade to hand it to him.

Antoff recognized the man as Captain Ver'Mear of the First Order of the Light. He spoke loudly, ensuring his words reached all ears, "When the High Bishop abandoned his post, I overheard him pledging his allegiance to Sib'Bal, the Veil of Darkness, beseeching her for salvation. High Bishop Er'laya and Diocesan On'omus departed with her." He signaled the Haven warriors to stand down, and they sheathed their swords and put up their weapons.

Antoff declined the captain's blade, remarking, "I do not require this; your assurance of peace is sufficient for us."

Al'len nodded at the captain, adding, "She attempted to kill me with her construct. I had always suspected her existence, but she had never made such a brazen move in the open. Not once, did she invoke the names of the old gods!"

The captain turned his gaze toward Al'len and inquired, "And whom might you be?"

She smiled at him. "I am Al'len, Captain Ver'Mear of the First Order of the Light. I am certain you have heard of me. Some also call me—El'Alue, the Maid of Light."

Chapter 14 Devotions Upended

"In the Grand Hall of Light, where gold and shadows danced in a solemn waltz, truth unfurled its bitter tapestry. Amidst the echoes of confession and the thunder of divine revelation, the faithful grappled with a reality reshaped by the hands of gods and mortals, tearing the fabric of faith asunder and leaving their hearts to reconcile with a new truth. The old lie upended."

Al'len and Antoff stood beside Lars before the elevated gold-worked dais, which towered five spans above the clergy as citizens packed into the Grand Hall of Light.

The great ecclesiastical hall, with rows of pews along the walls and seating in a gallery above, was now open to the public. There were no more private arrangements or paid credentials. The vaulted ceiling displayed vast murals painted in bold colors depicting glorious battle scenes and dramatic compositions of divine Power. Amidst these depictions, scenes of mercy, forgiveness, and love were scattered throughout the Grand Hall.

Lord Lars Haven stepped forward, his golden mail gleaming in the soft afternoon light that filled the great hall. He addressed the crowd, raising his arms and spreading his hands wide. "I know the past year has been difficult for all of us to understand. It's as if I have been here and among you, yet I was a different man—one you didn't know. I have indeed changed. While incapacitated, a member of my staff drugged me and subsequently possessed me." The crowd stirred, and some of the clergy made the symbol of the Light with upraised hands. "It's true. The entity that had taken control of my body orchestrated Lady Martin's possession, which also caught my son's attention. Some of you may be aware I banished him for Lady Martin's murder."

Edward, beside Tara at the hall's front, fretted over his father's words and their potential impact on his relationship. Tara, sensing his discomfort through their bond, entwined her fingers with his.

Lars' tone, both somber and reflective, pierced the hush of anticipation. "This past year has been a puzzle wrapped in shadows. You knew me, yet didn't. I was changed, not by choice but by manipulation. Unknowingly, I was shackled by deceit, while a specter within spun a web that ensnared Lady Martin and, after, my son. Imagine: a casual night at the inn turns into a chessboard for dark forces. Edward, asleep, unaware, became a pawn in a plot thickened by a constable, no mere bystander but a piece in the play. It was not a mere coincidence that the city constable was present at the inn during the time of the murder." The grand doors of the hall banged open, and two Priest Knights dragged the constable down the nave toward the stairway.

"They framed me!" he yelled. "I had no choice; they would have killed me and my family."

Lars pointed at the man. "You took money for the act and allowed one of your men to be drugged and possessed, accepting a part in a scheme that would have brought ruin upon your family, this city, and the entire Order of the Light. Under normal circumstances, I would send you to the gallows. However, as I am as much a victim in this plot as everyone else here, I will recuse myself and leave this matter to the church and its mercy." With that, Lars stepped back.

Al'len stepped forward, her gaze sweeping across the gathered faces. "Greed, pride, and the lust for Power have caused needless suffering," she said, her voice echoing softly in the vast hall. "For ages, the old gods have slumbered, while mortals consumed by greed have usurped the authority that solely belongs to El'Alue, the Maid of Light."

The crowd of city folk and merchants murmured. One clergy member, A Diocesan, stood just behind Edward and Tara. "Why are you addressing us, and by what right do you slander the holy El'Alue, who possesses neither male nor female form except in battle?"

As thunder declared its presence, Al'len's words, soft yet unwavering, enveloped the hall. "The truth is, as startling as it is simple—I am El'Alue. Not just in name, but in reality, I've grappled with my grief behind veils of secrecy and sorrow. I abandoned you in my sorrow. I injured you in my pain. It's an admission of my absence when you needed guidance, and the vacuum it created, filled by greed and Darkness."

The Diocesan, stricken with fear, attempted to speak, but his words came out ragged and confused. "It goes against our teachings. It's considered blasphemy by the Order of the Light."

Al'len took a step closer to him, and the clergyman sat down. "I founded the Order of the Light," her voice boomed through the hall as lightning crackled above and rain started to fall, "and when Ram'Del fell in battle at the Torn Flowage, I lost control." Tears began to roll down her face. "I couldn't bear the grief and agreed to sleep, so that we, whom you refer to as the old gods, would no longer cause harm by tearing apart the fabric of creation around our planet. And yet, we caused more harm. When you needed me, I withdrew and left you in the hands of these greedy men. They altered the very nature of the order and how it operates! For this reason, I strip all clergy of rank and I subject them to review by Priest Knights, Clerics, and the faithful people of our order."

The ranks of clergy stood and protested, but the lightning striking the square and the charged air of Al'len's Power silenced them. Al'len continued, "It is my judgment that the archives be opened to all people, withholding none of the knowledge of the Light. All ranks of the clergy shall be open to any Cleric or Priest Knight of the Light who has shown good service. I did not intend these positions for elevation but for a humbler service. As I, myself, have never attained a rank beyond that of Priest Knight of the First Order of the Light, the replacements will be selected from the remaining clergy, clerics, and knights based on their service, not only to the order but also to you, our beloved people." Al'len extended her arms wide. The crowd rose and cheered.

She quieted them, raising her hands. Al'len ordered, "Return all the wealth of the treasury, except what is necessary for good works, to the people of Haven, from whom they embezzled it during my period of grief. These are my words and shall be the next entries in the archives of the law." The sound of the boots of Priest Knights entering the hall filled the air as two hundred of them filed in, cutting off the exits. "I command that all these clergy members be arrested and held until they are cleared of charges of greed and embezzlement against my people, as detailed in the court articles in the archives. We will expel anyone who resists arrest or is not cleared of these charges. Those who are found guilty will be sent to the gallows to hang until dead. You may submit requests for mercy directly to me for my consideration."

"Take them away," Al'len commanded, her voice resolute amidst the charged silence of the Grand Hall. As the Priest Knights moved to arrest the clergy, she stepped back, the weight of her decree settling over the hall like an earthquake. In one fell word, the reign of the clergy was over.

***

High Bishop Er'laya's face flushed crimson as Diocesan On'omus walked behind him. Entering the grounds at the rear of the main Cathedral of Light in Alum 'Tai, the capital city. They emerged into the deserted alley behind the outbuildings next to the rectory's rear. A twinge of unease fluttered in Er'laya's stomach.

"Diocesan On'omus, we must put our situation into perspective," Er'laya said, his voice tight with tension. On'omus nodded, his face beet red and covered in sweat. "When we stand before the High Seat of the Light, Lord Gan'Vile and the High King Lord Mel'Lark, your words must align with mine. If the Holy Seat of Light deems our actions in Haven lacking, we face condemnation."

He raised a finger, "Foremost," Er'laya emphasized, "we allowed ourselves to be deceived by a goddess of Darkness and sought her aid to escape, abandoning our parish. Secondly, as members of the Order of Darkness and servants of the dark deity Sib'Bal, we betrayed our sacred duties and fled. These acts are punishable by death. Do you comprehend?"

Diocesan On'omus swallowed hard. "I was simply following your instructions," he murmured.

Er'laya let out a dark laugh. "If you believe that will save you, I'm certain the Holy Seat of Light will make an exception. What do you suppose His Excellency will do when he discovers that we sought aid from Sib'Bal, violating the very tenets of our faith? You can test that and let me know how it turns out."

On'omus's face grew even redder, sweat dripping from his forehead. "Well, when you put it that way, we are nothing more than cowards and traitors!"

Er'laya poked him in the chest with a thick finger. "That is precisely what we are, Diocesan On'omus. If you wish to survive, you must do as you're told. Is that clear?"

On'omus reluctantly nodded, though Er'laya found it far from convincing. "Did you forget our subservience to Sib'Bal? Our agreement to serve her and come here? Whether driven by fear or not, we are traitors. I will present our narrative, and you must support it fervently. I may yet buy us some time and secure compensation."

"I understand your point." Diocesan On'omus nodded in agreement.

Er'laya smiled wearily at him. "I thought you might. Now let's find a secluded spot to freshen up. We resemble guilty beggars, and I would prefer to present ourselves before His Holiness with some semblance of dignity."

"As would I." On'omus nodded again.

De'Nidra waited outside the Haven Cathedral of Light for Tara, Edward, Al'len, and Antoff to exit. It had become late long ago, but she couldn't bring herself to enter the grand temple after the history that existed between her and the Order of the Light for so many years. It felt sacrilegious, given the harm she knew her actions had caused. El'Alue had forgiven her, *kind of anyway*, but she hadn't forgiven herself. "Once again, I am the bearer of bad news. Tara, that poor child just starting her life, now I must tell of her mother's death. I have to inform El'Alue that Sib'Bal, the Veil of Darkness, is not a myth and has been disrupting the balance while the old gods slept, maintaining peace. During my time in the Dark Order, I was coerced and driven to cause harm. Now I'm left picking up the pieces."

Al'len and Antoff exited first, and De'Nidra released the inverted light that cloaked her form. It startled Antoff a little, but Al'len could sense her presence through their bond. "Al'len, we have a problem too big for me to handle. It will require careful consideration before you react to it."

Al'len raised an eyebrow. "Something beyond De'Nidra's capabilities? That sounds ominous. What is this problem?" Al'len appeared tired, if that were even possible for a constructed being willed into existence by a god. They all looked exhausted. The monks had been leading both city folk and nobility into the forbidden library of history, exposing them to the harsh reality instead of the controlled release of lies.

"Al'len, the issue that is beyond me is Sib'Bal, the Veil of Darkness. She is real, not a myth," De'Nidra revealed.

Al'len didn't seem surprised by this news. "She has been awake the entire time the old gods have slept, altering reality around herself. She has been discreet, not wanting to attract the attention of the other old gods, but she has been up to something for a long time."

Antoff and Al'len exchanged glances. Creation trembled around them, and all the sounds of the world faded away. It was like standing in an endless white void, without form or structure. No sky, just emptiness. This invoked fear in everyone, but Al'len reassured them with a few words. "Everyone, relax. This is my doing, a construct of reality with no form or substance, existing outside of time. It's too complex to explain briefly; we'll have to delve into it later. This is just a trick I learned to prevent eavesdropping. If she is watching, apart from this momentary pause, everything is frozen. It's like being caught between heartbeats, stretching out time. So, our puzzling myth has emerged. That certainly explains why reality isn't mending itself. She's doing just enough to extend the cataclysm and keep us all unaware while she plans our demise."

Tara marveled at the surrounding envelope of reality. She had never imagined it could be used like this. She could see the patterns forming around them, like a small bubble in space-time. "Sib'Bal, the Veil of Darkness? I've never heard that name before," Tara said.

Al'len nodded. "Few have, Tara. The old gods themselves considered her a myth. There was never any direct interaction, and she didn't have any servants or followers."

De'Nidra interjected, "Well, she has them now. Lord EL'Keet has joined her, and he sits on the Dark Order's council. If she had never taken any followers before, this is a significant and dramatic move for someone trying to maintain a low profile."

Al'len shook her head. "Her plans are coming to fruition, and she has reached a point where hiding is no longer an option. I'll ensure that everyone who needs to know is aware of her. I suspected something was amiss when a construct attempted to kill me earlier today. Initially, I assumed it was one of the old gods, given its Power, but its training resembled that of a regular soldier, not a god who had personally fought through epochs of war."

Antoff looked concerned as he joined the conversation, evaluating the information and piecing it all together. "Al'len, I think we should relocate most of the Priest Knights from Haven to Coth'Venter. We can leave the monks to watch over the city, and Lord Lars, having taken command of the entire guard, should be able to defend the city until reinforcements arrive. The Dark Order may not be as significant a threat as the High Seat will be when he finds out that Haven has fallen to a band of heretics. It's best if we remove ourselves for the safety of the people of Haven."

"I agree." Al'len said.

De'Nidra had reached the point she had dreaded. "Tara, you need to be strong. I have something terrible to tell you, and you must be prepared."

Tara clung to Edward's hand tightly. "What is it, De'Nidra? Just tell me." She could feel it was going to be bad. Like a blade hanging above her heart, awaiting the plunge.

De'Nidra hesitated, striving to be as compassionate as possible. "Tara, there was an attack on the Coth'Venter Cathedral of Light by the Dark Order. I'm sorry, but Cur'Ra was alone on the balcony, and demons attacked her. She managed to injure at least one, but there's no doubt it was meant for you, and she became a convenient target. I'm sorry."

Tara's world halted, a silent void swallowing her screams of disbelief. Each heartbeat echoed the shattering of her reality.

Edward felt her confusion through their bond, followed by an overwhelming surge of pain. All he could do was pull her close before she erupted. The anguish was unbearable, and it engulfed Tara in a world of pain. Deep, uncontrollable sobs shook her against his chest, and her hands clung to him like an anchor in a storm. She couldn't find the words to speak.

Edward glanced at Tara, noticing the subtle hardening of her jaw and the distant storm brewing in her gaze. The surrounding air seemed to thicken with an unspoken vow of revenge, a shadow creeping into the space between them, whispering of a darkness taking root. And he would make sure she got it. "I swear, Tara—by the suns that Light our sky—they will pay for this. We will make them pay together."

Reality shook, and the world resumed its normal state. "We'll discuss this further once we've all had a chance to mourn. Antoff, prepare every Warrior of the Light to move. We can't let harm befall these people because of us. We're relocating our base to Coth'Venter once again," Al'len declared. They huddled around Tara, embracing her as family.

High Bishop Er'laya and Diocesan On'omus knelt before the High Holy Seat, feeling the weight of his gaze upon them. Er'laya knew that this meeting wouldn't go well, but he had no choice but to face the consequences of his failures.

"So, what you are saying, Er'laya, is that the Dark Order infiltrated Haven right under your very noses, and you and your cronies were so blinded by your positions that you couldn't see the destruction happening around you. Is that what you're telling me?" The High Holy Seat's voice laced with disappointment and anger.

Er'laya took a deep breath, steeling himself for what would come next. "Your Excellency, we must recover Haven for the sake of its people and put an end to the influence of the Order of Darkness. There is a woman named Al'len, who claims to be the image of El'Alue, the Maid of Light. If this information reaches the ears of the populace, the consequences would be dire. I cannot disclose all the details due to Diocesan On'omus's position, but believe me, the threat is real. We were fortunate enough to call upon a god of Light and escape through a Mage Gate, or else we would not have made it back alive."

The High Holy Seat pondered Er'laya's words, his expression grave. "I understand your point, High Bishop Er'laya, and I appreciate Diocesan On'omus's support of the facts presented. As he is not yet acquainted with the liturgy surrounding this matter, I will withdraw and continue this conversation with the High King. He is entitled to act on behalf of the realm, and I believe a crusade is necessary to confront this threat and teach the Dark Order the price of their actions. We must confront darkness wherever it presents itself, and it is high time we put an end to this evil order once and for all."

Lord Gan'Vile, the High Holy Seat, had made a decision and now he would reveal the fate of Haven to Lord Mel'Lark, the High King, who would undoubtedly recognize the danger this rebellion posed to the realm. Er'laya and

Diocesan On'omus rose from their kneeling positions, knowing that their actions and failures had set events into motion that would shape the future of their world.

Chapter 15 Darkness Rising

"Darkness seeps into our hearts, its deceptions piercing, our honor dwindling as if it were the blood of a fallen warrior. Pride, untreated, festers. Adrift in a sea of loss, only the beacon of Light and the compass of truth can guide us to safety."

Twelve lamps cast flickering light across the glassy walls. Great Lord EL'Keet stood to address the Council of Darkness. Sparsely furnished, the room was large, save for a long table made of onyx stone. Seated around it were ten other Dark Lords, were each reigning over a distinct territory within the Blacken Lands. Except for EL'Keet and Amorath, the ten other Dark Lords, each clad in black attire, their faces obscured by veils. The other Lords had adopted this practice as a safeguard, a shield against the prying eyes that might pierce their veils of secrecy. Anyone who considered the matter would see the obvious connections. There were twelve territories along the border in their district and twelve of them. The only reason to hide their identities was a safeguard to deny membership should plans go awry.

"Cowards," EL'Keet muttered, his voice a low growl. "Our spies within Haven's embrace now stand exposed. Save for a scant few, they've left us groping in the dark, blind to the Order of the Light's plans. The gods now deploy constructs against us. A woman named Al'len is working with the Torrent at Coth'Venter, claiming to be the very embodiment of El'Alue, the Maid of Light."

Great Lord Amorath, his face contorted with anger, rose abruptly, and slapped the table. His voice trembled with rage as his face took on an expression of disbelief. "This is madness, EL'Keet. Our agents in Haven are silent, and now you speak of gods and constructs? Explain yourself."

"You should take better care, Great Lord Amorath. Slamming your fist down so, old friend, might just cost you a rotting finger." EL'Keet lowered his voice near to a whisper, straining them to listen, "Great Lord Amorath, once you cease squandering your time trying to contact your nonexistent agents, you may return to your previous practices of secrecy and decadence. These practices of yours have placed us in this perilous position to begin with." He raised his voice as the accusations tumbled out of him in a landslide. "Your mishandling of the Torrent issue has entangled us in the affairs of the ancient gods we have fervently strived to avoid. If you had been forthcoming concerning your desire to capture her and use her body as a vessel from the beginning, we would not find ourselves in this predicament. Now, because of your incessant meddling in the politics of the Order of the Light, we could have been otherwise steadily eroding their strength like a grinding millstone." Punctuating each point by forcefully pounding the table. EL'Keet continued, "The consequence of your greed and failures will be a full-fledged crusade against us, leading to the destruction of our lands and our order, unless we act now."

The council members exchanged uneasy glances, their veiled heads turning between Amorath and EL'Keet as the accusations flew. It was a silent, apprehensive communication, like children tossing a ball in a game of catch. One of them stood, face concealed. "Enough! What action is being taken?" Murmured assents from the other members rippled through the room, signifying their collective unease.

EL'Keet continued, "I am mobilizing the entirety of my forces for the defense of our borders. Also, I am in discussions with the gods of darkness, seeking their aid. While some of you may be too young to recall the notoriety of El'Alue, the Maid of Light, Amorath and I certainly do. She will slice through your troops, leaving behind a trail of blood all the way to your strongholds." He pointed his finger back at Lord Amorath in retaliation. "And you will be the first to witness her wrath. Have you considered the consequences once the Torrent discovers that you ordered the death of the woman she regarded as her mother?"

Amorath retorted, "We all agreed that De'Nidra, the Daughter of Shadows, needed to be flushed out of hiding so we could identify her agents."

EL'Keet laughed menacingly. "And now you find yourself facing an ancient god of Light and a rising one who perceives our annihilation as a mercy to the world and a retribution for her mother's murder. Amorath, you are a fool! Why don't you just place our heads on a stump and hand her the axe?"

Great Lord EL'Keet pushed himself away from the table and glanced at them before striding out. "Unlike you, I converse with an ancient god daily, and I have received instructions to prepare for a new cataclysm and a new balance! I suggest you do the same!"

In the square by the fountain of Ram'Del, the Mage Gate burst into a bloom of life, flickering, casting a purple light that danced upon his upraised sword and banner. Tara and Edward guided their mounts through the Gate ahead, followed by De'Nidra.

Coth'Venter Cathedral of Light was silent, the only sound being the gentle rustle of leaves in the breeze and horseshoes ringing on the cobblestone. It was late at night; the moons casting a gentle silvery glow that still illuminated the square as the Mage Gate vanished. Mic'Ieal, the First of Her Guard, hurried two volunteers down the wide steps. Tara and Edward had just made it to the landing by the time they trotted down the thirty steps of the grand entry.

Two house guards escorted the Stingers to the stables, and the scent of the grassy field wafted through the air. Inside, Mic'Ieal knelt before Tara, his voice heavy with remorse. "Forgive me, my Lady. I failed you. If only I had been more vigilant, Cur'Ra might still be here."

Tara bent, her fingers closing around his hands as she gently lifted him to his feet. "Rise, Mic'Ieal," she commanded firmly. "You are not responsible. You have served us honorably. The Dark Order is accountable and they will pay for it. Not you Mic'Ieal."

His face shone in the moonlight, and the glyph, a mark of an oath to the Light, stood out prominently on his forehead. "Thank you, Lady Tara, for your kind words, but you gave me the command and I am responsible."

"You are not, and I will hear no more of this. Cur'Ra went out for air at odd hours of the night to think, and you can't follow everyone around for their safety. I left you in command of the entire grounds, and it is still standing. My people are still here, and you are still in control until Antoff and Al'len get back." Her tone bore firmness, yet held kindness.

Mic'Ieal, the First of Her Guard, stood straighter and bowed. "It is as you command, Lady Tara. You both look tired; perhaps something to eat and some sleep would be in order?"

"You should eat and get some rest, Tara," De'Nidra echoed.

Edward took Tara's hand, leading her up the steps. "That sounds like a good idea," he said. "There will be time in the morning for everything else." *If I can just get her to eat something and sleep a little, she will be more up to dealing with the loss of her mother.* Tara's pain pulsed through the bond, raw and torn.

"No, Edward. I want to see her now. Mic'Ieal, take us to her, and afterward, I will try to eat and sleep if I can. I need to see Cur'Ra. I need to know that this is real. That I will never again find her waiting for me in her room." Tara held back bitter tears. She felt them forming, yet remained stoic. She wouldn't acknowledge it until she saw Cur'Ra for herself.

"Please, Lady, of course, this way." Mic'Ieal took her other arm to lead her up the stairs and to the chapel where Cur'Ra lay in state.

De'Nidra followed, but remained silent. The thoughts tumbled in her head. She thought about all the people she had lost over the long years of war. She felt the need to get back to Tem'Aldar, but resisted going to him. *Life is so easily lost. The love that was once known, torn from you and then it is gone. Left with your spirit empty and an unfillable hole.*

Their footfalls echoed down the silent hall and into the chapel. Cur'Ra lay before them on a cushioned stone altar.

Tara dropped Edward's and Mic'Ieal's hands and walked toward Cur'Ra. A white sheer veil of fabric lay over her. She wore her favorite earth-toned blouse and pants. Tara was empty, wounded, and angry, as if someone had cruelly ripped away Cur'Ra's very essence, which had so vivaciously infused her life. *I never noticed the energy and life that had been between us before she was gone. Not as I should have. There are so many things I needed to say and now I never will. She is gone.* It welled in her like acid bile. *Never will I forgive this! I will never rest until I avenge it!*

Edward waited with De'Nidra and Mic'Ieal to give Tara space alone with her mother. For some, they may not see her as Tara's mother. She was not her birth mother, but in the Elp'harean culture, they saw people for how they treated each other. The place Cur'Ra had been in was Tara's mother since the time she had set her as the troop's leader, and that was that. Even in death, the Power of her decision held.

Tara sat next to Cur'Ra. Her fingers trembled as they slipped beneath the shroud to clasp her hand, a torrent of tears breaking loose and mingling with her grief. Edward sensed the oppressive weight of her sorrow, and all he could do was stand there and bear it with her. Try to lend her strength through the oneness of their bond.

That evening, the kitchen sent up some stew. He coaxed her into a few spoonfuls of the rich broth. However, all she wanted was to sleep. She lay there against his chest, curled in an injured ball. She dreamed. Not the hurt dreams of a child. They were dreams of smoke and vengeance and dragons breathing hell's inferno. Her anger and anguish fueled those fires, the flames of her pain consuming the surrounding darkness.

Black and white shadows loomed in the night sky. Powerful rhythmic strokes of their wings lifted on winds as they passed over the Darkened Gate into the Blackened Lands. Heat from Zoruk bodies lit the battlements far below like radiating forge fires. The dragons passed visions between them, but kept them hidden from Tara. The pain these mortals had caused their bondholder had been too much. Tara's vengeance would begin tonight.

The Black and White passed a plan between them. It was a simple plan. A plan that brought Tara's pain and burning hell. They split in opposite directions, high above the battlements. Diving with their wings pulled tight to their bodies; they fell like javelins from the blackened sky.

All Zoruk's heard was the sound of popping like large sails opening and an exhaling roar as two long streams of hell fire blanketed the top of the battlement walls, melting Zoruk'ar and metal-clad ballista alike.

Swooping low over the wall, the White seized a large Zoruk, its taloned claws piercing his armor as spear-sized hooks tore through his trembling form.

The Black hovered before a tower's door, its wings beating with powerful strokes. An arrow bounced off its armor, and a vile gas ignited by the striker in its throat. Fire billowed forth as its muscles strained. A glut of liquid hell rolled through the tower and burst out of arrow slits like the billows from a smithy pumping the forges. It began with screams, but liquid fire swiftly snuffed them out. The Black's wings pumped hard as his bulk passed the wall. He snatched a Zoruk hiding behind a barrel of oil with dagger-sized teeth and gave a few healthy crunches, just to be sure. Zoruk blood was not sweet, but it was the beginning of Tara's vengeance and that seasoned the meat.

The Black listened; as the White's call pierced the night. *"Servants of old ones, we bid you come and answer our call!"*

Antoff and Al'len had arrived with an army of eight hundred and ninety-two Warriors of the Light. They had entered through a Gate forged by El'Alue, the Maid of Light. Antoff was not dressed in the normal chain over boiled leather. He had gone to the rectory and put on his burnished silver plate mail, and with him came twenty more retired clerics, monks, and Priest Knights.

The Square thundered with war beasts, clawing shoes and arching of necks as they passed through the fluid surface of the huge Mage Gate four abreast. The setting of the cathedral was familiar to all, even those that had never been to Coth'Venter. As with many of the Temples of the Light, this was a historical design.

Al'len and Antoff dismounted and handed their Stingers to an aging monk with a nod as they climbed the cathedral steps. It was very late and the entry of such a large force brought the investigation of the guard and a detachment of light cavalry on patrol in the main street.

Antoff raised his voice, "Get your animals tended and find yourselves a cell for the night. There are plenty. If you are hungry, go to the dining hall and give the staff a bit to get started. They will see you fed."

"Yes, Lord Captain!" The warriors saluted, their voices ringing out.

A breeze blew through the open window into Tara and Edward's room. She lay entwined with him while he slept in a seated position. Tara stirred. *Has he been sitting there all night holding me until he finally fell asleep?* He moved but didn't wake. She could feel the emotion and care for her that coursed within their bond. He was exerting a portion of himself to just holding her on the very edge of waking. Tara's hand lay on his chest. Cur'Ra had taught her to feel the flows of life and emotion and heal the injury of mind and soul as much as outward damage of flesh and organs. Tara reached out with a small flow of life and slowly untangled his knots of emotion. She loosened his struggle to remove her pain. She poured safety and joy into him through their unity and felt him relax. He fell into a deep and restful sleep.

Untangling herself from his arms, she got up from the bed and washed. The water poured from the clay pitcher was ice cold. She splashed her face, clarifying her mind. The feel and smell of rosewood and lavender soap filled her nose with a fragrance of the Garden Wood's childish memories and the washbasin was the clear water of the pond. She had everything she had wanted then and more. Home, a man that loved her, not the garden or the children yet, but those too would come. First, was the putting down of everything that could threaten them, every Darkness that yet wanted to take her dreams away. Just like they had stolen Cur'Ra from her while she was in Haven, they would try to take what she loved whenever she was distracted by everything else that the Dark Order had thrown her way.

No, you will take no more from me! Not one more person or thing that I love. I will find you. Every taker and murderer of spite. You will know the cost of folly! You will fear not just the day. Now you will fear the thief in the night! Tara promised herself.

"Mic'Ieal, I know you are there," Tara said. She wanted to make him feel useful to her and she could sense him there trying to shelter her from someone interrupting their sleep. He said he had failed her. Tara's protection had been part of the oath to the Light he had taken. For Mic'Ieal, that extended to family, friends, and property. If one hair was out of place, he would fidget, and she was sure he was out there in the hall.

"Yes, my Lady, I am here. Do you need something?" Mic'Ieal asked.

"Yes I do Mic'Ieal, I want some breakfast for myself and Edward and you can sit in here with us where you belong and tell me everything that happened."

"Of course, Lady Tara, right away." She heard Mic'Ieal's feet start his joyous run, bringing a smile from somber lips.

Tara gazed out of the modest window, her eyes fixed on the surging sea of grass in Dan'Nor. The twin suns ascended above the distant mountains, casting a golden hue upon the treetops. It was as if the Elder Brother guided his Little Sister toward the orbit of the first noon, painting the world in morning's promise.

Are'Amadon, a massive fortress of obsidian stone, rose like a menacing sentinel from the desolation of the Blacken Lands. Its ancient Citadel of Darkness stood against the backdrop of murky soil that stretched for leagues. The Zoruks, dark red and black ants, scurried with slaves in the vast fields below.

Great Lord Amorath clutched a twisted and disfigured mage's staff in his withered hand. The ancient relic's crystal flickered, ready to amplify his mages abilities.

"Rem'Mel?" He heard the swish of an elegant bow and the expensive fabric of value draped upon what was assuredly an almost worthless middle mage.

"Yes, Great Lord Amorath, I hear and obey," Rem'Mel said from the sitting room just outside of his chambers. He had been dutifully teaching Moros while they waited for their Lord to give the boy his next lesson.

"You may bring the child in now Rem'Mel, I am ready for him." *But am I ready?*

Moros walked in wearing black silk robes covered by the runes etched in gold that warded him against the searching eye that had the talent to use spy devices. He thought of De'Nidra, the Daughter of Shadows, "what a waste." He whispered. *I had such high hopes for her. I can't say which of us failed the other worse. You De'Nidra for your betrayal of the Order, or my failure of you.*

"What was that, my Lord?" Rem'Mel asked.

He gave a rusty giggle. "I said you are a waste of good fabric. Now bring the boy here."

Moros, his black hair now grown longer. It was down to his shoulders and fell loose perfectly straight. No doubt the result of Rem'Mel's incessant brushing. His bright brown eyes had taken on an almost fiery look. Like deep brown embedded with hot coals. "Okay, Moros, show me."

Moros gave a bow that smacked of the formal, almost worthless teachings of a middle mage, as grand as any Grand Mage of his day. Moros closed his eyes and the image of the Darkness and the Light rolled in upon him. In the higher reality, he sheltered in the blackest part of the void where the Light tried to hammer at him the hardest. The Darkness stood like a shield against its blows and struck back whenever the Light tried to withdraw. Reality shook around the child in a wash. Lord Amorath watched as the boy formed a creature that lived and took shape in the world. It was as real as any that existed. With blood and flesh over scaly skin. This one was a replica of Lord Modred, just smaller. Moros had a vast imagination, and he had given it not only body but soul and language and attitude.

Great Lord Amorath gave a cautious laugh. "You can create life from imagination. That is something I have only seen the High Mages do before the Breaking of the Balance. They broke all the rules using the Power of Darkness and that of Light to do it. Is that what you do, Moros?"

Moros' head shook vehemently, his dark eyes fixed on Great Lord Amorath, a silent but firm refusal in his gaze. "I do not use the Power that comes from Light to make the spark of life. I'm using fear and horror, which I learned of while playing with the mad souls that Be'elota took from a thing called the Dark Well. The insanity inside has a life of its own. Once consumed by it, I mean. I copied and then enriched that."

"I see, Moros," Great Lord Amorath said with a wonder and a dread that a child was beginning to watch outstrip his talent. He could create a false life, but it perished without purpose once its task was complete. The child had created something without material and from raw imagination. If he did not need this child as a vessel, he would have terminated the abomination there and then. Fear crept over Amorath. He was committed now to his dark god Mali'Gorthos, The Corrupter. He had given his word to be ready in one year and that time would soon be growing short. But the more he taught this child to increase his imagination and new knowledge of spells, the faster he outstripped his own ability.

Amorath glanced at the staff in his grip, a silent thought flashing through his mind: *With this, I can resist, even if the child learns to wield his control over reality against the living. He needs to learn much more and lay the pathways of understanding down in his mind before I take him over. Otherwise, I will have to relearn it all and the amount of the old wisdom and knowledge that I alone hold would be lost. I will risk it a while longer and teach this child, at a minimum, what I will need to know.*

"I think I can do bigger things," Moros said with an innocent smile.

Great Lord Amorath fought back a shutter, "Let's not. I forbid that, just for now. We should work on your lessons. Are you ready to learn?"

Moros nodded, with a child's interest and a smile.

"Very well, we shall begin." He watched the middle mage lean forward with interest. "Rem'Mel, you may go!" Amorath gave a dead, grinning smile.

In a chirping, demonic tone, Little Lord Modred pointed Rem'Mel to the heavy wooden black door.

That's right, Rem'Mel, Amorath thought. *Your master is a dick. You would do well to remember that.*

Chapter 16 Sea Of Fear

"Mortality floats on an ocean of sensation. It is like a deep sea. We go down and struggle with currents that either lift us to our heights or pull us under."

The mood was somber under the Second Noon as the Little Sister cast purple, blue, and red shades, illuminating the delicate kaleidoscope of cut glass within the Cathedral of Light. Reflections of scenes depicting mercy and courage that scattered light and imagery throughout the space. The statues of the old Priest Knights lined the nooks within the far wall, appearing almost lifelike as the rays struck the marble floor, reflecting hues of gilded flakes and bringing a supernatural atmosphere.

The Nave filled with souls from every corner of the Cathedral. Tara stood behind the veiled sleeping form of Cur'Ra, while the clerics and knights begun singing. Mel'Anor's baritone voice moved everyone to tears. It wrenched at the heartstrings, evoking a deep, unspoken sorrow. "Mercy was Cur'Ra's name. May Light and love embrace her. Grant her peace and rest. Throughout her days, she blessed, healed, and restored our lives. We will remember her sacrifice and live by her example. We will strive to bring truth and love. Let us all be like her, a saver of life, a lover of one another."

The words drifted into the background as she recalled the day they met in the desert before the stone wall of Forge'Wrath Keep. Cur'Ra's voice echoed in her mind. "You are welcome to our fire." From that day on, Cur'Ra provided warmth and comfort, and her memory would forever remain in Tara's heart. As the choir's song faded, silence reverberated through the expansive hall.

Addressing the crowd, Tara stood alongside Edward, Antoff, Al'len, De'Nidra, Va'Yone, Ivan, and the veiled Lil in the front row. Lil, Tara's friend, endured the brightness of the suns to lend Tara strength.

Struggling to find words as powerful as the song the Warriors of the Light had sung to honor her mother. "Cur'Ra loved life, not just her own, but all life. She willingly gave it to protect her family. It is how she would have selected to go." Her hand swept across the seated crowd. "Today, while we burn her body and she gives up her last Light, we will keep the flame she has ignited within us all alive, and she will exist within us all. I know she wouldn't want me to seek vengeance. But I cannot let her pass without crying out her name in the Blackened Lands, where her murderers live. I will confront the darkness that took my mother, ensuring they remember the heavy price of their acts. They will not attack our loved ones and children in the night without a response. She will not slip away unremarked. Not one of them will breathe her name for fear I will hear them. Fear that I will come." Tara's voice echoed through the room, raw and visceral, booming from every corner. "They will cower at the thought of doing my people harm. I must arise and confront this horror!"

Moved, everyone in the hall stood. "Arise!" They echoed.

Tara bent to kiss her mother's forehead. "Forgive me, Mother, if your loss has clouded my mind. I cannot let you drift away into the mists of night unremembered. If I do not answer this challenge, they will perceive us as weak, ready to fall. I must rise! Stand against the night, so we can carry on." She stood tall. Her god like thunder shook the room. "Rise and fight! I will ensure your memory becomes the catalyst that brings life to our dying world. For that, I stand. For that, I fight!" Tara lamented, her tears bitter cocktails of loss and anguish. Down her cheeks ran the burning rivers of war.

Every soul in the hall had stood, and a call echoed with divine Power, "For the Light, for truth and for love!"

Blood bats burst from the towers as dragons roared from above. Tara answered their call and ran from the temple hall toward the square. Led by Tara, the congregation poured out of the hall, just as dragons, majestic in their black and white scales with wingspans stretching fifteen meters, descended beside the statue of the Hero of the Light, Ram'Del. They tossed Tara's Zoruk offerings onto the stone, their eyes meeting hers, revealing that they had been aware of her plan all along. They had already begun the fight, knowing what she intended to do, and were willing to risk their lives to avenge Cur'Ra's death. The dragons bellowed an angry roar of vengeance that shook the square. Tara felt their minds respond.

"We will not finish it until you say," replied the Black.

"Not until you say it's over!" said the White.

Antoff and EL'ALue, the Maid of Light, had opened the Archives of the Light to the public to reveal the Truth. They instructed Lars not to resist any Warriors of the Light who might arrive, but to let them pass. It would support their fight against the Order of Darkness. Lars sent a page with information about what had happened to the king and the High Seat, seeking answers. Also, since the Maid of Light had taken every Warrior of the Light with her, he sent an affidavit from the Captain, stating that Haven's High Bishop and the Diocesan were colluding with the Dark goddess Sib'Bal to save themselves.

EL'ALue and Antoff had taken all the remaining Knights and Clerics of the Light from Haven to Coth'Venter. Sixty-six had died in battle. Before departing, they held a funeral in the square before the people, leaving Lars to manage the city of Haven alone. Lars watched as the large Mage Gate opened, allowing the Warriors of the Light, including the retired ones, to transfer to their new home in Coth'Venter.

Later that night, De'Nidra stood next to the construct of EL'ALue, whom everyone else called Al'len. The funerary fire burned. Sparks climbed towards the cloudless night, adding their colors to the stars. Burning wood crackled and wind blew a black cloud from Cur'Ra's fire, her ashes climbing high and free into a star filled sky. De'Nidra hoped that she had found peace. She hoped Tara would too, before the entire world ends in flames. She leaned close to Al'len and whispered in her ear. "I have had an idea that may be useful. I bought a ship for safety some time ago and it arrived in the Harbor Cities this last week. Originally, I got it to hide from you," De'Nidra said.

Al'len raised an eyebrow at her. "Go on."

"I want to get your permission to go set it up. I sent Tem'Aldar ahead to hire a crew and get provisions. He didn't like it, Al'len, but he did it. I don't believe anyone that is not on the ship could Gate to it because it will be moving. But because I am standing on the deck and am stationary, I can. I attach it to the distance in front of me on the deck rather than stationary, so the Gate just keeps moving with me in space. It is costly, but it works." De'Nidra said.

Al'len asked. "Does Sib'Bal know? If she catches wind of it, she will burn that ship before you get out of the harbor."

De'Nidra thought about that. "I don't think so. If I get it out, it may be the only safe place for Tara if everything goes poorly. Her dragons are bonded, so they will find her, but until we reach land, she will be safe. I was going to take Va'Yone with me so he does not get killed trying to keep up with Tara. You know he won't leave her unless he thinks she wants him to keep me safe."

Al'len whispered back, "I will talk to Tara and I am sure she will send him with you, but you are going to be responsible for him. You keep him safe."

"I will EL'ALue. I promise."

Below in the fortress of Are'Amadon Modred reviewed the Priest Knight in his burnished silver plate. Be'elota's training program had gone well, and he was ready to be placed into the ranks of the Knights of Coth'Venter to keep him informed and as an assassin. "Good work, Be'elota, but is he loyal?"

Be'elota's voice cackled with a shrill laugh. "Indeed, my dear Lord Modred. As loyal as one can be within the shadows of Darkness. You have seen with your own eyes what greed and pride can do. I still remember when you and the other Heroes of the Light underwent your slow change. The dark lineages of your construct slowly wearing you away. Long ago now, likely you don't even remember your fall from the Light. However, Lord Modred, I still remember when you laid on this floor screaming that you are a servant of the Light."

"Dear Lord Modred, you say," he thought out loud. "I only vaguely remember being that person at all, Be'elota. Yet, I am still here and you did good work. I have remained Modred. I could never go back. This Priest Knight must hold out at least as long as I need to use him. If that god of Light discovers our ploy, she will recover him and he will lead her right here. I hope you understand the fragile nature of our situation."

Be'elota was saner than usual when he answered, "I had not thought of that, my Lord."

"Well, you should have. Just remember what I did to the Light when the Darkness took me. I told you everything, as did my brothers, and we led you right to the very door of the Bastion of the Light. Remember Be'elota? Do you remember that night when you helped me betrayed the Light?"

Be'elota nodded. "I do, my Lord. Let's just make sure that problem does not come back and bite us. I will try to add some insurance."

"See that you do, Be'elota, because the last thing you will see is yourself falling into the hands of an angry god of Light, holding you responsible for every evil deed you have ever done. Do I make myself clear?"

"Crystal." Be'elota swallowed hard at that thought.

Sib'Bal sat in her garden enjoying the freshness of the sea air mixed with a perfectly fragranced garden. Her plans were proceeding well. Both sides were in motion now that EL'Keet had properly stoked the fires of the Dark Order. "With one deft touch, I will remove the competition of the other gods and factions by letting them destroy each other. That suits my purpose just fine." Now that the Order of Darkness knew the Seat of the Light's crusade was coming, they have time to muster their troops. "Will the other gods wake now and fight it out, or will I need to push them further? Only time will tell."

De'Nidra opened a Mage Gate to the library study just off the garden of her brownstone manor. Va'Yone walked through, wearing a backpack filled with his belongings, and there were also square outlines of books. She followed him in, letting the Gate collapse. It was late, and the light of the silvery moon highlighted fluttering silk curtains, open to let in the salt air of a cool night breeze.

Va'Yone stared at all the opulence. "Do you live like this all the time?"

"No," she laughed, "not all the time. Only when I have to," De'Nidra said. The return to Harbor City with Va'Yone had created a few complications that she had not accounted for with her original plan, but back then, she was a vaunted member of the Dark Council. So many things had changed. "Va'Yone, I want to teach you magic while I am setting up some business here. So, I thought it was a good time to get started on your lessons. If you're still interested?" She said the last part with a knowing grin.

"Stop teasing me." He returned her smirk. "You know I am, De'Nidra." Va'Yone said. "I just worry about Tara needing me and something going wrong because I am not there to help her."

"I know, but people surround her, and you will do more when you are further along in your studies. Our magic works the same, so it will be easier for you to pick up the lessons when I demonstrate them to you. Tara's magic works differently; she pulls images from her mind into reality. Our magic works with specific uses in mind, forming an exacting pattern. So, it's like learning to play a harp while someone is explaining the flute. You might pick up some things that help you learn. But in the end, what you need is someone that plays the same instrument."

"I understand. Still, I have a feeling in the pit of my stomach that something bad is going to happen, and I want to be there to help when she needs me."

"Study hard, and you may very well be able to get there on your own. You need help, Va'Yone, and your potential may not be as vast. But with hard work and practice, your skill with the craft will be varied and unique. I also intend to locate some new items in a dig. It came to my attention that, if fortunate, it would be of help. I have people working on it now. Would you like that?"

"What kinds of things, and what is a dig?" Va'Yone was getting interested.

"Professionals in Ancient Studies refer to it as an archaeological dig. These digs can yield a wide range of valuable or intriguing artifacts, including items of Power. If we find some of them, and if you're ready, because you have studied hard, I will let you pick one," De'Nidra said with a smile. "But only if you're ready."

"Oh, I will be ready, De'Nidra," a mischievous smile played on his lips, "you can be sure of that."

"Good. Now let's get you a room."

The morning light came early, and the sun heated the salty air. De'Nidra found Va'Yone in the garden. Mar'garete was practically spoon-feeding him eggs and meat. De'Nidra sat down across from him and smiled. "Mar'garete, I'll have whatever he's having. But I can feed myself." The old Lady of Deepwater, had arrived home with a friend and her maid was fussing over him.

Mar'garete dipped a curtsy, her cheeks flashing red. "Yes, my Lady." She bustled off to the kitchens.

"Sorry, Va'Yone. Mar'garete can be affectionate," De'Nidra said.

Va'Yone grinned. "I didn't mind. She's nice. She had a lot of questions about some guy she described as handsome and who had been staying here. I didn't know who she was referring to, so I told her so." He gave her a grin. "But he sounded a lot like Tem'Aldar."

"That girl never quits. She has been trying to attract his attention, but he was smart enough not to play along. He did find the whole thing a little too fun for my taste, though. The girl is becoming a nuisance," De'Nidra said.

Mar'garete returned with Lady Deepwater's breakfast, and she dismissed her with instructions to prepare the coach.

After breakfast, the black lacquered coach sat outside the brownstone on the white cobbled drive, and the liveried driver let them in. De'Nidra directed. "To the harbor." She stepped in.

"Yes, my Lady. Off to do more business, I see."

she answered with a nod as he closed the door.

He mounted the coach and cracked the whip, and they lurched and rattled out of the manor gate. Va'Yone sat across from her and held the curtain back from the window so he could watch all the people and buildings in the Harbor Cities slide by. It was easy to forget that until Tara had let him out; he had been living in the old underground Bastion of Light, sealed off from the world many ages ago. He bombarded De'Nidra with questions, his curiosity piqued by the people, buildings, and merchants they passed. She did her best to answer, but his questions kept tumbling out all the way to the docks. Then, seeing all the water, they stopped.

The coach came to a bumpy, lurching stop, and the door opened. "My Lord and Lady, we have arrived."

De'Nidra stepped out, looking like the old lady, and Va'Yone followed her. "You don't need to wait with the coach. I will hire a ride if I need one. You may go."

The driver bowed, closed the door, remounted, and they watched the coach go.

Va'Yone said. "Look at all this water. I didn't think there was half this much in the whole wide world. And these ships, I have seen pictures, but to see them like this!"

"Would you like to have a look at one? Come on Va'Yone, this way."

Men and women ran along the docks, working, and sailors moved along the deck of her ship as well, showing that the crew was hard at work. She led Va'Yone along the docks that extended like fingers into the water. Merchant ships bustled with activity, loading and unloading cargo, and sending wagons in and out of the ramps. The activity resembled a large, but profitable, messy dance. The Neal 'Lance' was a heavy Corsair design, named for its cutting lines and rakes. It was more of a frigate, with its three masts and deep hull, its sleek lines promised speed.

They walked up the gangplank. De'Nidra was wearing boots under her long dress this day. *Lesson learned*, she told herself, *no heels today*. They proceeded along the length of the deck, which was made of light-colored wood and had twenty ballista on each side. The doorway leading below, beneath the wheelhouse, was open, and sailors made way with a bow as she moved down the hall, dodging the line of mariners waiting to be interviewed by their employer. Wooden walls glowed a deep yellow in the light of brass ship lamps affixed to gangway walls. The lamps were designed to stay upright even with the ship's heaving. Tem'Aldar was in the captain's day cabin, meeting with some scruffy fellows. De'Nidra caught his eye, and he gave her a wink before going back to his interview without breaking stride.

"This way, Va'Yone," she opened the door to the patrons' room and shut it behind them. "Let's take a break for a bit and let Tem'Aldar finish those interviews." The lamps were lit in this room as well. Her wardrobe stood open—Tem'Aldar had brought her things—and from the looks of it, he had hastily stuffed them all in. De'Nidra took everything out and laid it on the bed before stowing it back in neatly.

Va'Yone pulled off his pack and sat down at the desk, watching her with interest. She was practiced and methodical in how she arranged her things, ensuring everything was in its proper place. "You sure know how you want things, don't you, De'Nidra?"

"Yes, Va'Yone, and there's a reason for it. This is your first lesson. If you place things a certain way, you don't need to search for them. You don't lose things, and when they are disturbed, you notice it. Thus, you are always aware. Magic is the same. You learn new techniques, and they operate the same way every time. Your thoughts and actions must be precise, and you must perform them the same way each time. If you live your life that way, it affects everything else, and your mistakes become fewer. Right now, you don't have many tools in your toolbox, but I am going to fill it up. So, you need to be organized from the beginning, or you will never keep track of it all."

It took Tem'Aldar two more hours to get the ship and crew ready. He walked into the room. De'Nidra was finishing a document, and Va'Yone was sleeping on the bed. "The crew and supplies are purchased and aboard. The captain has settled in, and from the sound of the feet thumping on the deck above, he is about ready to set sail. What is this I see, my Lady? Another man in our bed?"

"Yes, I see," De'Nidra teased. "And he is much younger than you, too." She gave a playful smirk. "If you think we are ready, let's cast off. I don't want to sit here a minute longer than necessary."

"They are bringing the last of the fresh water on board now. I will let Captain Tan'Near know that we are ready to sail. After we are underway, I will find our young friend a cabin of his own. You two stay hid until we are completely out of sight of the harbor."

Flocks of Mer'Gulls hovered, their scales a canvas of flashing greens against a world of sparkling water, as if the sea itself had come alive, singing their shrill chirping calls. Four leathery wings buzzed, almost floating above the slow rolling sea. She could see through the windows as sheer curtains ruffled open to the salt air, and the ship cast off the wrist-thick lines that moored her to the dock. Long poles stretched out from the upper deck and slowly pushed the Neal 'Lance' out past the docks into deeper water. Foresails unfurled with the sound of heavy fabric and a creaking of thick lines. The main sails unfurled, causing the ship to lurch as the upper sails fell open, and the ship slowly picked up speed. De'Nidra sat on the bed beside Va'Yone and watched the ship glide away from the docks and out to sea, the wind filling the sails and pushing the ship further away from the coast.

"We are off," she whispered to Va'Yone's sleeping form, her heart pounding. "Our new adventure awaits."

Chapter 17 Heart Darkened

"It is a subtle step across that line, nudged gradually over time, altering our perspective. We turn our heads, allowing the border of our inhibitions to slide by. The line just goes missing. However, the truth is it never moved—we have simply wandered miles beyond it, happily led away by desires to places we should have never gone. Now, all that remains is to pay for it."

In the Alum'Tai moneylender's waiting area, High Bishop Er'laya's face reddened with frustration. "Outrageous," he hissed to Diocesan On'omus. "A full hour!"

"High Bishop, the capital's money changers are not renowned for their speed. Furthermore, Lord Gan'Vile, our beloved High Seat of the Light, has not confirmed our parish's reinstatement. In the Diocesan quarters, rumors suggest your defrocking is imminent."

Unease fluttered in his stomach. Cupping a hand to his mouth, Er'laya whispered, "It's not like we intend to stay."

A clerk in gold livery entered, bearing a noticeably heavy black leather case, as if laden with secrets beyond its modest size. "I apologize, Bishop Er'laya. This place is a madhouse today with all the requests from nobles for the crusades."

"High Bishop Er'laya." On'omus corrected in a hushed tone.

"My apologies *High* Bishop Er'laya. It appears the information we had was inaccurate."

Impatience sharpened Er'laya's tone. "Never mind that. Just get on with it."

"Here are the requested funds," the clerk said, displaying a hint of discomfort. "I divided the coins into gold and silver denominations as you requested, and there are three letters of credit. They hold considerable sums, so you'll want to be careful. Now that you have withdrawn the money from the Haven accounts, anyone could cash them," the clerk said, as he placed the leather case on Er'laya's lap.

"We appreciate your concern," Er'laya said, raising his bejeweled hand adorned with the ruby ring of his office, waiting for the man's kiss.

The clerk cleared his throat, leaned down, and kissed the ring with feigned reverence.

"You may go." The clerk nodded and pivoted on his heels and was gone, an air of outrage wafting behind him.

On'omus leaned closer, his voice a mere breath. "The performance with the ring... it may cost us. He is certain to complain."

"Let him. We'll be long gone before this crusade even passes the gate tomorrow. I've arranged for a coach to be purchased, and we're going straight there, On'omus. I don't intend to dally," Er'laya whispered. He stood up, the weight of the black case considerable. "Come on, let's go."

They exited through the gold-inlaid doors, passing by splashing fountains and fragrant Wallander trees shedding white blossoms in the morning light. "I'm going to miss all of this." On'omus sighed.

"Yes, I will too. But crossing that Mage Gate sealed our fate. We're now bound to each other," Er'laya admitted. "You're too trusting, On'omus. To her, we're already forgotten, mere pawns for her crusade. Sib'Bal's concerns lie elsewhere now," he continued, stepping from the lush garden into the bustling cobbled street. Without hesitation, Er'laya boarded a waiting black lacquered coach. "To the Prince's Wagon Yard, and quickly," he instructed the coachman, his entry causing the coach to sway noticeably.

On'omus stepped in behind him, afforded an unpleasant view of Er'laya's ample posterior. He thought, *So, he thinks this is supposed to be my life now? I think not. I'm not spending it in service to this self-important idiot. We're going to have to redefine our relationship.*

High Holy Seat Lord Gan'Vile sat at the breakfast table of the High King, Lord Mel'Lark, dressed in their white robes with golden scrollwork embroidery, symbolizing unity between the crown and the church.

Gan'Vile rolled a grape between his fingers before casually tossing it into his mouth. "And how do we fare with the preparations, my High King?"

Lord Mel'Lark had a spoonful of egg halfway to his open mouth, stopping mid-bite with a sigh. "As well as expected, Your Eminence. The army is making progress, and we'll lead the first five thousand troops, along with the baggage, toward Haven tomorrow. The remaining troops will trickle in from the other provinces afterward. I've sent word to muster in Haven. That will give us time to assess the situation before charging in blindly. They have assigned me four senior mages from the conclave, and a High Mage will arrive once he finishes his preparations. What about your Priest Knights and Clerics of the Light?" He brought the spoon of the eggs to his mouth, which had been hovering in readiness.

"The numbers aren't all in from the individual captains yet, but it seems we'll have fifteen hundred troops leaving with you tomorrow. I've ordered the pressure to be maintained in the campaigns so that the Dark Order doesn't dare withdraw their forces. We need to keep the pressure on them where we can. However, I believe at least the same number will arrive in Haven after we muster," Gan'Vile said.

Lord Mel'Lark took a bite of toast. "That sounds light on troops for a crusade. It would have been good of you to consult with me before making the announcement, for preparation's sake. Defending the realm is my foremost responsibility, and with the High Seat demanding troops, it's going to be difficult."

"My primary duty is to the Order of the Light, and confronting darkness is the responsibility of the High Holy Seat, not the High King. That's the way EL'ALue set it up long after the Breaking of the Balance," Gan'Vile said.

Lord Mel'Lark paused; his chewing halted. Holding up rolled parchment to Gan'Vile. "This was brought to me by a Conclave Under Mage who happened upon it fifty leagues from Haven." Lord Mel'Lark flicked the parchment toward

Gan'Vile with a gesture that belied his calm. "EL'ALue's commands have torn the archives open to the public. Histories once sealed now breathe free amongst the people. Now that problem is yours, Holy Seat."

Gan'Vile's voice dropped to a venomous whisper, "Blasphemy, yes, but a noose that may just fit the neck of Er'laya, with his cowardice as the knot. His hands, once outstretched in benediction, now wring the coppers from Haven's folk. For now, I'm playing along, letting him believe that I'll return everything. But I intend to see him swinging from the gates of Haven, and this entire matter can hang with him."

"And what about the rumors surrounding the Maid of Light's reemergence?" the High King asked in a more official tone.

"No one has heard from the Maid of Light in ages. Everything I've studied suggests she has no interest in talking to us unless we acknowledge her. I, for one, won't reach out to a dormant god and tell her that the Order of the Light, which she founded, has usurped her authority, and placed ourselves above the people we swore to protect. That's precisely why we wait before granting access to the holy archives. By the time I became a bishop, I was already guilty, so I kept my mouth shut, just like everyone else," Gan'Vile said. "No, we'll let that dormant god be."

"Too late for that, my friend. That hornbee has already flown its hive. But as you say, it's the High Holy Seat of the Light's problem. Not mine. I don't envy your position. At least I can feign ignorance and be as outraged as everyone else. You, on the other hand, are stuck holding a burning bag of dung. I would recommend getting your house in order because if the nobility believes these reports, you'll have a lot of explaining to do. Remember, the rulers of the provinces have also had access to the archives. They know the truth, even if they don't speak of it. Maybe the usurpers should have thought of that before granting us access?" The High King raised an eyebrow at him. "So, if you fail to fix the problem, and when the truth spreads, the people will demand recompense, and the nobles will act outraged and demand that I grant it. You might want to consider that. Enjoy your breakfast, your Holiness."

Gan'Vile called after him as the guards opened the doors, "Is that a threat, your Grace?"

Lord Mel'Lark didn't slow. "No, if you don't regain control, it'll become a fact, Your Eminence." You might want to clean up the mess in your own domain before telling me how to rule mine." The doors closed behind him, leaving the High Seat to his breakfast and his concerns.

"What is all this ruckus?" Amorath's voice cracked like a whip. The Mage gate strobed, casting flashes of purple throughout Modred's tower quarters. Narean, an injured red demon, stood next to Modred and an inset table filled with black sand. The sand constructed three-dimensional views of the land at the very border of the Blackened Lands and there was a thick stone wall with battlements that ran between a mountain pass. Smoking bodies lay piled behind it. The sand writhed in bewildering patterns, generating smoke blown in the wind.

Modred and Narean turned and knelt at the sound of Great Lord Amorath's voice. His icy chill permeated the atmosphere.

Modred had one hand to his heart and the other on his blade. He stared at the floor, not wanting to answer, of course, but he had no choice. "Great Lord, they have attacked us. They destroyed the defenses of the Darkened Gates."

"Destroyed by who? And why?" Amorath said, growing impatient at having to drag it out of him.

Modred's eyes flicked to Narean, the suffering red demon kneeling next to him. Narean answered. "Great Lord, I have overflown the site and I could tell it was dragon fire. They decimated the entire guard, and the siege engines were destroyed."

Amorath's withered form limped forward on his staff. "And why were there no mages warding that dragon off?"

"Mel'Temdel had that watch and he is nowhere to be found. We believe he was incinerated in the attack. I've dispatched two middle mages from the conclave and a garrison to replace the dead. I want them Gated there by first noon sun." Modred said, thinking, *I'm going to point as many fingers as I have to, to keep from being drained dry, regardless of what the rest of these fools do.*

"What precipitated this attack so far from the campaign? There has not been an attack on The Darkened Gate's defenses in an age. Wild dragons do not hunt Zoruks. They don't enjoy the taste of the meat. They hunt the forested county or steal Hurdbeast from ranchers. No, this was either that bothersome Torrent at

Coth'Venter or a god. I would discount the last. Why would this Torrent put her own life at risk? If even one of those dragons died, she would die along with them. So tell me Lord, Modred, why did she risk it and why is your brother Narean wounded?" Amorath demanded.

"Great Lord, you ordered me to find agents of De'Nidra, the Daughter of Shadows. She was not contacting any of them, so I decided to shake her up a little to see if I could flush her out. I ordered an attack by my brothers on Coth'Venter Cathedral of Light to kill the Torrent. Narean was hurt during the attack."

"And did Narean kill said Torrent? Obviously not, or her dragons would have been dead and not attacking my gates."

Narean's hackles were up. *Somehow, Modred will make this debacle my fault if I don't head it off quickly.* He did not take his eyes off the stone floor. "Great Lord, my orders were to kill the Torrent or anyone important to flush De'Nidra. The Torrent was my primary target, but collateral damage was acceptable. I killed the healer Cur'Ra and was injured in the exchange. I followed my orders, did as I was commanded, and completed the task." *Let's see if Modred can shimmy his way out of that one.*

"I see," Amorath said menacingly. "Narean, get reinforcements to that gate. A single garrison will not do. If you killed that Elp'har healer and this was the result, she was important to the Torrent. While you may not have drawn De'Nidra out yet. You have drawn the anger of the Torrent and if she risked her dragons to attack my gate, it is because she is coming for us. She will want revenge, and she is naïve enough to believe in giving fair warning. No. She is coming and we must be ready to meet her." He smiled. "Modred, you have done well. I want an army ready to sweep them away. Reoccupy the Flowage battlements. I want every extra available mage and troop found to man that bridge."

Modred breathed a relieved sigh, perspiration forming on his brow. "Yes, Great Lord!" He answered alongside Narean.

Amorath walked back through his Mage Gate, and it winked out.

Coth'Venter Cathedral of Light teemed with activity, packed with wagons, animals, and carts. More of them curled their way through the broad streets of the once abandoned city toward the cathedral. Edward had ordered the streets to be cleared of debris, and work crews were out wrestling gray stone rubble strewn on the cobbled streets into a wagon.

A black lacquered coach, adorned with a sigil resembling a ship navigating turbulent waters, rattled through the bustling main square of the cathedral. With a sharp halt, it came to rest at the foot of the grand stairway, which ascended thirty steps to the imposing entrance. A tall man, wearing a long black travel coat, stepped out of the coach carrying a leather parchment case. He started climbing and two guards from Tara's house met him. A man and a woman. Their spears snapped to bar the door. They wore light gray garb with a darker green cloak. The cloak bore the house sigil—a depiction of two dragons facing a fist holding two lightning bolts.

Related to House Haven, I should think. "I am Attorney Jel'Dun for Lady Deepwater of the House of Deepwater," he said, as if expecting recognition from them. They did not. "I have arrived from the Harbor Cities to settle an affair between Lady Tara and Lady Deepwater. If you could kindly announce my presence."

The female guard whispered to a passing staff member wearing white livery. The man nodded, and the guard turned back to Jel'Dun. "You may wait here. It will be a few moments, sir."

"Very well," Jel'Dun replied, turning his attention to the view of the square. "Is Lady Tara restoring the place?" He observed the lines of light cavalry heading for a city watch patrol by a statue of the Hero of the Light Ram'Del atop a dry, three-tiered fountain. Wagons led by Warriors of the Light trotting in and out.

"As to Lady Tara's plans, it's for her to explain," the female guard responded. "It should not be long. Lady Tara will be with you soon."

Within a short time, the guards withdrew their spears and a young woman wearing black thieves' armor and carrying two silver-inlaid short swords at her hips emerged. She was Elp'har, if Jel'Dun's guess was accurate. Her black hair, with white bangs, framed her lovely, yet marred, face. Deep, swirling marks ran from the corner of her eyebrows to the top of her cheeks and down her neck. *Likely some Elp'harean custom.* A young man, related to the Haven royal house, accompanied her, wearing smoked plate armor and carrying a wicked-looking broadsword at his waist.

Jel'Dun bowed low. "My Lord and Lady?"

Tara nodded.

"I am Attorney Jel'Dun for Lady Deepwater of the House of Deepwater, here to settle an estate."

"Estate?" Edward asked. "Who died, and who did you know in the Harbor Cities?"

"Edward, I don't know anyone, except...," Tara left it hanging.

Attorney Jel'Dun cleared his throat, his gaze shifting between Tara and Edward. "I understand your confusion. If you wouldn't mind, I'll explain the situation briefly, and we can proceed without further delay."

Edward nodded. "Certainly, this way." They led the man to the dining hall, where he opened the door and ushered them inside. There, they approached a large gray stone table, one among many. The double doors to a balcony stood open, and a cool breeze blew in from the west, rustling the curtains. Beyond it, a battlement wall with a rippling banner and a field of tall grass waved toward a thicket.

Jel'Dun stood until they sat down. Clearly the young Lady did not stand on formality, though the young Lord observed the forms without thought. "My Lord and Lady, I am an attorney, and I am here to settle some affairs." Placing his leather case on the gray stone table, unsnapped the clasp, and unfolded it. He sealed the two parchments with the same standard as the coach, pressing it into melted red wax. He handed one to Tara and one to Edward. "You can see that I have provided the deed to Lady Deepwater's entire estate, including, but not limited to, her manor, businesses, and all associated accounts." He pulled out a quill and a small inkpot from his pocket and placed them neatly in the center of the table.

Tara stammered, "But why would she do that? I mean, I don't even know a Lady Deepwater of the House of Deepwater?"

Attorney Jel'Dun smiled. "She knows you and has left you her estate. If you would be so kind, my Lady, please sign the documents. I will leave an original with you and file the other with the Harbor Cities Guild Council when I return." He unstopped the inkpot and held out the quill.

Edward winked at Tara and gave his best smile. "Your Ladyship, give the man what he wants."

"Okay, Edward, but this isn't making any sense," Tara said. She signed the first one and handed it to the attorney. Then she repeated the process with the one Edward had given her and handed it back to him.

He took the quill from her, dipped it in the ink, and signed the documents. He then pulled out a candle, lit it from a nearby lamp, and sat back down. Then he retrieved red sealing wax, a stamp, and a ring from his satchel. Heating the red sealing wax with the flame, he dribbled it until it puddled, then used the seal and blew on it until it cooled. He repeated the process with the second document, then handed the signet ring, the wax, and the stamp to Tara. "These are yours, Lady Tara of House Deepwater."

"I don't understand," Tara said.

Edward took the ring and placed it gently on her finger, where it stayed securely despite being a little loose. "This ring signifies who you are, granting you certain rights. The stamp is used to sign drafts and letters of credit against your estate."

"But I don't even know what the estate is or what it's for," Tara said breathlessly.

Jel'Dun stood and bowed low again. "As for that, my Lady, you would have to come to the Harbor Cities and review your accounts with the guild money changers. I'm sure your secretary has your ledger at House Deepwater. However, I can safely say that if you require moneys for your remodeling project here, there would be no problem. Your estates are well-funded."

"You should stay for a night to rest, Jel'Dun," Tara said before he could turn. "You must be tired from your trip."

"No, my Lady. I have guards at the inn waiting, and I only have ten days to file this with the guild," he said, packing the parchment into his leather case. He left the inkpot and the quill on the table. "Thank you," Jel'Dun said. He slid an envelope from his pocket to her. "This was to be given to you when I leave. You are to read it and then burn it."

Tara took the envelope. "I understand."

They escorted him out and watched his coach depart. She furrowed her brow in confusion. "Edward, I'm completely baffled by all of this." She carefully unsealed the envelope with her fingers and unfolded the single piece of parchment. Tara opened it and showed it to Edward. It said, "Love De'Nidra, now burn it!"

"I'm sure someone will help us figure it out with time, Tara. But that would mean a trip to the Harbor Cities to review the estate." Edward said.

"Not until we are ready here, Edward. All the estates in the world wouldn't pay for what the Dark Order had done. If there's a bill for that, I intend to collect that debt in person."

Chapter 18 Daylight Memory

"In the heart of adventure, where the light of dawn meets the shadow of ambition, destiny weaves a tale of courage, mystery, and the unyielding pursuit of greatness."

The castle gates stood ajar, the stable yard abuzz. Mel'Lark's Stinger, silver tooled saddle and armor, gleamed in dawn's light. He approached it as an oasis, yearning to slip away—a feat never easy for a king.

"My Lord High King, it is unconscionable for you to travel by horse all the way to Haven! Let me open a Mage Gate and I can bring you right there." The elegant robes of the ancient High Mage swished as he followed, trying to keep up with the High King, Lord Mel'Lark. His balding head sweated from the effort.

"Why rush to arrive today, Heli'os? The ride will do me good, and the army won't gather for weeks," Mel'Lark said, pacing ahead of the tapping staff. "You might as well ride with his Holiness." He added, thumbing towards Gan'Vile with the casual indifference of a stableman.

Trailing the High King, Heli'os gasped for breath as if he'd chased a ghost through the castle all night. Each step seemed a battle, and his robes, though elegant, hung disheveled. "My Lord, your safety."

"Safety?" Mel'Lark's voice carried a touch of irony as he gestured towards the vast expanse beyond the castle gates, where the morning light danced on the armor of five thousand noble knights and three hundred bowmen. In addition to three thousand Priest Knights and a thousand Clerics of the Light. "The city bursts with an army too large for you and your conclave to move. Safety? Give it a rest Heli'os. Neither you nor his High Holy Eminence there wants to ride for the two weeks it is going to take to get there. I did not call this crusade, but I am going to lead it to Haven and then to the very doorstep of those dark Lords. Protect me through that, and you will have my appreciation and respect."

The High King, Lord Mel'Lark, swung into the saddle and booted his charger out of the yard. His knights and bannermen, clad in polished armor and bearing banners with the royal crest, formed a proud procession behind him, their horses' hooves clattering on the cobblestones.

Heli'os, the High Mage, watched him go. He turned and walked to the white lacquered coach drawn by a team of twelve Stingers. A monk opened the door, and he stepped in. His Eminence lowered himself onto the purple seat, the cushions sighing under his weight, enveloping him in their velvet embrace as if to shield him from the journey's discomforts.

"Well, Heli'os, what did he say?" Gan'Vile asked.

"He said *no*, your Holiness. We are going to have to ride all the way."

"For the love of the Light, Heli'os, the next thing you are going to tell me is he will be in the van of the fight."

"Indeed, he intends to march us directly into the Maw of Darkness, to the very threshold of the Dark Lords, is unwavering—a testament to his courage, or perhaps, more correctly, your recklessness," Heli'os sighed, his voice tinged with a mix of admiration and resignation. "And we," he pointed at the plump man across from him, "will keep his safe conduct. Your Holiness, that means we shall stand beside him through it all."

High Holy Seat Lord Gan'Vile's eyes went wide. "Is he mad? We could all die."

A laugh spilled from the High Mage, mocking his host—a sound as ancient and layered as the tomes he revered, laced with an irony born of centuries. "You called for this crusade, igniting a fire you thought we could control. All to cover your Orders ancient folly. What did you think would happen? We," his gnarled old finger swung back and forth between the two of them, "are going to defend the Light and put down the Order of Darkness! Remember…? You asked for a crusade, your High Holiness, and now you are going to get one."

De'Nidra and Tem'Aldar walked on the ship's balcony, the honey gold planking rich beneath their steps. Moonlight draped the sails in silver, and the water's chorus sang their passage. Harbor City's lights dwindled behind them, stars yielding to the sea's misty embrace. "Safety finally," she whispered.

Tem'Aldar took her hands and drew her close. "As for promises, De'Nidra, the future holds none I can make. Save that I will always love you. But this moment, this closeness, it is ours, and I will claim it," he whispered, his lips finding hers in a kiss that was slow, deliberate—a silent vow of shared solace amidst danger. It was a kiss that caused her world to disappear. A kiss hungry and consuming that would not let her go. Everything shifted, and she felt the world come back into view.

"You are a rogue, Tem'Aldar," De'Nidra accused, her voice a mix of mock indignation and undisguised affection, as she lightly slapped his chest, her hand trembling not from fear but from the thrill of their closeness. And more importantly, the desire for what she knew was coming next.

"Am I, De'Nidra?" he smiled roguishly, sweeping her off her feet and lifting her in his arms. He carried her to their room.

In the cabin allotted by the quartermaster, Va'Yone watched a displaced officer gather his belongings, his glance sharp but silent, before descending to the crew's quarters below. *Tem'Aldar has a knack for making friends*, he mused.

"Good night, young Lord," the quartermaster said, his voice trailing off as he ducked out, leaving a whisper of mistaken authority in his wake.

The door closed behind him. "Thanks, but I wear no lord's title," Va'Yone murmured, the words falling in the empty air between them, a gesture lost to thumping feet on the deck above. Worthless because he knew he did not hear it. The crew was always in a hurry and the captain drove them mercilessly. Talking about strapping their hides and lashing any procrastinators to a mast. They jumped at his every word as if they believed he actually would. Va'Yone threw his backpack on his bed and dug some small clothes from it. A book that Da'Vain the Chronicler had given him slid out so that the weathered edge of the rough leather cover lay exposed. He changed and hung his dark leather up in the wardrobe. Using a bucket discarded in the corner, he stood on it to open a small round window. He let the cool sea air wash over him. Moonlight danced on the rocking sea, churning his stomach.

Jumping down, he surveyed his cabin. It was not large by the standard of De'Nidra's and Tem'Aldar's, but it was larger and nicer than the stables of Coth'Venter, and he had a small table affixed to the floor. The stool swiveled. It could be locked in place for heavy storms. Those he did not want to see, but they happened, Tem'Aldar had said. They had bolted his bed to the floor so it would not slide, and there was a chest at the foot and a wardrobe on each side. A brass lamp attached to the wall swiveled in a pedestal with the rocking of the ship, which did nothing to help the queasiness of his gut.

Va'Yone went to his pack and pulled out a book. Carrying it to the small desk, he sat down and opened it. In silvery script, the title page read, "Memory of Daylight: Before the Shattering, Our Wonders, Our War." Signed and translated by Lil. Her distinctive hand was unmistakable. Lil wrote, "We Vam'Phire do not have the talent to use the book. This is a transliteration for the future, for the wisdom of the one who can read it, with the talent that can use it for good. Our hope is in you." Signed Lil'Emeran Doe'Minia.

Receiving Lil's full name felt like a sacred whisper. A bond forged in the silent communion of two souls. A sacred promise forming in the quiet spaces between words. It was lovely and a perfect name for her. In a way, she was like a sister. Half his physical construct was drawn from these Vam'Phire. The same coven. *In that way, Lil'Emeran Doe'Minia, I am your little brother. From a prince stolen during the Light's most desperate hour.* Va'Yone cherished this moment. It gave him connection. A deep sense of family. He did not realize it before, but now he knew he needed it more than anything.

Turning the page, "Within you is a well, and that well, filled by a trickle that comes from a flow. Endeavor, therefore, to understand the depth of your talent and to not only feel the heights of your well but learn to pull at the flow. Have care of your potential so that you do not burn it out, as the flow can overwhelm you."

Va'Yone's hand trembled on the page, his heart a mix of excitement and dread on the brink of an epiphany. He was afraid that the image that Lil had painted in his mind would disappear. He had always seen the trickle as something beyond his control. But, she was saying that you could fill yourself quicker by pulling on it, but not to overflow the potential of your well. It had never been that great anyway, but this idea, if he could figure it out, would refill it more quickly and that would allow him to do more with the little he had.

He breathed slowly and closed his eyes. The well of his potential was only half full, and the flow was only the smallest drip. He searched within for the opening of the flow. There the trickle of Power dripped. He pulled at it and it trickled faster. Sweat beaded on his forehead, drenching his small clothes again. But he had done a little to increase it. "Thank you, Lil, my sister," he whispered, a wave of gratitude mingling with exhaustion. In the quiet of his cabin, Va'Yone felt an unspoken bond strengthen, a silent acknowledgment of the journey they shared, even in absence. Going to his bed, he slid the book inside his backpack and pushed it over, laying down. He tried to remember all Lil had said, but sleep quickly took him instead.

Ad'ver was angry after being displaced from his cabin and sent so far from his quarry. He may be a construct, yes, but he had feelings, and a task. Further, he had a burning need to finish it. His maker, the goddess Sib'Bal, had built him for a purpose and this little Lord had moved him further from it. It would have been so easy to kill her in her sleep. Now he had no reason to be below on this deck at night. The best he could hope for was to pull some night duty, earning him time on the main deck so he could sneak below. When he had finished his purpose, he would save time to pay that little young Lord a visit.

"Deck officer," a woman's voice rang out, clearly for him. Positioned mid-deck, she clung to a rope, her feet perched on the railing, hovering over the churning sea. "There's an issue here."

Ad'ver responded with a hint of irritation. "What's the matter?"

She released the rail, landing agilely on the deck, her blonde hair cascading from beneath a white bandana. "We've got something dragging behind. Have a look."

Entrusting his belongings to her, Ad'ver gripped the rope, curiosity piqued. As he observed her, a thought crossed his mind: *she is strikingly attractive, a diversion before my departure*. Leaning far over the railing, he sought the supposed obstruction.

Before making her move, the deckhand ensured that the crew's attention was diverted.

Catching Ad'ver's glance, she returned a serene smile, resembling the freshness of a spring flower. "No draggers here, just a Bay Shark," he chuckled, convinced of her naivety. "Be wary; they're not forgiving to intruders. You're done for if you hit the water with one of them."

Her eyes sparkled with an unspoken plan as she let go of his gear and drew a knife from her belt. Ad'ver's expression shifted from amusement to disbelief. "You're a—" She cut the rope.

"Construct," she completed his sentence. With a swift motion, she sheathed her blade and called out, "Man overboard!"

The crew rushed to the rail, finding no trace of Ad'ver. "What happened?" one inquired.

The blonde deckhand replied, "Showing off. He was lecturing me about Bay Sharks and lost his grip."

As they observed the turbulent waters, it was clear: Ad'ver's fate was sealed. "Poor soul, those sharks leave no survivors." A crewman shook his head.

"Shame, he had a charming smile. His belongings are up for grabs, he'd not mind," she remarked, back to her duties with a mop in hand, the blond girl with the white bandana swabbed the deck. At that, she thought she heard a god whisper in the air. "*El'Alue! You bitch!*"

Awakened by the rhythmic thud of boots on the deck above, Va'Yone surfaced from sleep as if summoned by the heartbeat of the ship itself. The Little Sister's light was streaming in the porthole, shining right on his face. He felt a hollow in his stomach and realized he was famished. Unable to eat anything the previous night, he now craved a hearty meal. A hunger gnawed at him, fierce enough to devour a whole Hurdbeast. *Hair, teeth, I could eat all of it.*

Rummaging through his backpack, he retrieved the fresh clothes Tara had given him. Using a small basin and water from a clay container fastened to the wall near the wardrobe, he washed. Afterward, he emptied the water through the round window, which the crew referred to as a porthole. Heaving it high, trying amid the sway of the ship not to empty it on his own head. He put on his leathers from the cabinet and headed out to seek De'Nidra's guidance on finding breakfast.

He navigated the passageway toward the rear of the ship, known as the "aft," until he reached De'Nidra and Tem'Aldar's door, and knocked.

"Yes," De'Nidra's voice responded.

"It's me," he said.

"Va'Yone, come in," De'Nidra welcomed him.

He opened the door, noting its unique design that prevented hallway blockage, unlike the others. De'Nidra sat at her desk, engrossed in writing a document. A low growl echoed through the cabin, Va'Yone's hand instinctively pressing against the fabric of his tunic where his body betrayed his hunger. He entered De'Nidra's room with a sheepish grin. "I missed dinner last night," he admitted, his tone laced with hunger.

She smiled at him, a blush tinting her cheeks. Not that she wasn't already beautiful; she was flawless. But that made her even more so. "Good morning to you too," she chuckled. "You'll need to find the purser or join the crew for breakfast. The ship's kitchen is likely empty by now since they start early."

He grinned mischievously. "How did you sleep?"

De'Nidra's cheeks flush deepened. "Not very well. I'm sure I'll sleep better tonight. Thank you." She returned his smile and then waved him out. "Now, off you go before you faint from hunger."

Va'Yone's back straightened, his movements graceful and practiced, as he lowered himself into a deep, formal bow. Giving his best leg. He hoped she noticed. "As you command, my Lady." He backed out and closed the door behind him. Making his way down the corridor to the steps below the wheelhouse, he ascended to the deck. The salty breeze whipped through the port aft—sailor's jargon for the ship's left rear—tinging the air with the essence of the sea. The briny wind gusts made the Neal 'Lance' list, forcing Va'Yone to grasp the door frame for balance as he strolled on deck.

Approaching a man who seemed to belong to the deck crew, with his puffy sleeves, short pants, and bare feet, "Have you seen the ship's purser?" Va'Yone asked.

"Oy lad, he's up there, by the wheel," the sailor pointed.

"Thank you, friend," Va'Yone replied with a smile, extending his hand.

The sailor looked at the offered hand and then up at Va'Yone's face. "Well, you're right, welcome, young Lord." He gripped Va'Yone's hand, shaking it before letting go.

A stairway flanked either side of the wheelhouse, leading to the uppermost deck. There were indeed two wheels, one in front of the other, with handles protruding. Captain Tan'Near stood at the rail, sipping a steaming cup of Coffee, while another man held a decanter. Va'Yone walked unsteadily toward the rail, right beside them. He grabbed the honey colored wood, glad for its smooth surface to steady the rolling of the ship.

Tan'Near nodded. "The young Lord's, up to get some fresh air, I see."

"Yes, Captain Tan'Near, and perhaps some breakfast if I can find it," Va'Yone's hopeful smile on his lips.

Captain Tan'Near turned to the tall purser, who peered down at Va'Yone. "And what can I get for you, my Lord?"

The title of Lord works well, He thought. *No reason to spoil it. They can think what they want.* "Whatever you have for the passengers would be fine, if you could have it sent down to my cabin. Thank you."

"Of course, if you don't mind waiting a bit, I'll bring it to you shortly, my Lord," the purser replied.

Va'Yone nodded his agreement and turned away as a wave splashed across the bowsprit, showering the foredeck. Watching the rising and falling of the sea made him feel queasy once again. "I'll be waiting below," he said. Sweat forming on his forehead, born of a fresh wave of queasiness. His hand going to his lips to hold back the dry heave of an empty belly.

"As you wish, my Lord," Captain Tan'Near said, a knowing smile curving his lips.

Va'Yone drummed his fingers impatiently on the wooden table. A muffled knock resonated through the cabin's door, breaking the silence. "Come in."

The purser entered, carrying a covered tray, which he placed on Va'Yone's desk. "They'll collect this tray later, my Lord. Just leave it outside. If you want breakfast served in the morning, I'll ensure it's ready for you when you wake."

"That would be nice, thank you," Va'Yone replied, rising from his seat on the bed.

The purser nodded. "I'll inform the kitchen. Don't be startled when they come in. Good day to you, my Lord." With that, he exited, closing the cabin door behind him.

As soon as the door shut, Va'Yone removed the tray's cover. Despite his queasy stomach, he wasted no time devouring the meal. The tray held slices of zephyr fruit, its tangy sweetness and satisfying crunch a favored morning delicacy, accompanied by smoked silverfin and a steaming cup of dark Corel'lean coffee, a brew that warmed him with its rich, earthy aroma.

After finishing breakfast, Va'Yone returned to De'Nidra's room and knocked. She welcomed him in. A map sprawled across the bed, as it was too large for the desk. De'Nidra had changed from her nightclothes and now wore a lovely green dress adorned with silver and gold embroidered lace, extending from elbow to wrist.

"What is this map for?" Va'Yone asked.

De'Nidra tossed him a wry wink and replied, "Come and see."

Va'Yone walked over and stood next to her, leaning forward as she pointed. "This is the location we sailed—from the Harbor Cities—and here outlines the land." She traced her finger along their route. "And here is our approximate location, moving at a speed of twelve nautical miles or *knots*." She winked at him. "As the sailors say."

"Nautical knots? Like the ones on bootlaces?" Va'Yone asked.

Her laughter was light. "Precisely. These knots measure our pace through the sea. The log line, marked at intervals, tells us our speed in nautical miles per hour. To determine the vessel's speed, the log—thrown overboard—unwinds freely. The line has knots tied at uniform intervals. A sailor counts the knots passing through their hands within a specific timeframe, typically measured by a sandglass. The counted knots within that time period represent the vessel's speed in nautical miles per hour. Eventually, the term '*knot*' became synonymous with one nautical mile per hour, with three knots equivalent to a league, as you would understand it. So, when someone says a ship is traveling at ten knots, it means the vessel is moving at a speed of ten nautical miles per hour or a little over three leagues."

Va'Yone paused for a moment. "That's fast."

De'Nidra continued tracing with her finger. "We're heading from the deep waters to the island of Far'Mora, where an excavation is taking place." She tapped the island and then the dig site, located approximately ten or more leagues from Far'Mora's harbor.

"Eighteen hours at sea give us two hundred sixteen knots, or seventy-two leagues," Va'Yone calculated swiftly. "Given our thirty-one-hour days, we're looking at a three-week voyage to Far'Mora."

She nodded approvingly. "Yes, close enough, and this is a short trip. The island of Far'Mora is a main trade hub, facilitating the transfer of goods between continents along what is known as the Shelf. Those locations are not on the map, Va'Yone; they are too far away. If you're interested, there's a chartroom on the island, and I'll have Tem'Aldar take you there. Oh, and I have something for you." She opened the wardrobe, pulled out a small leather bag, and shook it. It emitted a clanking sound. "This is for you to buy the things you need when we reach port. You'll receive a weekly allowance, but be careful with your spending. Learn the value of things and don't simply pay the asking price. Understand?"

She handed him the purse, and Va'Yone bounced it in his hand. "Do I really need this much?"

"Yes, things are expensive there, and one of our first tasks will be to order you proper clothes," she said. "Now, put away your purse. We have studies to do."

Chapter 19 The Calling

"Fate calls to us. We need not answer. It places us in a state of becoming, molding us, casting us into a scene. In the end, fate's purpose is fulfilled, and its desires, without us knowing, have somehow become our own."

Above the Steps of Glass—two dragons soared, their eyes fixed on a monument to a deity's momentary sorrow, intertwined with awe and wary respect for the Power that sculpted beauty from grief. It was a genetic memory given by their mother as a reminder of the Power that filled them, and bondholders, wield over dragonkind and the world.

The Steps of Glass, sheer peaks of sunlit obsidian, rose majestically. Sparse game near these glassy summits drove the dragons beyond the otherworldly terrain. As they crossed, wind buffeted their wings, guiding them in a smooth descent to an open field abutting an ancient forest, unfolding into a verdant expanse of endless trees.

In the grassy tundra beside the forests, vast gatherings of wild Hurdbeasts graze, their movements mirroring the rhythm of nature. Excitement flared. Dragons exchanged ethereal visions heat radiating from the grazing animals, casting an image akin to a river of life meandering through the waving grassy savanna. The White turns eastward; the Black, westward. Using the edge of the forest, they drive the beasts away from the safety of the trees and deeper into the undulating meadow of waist-high grass. Wingbeats and echoing predatory roars drowned out all but the creature's fear.

The great herds scatter toward the center, where they fall prey to the dragons, who consume some but spare others, ensuring life's natural rhythm. Swooping low, the Black dragon's claws and teeth snatch prey, soon burdened by its kill. It beats its translucent wings, descending in a whirlwind of dust and grass. The White dragon follows suit, claiming a large squirming bull in his. He glides alongside his darker sibling, purposefully adding a touch of dirt and grass to his meal. They knew they were not alone. The little ones known by mortals as Dragon Hounds followed at a distance. This was no chance meeting. They had been calling them here.

Selecting a central spot within the field, they position themselves in opposite directions, guarding each other while they eat. Dragon Hounds, the two dragons could sense their minds drawing nearer. Guided by an ancient pact, five shadows approached through the sky, not just followers but partners in the cycle of life, their presence known to the dragons long before they became visible. Mortals refer to them as Dragon Hounds, a name far from the truth, for they are the faithful servants and guardians of dragons since long before these mortals tread upon Ves'Ral. A world mortals call the lands of El'idar.

The White dragon sent a mental image of permission, picturing them landing and sharing their bounty. The Black, mid-feast, snorted in agreement, tossed a partially consumed carcass nearby. It is a traditional offering, symbolizing their provision for the little ones for their unwavering service and loyalty.

The largest among the smaller dragons, decorated with bright red wings trimmed in black, landed first near the feasting dragons. A carcass was hidden in the tall grass, save for its heat and scent. The dragon crept slowly toward the offering, mindful of the potential for deceit, as some malicious beings among the dragonkind exploit these offerings to secure an extra kill. Are'Nok, the larger red dragon hound, sends his thought, "Are'Nok wishes to partake of your generosity, noble Lord," accompanied by an image of himself feasting on the Black dragon's kill.

The Black turned his head and reciprocated with the same mental image, conveying, "Then partake of our bounty, where we live and serve those we are bound to." The image of Tara flickers in Are'Nok's memory. Drawing closer to the meat, Are'Nok's acidic drool smokes on the bloody hide and flesh. He takes his first grateful bite, and as he does, the brood of lessor dragons above, with their malty-colored scales, swooped down by his side.

Are'Nok affirmed, "We are yours, Old Ones. You are our Lords."

These were the first to answer Tara's young dragon's call.

Beside Ram'Del's towering statue, Al'len sat perched on the fountain's edge, her shadow merging with Tara's, idly pushed around a pebble on the cobblestones with a boot. Inwardly, Al'len harbored a silent condemnation for El'Alue. She felt trapped between her love for Tara and the judgment of an elder god. Beside her, Tara waited in silence for the expected Mage Gate.

"Al'len, you've been quiet since Haven," She cautiously assessed the situation. Tara knew her actions burdened Al'len. What she had done was dark. It was wrong. Granting Edward, the mortal gift of life, at the cost of others' lives, had been Tara's darkest decision to date.

The air was heavy with unspoken things that needed to be said. Whether spoken by El'Alue or Al'len, the words carried the essence of the Maid of Light. "I see your point, child. But have you started to see? Our connections can hurt us, not just physically. We contort ourselves for their sake, yet they often remain unaware of their impact on us, driving us to extreme acts in the name of love. Their influence intertwines so deeply with ours that it can warp reality."

"Stop saying '*us*'," Tara said, her voice trembling. "I am not a god."

"Child, you are becoming one of us. You are in the process of transformation, though you haven't reached it yet. I've been trying to guide you. I knew what you were from the moment Antoff touched my mind, expressing concern for you. Mortals referred to us as Torrents, owing to our seemingly boundless Power. Believe me when I tell you that you will mature and grow even more disillusioned."

Tara exhaled, her shock and fear plain in the quiver of her voice. "No," she whispered.

Al'len's voice, barely audible over the passing guard, carried a solemn weight. "I am sorry, child, but it's true."

Tears welled in Tara's eyes, her voice a tremble of determination. "I can't lose him, Al'len—not after everything. Promises are all I have left, and I keep my promises."

Al'len reached for her, pulling her close, cradling her like a babe and smoothing her hair. "I know, but will you steal every mortal soul to fulfill that promise? How many lives will be lost, Tara, so you can keep just one?"

"Please, tell me what to do," she whispered into Al'len's chest.

"Tara, everyone you love who merges their life force with yours, if they die, it will probably kill you. If even one of your dragons perishes, it will claim the other two. Do you understand the risks of allowing them to roam freely? The odds are that one of these ascended Torrents, whom mortals call gods, is attempting to kill you to prevent the mistakes you have made and the ones you will make." Al'len rocked her gently, her words a soft murmur. To any observer, it would seem as though she was merely comforting a grieving girl who had lost her mother.

"Please, just tell me what to do, Al'len."

"I cannot," Al'len replied firmly. "I will not steer your fate. You must decide to join with him or not. I devised the ceremony of the Life's Vow so that mortals could experience what we do. To understand the connection and the loss beyond longing for who they loved and is now gone. Perhaps it was a mistake," Al'len said, or perhaps it was El'Alue speaking in her slumber. She no longer knew.

"I won't let him die. I'll keep my promise by siphoning life energy from the evils of the world, not the good," Tara declared, sitting up and wiping away her tears.

"And stealing life from evil makes it good, Tara?" Al'len raised an eyebrow, regarding her with a mix of curiosity and concern.

"No, it does not become good," she replied, Tara's gaze meeting hers with a hint of defiance. "If I connect him to my spark and he dies, I will also die. But I cannot save the ones I love if I allow Edward to join with me and I perish with him in some futile sacrifice." *But neither will I let him die.*

Al'len took a long, stuttering breath. "You see how easily we can become like those we consider evil, how swiftly our love distorts the very fabric of creation and fate. Even their dreams, while connected, can unleash horrors. The Warriors of the Light who bore witness to your actions knew they were wrong and felt fear. I assured them that love often breeds confusion. I promised you would not subject them to it again. Promised as the Maid of Light. Do you understand, Tara? I love them, and I won't let you harm any of them, regardless of how misguided they may be."

"Yes, I understand." Tara reached for her.

Al'len enveloped Tara in her arms. El'Alue, the Maid of Light, responded within, *"She is young but wise, and she accepts correction. I do not need to destroy her; she may yet choose love instead."*

A ribbon of light carved a bright, vertical rent in the air, larger than Al'len. It then blossomed into a strobing Mage Gate. The event horizon transformed, liquefying and opening into a room. De'Nidra and Va'Yone stood and waited.

"Come on, Tara, let's go," Al'len said.

They approached the Gate, its shimmering surface beckoning, and with each step, it felt like they were stepping onto a living current. Their bodies registered the subtle shift in momentum, even though the world around them remained eerily still. Al'len's boot touched the deck first, followed by Tara's. As soon as they arrived, De'Nidra released the Mage Gate, causing the strobe of light to vanish. All that remained was the colored glow of ship lamps reflecting on polished planking the color of syrup and the smell of recently cut wood.

"Welcome aboard," De'Nidra said.

"We are here, wherever this is," Al'len replied. "That was an intriguing feeling. The movement of the Gate compensated for the shift."

"Thanks for being my test subjects. I'm glad you're here. And that it worked. I also placed a bowl of water in the room so I can perform a sounding and viewing for you. Though, I don't think it would work the other way from movement," De'Nidra explained.

Va'Yone approached Tara, and she bent down to give him a hug. "You must be a stowaway, or perhaps a pirate?"

"I am not," he challenged. "De'Nidra is teaching me to use my talent, and I actually enjoy being at sea, though it feels strange after living underground for so many years."

"Wow, I can feel us moving, and the water is so loud," Tara remarked. The scent of salt was on the air.

"I would take you above, but De'Nidra said it wouldn't be possible since you didn't get on before we left," Va'Yone said, shooting a hopeful look at De'Nidra. "Maybe the balcony, though." A mischievous smile played on his lips.

De'Nidra didn't stop talking to Al'len, but winked at Va'Yone.

"Come on, Tara, let's go," Va'Yone said, grabbing her hand and leading her out the door onto the balcony. He placed her hands on the rail. "You're going to want to hold on."

A breath-taking scene. Moonlight dancing on the sea and the salty breeze invigorating their spirits. Billowing sails and the ship's movement created a soothing sense of freedom and an unforgiving quality. The sea was a Power that the ship's crew could harness but never fully master. As the ship heaved on the seas, and the wind carried a sense of healing. With time, those aboard learned to trust the Power of the sea with their lives.

Tara whispered. "Is that what it's like for mortals and the gods, Va'Yone? Do mortals trust the gods or goddesses they follow, not knowing what will come?"

Va'Yone looked at her with confusion shining in his eyes, but tried to answer. "It has always been that way with the gods, Tara. I don't have one."

Tara laughed at him, ruffling his hair with her fingers. "Oh, you do, Va'Yone, you just don't know it yet."

They enjoyed the sea air together while Al'len and De'Nidra worked until it was time to go.

It was late when Tara and Al'len returned to Coth'Venter. The Gate strobed behind them, and De'Nidra and Va'Yone's voices echoed goodnight just before it collapsed, vanishing from the square. The sound of insects filled the air, along with the familiar echoes of guards speaking and the shoes of mounted patrols ringing as they made their rounds. Tara thought about how much had changed in such a short time.

"So, what are you going to do about Edward?" Al'len asked.

Tara felt sorrow, a deep hurt dragging at her heart. "I am going to tell him the truth. A lot can change in a few years, Al'len, and he needs to know. I won't join my life to his until the breaking is repaired."

Al'len's eyes held hers. "Tara, you can come to me with anything, and I will try to help you work through it. But life isn't always like that. It won't always give you time for discussion. Try to look ahead and consider the choices you'll be confronted with. Don't just leap. When you have to leap, you have to give yourself time to think and make the best choice you can."

"Okay, I will," Tara said.

They walked together in a new closeness. The kind that comes from sharing the truth, whether desired or not. They parted ways at the entry hall; Tara and Edward's room was in the opposite direction. "Good night," they told each other, then separated.

A single lamp that Edward had left lit for her illuminated the room. He was sleeping, and she stood there watching him before changing into her nightclothes and climbing into bed next to him. She snuggled up to him, and in his half-awake state, he pulled her closer without saying a word. Everything she needed to hear was in the unity of their bond, and she fell asleep.

As dawn broke, a chorus of thunder heralded a storm, its raindrops like the heavy heartbeats of a world in turmoil, mirroring Tara's inner tempest. Rain splashed down with large, fat, rhythmic drops that blew in gusts, splattering off the open window ledge and landing on Tara's and Edward's faces. "What in the name of..." Edward got up, untangling himself from Tara to look out the window.

The Field of Dan'Nor stretched before them, its long grass whipping in waves with the driving rain and wind. Lightning and thunder answered with long rumbling crashes. The trees bordering the Lost Kings Highway, running north toward the Harbor Cities, shook violently with each gust.

"Oh boy, Tara, it's really coming down." Edward closed the small window. "So much for mustering and loading wagons. What ever will we do?" He lay back down next to her, wearing a roguish smile.

"Edward, you're still injured. That side is an enormous bruise," Tara said, wiping rain from her face with a half-hearted laugh. "Besides, I have something to talk to you about, and I need you to listen."

"Tara, I sense there's more weighing on you. Just say it," Edward urged. "Speak your heart."

She looked up at the ceiling, struggling to find words that just wouldn't come out.

Edward sighed. "Come on, Tara. Quit stalling and just say it."

"Fine, Edward," Tara's voice cracked, a tear tracing her cheek. "You're going to die."

"We're all going to die, Tara. It's just a matter of when," Edward said with a royal command in his tone. His green eyes locked onto hers. "Stop stalling and say it. Don't force me to drag it out."

Tara looked down at the floor. "He unhorsed you. It tore away your spark. It was fading, Edward. I did something I shouldn't have to save you. But it didn't work out as I had hoped. I took the lives of two other men who attacked us, and I gave that life to you, Edward. It was a terrible thing I did. I robbed them of their fate, their choice. There's more to it than you understand. These mortals were merely following orders from greedy leaders. First, their leadership misused them. Then I misused them to save you. I don't regret saving you, Edward. But the cost. I took the rest of their lives and destroyed their souls. And you gained five years of life, maybe eight. Do you understand now, Edward? What I did was dark." Tara's steel-gray eyes brimmed with sorrow and uncertainty.

Edward nodded. His hand reached, pulling her chin up and drawing her eyes to his. "I understand, Tara," he whispered. "You acted as you had to. I'm grateful. Your decisions always weigh heavily on you. I believe in you Tara. I believe in your judgment. And whether it's five years or eight, I'll still be by your side, cherishing every moment we have together, every single day." He leaned close. Pulling her tight to kiss her.

She clung to him, her heart aching to reveal her ascension and the hope of merging their sparks to escape reality's harsh grasp. There was still hope in her to save him, but it was a childish dream. Instead, she kissed him and vowed to bring him joy in these remaining years. At least he knew now. He knew that part. They stayed together in that little room, wrapped up in the unity of love for a little while longer.

By early afternoon, the storm finally subsided. The sun's rays baked away the moisture, bringing a pleasant warmth. White puffy clouds replaced the gray ones, and the wind had calmed. Tara finally started her day.

Chapter 20 Kings Of Light

Noble blood does not make you great. Character and upright choices grant a noble bearing. Keeping your word and putting your people above yourself, make you a person worth following.

Antoff and Al'len took their places in seats near the open balcony doors of the dining hall, close to a cold fireplace stacked with tinder and wood, ready for the evening's blaze. Warriors, guards, and the local folk shared meals together, their movements flowing like streams. A gentle breeze rustled the sheer curtains, carrying the scent of fresh, moist air. This rhythmic pattern had become the norm—a spot where everyone had their designated place and purpose, akin to the whispering wind that brought a breeze of hope for a better future.

Al'len watched as Antoff's eyes surveyed the room, lingering with a soft intensity on each face. His brow furrowed slightly, a silent testament to his deep concern for those around him. This quiet, almost imperceptible gesture drew Al'len's attention, binding her gaze to his. He wore dark brown leather britches and a tan puffy shirt she had gifted him, his longsword forgotten at his waist. He appeared as youthful as when he first served as a Priest Knight, his life intertwined with the very essence of her own. "You treasure them—the mortals, I mean?"

"What do we have without them?" Antoff asked.

"I also noticed an increase in the number of people today compared to a week ago," Al'len remarked. She had donned tan leather garments that emphasized her curves, the same ones she had worn the first time they danced. Her gaze held Antoff, captive.

"You always know when I'm thinking about you, Antoff," she said, giving him a reassuring smile. "The answer is, you have me."

He cleared his throat, and Al'len grinned, responding with a melodious laugh. "Okay, Al'len, you can stop teasing me. How many Priest Knights and Clerics have arrived?"

A playful smirk danced at the corners of her lips, barely contained, as she prepared to speak. "Mel'Anor mentioned that around two hundred and fifty more have joined. The Light has called for a crusade, and some meant to gather at Haven decided, after conversing with the monks and locals there, have come here instead." She savored a piece of buttered bread, chewing thoughtfully.

"It's fascinating how a mere sliver of truth can alter one's perspective." Antoff said.

A serving girl, one arm full with steaming plates, approached. With a graceful curtsy, she balanced the plates in one hand and a decanter of coffee in the other, ready to refresh their table. Al'len poured some into Antoff's cup and did the same for herself, expressing gratitude to the server with a warm smile.

"Truth brings clarity, and there's more where that came from. People are flocking to Coth'Venter from Haven and the Harbor Cities, not only the destitute but also nobles and merchants. Despite the best houses already being claimed by the poor, they are vying for spots closest to the cathedral square. Mel'Anor plans to deliver sermons from the Bishop's balcony for those who can't find room in the Nave. It's boosting the local economy, and more shopkeepers are opening new stores," Al'len explained.

Antoff's gaze lingered over the bustling room, a shadow of worry etching deeper lines across his forehead. "This is both remarkable and worrisome, Al'len. We must secure provisions and fortify our defenses for the influx. I'll talk with Edward on bolstering our forces and expanding the patrol's outer cordon."

Just then, Tara and Edward entered the room, hand in hand. Tara's steps lightened, and a flush of color tinted her cheeks. Edward guided her to Al'len and Antoff, greeting them both. "Good morning," before taking a seat beside Antoff. "How's lunch?" he asked. "I could devour a whole Hurdbeast."

Tara glanced at Al'len and Antoff, her blush deepening. "I'm sure you could," Al'len replied with a smile. "And how is your wound?"

"Getting better. I'll be ready in a week or two," Edward replied. Dressed in simple black leather britches and a white shirt, with his broadsword buckled around his waist. Tara wore her blue spring dress and black flats.

A serving girl approached, bearing plates for Edward and Tara, and executed a graceful curtsy. "My Ladies and Lords," she greeted.

Tara looked at her with curiosity and asked, "And who might you be?"

"An'Na, the tailor's daughter," she replied, curtsying once more.

"Please tell your father that I am very proud of the work he has done and how glad I am that you are here," Tara said, smiling warmly at her.

An'Na curtsied again, "Yes, my Lady Tara," before hurrying away.

Al'len murmured to herself, "If she keeps it up, Tara's halls will spill over with people soon."

Tara, already enjoying a bite of meat and cheese from the plate, replied, "Yes, large families are nice. How are the preparations coming along?"

Antoff, stealing another glance at Al'len, cleared his throat. "Everything is progressing steadily. However, we need to secure additional funds. Mel'Anor mentioned people are making donations, but it won't be enough to meet our needs. We have more troops arriving each day, and I cannot hazard a guess how many we'll have when we depart."

Tara bit her lip, looking up at Edward with a mix of hope and hesitation. "Edward, would you guide me through drafting a letter of credit? I'm not sure where to start."

Edward, mid-bite, nodded enthusiastically.

Antoff raised an inquisitive eyebrow.

Tara whispered behind a hand, "De'Nidra has granted me ownership of the House of Deepwater in the Harbor Cities. It holds some funds we can use if necessary. Edward and I might find the time to visit the Harbor Cities and explore its potential."

"De'Nidra always seems to be one step ahead of us, doesn't she?" Antoff said.

Al'len smiled at him. "Indeed, I'm grateful she is on our side. A journey to the Harbor Cities could benefit us all, if you don't mind, Tara. I have some matters to investigate there and some history to share."

"That would be wonderful, Al'len," Tara replied.

Antoff and Al'len stood up, signaling their readiness to address their respective tasks. "Let us know when you're ready to go, and we'll make time. Edward, I suggest increasing conscription and expanding the outer cordon. People are flocking here, and as the Lord and Lady, it's your responsibility," Antoff advised.

Edward suggested agreement once again with a happy nod and a mouth full of food, his smile widening as his plate neared emptiness.

***

Candlelight flickered on the stone walls of Mel'Temdel's current abode, which served as his temporary sanctuary. Deep within the ancient Bastion of the Light, nestled amidst the mountains in the Twisted Lands, he immersed himself in the study of an age-old instruction book. Its single metal page crawled with the characters of a long-forgotten age. Holding the pulsating teardrop crystal between his knobby thumb and forefingers, Mel'Temdel flipped through the intricate diagrams and archaic Scripts.

"The metal composing this instruction book is astounding!"

Mist's dark, enthusiastic face and bright red-brown eyes peered over his shoulder. "Yes, but how does it raise the letters and images like that?"

Mel'Temdel pondered for a moment, then replied, "I don't know, my dear. Well, that's not entirely accurate. Although it appears to be solid metal, it also possesses qualities of a liquid or particles. I can't perceive at a small enough scale to tell you the truth, but I believe the metal is akin to sand held together by some deliberate bond."

Furrowing her brow, Mist responded, "That explanation hardly makes any sense. How can particles of metal hold together by design or deliberate bond?"

Mel'Temdel smiled at her. "You possess an inquisitive mind, don't you?"

Mist simply nodded.

"Very well, I will try to explain. Do you recall how the sand works?" Mel'Temdel asked.

Mist mimicked the gesture with the crystal.

"Exactly. It functions similarly to the sand images I create, except the image embedded in them has a construction set, holding everything together. That's what I meant by purpose. Do you understand?" Mel'Temdel clarified.

"Yes. So, without purpose, it would resemble ordinary black volcanic sand," Mist concluded.

"Are you sure there isn't a hint of magic within you?" Mel'Temdel playfully pinched her cheek.

Mist shook her head sadly. "I wish."

"Well, that's the best explanation I can offer, though it doesn't automatically guarantee its accuracy. Let us delve deeper into this, shall we?" Mel'Temdel suggested.

"Okay," Mist agreed. "I will try to keep up."

Rubbing his chin, Mel'Temdel contemplated how to articulate the vision in his mind. "Imagine if each grain of sand were like a construct, a magical machine of sorts," he began, raising a bushy eyebrow to gauge Mist's comprehension.

"Please continue," Mist urged.

Mel'Temdel proceeded once he was confident she understood. "Suppose some of these grains possessed the complete set of images comprising their instructions. In that case, they would be capable of forming something permanent, like this book."

"So, the sand in the box near the portal doesn't know what it is until you send it the image, whereas the book already does?" Mist asked, breathless with excitement.

"You should have been a Mage, my dear. You possess a vivid imagination. Yes, that's what I believe I'm observing. You must go to the place I sent your master because I am gathering the Power to bring his army over. I'm sure you know. At present, it is easier for me to send you than to bring them all back," Mel'Temdel explained.

Mist looked at the distracted wizard, who was rubbing his chin. "What? You want me to go to him? I don't even know where he is, and besides, I've never been there, wherever *there* is. How can I find him and deliver a message?"

"Don't fret, Mist. I will open the portal two weeks from the day I send you, allowing you to return. Bring food and water, and if you cannot locate him, simply come back. He will probably be in the vicinity. He's expecting me to open the portal. Is that satisfactory?" Mel'Temdel reassured her.

She pointed a finger at him and place the other on her hip. "I am uncertain if I can trust you that far, Mage."

"Well, you will learn to trust me if you wish to become my apprentice," Mel'Temdel said with a grin.

"Apprentice? Are you saying I can learn magic?" Mist's excitement was palpable.

"Yes," Mel'Temdel replied, tweaking her cheek. "I believe so. Is it a deal then, my dear?"

"So, the agreement is that if I follow your instructions, you will teach me magic?" Mist confirmed.

Mel'Temdel extended his hand, raising a bushy eyebrow. "I will teach you as much magic as you can learn, and if you prove capable, as much as I know. Do we have a deal?"

After a moment's hesitation, Mist took his hand and shook it. "Deal, but you mustn't tell anyone, Mel'Temdel. The master would likely forbid it or exploit me if he discovers my abilities."

Mel'Temdel sealed the pact. "Deal," he said, firmly shaking her hand.

The following morning, Mel'Temdel and Mist stood before the portal near the sandbox. Mel'Temdel wielded his staff, while Mist carried a narrow chest pack and three bags of water. Mel'Temdel held the teardrop crystal before him, and its flickering light intensified. The sand within the sandbox assembled into an image of the world Mist had witnessed before, complete with liquid on its surface and blinking glyphs. The world spun until one glyph illuminated fully. Mel'Temdel raised his staff, and the portal arches began rotating. Slowly at first, then increasing in speed until the arches burst forth with light. The velocity escalated further until the portal erupted into a dazzling, singular bright sphere, blurring before the High Mage. He focused his attention on a piece of paper he held—his final preparations took shape. With one magnificent flash, the portal transformed into an event horizon, and a shimmering pool materialized, reflecting a room identical to the one they occupied.

Sweat beaded on Mel'Temdel's forehead. "Hurry, my dear. This endeavor is costly."

"Two weeks, Mel'Temdel, and I hope to find my master," Mist said as she stepped onto the platform and descended into the flickering light within the bowl, crossing over to the other side.

Mel'Temdel yelled after her, "Two weeks, my apprentice!"

The portal on Mist's side lost Power, and the glow flickered out as the revolving arches decelerated.

Amorath watched the lands surrounding the fortress, the field of Aram 'Adan empty from the balcony on the towering battlements above. Only the field taskmasters and a garrison of defending troops remained. Zoruk'ar marched in long lines, five abreast, totaling five thousand Zoruk foot. The lances of lizard and horse had departed earlier, their black trail of dust still visible on the brightening horizon.

The road to the Darkened Gate would take time without a Mage Gate. However, he had forbidden the use of mages, since they had already moved the previous troops in that direction. Exhausting his mages and taking them out of the fight was a poor idea, much to Modred's chagrin. Even he and his demonic brothers had been forced to fly the distance to reinforce the gate, which would take hours by flight and days if you walked.

Amorath and EL'Keet were working together to reinforce the defensive outposts, sharing responsibilities for the two connected provinces. The problem was that Modred had lost a significant portion of his forces in his failed attack on Coth'Venter nearly a month ago. Although Zoruks reproduced at the speed of bloodbats, it still took time to train them—years, in fact—and they killed many of the young ones during their rites of passage. *What a waste.* Aram 'Adan was now nearly empty and did not escape Amorath's notice. He was almost alone, except for the child who would serve as his vessel, and a worthless middle mage whom he had assigned as the boy's babysitter. It stretched the Dark Conclave of Mages thin, guarding unlikely points of attack. The issue was that the self-proclaimed Great Lords, who were nothing more than fearful and inept fools, were unfit to lead a province, let alone defend their lands.

"Maybe I have been a fool," Amorath whispered.

"What was that, Great Lord?" questioned Rem'Mel.

"I said you are a fool. Now, why are you not tending to the boy?"

"Moros is sleeping, my Lord, and will not awake for at least an hour. I had an issue to discuss concerning the child," replied Rem'Mel.

"What could concern you regarding my decision about the child? If Moros drops his bottle, that is your concern. Leave the thinking to me, Rem'Mel." Amorath intended to dismiss any thoughts from this incompetent individual that he could know what is best.

"If you would forgive the intrusion, Great Lord..." the middle mage started again.

"I may not forgive it, but it's your grave. So, dig," Amorath said, a dead grin forming on his face.

"My Lord, I am concerned for his safety. If the crusade reaches the Darken Gate, we should move Moros for both his and your future's sake," Rem'Mel's voice was squeaky, but he did well to get it out.

Great Lord Amorath contemplated the middle mage's query. The mere fact he was right had upset him. "Well, don't you like to walk yourself into a premature death? Normally, you would be drained of life for intruding on what I do, Rem'Mel. Actual work. As much as it pains me to admit it, you are right," he pointed at Rem'Mel with his gangrenous finger, "Dam it Rem'Mel, I thought I was going to get to kill you. I'm not sure I would risk that again if I were you." A grey grin formed on bloodless lips.

Unsure how to respond. Sweat dripping from his brow, he swept a bow. "Thank you, Great Lord?"

"Oh, you're very welcome, Rem'Mel. Just so you know, that's one I'll owe you," Amorath said with a gray-faced grin. "And I always collect my debts."

The suns loomed overhead, and the curtains to the Holy Seat's coach remained closed. Time marched on, and while the individual days passed slowly, weeks went by quickly. But for the ancient High Mage Heli'os, fidgeting with his elegant robes, getting out of this plush twelve-beast coffin could not come soon enough. His High Holy Seat, Lord Gan'Vile, complained about every free movement of the day, and the High King, Lord Mel'Lark, had placed them as far away as possible, just ahead of the baggage, while he rode in the vanguard of the foremost lance. *Can't say I blame him; this Holy Seat is little more than a bag of gas*, Heli'os thought idly.

It was a relief when the sound of their team's steel shoes began ringing as they struck the cobblestone. Not long after, they passed through the easternmost gate of Haven. Gan'Vile, the Holy Seat, opened the curtains of his white lacquered coach, expecting to see the normal fanfare, but it was not there. There were signs that a reception had taken place, but he was so far back in the line that the High King had already passed, and the excitement had followed him all the way back to Haven castle. The streets were still busy, with plenty of townsfolk walking about. The city teemed with activity—wagons and merchants of all sorts. People stared at him as he went by, and it was far from friendly. An old, gray-haired fellow, who looked like he had fallen on hard times, actually spat on the walk while eyeing him with disgust as he passed by.

Gan'Vile flipped the curtain shut. "Outrageous! A man actually spat on the walk as we passed!"

Heli'os looked up from his thoughts, fidgeting with his robe. "What did you expect? We have been reading these," he pulled out papers from his pocket, "facts pulled straight from the Church's Archives of the Light. You are lucky that the High King left an escort with us, or they might have stripped your skin from head to boot. Do you realize that these people have seen who they believe to be the Maid of Light? You do, don't you?" He held out a decree. "Look here. This says, by her order, she has defrocked you and all your clergy for lying to the people and defaming EL'ALue."

High Holy Seat Lord Gan'Vile took the decree, looked at it, and tossed it on the purple carpet. He kicked it with his white silk slipper. "It's worthless. She does not have the Power. She gave that up when she abandoned us."

"You are mad if you believe that. If she is EL'ALue, the Maid of Light, and these people abandon you, how are you going to resist her?" Heli'os peeled notices sent out from Haven onto the floor as he read them. "This one says the Warriors of the Light glowed like holy fire as they plowed through the ranks of the misled and confused servants of liars. And this one is a wonderful rendering of her standing before the High Bishop Er'laya's throne, bringing down your clergy. Here, look at it. Doesn't she look familiar? If that is not EL'ALue, the Maid of Light, I am a vegetable farmer. I have seen the ancient artwork in the Archives of the Light, too, you know. I'm telling you, it's her."

Gan'Vile took the rendering and looked at it. "It looks like her, High Mage Heli'os, and nothing more. You yourself could make me look like her if you wanted to and even sound like her using magic. It is a farce. Naught more than that." His Holiness did not release the rendering, though he scrutinized it, and his face grew redder by the second.

"That may very well be true, but no self-respecting mage would do it. I wouldn't. She is not dead, just sleeping and I imagine she would take exception to it, being EL'ALue, the Maid of Light—a goddess, I might add. She would punish anyone who tried it. So I would advise you against it," Heli'os said.

High Holy Seat, Lord Gan'Vile took on a look of shock. "I was not asking you to do it. I was saying it was more likely the way they did it. And I am *only* saying they used magic, and it is within your Power."

High Mage Heli'os looked Gan'Vile in the eye. "I know what you meant, Your Eminence." and as far as hiding the truth or covering things up, it is already too late for that. I have a crusade to fight, thanks to you, and it is going to cost the lives of brave men and women who believed in you. Beyond taking care of them and protecting the crown, I am out."

Lord Lars of Haven stood beside High King Mel'Lark, reviewing his units and the noble knights on parade, followed by the Warriors of the Light from the capital city.

"The troops are plugging Haven, my king, so I have set up a camp just outside the western gate," Lars reported.

"What a mess, Lars," Mel'Lark said. "And now I hear that the former High Bishop is on the run with a large sum, so His High Holiness won't be able to hang him from the gate to appease the people. What I want to know, old friend, is she real? Is it her after all this time?" Mel'Lark's voice was deep and commanding, yet there was a slight tremble in it.

"I think it is, my Lord. She herself delivered me from possession and then brought me here to my throne. I have seen it all, as will you. It is not a lie, and she is no joke," Lars said.

They observed the white lacquered coach pulled by a team of twelve matching Stingers. "His High Holy Seat will be the one who answers for this mess in the end. To think, Lars, the Maid of Light is with your own boy just down the road in Coth'Venter. What is she like?" Mel'Lark asked.

"She is like trying to hold liquid fire with your fingertips, and she is not the only problem we have there. Tara, a Torrent mage, is the Lady of Coth'Venter, and my son has given her his life vow and his sword."

"Normally, I would offer you my congratulations, but I can't see how this is going to work out," the High King said. "Are we at war with the Maid of Light?"

"No, my dear High King, we are not. As for the High Seat, that will depend on his pride and whether he will take the oath of a monk," Lars Haven said.

They watched the High Mage follow the Holy Seat out of the coach. "Yes, we will see about that, my old friend, but I doubt it. He will not stoop to feed the poor or serve the needy. He is a product of the lie, and she will kill him," Mel'Lark said.

"We could just take a ride to Coth'Venter, my king, and you could meet her. Your High Mage there can authenticate the Maid of Light for you, and we could use the Mage Gate to return," Lars responded.

"That is a fine idea. We will do it in secret, Lars. I think you and I should have a hunting expedition while we wait for the remaining troops to arrive. I can move some of my guards outside the gate before we go, so it appears as a hunting party when we leave. Is it safe?" The High King asked, one eyebrow rising on his noble face.

"It is EL'ALue, the Maid of Light, my king. The word '*safe*' is a matter of perspective. Going to see her and authenticating the truth is better than her seeking you, don't you think?" Lars asked.

"Point made, old friend. Hunting sounds nice this time of year." The High King watched the guards flank the High Seat into Haven Castle. "I noticed the Seat was not so brash as to try to spend the night in the cathedral. He is aware of his predicament and wants to avoid the wrath of an angry deity or her followers. He is smarter than he looks and an even bigger coward."

Riding through the grassy field, Tara and Edward were a striking pair. He, in his noble finery, and she in her elegant blue and white dress. They complemented the robust grace of their Stingers surrounded by a hilly landscape, bordered by a forest of Thay'Oum trees southeast of the Harbor Cities. Tara raised her hand against the glare of the Little Sister, its crimson orb hanging lazily overhead, carving a slow arc in the mid-afternoon sky. The Mage Gate flickered with anticipation, awaiting Antoff and Al'len.

The Thay'Oum trees, swayed in the wind, their ringleted strips fluttering like ancient parchment in the mid-summer breeze. They got their name from the ancient word, meaning "paper" or "parchment," and their bark was showing the effects of mid-summer as it peeled away in long ringleted strips that fluttered in the gusting breeze. The wind, even at a distance of ten leagues from the Harbor Cities, still carried the scent of the sea mixed with the field of grass and the sweet resin given off by molting trees.

Edward rode alongside Tara, his cloak fluttering behind him. The embroidered dragons and a fist clutching lightning bolts seemed to come alive with each gust of wind, a silent but powerful statement of his presence. Dressed in gray britches and a crisp white shirt, Edward wore his readiness not just in the broadsword that hung at his waist but in the set of his shoulders and the determined tilt of his chin. Tara had put on the fine blue and white dress she was saving at Edward's request, along with a cloak that matched his in every way. She wore her knee-high black riding boots, and of course, Edward had protested when she stuffed her daggers inside.

Antoff was the next to ride out, his Stinger's claws tearing at the ground in a spirited dance. Al'len followed, and her mount took on the same mood, stomping a few steps before returning to a more natural gait. They both wore burnished silver plate armor, with swords on their hips and lances raised in stirrup cups as soon as they cleared the gate. Priest Knights of the First Order of the Light, they looked every inch like heroes and legend.

"Let's get a move on. We still have ten leagues to go, and it will be nightfall by the time we get there, even at a trot," Antoff said as he moved next to Al'len. They cantered through the field, and Tara and Edward fell in behind.

"Al'len, I would have thought, well, we would have wanted to make an entrance into the city less obvious," Tara said.

"No. You are taking charge of a major trade house, Tara; it needs to leave no doubt that it is official. Besides, being escorted by Priest Knights adds a certain statement of weight to someone of a lesser guild that would think to move against you," Al'len answered.

Tara whispered, her words tinged with disbelief, a cloud of confusion shadowing her usually bright eyes. "Why would they move against me? They know nothing of me."

"Greed," Antoff said, his voice low, eyes dark with the weight of his knowledge. "It's the dialect of the heart they speak most fluently, Tara."

Edward chimed in, "They have soldiers and guards too. Tara, some are little more than gangs of thugs. As the partner to the son of the Lord of Haven, and escorted by just two Priest Knights, it says you don't need to bring more soldiers. You are in a position of Power, and they would be fools to underestimate you. You will also have a house and merchant guard sufficient to be a worry. They are going to want to size you up a bit before deciding to move against you."

"Move against me?" Tara breathed. "Why? These people don't even know me."

"Greed," Al'len said. "It really is their only motivation. Either way, Tara, we will face them. Let's pick up the pace." Al'len nudged her mount with her knees, and it broke into a slow gallop. Antoff joined her side. Tara and Edward smiled at each other and urged their Stingers to catch up.

Chapter 21 Affairs Of Fate

"Memories can become twisted. We recall them repeatedly, inserting details from our own imagination where the Darkness has crept in. Be careful to sift the reality of the past from the vision that we would create, or the memory of what we wanted becomes the lie our future must eliminate."

Sib'Bal trod lightly across the Smoking Plains, her silk slippers whispering through ancient dust. Twin suns blazed overhead, their heat relentless. She wove a purifier, a mesh of charged particles, casting a protective shroud around her. This knowledge, ancient and arcane, shielded her from the toxic air, a secret not even the elder gods could claim.

Each step Sib'Bal took was a haunting echo of the past. Visions of starships piercing the skies above and the vibrant hum of crowded city streets clashed violently with the silence that now embraced her. It was a stark, painful contrast that tugged at the remnants of her heart. Back when she was a humble schoolteacher, her talents went unnoticed.

A smile touched her lips. "I, at least, can still remember what we are. I am the only one who still holds that vision." She allowed her mind to see it, even if it was beyond her Power to recreate. The Smoking Plains shimmered as images from the past overlaid the area, yet they couldn't solidify. It was too complex and vast a vision. Structures rising higher emerged from her memory—level after level of buildings and grand spires. Streets of paving, not stone, and ships and vehicles flew above, rising from the Grand Hub. The air filled with personal transports of every type, and the sounds of the city echoed with pedestrians engaged in forgotten conversations using personal communication devices, discussing things that today meant nothing.

"Lost," Sib'Bal murmured, a lament for a past devoured by time and the gods' careless wars. A tear betrayed her stoicism, marking the grief for her lost loved ones and the civilizations reduced to dust. Her fists clenched on silk, knuckles going white, as the surrounding desolation mirrored the void within. It was the fault of these elder gods, the ones who came after her. When they came into being, they had, by their very birth and existence, destroyed it all. With a heavy heart, Sib'Bal, known among the gods as the Veil of Darkness, released a breath laden with centuries of sorrow. Around her, the grandeur of her memory faded, leaving behind nothing but the ghostly outline of a once-majestic tower's door — a mocking echo of a colossal tower in the Transit District. *I will have it all back, and none of you broken gods will be in it!*

Sib'Bal walked slowly, picking her way through the shimmering illusion of the building, the crunch of crust beneath her slipping feet. It was little more than melted ruins, resembling any other blackened rock after the Shattering of the Balance and eons of erosion. She passed through the shimmering doors and walked into a dugout section that resembled a small asteroid strike. The image from her memory simmered where the lift used to be, and at the bottom, a melted and deformed lift door looked like the rest of the rock and soil of a forsaken place.

Back before EL'ALue accidentally melted it in an argument with that stupid Dark Order, the place still had Power. The Maid of Light had taken care of that.

Her blast of anger had detonated the Power plant. A dark laugh of amusement escaped her lips. "Vain bitch! She fueled that devastating blast with her own Power. But it was the destruction of the Power plant that did the work."

The metal warped from an elder god's tantrum. The heat of a memory brought back images of the fall of the once-grand civilization on the planet El'idar. Sib'Bal felt dizzy, and she swayed. Her mind grasping at the cost, trying to reconcile the loss of her husband and children. *I never said goodbye.* Their faces danced like visions in memories floating before her eyes. She braced herself with a hand on the deformed wall and vomited on the charred ground. Visions of a life forever gone, spun wildly in her mind, each memory a blade that carved deeper into her soul.

Sib'Bal's mind spun out the memory, visual and real. The sprawling metropolis of New Horizons, a bustling interstellar transport hub, hummed with activity. Set against a backdrop of towering futuristic architecture, this scientifically advanced transport hub served as a vital gateway, connecting worlds across the galaxy. However, an unforeseen tragedy triggered a cataclysmic event that shattered the very foundations of this technological marvel. As day turned to night, a deafening boom echoed through the air, shaking the entire city to its core. A gargantuan detonation of otherworldly origin ripped through the heart of the transport hub, tearing apart the sky and unleashing a maelstrom of destruction.

Once-majestic structures that had pierced the heavens lay in ruin, their gleaming surfaces pitted and broken, tumbling down in a slow dance of destruction. Thunderous roars of collapsing structures filled the air, sending plumes of dust skyward. The shockwave emanating from the epicenter radiated outward with relentless force, shattering glass windows and sending shards flying like deadly projectiles, while steel beams twisted and groaned under its own pressure. The ground trembled as if the city itself were convulsing, swallowing entire sections into gaping chasms. A palpable sense of chaos and desperation filled the air as people scrambled for cover, their lives thrown into disarray in an instant.

Chaos reigned within the transport hub, a thriving hive of galactic travel and commerce. The concourse, bustling with interstellar voyagers, transformed into twisted corridors of destruction. It appeared as if the fabric of the universe itself had been torn open, revealing the darkened sky through the gaping holes in the ceilings. The devastation wasn't limited to the physical realm alone. Amidst the rubble, echoes of energy fluctuations danced in the air, casting an eerie glow that pulsed with an otherworldly energy crawling crossed its surface. Arcane patterns of shimmering light illuminated the wreckage, hinting at the unfathomable Power that caused the catastrophe.

Rescue teams hurried about, their faces etched with determination raced against time to save lives trapped beneath the ruins. Emergency sirens wailed in the distance, urgent cries swallowed by a cacophony of destruction. The once-vibrant transport hub now stood as a haunting testament to the fragility of civilization in the face of unimaginable forces.

"Resonance Nexus: The Shattered Gateway." Escaped from her parted lips. She just needed to hear the name in her own ears again. Sib'Bal was the last witness to the grandeur of a fallen Transport Hub. A tale told by the only one who remembers it. The only one left who could rebuild the ruins of a gateway to the stars. Somewhere their people were out there among the heavens. If she could, Sib'Bal was going to find them.

Shaking her head to dispel the memories, Sib'Bal summoned a Mage Gate—an ethereal ribbon of light that split the air before her. The energy coalesced into a pulsating sphere, revealing a small room beyond with a panel mounted on the wall. Stepping through the gateway, she let it vanish from sight. The room's dim illumination came from a small floating orb of light, casting eerie shadows upon the twisted, ancient metal—a testament to the fury of an elder god's tantrum.

Pushing back the darkness, Sib'Bal focused her energy on the crystal pendant hanging from her neck. Its faint light flickered within, awakened by her concentration. The panel responded, its dormant circuits now aglow. With a graceful wave of her finger, she began her descent to the lower floor. The Power fluctuated sporadically between the nodes, causing the lift to sputter, nearly hurling Sib'Bal off her feet. Yet, she resisted the temptation to override the automated systems, aware of the dangers that lay in interfering with mechanisms she did not fully understand.

Finally arriving in the control room, Sib'Bal ascended the steps to the central seat—a place of paramount importance. From here, she surveyed the array of control cockpits encircling her, their dark displays meant to reveal the world's secrets to their respective overseers. The shattered orbital system, once under their watchful eyes, now lay in ruin.

Sib'Bal directed her attention to the communications system, which employed the mysterious Power of quantum-entangled particles. She fed Power through the circuit. Out of the silence, a voice surged, urgent and clear, from the heart of the micro-quantum system. "Yea'Ta Vec'Co De'Nouma Ad'Drain! Yea'Ta Vec'Co De'Nouma Ad'Drain!"

With a swift gesture, Sib'Bal muted the clamor, the once-familiar words now strangers to her ears. Out of curiosity, her mind translated the phrase: "Warning! Localized orbital disturbance. Action required! Warning! Localized orbital disturbance. Action required!" No further details were provided, except for the altered orbital tracks traced a path cross a large, cracked screen on the wall. Though she lacked expertise in the realm of intelligent computer systems, she knew that comprehending the situation fully would require accessing the main computer core—the Power source lost to her thanks to EL'ALue, the Maid of Light, and her Torn Flowage incident.

Yet, there it was—a ship drifted in orbit, its track tracing crossed the large view screen. If she could reach it or bring it under her command, she might uncover answers and harness its potential Power. But the risk of destruction, her fellow gods mistaking it for a rival to their dominion, was too great. No, she would bide her time, patiently awaiting the demise of these ancient destroyer gods.

With anticipation and caution entwined, Sib'Bal prepared to navigate the treacherous path ahead. She knew that reclaiming her lost world would be difficult and fraught with unforeseen challenges. One of which was restoring the Power to the facility and the computer core.

It was night, and the moons had already cast silver light on the walls of the Harbor Cities when Al'len, Antoff, Edward, and Tara reached the crest of the last hill, overlooking a slow sloping valley that led to the shining sea. Enormous towers, three for each league, rose above the battlements that stretched along the length of the cities and down to the harbor below. The broad bronze-strapped gates stood closed, guarded by archers patrolling the battlements as the group approached.

"Who goes there?" A helmeted face peered through a slot in the gate. "We are closed for the night and won't open until first light tomorrow," the man said.

Antoff called back in an official tone, "It is the Lady of House Deepwater and Edward, the young Lord Haven, Lord and Lady of Coth'Venter."

The guard opened the small door and stepped out for a closer look. "Pardon me, but we often have people trying to sneak past the gate at this hour. Which one of you is Lady Deepwater?"

Edward's voice was a soft caress against the cool night air. "Your ring," he whispered, his eyes not just seeing but feeling the weight of its meaning in the dim moonlight.

Tara's fingers trembled as she raised her hand, the ring catching the faint moonlight.

"Apologies, my Lady, but I was expecting someone older." The guard approached, bearing the pyramid of middle rank, and took Tara's hand with a bow, inspecting the ring. He glanced at Edward and the two Priest Knights. "Only two Priest Knights as an escort, my Lady. Shall I send a guard to accompany you to your manor?"

Al'len spoke up. "That won't be necessary, sergeant. They would only get in the way." She inclined her head with the confidence of a skilled warrior. She smiled at him. "You have my permission to note in the log that we declined your offer."

The sergeant bowed and motioned them inside. "Open the gate!" The bar slid, and the hinges groaned as the gate swung open.

They rode through, the echo of their shoes resonating as they passed the porticos, gradually fading into the distance along the expanse of the four-lane cobblestone street. The buildings surpassed those of any other city Tara had visited, except Coth'Ventor and its towers. Stone structures rose to five or six floors, with slate or tile roofs. This first area consisted mainly of storefronts and the commercial district. The main street still had some northbound traffic heading towards the harbors, where warehouses stood, and eastward to more upscale businesses, some made of marble, others of the local brownstone. To the west, the intersecting avenues led to manors, and further down, closer to the sea, were slums and shanties.

Antoff led them west along the first row of manors until he found a large brownstone with a matching banner flying, similar to Tara's ring. They trotted down the main stone drive to a wrought-iron gate flanked by two stone towers embedded in the thick wall outlining the property.

A man named Nor'Ray, accompanied by some stable boys dressed in leathers, held hats and bowed low. They eyed her ring. "I am Nor'Ray, my Lady. May we take care of the animals and bring them to the stable?" After speaking, he ducked his head, as did the boys. The guards opened the gate.

"Yes, you may, Nor'Ray. Thank you," Tara said.

Antoff and Al'len dismounted, handing over their lances and Stingers to two waiting stable boys at the rear of the lovely brownstone.

Tara and Edward walked past the row of servants, as if inspecting troops. The staff bowed and curtsied low as they passed.

"Are you satisfied with your staff, my love?" Edward asked. "I, for one, am tired after the ride and could use a meal and some rest."

"I am, Edward. Everyone, please attend to your duties and show us to our rooms so we can freshen up. Prepare a light meal in the dining room for the four of us. Inform us when it's ready," Tara said with the grace and poise of a noblewoman.

A young woman eyed Edward as she stepped forward and curtsied low. "I am Mar'garete, my Lords and Ladies. If you would follow me." She had almost red-blonde hair that reached her waist in a single braid.

Tara's jaw tightened as she observed Mar'garete's smile, a storm brewing behind her eyes. A forced calmness coated her words, but the rigidity of her posture betrayed her irritation. *She likes Edward, and not in a good way.*

"Mar'garete. Please lead the way," Tara said with a patient smile, while thinking, *I'll have to watch her around Edward, or she will try to corner him for sure.*

Mar'garete led them to the garden room, which boasted an enormous bed and luxurious furnishings. Tara dismissed her and, after the door was closed, she looked around at all the things she now owned. But it was the books and the garden overlooking the sea that took Tara's breath away. Her hand sought his and their fingers intertwined. "Edward, look. A garden, a house, and the man who loves me. It's my dream come true." A tear trailed her cheek, and she blinked it away. "I wish Cur'Ra were here to share it with us."

"Oh, Tara, you're right. But we're missing a few things." Edward turned her to face him and kissed her. "Once all this worry is behind us, we'll work on completing the rest of it."

Tara looked at him questioningly.

Edward nodded. "Yes, our children. We can start planning for them then." He drew her close and kissed her again. "But for now, let's freshen up, Tara. We should get our meal."

The thought of that time and its safety seemed so far away, but she answered him anyway, with a forced certainty in her voice. "Yes, I know how much you hate missing a meal, Edward." she replied affectionately.

Dinner arrived quickly, an hour later, when young Mar'garete knocked on the door. Tara answered.

Mar'garete curtsied. "Dinner is served, my Lady. Allow me to lead the way?"

"Please do. Are you ready, Edward?" Tara asked.

Edward joined her, taking her arm. "I'm always ready to eat, my Lady." He gave her his best grin.

Antoff and Al'len had changed out of their armor and were waiting in the richly paneled hall. Mar'garete led the way to the dining room, a large space with a long wooden table and red cushioned chairs, enough for twenty people. Windows with carved trim overlooked the main drive, although they were now closed. Lamplight played on painted pictures depicting the history of Harbor Cities' growth, and a fire crackled in the dark stone fireplace, providing atmosphere rather than warmth. The flue had been opened to let out the heat.

One by one, liveried servants placed plates of sauced meats and vegetables in front of each of them and filled their cups with deep red wine. The last servant, Mar'garete, brought Tara a bell. "Ring if you need anything, my Lady." Departing Mar'garete dipped a quick curtsey, and the servants closed the room for, privacy.

Tara took a sip of the wine, enjoying its fruity sweetness that lingered on her palate, enhancing the flavors of the meal. "This really is delicious."

Al'len and Antoff smiled with satisfaction, their soldier-like expressions speaking for themselves.

Edward also ate well, his body still in need of nourishment for healing.

When they finished eating, it was Al'len who spoke. "That was a delightful meal, Tara. Thank you. Now, there's something I need to discuss with all of you. Come to the window." Al'len drew back the curtains, and they gathered behind her. "Do any of you notice anything here that doesn't belong?"

"It appears unchanged to me, though it has been a year since my last visit," Edward remarked, savoring the last sip of his wine.

Al'len looked at each of them, receiving only quizzical looks or shakes of the head. "There," she pointed to a mansion high above the city on the ridge. "Do you see it? With the long, steep drive?"

Tara and the others nodded in agreement. "It seems fine to me," Tara said. "What's wrong?"

Al'len's gaze hardened as she stared at the mansion. "De'Nidra warned me," she began, her voice a mix of wonder and bitterness. "I braced myself against believing it, against accepting it as real. And now, it's like a sore thumb amidst the familiar, a glaring aberration only my eyes can see. It's the work of the goddess Sib'Bal, the Veil of Darkness. She's quite the perfectionist when hiding her work. None of you would have known because you simply accepted it, and the history of its existence became real for you. That's the danger. Who knows how many lives altered or destroyed just so she could have what she wanted?"

"Are you telling me she killed people to achieve this?" Tara's voice caught. Shocked by what she had just learned.

Al'len nodded grimly. "Most likely, yes. Anyone in that area during the creation of the new reality, whether they were hiking or hunting, would vanish from existence if she didn't bother to preserve them. Before we understood the cost, all the gods did it. But once we realized we were destroying everything, we stopped. Well, mostly stopped. Making things permanent goes against the natural order. They come into existence, serve their purpose, and then fade away, returning existence to its original state. It's costly but necessary."

Antoff shook his head, disbelief written on his face. "Why would she do this? Doesn't she realize she's only prolonging the Breaking?"

"She is aware, and she doesn't care," Al'len said. "No, she doesn't care about these people, their lives, or even this reality. She wants what she wants, regardless of who she hurts or wipes away to get it."

Tara's breath caught in her throat. "We'll have to be cautious."

"Al'len and I will return to Coth'Venter, as usual," Antoff explained. "We'll take all the mounts with us. You'll have transportation here, Tara, and when you're finished, find a secure and inconspicuous place to Gate back. You'll have to maintain appearances. Do you understand?"

"I do, Antoff, but it won't stop me from holding the Dark Order accountable for Cur'Ra's murder," Tara asserted. Thinking of Cur'Ra brought fresh anger and the loss to the surface. Tara would not forget her mother or the one that had killed her. "We're all tired. I think it's best to rest now and discuss this further in the morning."

The heavy Corsair vessel, Neal 'Lance', rode the rough sea, waves lifting and slapping the hull, covering the decks in the spray. Dark clouds obscured the moon's light, leaving only the deck lamps to carve out a small oasis within the watery abyss. Wind blew with such force that the sea churned, forming whitecaps that rose five spans in height. The captain altered the course to avoid the risk of capsizing. The storm had torn one small sail, which would need to be replaced, but fortunately, that was the extent of the damage. De'Nidra, Tem'Aldar, and Va'Yone all stayed together in the larger cabin.

The ship lamps swayed rhythmically, serving as a reliable indicator of how much the sea boiled and tossed them about. The constant movement did nothing to relieve Va'Yone's sensitive stomach. "De'Nidra, I'm going to be sick again."

They sat together on the large four post bed, and De'Nidra handed him a bucket. "Hold on to the bucket, Va'Yone, and don't lose it. Every time you throw up, I have to as well."

Tem'Aldar averted his gaze, avoiding watching Va'Yone empty his stomach and pass the bucket to De'Nidra, who promptly vomited because Va'Yone had done it. Swallowing hard, he said, "Will you two stop? Please! We only have one bucket, and if you get me started, one of us will be in trouble with all the passing back and forth. There is going to be a timing issue." He chuckled in between gasps of air.

De'Nidra shot him a look and made a gesture that would have curled a sailor's hair. "It's not just the ship and Va'Yone throwing up that's making me sick, you oaf. I'm pregnant! And it's your fault." The ship rocked, and she took the bucket back from Va'Yone and retched.

Tem'Aldar's face flushed, and Va'Yone stopped breathing. "What?" they both exclaimed. They turned to face her as if to read something hidden behind her shining eyes.

That declaration had caused a certain level of fear in Tem'Aldar to bubble up in his gut beyond the sickness he felt from all the throwing up. It was strange to him.

He had been in the line of battle and never felt this kind of fear of responsibility. He needed to grow up.

"I am going to be a father?" Tem'Aldar whispered, the words feeling alien on his tongue, as though he was speaking a truth too vast to fully comprehend. He did not, and that scared him. Shuddering he heaved a breath, but it just did not seem to fill his lungs. He felt like he had been holding his breath or his lungs were not working. Whichever it was, he could hardly breathe.

De'Nidra wiped her mouth with a towel. "That's right, you rogue. You're going to be a father." She tried to smile while cradling the bucket in her lap.

"So, I'm going to be an uncle," Va'Yone remarked, taking hold of the bucket.

Tem'Aldar laughed. "It's great, De'Nidra. When did you find out? And why did you wait to tell me?" He felt the fear of the unknown flutter again. He had to get his footing again before she saw his uncertainty. The last thing she needed to see was his fear and think of him as unwilling. He was willing, just scared of the responsibility and unsure if he was going to do the job justice.

"I've been sick every morning for two weeks now, and I wanted to save it for something special. But since you're giving me a hard time, I figured I might as well tell you." De'Nidra said.

Tem'Aldar reached over Va'Yone and embraced her. "You're going to be a great mother and an even better wife. If you will have me forever?" He hoped she was not feeling trapped with him now or unwilling.

"You oaf, I joined my life to yours ages ago. What do you think I was doing when you were in that dungeon? I was sneaking around, looking for you. I promised to love you forever," De'Nidra said.

Tem'Aldar raised his hands. "I was praying. Besides, I just want to hear you say it. I want to hear you say you want to be with me forever."

"I will be with you. You are ridiculous," she said, a laugh forming on her lips.

Eventually, the sea calmed, and so did the passing of the bucket. Va'Yone took it out, emptied it into the sea and washed it, then stowed it in the corner. When he returned, they were kissing again, but they stopped when he entered. "I left your bucket in the corner. I think I'll head back to my room. He gave them a little space." They bid each other good night, and he left. After the ordeal, he was tired and wanted to read a bit before falling asleep.

Chapter 22 Sea Or Dirt

"Sea, only sky and water exist—a boundless expanse that leaves one yearning for the safety found within port or harbor. Eyes tirelessly scan the horizon as the weary crew longs for a glimpse of the Lands of El'idar. A desire to feel solid ground beneath their feet. Perhaps that is why we wait so eagerly for those we love, those who provide us with a sense of security akin to an island amidst the waves. Without them, we are adrift, lacking mooring and anchor. Our ragged souls are the tattered sails, our yearning hearts the rudders."

Orbiting El'idar, Mali'Gorthos' ship lay silent against the backdrop of a world in decline. Within the ship, though his body lay in hibernation's grip, his mind stirred, roused by an orbital array's unexpected pulse, a ghost of civilization's echo. Hope surged within him, prompting a surface scan. Though the signal was feeble, it undeniably existed. Someone proficient in ancient technology had awakened the array and scanned his vessel.

The scan came and went, revealing the source of the signal. It originated from the subterranean remains of a former galactic hub. The usage of such advanced technology was no mere accident or oversight. Someone must have deliberately activated it. The entrance to the exterior of the complex appeared on his scan as inactive and sealed. There was only one type of being he knew possessed the ability to transcend physical barriers. Whoever had entered that location and used that technology was an ascended and a remnant of a destroyed people.

Mali'Gorthos ran a quick inventory check, his thoughts a mix of prayer and strategy. *Let them scan again*, he mused, the idea of dispatching a shuttle to reveal himself to the deity—a calculated risk that reignited his hope. All that remained was to bring them aboard this vessel.

Ivan moved through the cavernous chamber, his gaze following the Scripts and images that danced like shadows across walls and ceiling—every surface alive except the steadfast floor and the shadowy portal arches. He thumbed through a pile of research he had taken from the nearest stack by the vast arches. "The documents and notes were a part of the De'Moggda Lucida. 'The Clarity of Dimensions' or 'The Illuminated Realms'—why is the idea of such limitless travel through a multiverse such a hard concept? I cannot understand how it works. Let alone how it was done."

"Not really, my Lord Prince. Lil smiled, no longer emphasizing the title *'Lord'* as she once had. Old scholars didn't just dream up the multiverse. It's the backbone of the math that breathes life into this room." Lil said, her hand sweeping across the air, as if stirring the very theories into visibility.

Ivan turned towards Lil, who was retranslating the missing De'Moggda Lucida that the Dominion's servant had stolen. She was wearing a dress with a low cut, and the dark silks draped her curves. It made him want to stop working and simply watch her move. Ivan shook himself free of what he now recognized as her deliberate attempts to fill his head with intrigue and allure. He sent with a light-hearted smile, *Stop that, Lil. You know I'm trying to work*. His tone was playful, yet she understood the earnestness behind his thoughts. Well, partially at least. Watching her was quite fulfilling. He never tired of it.

Lil spread her arms and placed one hand on her heart, curtsying deeply. *I apologize, my prince. My concentration is wandering.* She sent him a blush that would have almost matched the sincerity of her inner voice. If he didn't already know her better.

Ivan noticed the other Vam'Phire working in the room, occasional smiles curling their lips. They were enjoying his emotional interplay with Lil. He blocked them out, and they returned to their tasks. Not that they had ever appeared to have stopped, but it was clear they were putting considerable effort into savoring every emotion he felt for Lil. He sent her a mental image of him shaking a finger at her.

Lil's voice flowed into his head like silk, and he couldn't, or wouldn't, block her out. Doing so would violate the trust and the life their relationship had become. *Ivan, don't shield our life from those who serve you. They intertwine their happiness with your thoughts and emotions. Our love, with few exceptions, should not be private. We must share without mental filters. Understand? They live to learn, and for some, without you and their studies, life would lose its meaning. We should share every aspect of life that can be, with only a few exceptions.* She repeated. *I am not embarrassed to love you, my prince. I want the world to know it.*

He opened his mind to everyone again. *Forgive me. I want them to know I love you.* It came out as a mental shout, and everyone looked up from their work, startled. Then returned to it with a smile on their faces. *I need to learn better control. I am like a screaming child.* He thought. Deciding to use his voice, fearing another slip. Lil did that to him. The worst part was she knew it. "Lil, how close are we to completing the translations?" He wanted to redirect the attention of everyone he had shouted at back to their tasks.

"We are working on the last one. Everyone is providing me with translations, and I am reproducing the images and text. It won't take long to finish," she replied, a gleam in her eye that said she had gotten to him again. *You need to focus and prevent your thoughts from wandering.* She chided like honey in his mind. *The De'Moggda Lucida's restoration to its former state of research will take time. There is still much to do. Many worlds and locations have yet to be translated.* Lil explained, sensing his unasked question, *Our challenge lies in the unfamiliarity with what should be commonplace to us, as it was for our predecessors who used the portal gate daily,* Lil explained, sensing another question. *It's akin to grasping a concept that's second nature to an expert, yet elusive to those without the daily contact with the concepts. You catch the words, but the years of experience behind them remain a mystery.*

Ivan refused to be led deeper into her mind. She delighted in setting romantic traps for him. He enjoyed them, but he needed to concentrate, so he used his voice. It came out in a rasp. "You could at least let me ask first. Lil. Before you answer. But I grasped the meaning of what you said to some extent. So, you're likening it to a blacksmith, explaining complex metal work to a vegetable farmer?"

"Yes, Ivan, that's it," Lil laughed at the simplicity and ingenuity of his explanation. She loved Ivan, the leader, the warrior, the poet, and his humor. She savored every part of him, even his frustration. Lil found his attempts to ignore her wiles best of all. He could not. Nor could she resist his charms.

"Sometimes you're too smart, Lil. I feel that way when you explain things to me about all this stuff. He waved his hand about the room. I'm ignorant of all of it," Ivan confessed.

She sent a blush in response. "I enjoy teaching you many—things, my Lord." she teased. Her eyes tracking over him. She gave him a wash of inner desire. Just for effect, of course. No sense overdoing it. She felt her cheeks growing hot.

He knew she wasn't just talking about their work. She was trying to corner him again. *I'm simply not going to fall for it again.* He told himself, but inwardly he knew he would.

Abruptly, the Chronicler Da'Vain emerged from the shadow, wisps still clinging to him as if walking out of a hall. He held up two staffs, smaller than him, more sized for mortals. "I think I found what you and Tara are looking for, Lil," he said, extending the staffs.

"Yes, they seem to be the right size," Lil replied, walking towards Da'Vain to meet him halfway between the door and the depression of the arches of the portal gate. Lil examined the staffs, twisting the aged metal in her hand, and then the other. "Both store Power. This one resonates with positive energy, according to the script and this device resonates with negative," she said, reading symbols, as the light flickered in the crystals embedded in the top.

Ivan looked at the devices in Lil's hands. "Oh yes, I've seen those before. They are mage's staffs. They store Power, and by tapping into them, they enhance their own abilities. I've been told that as long as they hold the staff, it continues to charge."

Da'Vain nodded in agreement. "I've seen that too, Ivan. But it's more likely that these devices had other purposes. The mages learned to use them in the way you described. It aligns with its original function, so it works. However, this portal is one reason they created the staffs. I'm quite certain that there are other devices that people originally made for different reasons, and the mages adapted them to their needs without truly understanding their original design or intention. They only know that it works, my prince. Likely the positive energy charged by the Light and negative Darkness. It seems right. However, Lord Ivan. I am no mage. Lady Tara would have more insight than I."

Lil appeared puzzled. "Tara said we can use them. I'm tempted to try, but I'll wait for her," Lil said, laying them on the table. "We cannot pass through time compression. It has something to do with how we use life energy, and the compression exacts a toll on time, draining us. A thousand years could pass in a second and leave us depleted. Mortals don't have that problem because the spark of life is innate to their existence, whereas ours is not. If time doesn't change when we pass through, it shouldn't matter. However, that's my theory, and I won't be the first to test it without Tara's presence. She has the mental capacity to understand it because she exists in a higher and lower reality contiguously. I believe she sees it in a way we cannot." Lil trembled, still shaken by her brief connection with Tara's mind. It was just that once. She feared seeing it again. The memory alone was enough to cause a physical reaction.

"As soon as Tara returns, let's have her look at it. By then, we should have completed the translation." Ivan suggested. Da'Vain and Lil mentally affirmed their agreement.

At dawn, beneath a cloudless sky, the Elder Brother sun revealed itself, casting its majestic reflection over the rolling sea. The fragrant breeze from the garden mingled with the briny scent of the ocean. The wind gusted, causing the manicured trees to sway and sigh gracefully.

Al'len stretched before rising from her plush, roomy four-poster bed. Not wanting to disturb Antoff, who was still pretending to be asleep, she slipped out of bed and filled the stone basin with cool water. Splashing her face, she braced herself for the challenges that lay ahead. Tara's household staff had thoughtfully stocked the washstand with all the amenities, including teeth paste, brushes, fragrant soaps, oils, and lotions. Al'len chose a bar of lavender-scented soap, applied some oil to her skin, and then brushed her teeth and hair.

As she dried herself off with a towel, Al'len noticed that the morning hadn't warmed up yet, although the humidity from washing still clung to her skin. Preferring to sleep in the nude, she was accustomed to Antoff watching her morning routine unfold. With a playful smile, she asked, "Is there something I can do for you, soldier?" *I know you are watching Antoff.*

Antoff, clearing his throat, replied, "Do you know, Al'len, no matter where I wake up with you, I always have the best view?" His gaze lingered as she dressed.

After Antoff washed and dressed, they helped each other don their armor, going through their usual ritual. Following this, they made their way down for breakfast before their return to Coth'Ventor.

Tara and Edward were already enjoying their meal at a wrought-iron table on the patio, nestled under the shade of a large redleaf tree. Its broad branches swayed with the breeze, casting spots of warm light that danced in the filtered sunlight of leafy branches.

Mar'garete, standing with a coffee decanter, diligently kept Edward's cup filled. Tara almost had to ask for a refill, but Mar'garete managed to anticipate her needs, all the while attempting to dazzle with her smile and slim waist. Edward, to his credit, seemed oblivious to her charms.

Antoff and Al'len followed a member of the kitchen staff to the table across from Tara and Edward, who were sipping their coffee, patiently awaiting the arrival of the morning meal.

Antoff quickly assessed the situation and understood what was happening. He looked from Tara to Edward and greeted everyone, "Good morning."

The kitchen staff brought in the morning meal on polished metal trays with lids. As steaming lids lifted, they revealed a delectable spread of meats, cheeses, eggs, sliced fruit with sweet and tart sauces, piping hot bread, and honey cakes.

The aroma of honey cakes swept Tara into nostalgia, transporting her back to the carefree days of her childhood in RavenHof. *Things were simpler then. Reading books and stealing honey cakes were the worst of my problems back then,* She mused.

The staff placed thin pottery plates resembling glass from across the sea in front of them, accompanied by fine silverware. "You may all leave; we will serve ourselves. Thank you for your service," Tara said appreciatively. The kitchen staff withdrew, leaving Mar'garete to place the coffee decanter on the table, offering a curtsy as she left with a smile for Edward.

Edward rose from his seat and attended to the needs of Tara, Al'len, and Antoff. Antoff whispered audibly, "Keeping your head down, son?"

"Trying to, Antoff," Edward replied.

"Good idea. Thank you, Edward," Antoff acknowledged, loud enough for everyone to hear.

"It is my pleasure," Edward responded stoically.

Al'len, a faint smile on her lips, chewed a bite of her meal before saying, "Mar'garete seems nice."

Tara huffed in response. "A little too nice, if you ask me! She's practically drowning Edward in coffee and bodice all morning."

"Tara! She hasn't done anything of the sort. I hardly noticed her," Edward defended himself.

"Lucky for you, Edward. If you had noticed, you would've been in trouble. But thankfully, you're not, and you can count yourself fortunate for that," Tara quipped. She did not know why she was mad at Edward. It was not like being handsome was his fault.

Antoff and Al'len smiled at Tara's remark, but it was Al'len who spoke up. "She is friendly, Tara. Perhaps a bit too friendly. But remember, you can always assign her some tasks if she upsets you. That usually gets the point across. Once she becomes familiar with you, she will better understand your preferences. De'Nidra hired her for a reason, so she is not a fool and likely has other duties beyond what we are aware of."

"No doubt," Tara said, sighing heavily. "I'm just not accustomed to other women openly fawning over Edward like that. Well, not so blatantly, anyway. You're right, of course. She just needs some guidance to understand my expectations. I intend to ask De'Nidra what she was thinking, or rather, what other roles she had in mind. I'm hesitant to speculate."

They enjoyed their meal together and were left alone until it was time for Antoff and Al'len to depart.

As Antoff and Al'len rode away, a small brown coach pulled up, guided by a single animal and driven by a young coachman. The driver swiftly stepped down and opened the coach door for a middle-aged woman, who curtsied politely. "I am Libby, your ladyship, your secretary. When I received word that you were in the city, I came immediately to assist you with your holdings and address any inquiries you may have." The coachman handed Libby a leather case, bowed, and retreated to the stable, awaiting further instructions.

"Please, make yourself comfortable, Libby," Tara said graciously. "This is Lord Edward of Haven."

Libby dipped a curtsy once more. "An honor, my Lord."

Edward reciprocated the gesture with a bow. "The honor is mine, Libby. Pleased to meet you. I'll leave you two to work. You won't need me, Tara. Libby is your secretary and knows her job well. Fill me in later."

Tara nodded at Edward. "I know you need some rest, Edward. I'll wake you when we're finished. Shall we proceed inside, Libby?"

Two hours later, Edward rose and headed to the library office, where Libby was assisting Tara. She handed Tara parchment after parchment, which Tara signed and sealed with wax. Edward listened attentively, a loving smile gracing his face.

"And this one pertains to the funding for the additional guards and sailors you requested," Libby informed them.

"Very well, Libby. This is the last one. My hand has gone numb," Tara said with a light giggle.

"Apologies, my Lady. However, with your absence, I must be prepared to handle your orders, purchases, and outstanding bills of lading. I will send your instructions to the relevant parties this afternoon by second sun," Libby stated, as she neatly folded and sealed the papers before placing them into the leather case. She curtsied and quickly departed upon being dismissed.

"That woman is a Dark Order taskmaster, I'm certain of it, Edward. She is highly efficient, albeit pleasant. I was struggling to keep up," Tara said, dabbing her moist forehead with a handkerchief.

"Did you acquire the information you needed about the holdings?" Edward inquired.

"Yes, though I don't fully comprehend all the terms, Libby assured me that we needn't worry about the financial requirements of Coth'Ventor. I have approved the recruitment of more guards and sailors. De'Nidra has ordered the construction of five additional ships, and I wanted to plan for the crew before their arrival. Finding the right individuals may take some time. In the meantime, we can assign them among the existing crew for training purposes," Tara concluded, her breath labored.

"Would you like to stay another night and rest? You appear exhausted, my love. I could massage your feet and help you out of that hot dress," Edward proposed, his smiled bordering on mischievous.

"Edward! What has gotten into you? You know we must return," Tara responded, attempting to sound serious.

"I was merely suggesting Tara," Edward replied, attempting to feign seriousness.

Tara narrowed her eyes at him. "You have one hour, Edward." She grinned at him and ran.

Edward chased her to their room.

Led by the High King and Lars of Haven, the hunting party emerged from the gates of Haven Castle, a retinue of noble knights and eager hounds in tow, all primed for the hunt. The party was of a typical size for a hunting expedition, except to include High Mage Heli'os, who was likely there for security reasons. From the safety of his bedroom in the tower, High Holy Seat Lord Gan'Vile watched them depart. "Ridiculous," he muttered. "The High King, Lord Mel'Lark, has nothing better to do while my life and our order hang in the balance. Enjoy your hunting trip, my Lord. I intend to work. You can busy yourself with play." Gan'Vile's face flushed with anger. "Not that I would want to go, but the least you could have done is extend the courtesy of inviting me, so I could refuse!"

Mel'Lark and Lars wore leather armor and dark hooded cloaks, with bows and quivers hung at their backs. They each carried a hunting dagger, and a sword belted around their waists. Their attire resembled that of hunting Lords or travelers, allowing them to blend in. With their hoods pulled up, they would be nearly invisible in Haven if not for their noble guard and the baying hounds. The High King raised his hood, and Lars followed suit as they rode through the city streets. It was quite a spectacle, but not an unexpected one. In fact, that was the very purpose of the entire endeavor. Riding through the bustling streets of Haven, filled with people going about their daily activities, the wagons made way for the obvious noble procession. Mel'Lark had forbidden any yelling of "make way for the king" and such. Pomp and circumstance were to be avoided when attempting to appear as though they were slipping away for a secret hunting expedition, orchestrated by a spoiled High King and his retainers. Passing through the area that some in the city had long ago named the Gray Gate, the people made way, and a weight seemed to lift from Mel'Lark's chest, relieving a breath he hadn't realized had been stifled.

"We made it, Lars," Mel'Lark whispered. "I won't say we're in the clear, but at least we're away from that foolish old man for a day or two."

"My Lord! That's our High Holy Seat, Lord Gan'Vile you're speaking of. We must mind our tongues!" Lars feigned outrage, placing a leather-gloved hand on his forehead. The noble knights around them chuckled. They were all noble Lords, some more distinguished than others, but all loyal and aware of the canonical texts and histories of the Order of Light—the lie the church had perpetuated for ages. The difference was that they were all obligated to continue the charade, until they weren't, leaving High Holy Seat Lord Gan'Vile holding a metaphorical bag of excrement. The one chance he had to hang it around High Bishop Er'laya's and Diocesan On'omus's necks was lost. No, they were long gone, like smoke in the wind.

"What about High Bishop Er'laya and Diocesan On'omus?" Lars asked absentmindedly.

The High King answered, "I issued warrants for their arrest, as did the Holy Seat. As futile as it may be. I had to do at least that much. I seriously doubt they are traveling openly, wearing the robes of the High Bishop of Haven and his loyal Diocesan. No, they stole gold from the church and fled. It was foolish to leave them with a line of credit, but 'Lord Gan'Vile' believed that by cutting off their access, they would realize he was onto them." Mel'Lark lowered his voice during the last part of his statement, but his face displayed a mix of bewilderment and disgust.

"It might be best if we don't find him unless necessary, if you catch my drift, my king," Lars whispered back. "Having a little leverage might keep the High Seat in line, should he come out unscathed."

"I'm not actively searching for him, Lars. It only appears that way. I thought of that too," Mel'Lark said.

The second sun had passed its zenith and was descending toward night. The Elder Brother, the largest sun, hovered an hour from gracing the horizon, and darkness would set in within four or five hours. Sweat glistened on the High King's forehead beneath his hood. "Let's pick up the pace. I want to be out of sight of the wall and hunting before dark." He winked at Lars and spurred his mount into a prancing canter. The others followed suit.

A ribbon of light sliced through the air in the main square of the Coth'Venter Cathedral of Light, blossoming into a sphere and then into a pulsating purple ball larger than a man. The oculus, resembling a great eye, transformed into a pool, revealing a well-furnished bedroom. Tara and Edward stepped out onto the square near the Ram'Del fountain, and the Mage Gate collapsed, leaving residual energy that drifted and dissipated in the warm evening air. The smaller sun had almost reached the horizon, casting a reddish-orange hue against the fluffy clouds scattered across the sky. Wagons rumbled through the square, either departing or making last-minute deliveries before nightfall. There was no longer a sense of urgency. Edward had increased patrols; doubled the guards; and even ordered the streets if RavenHof to be swept twice a day and again at night. Coth'Venter was now safe. Well, mostly safe, Tara thought.

They climbed the flight of thirty steps to the main entrance, which now featured new double doors made of dark, sturdy wood banded with steel. Tara recognized the stamp of the metalwork, crafted by the cathedral's smithy. As the house guards opened both doors, they placed gloved hands over their hearts. Edward nodded in acknowledgment, and Tara said, "Thank you," as they entered.

The halls bustled with servants and guards on their way to the evening meal. Some carried trays or pushed laden carts, while others headed to the dining hall. Antoff had instituted a cherished tradition: everyone dining together as a family. It provided an opportunity for shared thoughts, laughter, and savoring delicious food. Occasionally, musicians from local inns would spontaneously arrive, leading to impromptu dancing.

Tara looked at Edward and asked, "Do you think there will be music tonight, Edward? I can manage a light meal, but I would love to dance."

Edward's laughter rang out. "Should music grace us, I'd gladly risk stepping on your toes."

"Your dancing has improved, Edward, truly. Promise me you'll dance with me." Her smile suggested she already knew the answer.

"Tara, you know I will. But it'll cost you a kiss," he replied, grinning mischievously.

She took his hand in hers and smiled back. "Do you want an advance?"

Edward's cheeks tinged red. "No, Tara. The last time you did that, I had to dance with you in front of everyone, and there was no music. They all hummed and sang along. It was embarrassing."

"I'm just teasing, Edward." Tara said.

As they passed, men bowed and women curtsied, murmured "Lady Tara" and "Lord Edward." They entered the dining hall, which was filled with people. The heat and humidity of the day were slowly dissipating thanks to the open balcony door and the entrance to the hall. Tara motioned for people who attempted to stand to remain seated and enjoy their meals. They complied, bowing their heads to show their happiness at seeing both of them and expressing their respect.

Edward and Tara sat down with Antoff and Al'len. "You're back! Well, that took a little longer than expected," Antoff remarked.

"What did I do?" Edward said.

"The secretary took hours, and Edward had some things he wanted to take care of," Tara explained, with a smile that emphasized her blushing cheeks. Edward was going to get it later. He knew very well what he did, too, and if he did not, she would explain it.

Edward heaped meat onto his plate, prompting Tara's amused inquiry. "How can you be hungry again?"

"Ever since the injury, I eat like a starving beast, and it was—energetic earlier," he smirked, his tease warming her cheeks.

Al'len smiled and said, "Tara, his body is still trying to recover from the loss of life energy. He was gravely hurt. He is not completely healed yet, although I must admit, he's looking better every day. Don't let him fool you, Tara; he knows he's being spoiled."

Edward grinned, his mouth still full of food.

Chapter 23 Maids And Lords

"You cannot give away what you do not have. A soul cannot whisper in an ear that will not hear. Hearts mend hurt in the confines of creation. Give love and compassion, and store it up in those around you. So that when you need it, your storehouse will be full. Your harvest will wait there when you hunger for it most."

The hunting party of High King Mel'Lark and Lars of Haven emerged from a Mage Gate near Haven. They had left the hounds and handlers behind as an alibi. High Mage Heli'os followed, with fifty noble knights trailing behind him.

"Remember, this is not our land, and here I am, not the High King in Coth'Venter. Like you, I am a guest. So, be on your best behavior. We are not here to start a war with Lady Tara or Lars's son. The same goes for the Priest Knights of Coth'Venter. Remember the rumors—if they're true, fifty of them defeated three hundred with the help of some villagers. And let's not forget the Maid of Light. So, my Lords and ladies, be careful with your words. We are here to verify her authenticity, not to make an enemy," He said.

A chorus of "Yes, High King" echoed, though he was uncertain if they could control their tongues. Most didn't believe in gods, dragons, and all that—at least not yet.

After a journey of just half an hour, they arrived at the RavenHof gate, which stood closed in the deepening night. However, before they could call for it to be opened, it swung wide, revealing a light cavalry of twenty.

"Lady Tara has sent us to offer you warm lodging and a meal, my Lords and Ladies. Will you accept my lieges invitation?" the woman said.

Lars nodded. "In that case, we accept with gratitude. Your Lady Tara is very kind," Mel'Lark replied, sweeping a bow.

"The Lady Tara has ordered musicians from the inn, and they arrived an hour ago, my Lord," the woman added.

"How did she know?" Mel'Lark inquired.

The cavalry officer pointed upwards, and he followed her gaze. "There they are, my Lord."

"It looks like a flock of Leatherwings to me," the noble knights broke out in laughter at the High King's remark.

The officer smiled, her expression tight, as if she were baring her teeth. "They get bigger if our guests don't behave themselves." The laughter quickly subsided.

"Very well, good soldier, lead the way," Mel'Lark said, bowing from his saddle.

High Mage Heli'os gazed upward, swallowing hard. "Two large, six small–I believed she had but two. Bonding with both was impossible. But whence are the six smaller ones?"

"I don't know, my Lord. They seem to keep appearing on their own. But I know that the two larger dragons are hers," the officer replied.

They headed to the inn to await the musicians and their instruments. Soon, a blonde woman and five musicians carrying cases arrived. After loading into the wagon, they set off at a leisurely pace, considering the comfort of the riders and the safety of the instruments. The nobles grumbled, but Mel'Lark appreciated the care they showed towards the common people and their property.

"Your Lady Tara is a kind woman, sending a guard to open the gate and provide an escort," Mel'Lark remarked, trying to glean more information from the lance officer.

"She extends hospitality to everyone, my Lord," the officer replied. They approached the cathedral, and lights burned everywhere. She gestured towards the houses. "If anyone wants a house, they'd better hurry, as the best ones are going fast. Choose an empty one, and she will grant your family a deed."

"Is she selling the properties, then?" Mel'Lark inquired.

"No, my Lord, she is giving them away and helping the poor with renovations," the lancer answered. "Most of the sizable mansions next to the Cathedral of Light are now owned by the less fortunate."

"What? They always reserve those for the nobility!" one of the noble knights harrumphed.

Mel'Lark silenced him with a wave of his hand.

The officer shook her head. "Not here, not anymore. We give priority to the ones in greatest need to be close to a free meal and help. Many of them work for her on the orders of Lord Edward and Lady Tara." She raised an eyebrow challengingly at the knight who had spoken, but he didn't take the bait.

The cathedral square bustled with patrols coming and going. The waterless three-tiered fountain in the square beckoned, and the Hero of the Light, Ram'Del, stood ready for action. Everything about the place exuded life and an active commitment to protecting the people.

The officer and her light cavalry escort led them to the grand entrance and dismounted at the bottom of a long flight of thirty dark marble stairs. It ascended to the landing before the front door. "Allow us to take care of your mounts, my Lord. You can retrieve them from the stables when you're ready to leave. I would recommend spending the night. Someone will guide you once you're inside, so you won't get lost. Lady Tara has granted you access to the dining hall, my Lord."

Mel'Lark gave Lars a shrug. They dismounted, and the noble knights followed suit. At the top of the broad landing, two house guards in dark gray cloaks opened the doors and nodded for them to enter. "Enjoy your visit, my Lords and ladies," they said.

Inside, a white-liveried servant, a young and visibly nervous girl, awaited them in the hall. Mel'Lark smiled and asked, "And who might you be?"

"I am An'Na, the tailor's daughter," she curtsied. "I am here to escort you to Lady Tara." Her smile was radiant in her white livery.

"Well then, my Lady," the High King indulgently bowed, "lead the way." He gestured for his noble knights to do the same, and they bowed formally.

An'Na, the tailor's daughter, gave a dimpled smile, and guided them through a busy corridor to the main dining hall, where she curtsied and ushered them in.

The dining hall stretched before them, adorned with sturdy, dark stone tables, each hewn from the same material, capable of accommodating hundreds of guests. It was packed to capacity with many folks. An'Na led them to a table where two Priest Knights, a stocky man with icy eyes and brown hair, a stunning woman with long blonde hair, and a young Elp'harean girl with swirling lines on her face and black hair streaked with white at the bangs were seated. And, of course, Edward, Lars's son, was there. He had grown older, but Mel'Lark recognized him immediately. The rest of the table was empty.

Musicians hurried past them and took their places on an open balcony. The doors stood wide, allowing a gentle breeze to ruffle the curtains, cooling the room. Mel'Lark, Lars, and Heli'os followed young An'Na forward, and the people at the table with Lars's son stood up.

Mel'Lark turned to the young girl that had escorted them. "Thank you, An'Na," The High King said. She flashed him a smile, bobbed a curtsy, and left.

"I am Tara, and I welcome you to our fire," the young Elp'harean girl spoke. She gestured for them to take the empty seats at her table, then went to Lars and kissed him on the cheek. "I'm glad to see you again, Lars." She led him to the seat next to Edward.

Lars nodded to the High King. "Please, take a seat. Lady Tara isn't bound by formalities."

Mel'Lark gestured for all to sit. He took a seat opposite the blonde Priest Knight, with the commanding figure taking the head of the table. High Mage Heli'os chose a seat next to Mel'Lark, and as soon as he sat down, the others followed suit.

Tara nodded to the staff, and they promptly placed food in front of them. Plates, silverware, and serving staff in livery attended to them. It lacked the refinement of his own staff's service, but it was still well done. Mel'Lark tried to find the right words to describe it—it was like feeding a large family.

The musicians began playing, their music unfolding slowly and lyrically, a gentle invitation for bodies to sway and hearts to soften. The melody wove through the air, an embroidery of sound, its threads hinted at stories of love lingering on the edge of song. Some couples, drawn by the tender call, stood to dance in the area before the open balcony, their movements a testament to the song's pull.

As the singer's voice climbed, threading through the melody with grace and fervor, the beat of the music subtly shifted. What began as a slow caress of sound gradually quickened, as if the night itself whispered secrets of a faster, more joyous dance. The singer's tale evolved from the sweet anticipation of love to the exhilarating chase of hearts destined to meet. Just when the narrative reached its crescendo—the moment when the lass finally let the lad catch her—the music halted. A single tambourine shook with a loud, surprising jingle. The room erupted in laughter, a shared delight in the playful twist.

Then, as if the pause was a breath, the musicians leapt back into the song. The tempo soared, sweeping everyone into a rhythm that celebrated the joy of connection, the thrill of the dance.

Edward gave Tara a smile. "You set me up again, Tara." He stood, offering his hand.

Tara took it and stood, returning his smile mischievously. "Yes, I believe I did, Edward. You owe me a dance." They glided to the floor.

Edward and Tara, amidst the whirl of colors and laughter, found themselves caught in the music's embrace, their movements a dance of stories waiting to be told.

Edward spun Tara in a dance that felt like the heartbeat of the evening—each step, each turn, a word in the story as they wove together in the middle of the crowded hall. Tara's laughter mingled with the music, a melody in its own right, infectious and bright.

"Lars, your son is smitten," Mel'Lark remarked, watching the pair with a mixture of amusement and admiration.

Lars simply nodded, his eyes reflecting the pride and affection of a father witnessing his son's journey into love. "Yes, he is. But she is good for him, and he loves her."

As the music drew to a close, the applause filled the room, not just for the musicians, but for all who had shared in the dance. It was a moment of unity, a celebration of the many paths that had converged in this hall, under the banner of music and camaraderie, shared joy at the moment's simple beauty.

Edward and Tara returned, her cheeks flushed from laughing.

Lars then introduced the others. "High King, you've already met Lady Tara, and of course, you know Edward." Edward nodded. "This is Antoff Grant, the Lord Captain of the Warriors of the Light in Coth'Venter, and this is Al'len." They both nodded politely. "And this is High Mage Heli'os. I'm sure you've noticed his attire and staff. And these are the noble knights, our escort." Lars gestured towards them with a wave of his hand. Then he smiled at the food and the empty plates. Clapping his hand together with a fervent rub, "Let's eat."

"I see the son gets it from the father," Tara laughed. "I hope one day to meet his mother." The others joined in the laughter. Deep within, though, she regretted not taking the time to meet her while they were last in Havan. Edward and Lars made it clear Edward's mother would not accept her because she was not highborn. She had let it pass. But it hurt. She wanted so much to be her daughter.

Mel'Lark chuckled as well and started filling his plate. The Priest Knight with long blonde hair offered him a basket of steaming hot bread. He accepted one with a grateful smile. "Thank you, Priest Knight. You are too kind."

"Am I? I don't think you can be too kind, High King of the Lands of Light. Nevertheless, I am pleased to serve you," Al'len replied with a smile and a nod of her head.

Edward stood and extended his hand in a bow to Tara. She smiled and took it graciously. They moved to the dance floor, and the applause and music filled the room. More people joined them in dancing. Edward spun Tara around, and her laughter filled the air.

Mel'Lark surveyed the room, filled with people of all ranks—Lords, ladies, Priest Knights, clerics, tradespeople, merchants, and the poor. Everyone sat together, united as a people, one family. It defied conventional norms and societal rules, but it worked.

"So, where is this Maid of Light of yours, Antoff?" Mel'Lark inquired.

Antoff smiled at Al'len and then at Mel'Lark. "Oh, she's around."

Al'len stood up and looked at Antoff. "Where is my dance?" Her tone was more of a command.

Antoff rose as well. "As always, my Lady, I stand ready." He bowed formally and offered his hand.

Al'len accepted it, her deep blue eyes fixated on him. They glided to the dance floor, and the music slowed once more. Their dance was a seamless display of harmony, as if they were one.

Men and women approached the noble knights, asking them to dance. Initially, it seemed some would decline, but the High King's pleasant voice rang out, "Dance." And they danced, shedding their reservations, mingling, and smiling. The stiffness among them dissolved.

Lars stood and approached the dance floor, stepping into his son's dance with Tara. She smiled and danced with Lars, while his son stood by and waited until Lars graciously handed her back to him with a grin. A woman around Lars's age smiled at him and offered a dance. He danced with her and then with another. The music was warm, the singing enchanting, blending with the instruments.

Heli'os leaned over to Mel'Lark. "My Lord, this place is peculiar. The people are free, unbound by privilege or status. I don't understand how it works."

"Here, perhaps we can learn something, High Mage. Maybe it's not the place that matters, but the people. Maybe it's us who are strange." Mel'Lark thought.

Tara returned with Edward to the table, and he took his seat while she offered the High King a dance. Mel'Lark hesitated for only a moment before standing and taking her hand. Towering over her, just like Edward, he led her to the dance floor. She waited, and he placed a hand on her waist, beginning to dance. Tara exuded joy and grace, and he couldn't help but laugh along with her delight. This was who she was, and she shared it with him. She had noticed that he hadn't danced and that no one had asked him, so she took the initiative and made him a part of the wonderful celebration.

Mel'Lark studied Tara's face. The swirling lines that marked her as a Torrent Mage marred her beauty, but she cared for people, including him. "You are a Torrent Mage?"

"I am," Tara affirmed. "Does it frighten you?"

"I should be scared, Tara. You hold my entire realm in your hands," Mel'Lark responded. He gestured toward Heli'os. "Poor Heli'os is on the edge of his seat with fear. But no, Tara, I am not afraid. I gladly surrender." He bowed his head.

As the music ended, everyone applauded each other. The Warriors of the Light cheered for Antoff and Al'len. Mel'Lark led Tara back to her seat next to Edward.

"Thank you for the dance, Lady Tara. Edward, she is a remarkable young woman," Mel'Lark said.

Edward smiled at him. "She truly is. Just don't make her angry."

"Edward, you excel at that," Tara replied with a grin.

"I do not, Tara," Edward protested. "I can show you what I excel at after the dance." He gave a wink that colored her cheeks. *Oh, I am going to get it for that. But it was worth it, whatever the cost.*

Mel'Lark looked at Antoff. "I really need to speak to the Maid of Light."

Al'len answered him, "Come then, I will take you. You too, Heli'os, I know you have tests."

Al'len led them to the main chapel of the Cathedral of Light. It was getting late, and the nave lay empty, save for a monk who lit candles and left them to talk. Al'len led them to the front.

"Do I call her, or do we pray?" Mel'Lark asked.

"No, I am here." Al'len said. "I, Al'len, am her construct. EL'ALue, the Maid of Light, sleeps lightly yet. She wanted to be close to people, and I am approachable. Well, if you have something to say, say it. She is listening. I am listening."

High Mage Heli'os said, "I have tests to perform. If I may."

Al'len nodded. "I am ready."

Heli'os raised his staff, and the crystal burned bright. Liquid Power burst forth from his free hand in a stream that struck Al'len in the chest. She flinched slightly but stood tall; the Power did not breach her shield. The High Mage poured more Power, and the beam of light crackled with energy. He released it, and the staff stilled to a flicker. "I cannot damage you. Even as a construct, if you were not a god, I would have destroyed you. Lord High King, I certify that this is EL'ALue, the Maid of Light, even though she is a construct." They tried to kneel.

"You don't need to do that. I will keep that for those who have sworn to serve, and I will not allow that as long as you lie to the people," Al'len said.

Mel'Lark flinched as if she had slapped him. "I don't understand?"

"I needed time to recover. Ram'Del's loss was too great. It was my fault, and if I had been wiser…" Al'len shook her head. "I was mortal once. Did you know that?"

Again, Mel'Lark was taken aback. "No, I did not."

"We were all Torrent once. Like Tara, we emerged one day and, in time, ascended. She does not know that she emerged. The things she is dealing with are difficult, and she does not need the stress. Can you understand?" Al'len asked.

Mel'Lark shook his head. "No."

With a compassionate smile, Al'len replied, "There, you see, the truth is better. I don't remember being born. One day, I just was. I was a child and grew and learned, and then I ascended. I live in the higher reality and the lower at the same time. People are important to me. I need them. Without them, I would vanish. I would lose my connection and completely disappear into the higher reality. I don't know what I would become or if I would even care anymore. We need each other. It is a secret that we don't tell anyone. Connecting ourselves to people is an anchor in the lesser reality. Now do you understand?"

"I think so," Mel'Lark said.

"I cannot accept less. It would diminish me and bring me closer to the abyss. Everyone joined to my life affects the surrounding reality. This can hurt people if you are the wrong one. I will not risk it. Make things right if you want to give your oath. But it's your choice. You can join the fight if you want in the condition you are in, but know this: Right now, you are both frauds," She accused. "Now, if you're finished with your test, I will return to the people I love." Al'len turned and left them there alone.

High Mage Heli'os looked at Mel'Lark. "She speaks the truth, my Lord. We have been complicit in the deception. It is time to make amends and stand on the side of truth."

Mel'Lark nodded solemnly. "You are right, Heli'os."

In the chapel's hushed stillness, Mel'Lark and Heli'os vowed to rectify their past deceits, pledging allegiance to EL'ALue, the Maid of Light's true mission. Their journey had taken an unexpected turn, but they were ready to embrace the path of honesty and loyalty, not just for themselves, but for their people.

Chapter 24 Blood And Blades

"A heavy darkness looms, enveloping the heart's last hopes. You find yourself adrift. Every attempt has faltered and your cries have fallen on deaf ears. The aftermath of decisions bears down incessantly, an unyielding burden. This is a test. Be cautious when the malevolent force offers its sinister invitation and tempting bargains arise. In that moment, the balance irreversibly shifts, spiraling into depths unknown. If you accept it, you may already be beyond redemption."

Dust devils twisted across dark plains, dancing like masterless creatures beyond the looming fortress of Are'Amadon. Silver moonlight bathed the jagged mountains that bordered the Twisted Lands.

Seated cross-legged between two crenels above the gate, Moros seemed lost in contemplation. Beneath obsidian leather, the boy's charcoal-gray silks fluttered in a biting, thirsty breeze. He faced the border of the Twisted Lands, his gaze fixed on something beyond Rem'Mel's perception. A dark aura pulsed from the child's body, electrifying the air.

The swirling markings adorning Moros' cheeks, a fading remnant of a perilous experiment with the Power of Darkness that had shrouded the Blackened Lands. Great Lord Amorath had sternly forbidden him from attempting it anew, yet Rem'Mel had glimpsed fear in his master's undead eyes. The boy was on the verge of overpowering him, and Amorath knew it.

"What are you watching, Moros?" Rem'Mel asked, his voice quiet so as not to startle the boy.

Moros turned, speaking as though his words traversed distant realms. "I'm currently winding back time to witness dragons melting Zoruks at the border. A few days ago, I sent little Modred with the mages through their Gate. By seeing through his eyes, I can walk time back."

Rem'Mel shuddered. "You are here, and that is many leagues away. The images are gone; time has moved on. How can you see what is already gone?" *If I didn't know the child better, I'd think he was lying.*

"Time is not lost." Moros explained. "It's different in the higher planes, like looking through a warped lens. Amorath forbade me from sharing this with you. I disagree with his decision. I find it unfair. What say you, Middle Mage?" Moros asked, his smile spreading across chapped lips, eyes glinting with knowledge. Anticipating Rem'Mel's eager nod.

Why is he using my title? He's only ever called me Rem'Mel, he thought, his red office garb fluttering in a sudden gust of stinging sand. "I would like to know, but not if it is going to get you in trouble with Great Lord Amorath."

Rem'Mel watched Moros' lips curl into a wicked smile. "I adjusted his teachings to combine viewing and sounding. Are you familiar with these concepts?" Moros probed.

"I am, Lord Moros," he said, giving the boy the same formal respect he received.

Moros nodded. "As long as you know where you are in time, you can walk it back, but never forward. That cannot be done with the Power. Though I have read a tome that spoke of premonitions, and I believe it is an echo from the future. Okay, do you remember the little copy of Modred that I constructed?"

"Yes, I have not seen him for days. I did not know where he went," Rem'Mel said, raising an eyebrow. He hung on the boy's every word.

"I sent him through the Gate the mages made," Moros continued, sensing Rem'Mel's growing anticipation. "I've maintained a connection since, watching their actions—like using a viewing and a sounding combined. His eyes have liquid, as does his blood. Once rooted, I froze one image in my mind: the wall and gate as they were. Then I moved backward until the outlines of the dragons overlapped. It's grainy and distorted, yet I could watch it. And now that I have seen them in time, I could make it." Moros gently tapped his temple with a finger, his eyes distant. "It makes me dizzy, which is why I'm sitting while doing it."

Rem'Mel's mouth gaped, and his teeth clamped shut in realization. His thoughts raced as he absorbed what Moros was saying. "So, you can see past events as if they're still happening?" He questioned, his curiosity piqued. "The idea of the liquid in the eye is a fascinating one, but if the creature is moving, how do you maintain your connection? I mean, the liquid has to be still to keep a seamless connection for me to use it," Rem'Mel questioned, waiting for the boy's answer.

"Possession, Rem'Mel. I employ possession," Moros replied, turning his gaze back to the border.

Rem'Mel's face paled. "I thought only the entities alone have the talent of possession, my Lord?"

"Yes, it was theirs alone until I took it." Moros fell silent, and Rem'Mel's class was over.

Firerocks smoldered, plummeting through a torn sky, resembling meteors ejected from the volcanoes that dominated the jagged mountain flanks. From there, molten stone cascaded into a vast crevasse, forming a river that spanned leagues in width. Amidst the smoke-shrouded peaks, bolts of lightning split the orange sky. The mountains exhaled a rancid, acrid plume that veiled the air in choking ash.

The lone red-amber sun hung low, its light quivering, as though viewed through a viscous, heat-soaked haze. Bat-like creatures waged war in two massive flocks, feasting on the fallen. "Demons," Mist mouthed, tasting the words—laden with cinders and sulfur. She searched for her master and avoided the battle that raged in a mass of tangled forms tearing at each other.

This world's cruelty was only rivaled by that of the Dominion. In this realm, her master had once been the strongest demon ruler before vanishing a millennium ago. *This war no doubt had erupted because of his return*, Mist thought. He would need to gather followers and reassert his dominance to rule the realm once more.

Unlike the demons surrounding her, Mist stood as a unique hybrid, her existence a blend of her master's essence and her Vam'Phire lineage. She feared them, finding their existence aimless beyond their insatiable desires for war and feeding. It was not her demon side that had saved her in this horrid place. It was her Vam'Phire lineage that granted her the ability to fold into shadow. *Clearly, my yearning for books and civilized society didn't come from these creatures.*

For days, the hunt had sapped Mist's supplies. Surface water was scarce, and what bubbled up was tainted with sulfurous brine. No, the water was in deep pits within caves and they guarded it as treasure. In this realm, they were treasures surpassed in value only by the rare forms of life that the weakest of the demon kind, unfit for war, could cultivate. In the cover of darkness, Mist had stolen water—a feat not to be underestimated considering the strength of their guarding force.

Her Vam'Phire lineage had guided her through the crisis. Shadows clung to the cave walls, where dim light flickered from braziers spaced every twenty feet within the cavern's depths. She employed the shadows as her cloak, venturing out briefly to get what she required, then seamlessly melding back into the obscurity. Food, however, was something else. *I am not eating what these barbarians do. That is certain! If it comes to that, I'll abandon both this realm and my master.* The conflict between wanting to please him and fearing the introduction of this madness into her world was too great.

Mist's gaze locked onto her master, the towering figure commanding his faction's forces from the epicenter of the battle. He tore into flesh with the ferocity of a starved beast. *This entire world is madness, even worse than ours. I cannot release it on us.* Crouching within the shadow of the mountain, Mist concealed herself among the scorching, twisted rocks. When her master's gaze met hers, a surge of fear gripped her—not just for her own safety, but for the fate of her entire world. *I should've left him,* she thought, her heart sinking as regret washed over her. *What have I done? These creatures are eaters of worlds.*

The Dominion descended from an embattled sky, landing nearby. Raising a hand, he signaled for her to remain hidden. The imminent danger was apparent, one he wasn't certain he could shield her from. *Now that I'm trapped, I have made my decision.* He walked over to her, his steps stirring up the volcanic dust that covered the ground, sending a fog of particles and dust that cloaked her. Lowering his mass to sit on the rock, she huddled by the cover his bulk provided.

His hiss barely broke through the world's roaring fury. "I am not ready to leave. The political climate is unstable, and I'm battling to reclaim my leadership. A usurper sits my throne, dug in deep after an epoch, and destroying his rule is going slower than I hoped."

A thick stench, a vile mix of blood, sweat, and sulfur, enveloped him, and Mist felt a wave of nausea. "I've invested time that I hadn't believed necessary. I trusted that, when I came back, the world would be as it was. The new Reaver is of my blood and, though he is not as powerful, he has most of the Firewrought following him. Go home Mist. In one month, have the mage open the portal. Either I established my rule by then, or I will have died in the attempt. Have no fear your world's reckoning is coming. Now go."

Consumed by fear, Mist folded herself into the shadows and vanished.

***

The plain coach rocked violently as it transitioned from the hard-packed dirt road to the cobbled paving of Scale Bay. The Mer' Gulls cried, their leathery wings flapping, hovering above the gray-green harbor. On'omus peered through the curtained window, watching seaside buildings roll by.

The coach shuttered to a halt as they reached the inn. A large sign painted in the blue-green of the bay trimmed in a red and held a picture of a tall ship docked and the words Harbor Inn across the top.

With a sigh of relief, Er'laya exclaimed, "Finally." His general attitude during the trip had slid from frustration to snapping at everything and then silence for the last day of travel. The mood being brought on by On'omus incessantly babbling about warrants and some such. His belief was that the withdrawal of money from the Haven parish was theft, and he expected it would result in the issuance of a warrant, possibly attracting a tracker or bounty hunter. Er'laya scoffed, *The High Seat, otherwise known as the "Grand Pilferer" in the bishopric circles, had laid hard levies on each parish for years to fill his personal coffers. It is what I am due.*

When the coachman opened the door, Er'laya and On'omus piled out. On'omus, the last to step out, followed his *'High Plumpness'* from the coach and took in the night air, filled with the salt of the sea and the relaxing sounds of the Mer' Gulls, only broken by the laughter drifting out of the open window of the inn's common room.

The footmen carried the chest containing all their belongings and a considerable number of gold coins, On'omus noted, during their brief stop to stretch. The journey required brief stops to water and feed the horses. Er'laya had taken time to pack the trunk at the last village and buy new clothing. Not a bad cut mind, but a fine local stitch that well-to-do travelers or merchants would wear.

Er'laya's new blue attire contrasted with his light brown jacket, a change from the robes they had burned.

Er'laya had given him a purse to purchase new attire in Scale Bay while he hired a ship to take them across the sea. On'omus had never been to the Shelf. It was a completely different continent and it would be a long voyage to get there if they could find a fast ship. If it was a cargo vessel, it would be intolerably long. This, however, was the choice he had made to throw his lot in with Er'laya, and he was now stuck with it. The only hope was that they could find a ship, any ship, to get them off this island before the bill came due and the High King collected.

Er'laya led the way into the common room, bustling with sailors. On'omus followed to the bar, greeted by a gnarled old sailor who seemed to have taken over from another just as crooked. They ended up belly-to-bar, greeted by a sea-hardened old' coot who looked like he'd won the place in a wager from the last old' coot who ran it. "Arr, me fine gents, reckon yer in the market for a bunk 'n a bellyful, aye?"

Er'laya gave him a perfunctory nod, "and we are looking to hire passage to the Shelf. If you have anyone in mind with a fast ship, I will make it worth your while to make an introduction." He slid a gold coin to him under a pudgy finger.

"Ah, ye heard right, ye did. Aren't many that go straight to the Shelf round here? Ships drop anchor and weigh it by the day, so ye won't be high 'n dry for long. That's me salt's promise." With a flick of his wrist, the gold coin vanished into the depths of his jingling pouch.

Leaning forward, Er'laya lowered his voice. "I don't want anyone knowing my business. I have a deal cooking on the Shelf, so I want to keep it quiet. Ya get me?" He gave him a wink.

The old sailor nodded. "As ta dat, no one be hearing it from me."

"Good, we need a room for the two of us, and the footmen can sleep with the coach and horses in the stable. We will take our meals in our room. Please send the captain to us when you locate a ship and I will give you five more gold marks for your hard work and your silence."

The following morning, High King Mel'Lark and Lars departed for Haven through a Mage Gate. High Mage Heli'os had chosen the return Gate's location with confidence, ensuring a swift return if his Lord desired it. It looked like the whole of Coth'Venter sent them off. There was little question but, it was for Lady Tara that they turned out.

Heli'os returned to the same location where they had left the hunters and beaters, so as not to take a risk of harming anyone when the Gate opened. From there, it was only a brief ride of several leagues from Haven. High King Mel'Lark and Lord Lars went through the Gate first, followed by the knights. Heli'os waited, shooting one last glance at Al'len as he rode his mount through. Purple light strobed near the forest, causing the forms of mortals to shutter in the light. As soon as he was clear, he let the gate drop. Already he could hear his liege giving orders to pack up for the trip back to Haven.

"The hunt went well." Lars commented to Mel'Lark, eyeing the deer and the razor-sharp tusks of Ne'lear boars, now safely covered in leather and secured on the horses. The hounds danced around the kills, barking.

"After our visit to Coth'Venter, my taste for the hunt has waned. I intend to present Al'len to the Holy Seat for explanations. She has given us a way out for ourselves and the rest of the nobility. I intend to take her up on it."

"Surely, you don't intend to tell him the truth? He would never consent to go." Lars had a little curl on his lips, as if he already knew the answer.

Mel'Lark gave a laugh that sounded more like a bark. "No, I do not. I will tell him the truth. We are moving the army to Coth'Venter because half of our Priest Knight and Cleric troops are going there anyway. I would just as soon have no misunderstandings when we march for the border."

"He is going to have questions." Lars said.

"Let him." Mel'Lark nodded. "Yes, and I am telling him I met Al'len and have come to terms with her. That will be beneficial to the realm. I am waiting for him to meet with her and confirm that she is who she said she is. I can tell him in honesty that she gave no signs of divinity to me and therefore he can deal with it in whatever manner he sees fit."

Lars' smile spread across his face. "You know, he is going to think you are telling him she is a fake and that he will figure that he can denounce her and divest himself from the situation for good. That is a nasty ploy, my king. Let's hope it works."

Chapter 25 Discovery

"Wounds of trust make hollow echoing spaces in others. Places filled with brokenness and bitter loss. Like a man in chains plunged into a bottomless sea and drifting amidst the wreckage of promises uttered. Seek not hope or rescue from these depths, for they will elude you. For those who forsake others, have sewn the wind, only desertion's icy embrace awaits beneath the weight of faithless words."

Ivan knelt, shadows from the arches above engulfing him, the chill of the stone seeping deep—a stark reminder of his solitude. Lil's absence carved an inescapable void within him, her silence a labyrinth with no exit. He clenched his fists, the cold, lonely stone beneath his palms a physical echo of the turmoil within. He knew he'd done something wrong. In the past, Da'Vain had always sought him out when troubled. This time, he hadn't. *Whatever I've done, it must be serious if he won't speak to me about it.* Anger flared within him. *The Seven Hells! I don't even know what I have done to drive her away.*

Ivan's fury surged at the end of his patience. There was nothing else left to do. If Da'Vain would not come to him, he would command his presence. His mind spread like a shadowy veil permeating the halls. Every member of his coven would hear it. They had wanted to know him; now they would. *Da'Vain!* Ivan's mind bellowed like a gong, echoing through the thoughts of all who dwelt below—and likely some who did not—for all he cared. *The entire world could hear his call for all he cared!*

Da'Vain appeared as though conjured from the shadows. Hand on heart, he bowed deeply. "As you summon my prince, so have I come."

Normally, there was mirth and even closeness between them, but Ivan cared little for that now and had no patience for trifling. Ivan refrained from using his mental abilities, knowing he was but an apprentice against Da'Vain's mastery. The older Vam'Phire far outmatched him in mental maneuvering. His voice emerged like a blade, a rasping edge of steel. "Tell me where she is. Tell me what I've done. And never withhold information from me again. This, I command."

Da'Vain fidgeted with the buckle of his leather overcoat. "I did not want to tell you, my Lord prince. Lil, she is like a daughter to me and made me promise to keep you from danger."

Ivan's voice cracked like a whip. "Speak!" The word wasn't just a command; it was a plea, laced with the sting of betrayal. His eyes narrowed, a silent testament to the trust fraying at the edges. "Keep your mind open to me," he continued, each word measured, heavy with the weight of his authority and the unspoken hurt beneath. "Your secret dealings with Lil—they've chipped away at the trust you once held with your liege." His posture stiffened, the next words coming out as a cold, hard truth, "Deceive me now, and what's left of our friendship will crumble to dust."

"My Lord prince, I told Lil that I would only do as she asked this once, and only until you demanded it of me." His mind was open and crystal clear. Da'Vain replayed the conversation in his mind, encompassing the imagery from his perspective. First, Da'Vain shared his own perspective of the conversation, and then he shifted to present it through Lil's eyes—all complete with the rich emotions that had accompanied the original exchange.

"You must tell him, Lil. Ivan is your prince and your lover. I have waited until now to speak to him about the lottery. Waited for you to explain the fundamentals of our existence. The very thing I assigned you to him for. You have shirked your responsibilities for the sake of your desires for each other. What did you think was going to happen when he finds out? Lil, you are not an untrained child."

Lil's voice, a chided daughter. One who had failed a father in a duty. "Forgive me, Lord Chronicler, he took me, my heart and mind, the first day. I believed I would have time before the next lottery to tell him. It had only been a year since last chosen and then five before. I hoped for more time."

"Time for what? To ensnare him deeper? Time does not wait for us, girl; we wait for it. And failing time has its consequences. You've left me with little choice, child." His voice went soft, but only for a moment. Then it came back deep and powerful. "I must now inform the prince and you will be there when I do it." Da'Vain's voice in Lil's mind shook with a father's anger. "You have placed us both at the hazard of our Lord and his friendship to foster your love. You have sacrificed one for the other." Da'Vain's mind, a father that wanted to turn a daughter over his knee.

"Let me do this, please. It is my fault. I will return in a day or two and you need not get involved. I will confess it all to Ivan and do my duty as I should have. His training is my responsibility, and I have failed you in it. Allow me to make it right." There was a daughter's pleading in that voice.

"Lil, you have been my greatest student. See that you do not become my worst failure." Fury welled up within Da'Vain, becoming too powerful to contain.

With that Lil curtsied, hand on heart and was gone. She fled, the shadows took her.

Evenings salt air echoed with the screeches of Mer' Gulls. On'omus stood on the balcony, surveying Scale Bay's bustling street, his fingers tracing the rough wood rail. The nights were pleasant, thanks to the sea breeze, if one could overlook the drunken sailors and their fistfights over women. The wooden balcony stretched the length of the inn. Back when this had been a smugglers' port before, with muddy streets, beneath the notice of the Order of the Light, this had been an establishment for other comforts. Long lines of different flavors would stand up here and display their wares while calling out to smugglers fresh into port. On'omus felt as if he needed to wash his hands after that thought. Still, the Little Sister's sun sets were without peer, as they reflected the last light on to a rolling green-blue sea.

Er'laya sat in the inn's common room, enjoying time alone without On'omus. The wine was watered, far from fresh, and expensive for swill. Still, he enjoyed the liveliness of the place, despite the half-eaten plate of fish before him. The fare hadn't been bad—if you could hold your nose while eating it. Abandoning his meal, he turned his attention to watching drunken patrons attempt to dance with an uninterested maid, only to be ushered away by bouncers. Then tossed out for their trouble, leaving a weak smile on Er'laya's face.

While lost in his reverie, Er'laya was oblivious. He didn't notice the woman with a cutlass and a wide-brimmed leather hat step up. She cleared her throat on a bit of ale, lifting the mug to a thirsty mouth. Er'laya nearly leaped out of his skin before recovering a shred of dignity. "May I help you?"

"The innkeeper tells me yea be lookin' for a ship headin' to the Shelf. I'm Jen, captain of the Sea Mare. Interested in comin' aboard?"

Er'laya eyed her, dressed in all brown leather with a green blouse and hooped rings dangling below her hat. The one thing for sure was she had a penetrating stare, brown eyes that could burn a man to ash if he wasted her time. "Take a seat, captain Jen and tell me of this ship of yours. How soon are you leaving?"

"The Sea Mare's a sturdy vessel, fast and well-stocked for island trips. We'll be breakin' bay waters in a bell—that's three hours to you. As for the cost, that depends on yer cargo."

"Just two people a trunk and no questions, captain." Er'laya answered.

"So ye're lookin' to slip out unseen, eh? The Port Master's got eyes everywhere—you won't get by without help. Fifty gold per head for passage, and another fifty for discretion. Yer three trunks stay hidden till we're outta port. Yea, catch me drift?" She flipped a rolled paper at him.

Er'laya gingerly opened the paper, his throat tightening as he swallowed hard. It was his and On'omus likeness on the paper. His voice came out as a squeak. "We will take the passage, captain. Follow me to the room above and I will get the first half of your gold in advance and get packed for the voyage." He stood and led the way.

Life pulsed, and it called to Lil. The blood of mortals thundered in her ears. Images flooded her senses; their forms were akin to the branches of a forest, and the veins of hammering hearts bathed her in hot vitality. She prowled like a predator among bleating prey. Outwardly, she was a passive traveler, dressed in black leather britches and a matching coat that curved with ample hips, bearing a short sword. Her unbuttoned jacket and open gray silk blouse granted a view that kept few secrets. Her hair of black ringlets spilled to her waist. Mortals, regardless of their persuasion, could only describe her breathlessly, as hauntingly perfect.

She was searching, employing every advantage like a hunter in a blind. Lil's physical form was just part of the bait. She was not just a physical lure; she exuded pheromones that attracted subtle glances and desire. Yes, a huntress in the blind and Lil had spied her target. Her ears pulling words at a distance and their untrained mind ejecting every thought for those who possessed the powers to listen.

Er'laya walked up the stairs to his room, a woman with a leather hat in tow. Their eyes tracked over Lil, far from dismissive. They'd remember her.

Jen, captain of the Sea Mare, had another plan and secreting them away was just the first part. Once confined to those trunks, bidding would start at another port, and only the highest bidder would release them, like opening a gift. The price on the warrant was ten thousand gold, dead or alive. Lil would get that plus all the essence of his life for her coven. She had meant to tell Ivan how they survived. She had just not gotten around to it yet. Indeed, he'd wondered how they'd endured epochs without openly hunting mortals. This pact with the rulers and authorities of El'idar was ancient and would require a great deal of explanation for him to accept it.

That was not the reason Lil hesitated. With each explanation, Ivan would draw closer to her most hidden secret and it would rock the very foundation of the coven's relationship with the people now living in Coth'Venter. More important to her than that was her friendship with Tara. She needed to figure out how to explain it to her first, before it all came out.

Chapter 26 Overpriced Package

"Desire—a relentless swelling storm. It swallows you up with endless hunger, smashing down in waves of want, shattering faith, and scattering the fragments of a blissful existence."

The thick air of the Harbor Inn clung to Lil's skin like a humid silk shroud, rich with the primal scents of blood and sex. A storm of mortality and carnal desire enveloped her. Like a lover's urgent embrace, each heartbeat, a drum of forbidden desire thundered, quickening her pulse. Restless within, a ravenous creature stirred and paced, wanting to break free and devour the world beyond her skin. Her thoughts became a whirlwind of want, shattering the fragile facade of self-control. If they could read her thoughts as she read theirs, would these people reckon her among the undead? But she was not. To call her undead was imprecise; it hinted at a lack of self-contained life rather than true death. She had a life, one with Ivan, and she wanted to live it. Vam'Phires sustained themselves by stealing life from others. She had to be vigilant, for in her darkest moments, she could see them as little more than cattle.

The coven's lottery system for assigning contracts introduced ethical complexities that burdened Lil. *It is not as if I want to do it.* Her mind interjected. They randomly choose within the coven to perform the assassination for the agreed-upon price. They relentlessly hunt until they successfully catch the subject, regardless of the effort required. The service must never fail. The service was infallible, offering a reliability that surpassed ordinary mortal capabilities. Only the life from the condemned extracted, not the innocent. Not lost in a senseless killing. This had a purpose. The vita refined to its essence, then distributed among the coven. No mortal would see the justice in killing for a price, discriminately or not. *What will Tara think? Will she think me a monster when she learns? And when she does, will she call me her friend or rid herself of me, like a serpent shedding a filthy skin?*

After Er'laya and Captain Jen disappeared upstairs, Lil abandoned her watch. Moving like a silent specter, she navigated the tavern's maze of tables, adrift among fading laughter, the clink of mugs, and minds leaked their darker mortal appetites as their eyes passed over her. Lil felt coated in a coil of mortal slime. She wanted to suppress it. If she did not, her emotions would overwhelm her and her control would slip away. *I will need a bath when this is over.* Stepping outside, the night wrapped around her, a cloak of sea salt and a musty stable. Her presence, as light as a whisper, silently crossed the inn's yard to the wagon gate. The street, marred by missing cobbles and deep etchings from countless unseen passersby, lay shrouded in the night's embrace—a silent witness to untold stories.

An hour later, six sailors labored with two heavy trunks, their muscles bulging, before returning for a third. Captain Jen's authority was clear not in her stride but in the casual yet confident grip on her cutlass—a silent vow of the peril hidden beneath her calm. "Gently, me boys," she purred, "We wouldn't want to spoil the goods, would we?"

Shadows danced in serpentine swirls around Lil, enshrouding her in a cloak of darkness. Suddenly, with precision, these tendrils of blackness slid towards her. In a movement as quick as a strike, the shadow consumed her. The mist lingered momentarily in long wisps of smoke. She became a shade of death, moving in eerie silence, cloaked in supernatural Darkness. The lamps and torches shone through like a bright fog, vivid against the black backdrop. The captain and the sailors, carrying trunks, appeared as mere specters, outlined but devoid of shadow—a pale semblance of life.

Lil followed to the harbor and down the foggy docks, using the shadows of crates and barrows to hide. Only just keeping her prey in view. The harbor guard briefly halted the procession to accept a bribe, passing ghostlike figures of sailors and dock hands at work. Reaching their ship, the Sea Mare—a tall, sleek two-master—loomed out of a supernatural fog, as if straddling the realms of the living and the dead. If she had known how long it would take, she might have investigated the ship first. Yet too many variables had made that risky. This time staying the course had paid off.

Lil hesitated at the gangplank, her heart a tumult of fear and resolve. She followed up to the deck and then went below.

The Neal 'Lance glided through a windblown sea. The ship split the swells, topping the liquid hills that rose and fell in rhythmic waves. Wet sails billowed and snapped with each gusting spray. Bare feet thumped on deck planks above. Then the call echoed.

"Land!" The shouts through the open porthole drew Va'Yone's nose from his book. Bounding up, he ran for De'Nidra's and Tem'Aldar's room. His hurried steps nearly sent him tumbling as the ship pitched and rolled. Sliding before the door, he excitedly hammered on the hardwood surface. "De'Nidra, Land!"

"You better come in and escort me on deck before Tem'Aldar steals the job," she said, her voice filled with amusement.

Va'Yone burst through the door, his youthful energy lighting the room. De'Nidra, in a scarlet gown that emphasized her curves, laughed warmly at him. "Eager, aren't we?" she teased, her voice mixed with amusement. The lace at her gown's hem flirting with her sturdy boots, a contrast of delicacy and strength as her quill scratched away. Va'Yone fidgeted. He would burst if she didn't finish soon.

The dark leathers hugging his form made of the skin of bats. De'Nidra was eager to discard them as rags. He was her charge now, and he was going to have a proper education and that included dressing the part. Besides, everything was so new for him and she loved watching him discover. Clothing and all the different styles were just one more thing new to learn.

"Come on, De'Nidra," Va'Yone urged, "let's not miss it. I bet Tem'Aldar is already on deck, waiting for us." He said with sincerity. He was missing out on the excitement and wanted De'Nidra to be part of it.

She winked. "Very well. Escort me to the deck for a view of the island and some fresh air." She found amusement in teaching him to wait on a lady. Pitting Tem'Aldar and Va'Yone against each other for her affection was entertaining, and their efforts to win her time always added a special touch. She stood and smoothed her dress. Va'Yone was awash with anticipation when she offered her hand with a smile.

He couldn't contain his excitement. Seizing De'Nidra's hand, practically pulling her from the room. "Please, De'Nidra," he urged, "let's not miss it. Tem'Aldar is probably already on deck, waiting." His eyes sparkled with youthful enthusiasm.

She quickened her pace to appease the young man, and they nearly stumbled as they reached the deck, slick with sea spray. True to form, Tem'Aldar stood on the top deck, using the captain's spyglass to survey the harbor. He was dashing in his roguish way, and he gave her an appraising eye and a presuming smile when Va'Yone dragged her to a stop before the rail.

He handed Va'Yone the glass, and the port harbor of the Island of Far'Mora leaped into view. A tower stood atop a stone foundation. A lone globe of light floated above it. "What is it?" His voice was breathless.

"Shoal Tower," De'Nidra answered. It rode out the waves alone atop a stone foundation. Beyond it, fern covered branches of the Frump trees intertwined overhead, creating a lush canopy like a jungle. It spread across the shoreline and extended deep into the interior. The late morning suns, Elder Brother nearing its zenith and its smaller companion, a swollen red orb just above the horizon, bathed the world in radiant light, promising heat to match the sea air's humidity.

Far'Mora Harbor, its jetty extending into a foam-tossed sea, and its busy wooden structures clinging to the shoreline, presented a lively scene. The buildings, capped at two stories save for their flood-proof stone foundations, boasted roofs of shake and red clay tile. Balconies wrapped the structures, overlooking streets that turned from muddy to solid as they climbed the hill.

Va'Yone froze. His eye fixed on the spyglass, utterly captivated by the approaching harbor. Holding onto the rail with the other hand, he drank in the newness of it all.

A gentle touch on his shoulder jolted Va'Yone back to reality. "We can't linger. We need to pack and secure lodging at an inn for tonight. Tomorrow, we'll need fresh clothing for our dig."

Va'Yone lowered the spyglass and gave it back to Tem'Aldar. "You're right. I have little to pack, but the sooner I get it done, the faster we can get to exploring. When we have our rooms at the inn, I mean. You're coming with me when I go shopping, right, De'Nidra?"

"Yes, and after, we are going to buy horses, tack, and supplies. It will be a full day, and no time to dally." De'Nidra held out a hand, and he took it. Tem'Aldar stayed above while they went below to pack. He was a Priest Knight, after all, and was likely packed all ready.

Soon, the ship sailed into the calm waters of the harbor, its wooden hull thumping against the docks roped and moored. Sailors extended the gangplank, and Va'Yone waited at the rail until De'Nidra and Tem'Aldar joined him. Va'Yone carried his backpack, and two sailors carried an enormous trunk to a red wagon. It waited on the docks when they walked down the plank, bouncing a little under their weight. After so long at sea, he found the land's stability disconcerting. Having grown accustomed to the ship's constant movement, Va'Yone now found the ground unsettlingly stable. The sailors had called it having your sea legs, but he was just glad to be on a substrate that did not pitch nor roll out from under him while he walked.

Tem'Aldar, Tem for short, placed him in the back of the wagon alongside the sea chest. "Up you get lad," He said before helping De'Nidra to her place on the wagons bench. He took a seat beside her. The wagon master, a burly figure with a thick leather whip in hand. It cracked across the backs of the two Hurdbeasts pulling the wagon. With a sharp crack and a surge of effort, the creatures lurched forward, their muscles straining against the load. En route to the inn, every divot and rut in the road jostled the wagon, its metal-clad wheels clattering noisily.

Above, Mur 'Gul's soared in graceful circles, accompanied by a larger, pink-scaled lizard that plunged into the water and emerged triumphantly with a wriggling fish in its hooked talons. Like the animals, the people wore bright colors, baggy shirts, and britches; they were boisterous in a good-natured way. Women in colorful, low-cut dresses leaned over the balconies, their voices ringing out with affectionate greetings. "The women are friendly here, De'Nidra."

"Yes and expensive, that affection cost coin, my young apprentice. Coin that you can't spare." That last part said with a note of disdain.

Va'Yone's brow furrowed in confusion. "What do you mean it costs good coin to give affection?"

Tem, with a knowing smirk, leaned in. "Lad, affection in these parts can be more costly than you think. And if De'Nidra catches you spending your coin foolishly, you'll learn a whole new kind of expense. But that's a tale for later."

"Proper women don't require coin to be affectionate. You will not explain more than he needs to know," De'Nidra said with a sniff, as though that answered everything and put an end to it. Her cheeks colored, and that made her even more beautiful when angry.

"Of course, master."

That earned him a wink and a lovely smile.

"One day, a young woman will catch your eye and hold it all your days. Do not waste your time on the meaningless. The memories of it will taint the worthwhile with regret." There was a sad wisdom in her words laced with experience and hope that Va'Yone would have better than she had under her watchful eye. "I will make a man of you. One for which I will have a deep respect. You will be a man that towers above his stature."

Tem grinned with a hint of mischief. "You've stirred the pot, lad. She's taken an interest in you. That means your current state is in jeopardy, and likely to change." His face both held a look of hope and pity at the same time. "De'Nidra is relentless, if nothing else. You're trapped, and the best you can do is buckle down and work hard. Less than that will be—painful."

"I love her. As a sister, I mean you understand, Tem?" Va'Yone said. "And she is wise, having knowledge that I cannot find just anywhere else." He looked around, making sure his words were for them alone. The wagon driver seemed engrossed in avoiding pedestrians who had a talent for bounding into traffic without looking. "She is worth it. If there is a price. I will pay it."

De'Nidra's dark eyes bore into him like a stern schoolmaster. "You will pay in hard labor, sweat and tears. You will curse me and praise me. Struggle to understand. You will fail and triumph. In the end, I hope you remember you love me."

The wagon came to a halt outside the Jib and Prow inn. The building's sign had a ship's prow extending out with a blowing sail carved from a light wood. It was painted a green sea and white spray coming off a tall ship. The side of the ship bore the name Jib and Prow in deep red letters.

Tem jump to the hard-packed street rutted by wheels from the last rains. Offering his hand to De'Nidra, he helped her down and then lifted Va'Yone out as well. The wagon driver helped Tem carry the sea chest inside. De'Nidra waited for them at the bar with the keys to their rooms next to an open stairway. Tem and the wagon master struggled under the load of the sea trunk as she led the way up a narrow set of stairs above.

The rooms mirrored a ship's quarters, with tables and chairs securely bolted, beds and sea chests at each end, and square windows lit by swiveling ship lamps. Every detail whispered of the decorator's nautical penchant. After spending the time at sea. It made Va'Yone feel more comfortable in a strange land.

Va'Yone pulled off his backpack, the outline of the book of magic that Lil had translated clearly embossed in the leather. He placed it in the sea chest at the end of his bed, before heading for De'Nidra's and Tem's room. The rooms were stuffed along a narrow hallway. The inn's staff passed, carrying laundry in from the wash. He barely had room to turn sideways before a young woman with arms loaded with a basket nearly knocked him down. She gave an embarrassed smile and a curtsy—well, almost a curtsy, loaded with a laundry basket as she was.

"Sorry my Lord." She said with a rosy-cheeked smile.

She was appealingly tall, even in a world where height was the norm. Long blond, brown hair and deep almond eyes as equally brown and inviting as her face. She was attractive. In another dress, not the drab gray of a servant. Something bright and expensive. She would look every bit the high-born lady. Va'Yone swept a bow and gave an impressive leg. "My Lady." That brought a deeper red to her cheeks that set off an even warmer glow, adding to her charm. She raced past almost at a run.

Va'Yone turned to knock at the door and nearly jumped out of his skin. De'Nidra was standing there watching him.

"Va'Yone! You are a flirt." There was a little sparkle in her eyes. Half outrage and the other half pride. He was not sure which came first.

"I was just trying to be nice, that's all." He felt his cheeks growing hot.

Tem'Aldar rolled with laughter. He gasped out loud and placed his hands on his knees to keep himself standing.

De'Nidra looked Tem up and down. "This was what comes of spending time with a scoundrel."

"Leave over De'Nidra. He is a young man, interested in women. He has to try some charms now and again so that he knows he has them." Tem said.

"Is that what you did with me? Practiced your charms?" she said, her fists balling up on hips.

"No. I chased you until you caught me. That is how I remember it. And, an epoch later, I am still trying to figure it out."

De'Nidra bustled past them and turned, "Come on, you two rogues. I have a young scoundrel to get appropriately dressed." Outwardly, she looked properly angry, but her eyes bore humor.

Va'Yone fell in behind Tem'Aldar. "What did I do?"

"Lad, I don't know. But you'll be asking yourself that question about women your whole life."

It was first noon, and the heat made the fabric of his small clothes cling beneath leather. Va'Yone was starting to wonder whether De'Nidra was getting lost. What, with all this twisting and turning down muddy roads! When finally she turned into a shop nearer to the docks with a roll of cloth on a brightly colored sign. "He we are." De' said.

"We wove through the streets in such a maze-like fashion, I nearly lost track. Had I not paid close attention, I might have." Va'Yone answered.

"Boy, that is the next thing you better learn about women. They have keen minds for remembering shops." Tem smirked.

De'Nidra muttered under her breath, "If men could dress their self a woman wouldn't have to remember the best shops to buy clothes for men. Would we now?" She shot a glance at them, a questioning eyebrow raising.

Va'Yone was going to answer, but Tem shut it down with an upraised finger and a shake of his head. "That is a trap, lad. The next thing you have to learn is when it is time for answering and a time to keep your mouth shut." He said that out of the side of his mouth while maintaining a dashing smile for De'Nidra. He was good. Real good.

"Tem'Aldar, when you learn to keep your mouth shut, let me know. I will listen for it." De gave a sniff and went in. They followed. Tem was doing a good job of looking like he was exactly where he wanted to be at that moment. Va'Yone looked more like a lost pup looking for his mother.

The shop had every kind of colorful cloth. In long rolled bolts along a wall lined with shelves. A carpet of a tight weave adorned with a colorful scene of fish and mythical sea monsters as the centerpiece of the room. On it was a pedestal, and a woman with a cushion tied to her wrist was pinning lace to a jacket cuff. She was an older woman with black hair tied in a bun and dark eyes that took them in as she worked. "I'll be right with yea, my Lady."

De'Nidra gave a nod. "Take your time. I will look at the fabrics." She walked the line of shelves, touching different ones, feeling the softness.

The woman on the pedestal straightened. "There, have you found something you like, my Lady?"

Va'Yone noticed that, apparently, men did not exist for this woman because all the conversation was with De'Nidra. What he liked or did not like was not even part of the equation.

"Yes, I have a young rogue to dress. We are going into the jungle, so he will require something off-the-shelf. However, I have chosen some fabrics for you to make some outfits for him. For chasing the girls with you, understand?" De'Nidra said the last part with a little smile.

"Oh, I see, my Lady. What have you picked out for the young Lord?" The seamstress asked.

"The young Lord," De' glanced at Va'Yone with an appraising look. "He will need one jacket with this red. One of this tan. And one of this green. They need to be attractive with long cloaks. Something with stitching, as counterpoint to the color. Matching trousers for each and then an assortment of fine shirts. Twelve, I think. Also, the same number of small clothes and have the cobbler make boots, mid cut and two pair of shoes." De'Nidra finished.

The seamstress looked at Va'Yone like a hound, deciding to go after a rabbit. "Come here, young man. Let me have a look at you."

Va'Yone suddenly felt like a man heading for the gibbets. "What do I need to do?"

Tem gave him a push toward the seamstress. "You just stand there and get measured in all kinds of uncomfortable ways."

Before long, she had him measured and sent to a dressing room to try on the off-the-shelf work clothes. They were finer than anything he had ever owned. With each change, they paraded him before De'Nidra to see. She either excepted or rejected with a nod or shake of her head. Va'Yone got to do little of the choosing. And when he was done, he paid for all of it. De'Nidra had to add some besides to make up the difference in the bill. His purse was now empty, and he dressed in a new outfit of a green shirt and a matching brown jacket and britches.

He was almost done, but she added cloaks and seven changes of small clothes. The clerk took the coins and tossed in a bag for carrying.

De' snatched his black leathers off the top and tossed them on the counter. "Burn this."

The clerk nodded. "Of course my Lady."

Va'Yone was going to object, but Tem shook his head no. "Got to pick your battles, lad, and you are not winning this one. She hates them. Let them burn and save yourself the discomfort."

It was frustrating, but he gave De' her way. She watched him decide and then he gave in without objecting. She bent down and kissed him on the forehead.

"What was that for?" Va'Yone asked.

"For loving me more than your leathers." De'Nidra said.

He really did not understand women.

They went to the open market next. There, they purchased horses. Va'Yone choice was a small bay with black tip scales on its edges, while Tem and De' opted for a pair of matching tall blacks with heavy-bladed tails and a graceful, long stride. They also got the needed tack, including saddlebags, which added to the overall cost. In addition, Tem selected a short sword and a new belt, complete with a thick metal buckle.

They bought gear for cooking things and stuff for lighting fires or digging. A small tent for him and a larger one for them and blankets. Large saddle bags bulged and tent rolls hung behind saddles when they headed back to the inn and the first sun lazily slipped below the horizon, turning the clouds pink. The Elder Brother's retreating brought cooler air in from the sea. The humidity hinted at the promise of rain. Everything purchased, they returned to the inn for supper, a bed and to await the morning.

Chapter 27 Wraith Walk

"Vam'Phires drift between shadowy misty spaces and luminal spheres, bridging the realm of the living and the land of the dead. Their existence, ephemeral, as wisps of smoke. Their transient presence persists, like a candle flame untouched by the winds of time. A fire it can never blow out."

As day declined, the atmosphere's canvas, bruised and shifting from blood-red to deep black at nightfall, displayed volcanic tears weeping from a dying world, weaving smoky, chaotic trails across the star-flecked sky.

Mist found the portal's housing structure, a battered sanctuary amidst chaos, seeking relief from this deadly hellscape. Sulfurous ash buried its entrance. An inset doorway, buried ten spans deep, served as a shield against the fiery assault. She heaved the metal door open and left a trail of cinders in its wake. The portal arches pulsed to life, bathed in an explosion of light, as the event horizon opened into Mist's world.

Using her remaining strength, Mist pushed through to the Bastion of Light, where a mystic chill mixed relief with apprehension. Mel'Temdel lowered his staff, and the gate closed behind her in a flash; the archway slowing its frantic spin. She crumpled to the floor, gasping for clean air. Mist exhaled a relieved sigh, her breath stirred a dusty trail on the tiles.

At his end, Mel'Temdel's metal staff rang out as it struck the floor, its clear, resonant tone echoing a note of finality through the chamber. He leaned on it, using it as much for support as for emphasis, his shoulders slumped with exhaustion. Every clinging step towards her seemed to sap his remaining strength. "What's wrong, girl?" he puffed.

Mist sucked in pure air before speaking. Mel'Temdel reached out to assist her, and she gratefully extended her hand, allowing him to haul her to her feet.

Tears streaked her graying cheeks, and her lips quivered, caught between the Bastion's chill and the lingering heat of terror. Each word she attempted to form seemed to tremble with the echoes of the screams she had witnessed, the horror that lingered in her mind like a haunting melody. "It's beyond madness! A living hell where worlds are devoured whole." She gasped. The otherworldly air had scorched her lungs. "Mel'Temdel, we can't... we simply can't allow that terror and destruction into our world." The memory of the suffocating, blistering atmosphere haunted her with every burning breath.

"But what about your master?" He inquired. "Are you finished with him now?"

Mist squeezed her eyes shut. Dark memories of that world played in the depths of her mind. Each breath was a labored fight, her lungs grappling for air. "Screw him. He belongs there, Mel'Temdel!" she shouted, her voice carrying layers of betrayal and a deep-seated fear born from years under his shadow. "The Order of the Light was insane to kidnap him. He revels in misery, seeking only his revenge, delighting in the pain he can cause our world. He wants the death of those he believes are responsible. Will he stop there? Never mind the fact that everyone involved is already dead. No, he will not. I saw him, Mel'Temdel. I saw the endless ripping of flesh and the devouring of the dead. Please do not release that on our world." Her voice trembled, a parched plea teetering on the brink of panic.

"Okay, calm yourself, girl. I won't let him hurt you or our world. I can promise you that. Now, let's get you cleaned up. There is a place that we can go. I am done with the Dark Order. There is wealth here that we will take. If we leave it, they will use it. But that is not the prize for me, girl. You are my prize, my new apprentice." Mist clung to Mel'Temdel, her tears of relief flowing freely. After that, now, she had faith that the elderly War Mage would honor his word.

Mist and Mel'Temdel Vanished deeper into the old Bastion of the Light. Sib'Bal unwrapped herself from the weave of inverted light that had concealed her presence. This clever inversion, mirroring her surroundings, rendered her invisible, a mere bending of light. Wavering into view, having meticulously observed the mage's every move. The world, the glyph and the use of the crystal. Unlike them, she understood the technology. *Now all that remained was to figure out how I can use it to fit my plans?*

Sib'Bal studied the portal, her molten gold eyes and crimson lips revealing mysteries and dark charms, hinting at forbidden longings. Ebony skin shimmered beneath layers of translucent black and gray silks. Dark hair, braided with silver and seashell beads, clicked with her movements, cascading over her shoulders. She glided gracefully beside the torch-lit arches, casting dancing shadows. *I will wait for the right time to use it. And when I do, it will put an end to the broken gods and their twisted reality.* Bending the very light around her, she vanished once again.

In another part of the world, the heavy door of the Harbor Inn creaked open, and a hush fell over the room. Ivan and Da'Vain walked through, radiating an intimidating presence. A wave of fear slowly swept through the room, damping its lively spirit. Heads turned in a synchronized motion, transforming laughter and chatter into hushed whispers. Their dark silhouettes stretched across the floor, silent harbingers of latent threat. Unconsciously, patrons edged away, their eyes wide, as if the very air around them thrummed with authority.

The tense atmosphere filled the common room with a distressing, undead chill. Da'Vain had asked to do the investigation alone, but Ivan wouldn't hear of it. Da'Vain, like Lil, had ways of concealing their height and predatory nature. Ivan did not. Ivan, though a novice in the art, could project memories to a select few. He concentrated, considering whether he could influence more people, but swaying an entire room of mortals remained beyond his still-developing mental abilities. Da'Vain had argued for a more subtle approach, of course. But Ivan had authority he did not. Besides, he was the prince, and Lil belonged to him. He would not let her go for the sake of any law or custom.

The crowd was silent, scattering like sheep before dire wolves. They shrank back from Ivan's cold fury. This approach would have been brazen in the Grey Area, or the Darkened Lands, but in the Lands of Light, it was tantamount to an open declaration of war.

Da'Vain's voice whispered in his mind, *My prince, if there were any remaining doubts as to our status as a myth, that certainly is over now.*

I am here to find Lil, and if that disturbs the mortals, so be it. There is something amiss here, and I intend to find out what it is. If I need to empty this place to do it, I will, Chronicler. You and Lil should have told me about the lottery. If they harm her, our relationship with the mortals will be the least of your concerns.

My Lord, there are traditions and rules that govern a coven's behavior in these matters. These rules keep us beneath the notice of the mortals. It is for their safety as well as ours. Da'Vain cautioned.

Ivan countered, *Yes, there are many things you and Lil should have taught me but didn't. Things which you shall reveal once she is safely back home. But until then, I will hear no more about our customs.* The finality in Ivan's inner voice cut off the conversation.

The innkeeper watched as they entered, towering above everyone else in the room. The wary mortals noted their skin as white as bread flour. Ivan, in the lead, moved with the grace of a wolf. Clad in black leather armor adorned with red-edged scales, he bore a two-handed longsword at his hip, its red gem pulsing with a furious rhythm. Behind him strolled Da'Vain, a taller man by a head, with a face lined with age and a black leather coat flared at the knee. Over it, he wore a set of daggers that, for anyone else, would have been short swords.

Ivan's raspy voice held a hypnotic edge as he leaned on the bar. "I seek a woman whose beauty is perfection and hair of black ringlets. She would be hard to miss." He projected Lil's image into the innkeeper's mind.

The innkeeper swallowed hard, fearfully averting his gaze from Ivan's eyes. Those silver orbs, flecked with gold and rimmed in crimson, seemed to delve to his depths, a silent appraisal that forced a shiver down his spine. Judged by an immortal? His worth in the grand tapestry of life and death in question? An unheeded bead of sweat trickled down his temple.

He knew in the deepest recesses of his mind that if he did not answer true, they would find him wanting. And at this moment, being wanting sounded like a terminal condition. "She was here. I did not see her go, me Lords."

"She was here looking for someone?" Ivan said, the image of the bishop surfacing in his mind.

"Aye, he was here," the innkeeper said. "Paid well for secrecy, he did. Not two bells ago, he and his man left with the captain. The lass you seek was already gone by then."

Ivan nodded and said, "Then, I shall bid you good night." They turned and left the inn. The innkeeper let out a sigh as he slumped against the bar.

Ivan and Da'Vain, their presence like shadows lengthening with the light of the ascending two moons, moved with purpose through the mist-filled docks. Each step measured a silent dance with fate. But as they reached the edge, where land conceded to the relentless sea, they found only the whispering mist greeting them—the ship, like a phantom, had already set sail for the island of Far'Mora, swallowed by the hungry night.

Beyond the harbor, amidst the surging waves swaying, the ship battled the oncoming storm's crashing white caps. Lil sought refuge in a cramped hold. There, three tightly secured trunks lay, bound with ropes and formidable iron locks. Muffled voices resonated from within, and Lil listened intently, her breath barely audible.

On'omus' body curled into a fetal ball inside his trunk, pounded a fist against its confines. "When are they letting us out of here? Hey fat man! I'm talking to you."

Er'laya, similarly positioned, more tightly compressed because of his bulk. Gasping for air, he managed a strained breath to speak. "You are a bigger fool than I thought!" He sucked a ragged breath, "If you think we are going to be let out. They have captured us." He pulled another labored breath into his lungs.

"You are the one that paid for passage. Arranged for it without me. If anyone is an idiot here, it's you, Er'laya." On'omus said. "I can't believe you negotiated our capture, and then you paid them to do it. Idiot!"

The silk of Lil's voice touched their minds. *"Want to get out? Be quiet, or I'll hand you over to them myself."*

Lil navigated the cramped hold quietly. They had deliberately positioned three chests for easy access and securely tied them to the deck among crates held in place by cargo nets. That being the case, it would not be long before she had company. They must be out beyond the breakwater now. The ship lurched as the crew lay on extra canvas. The rolling and rising had subsided a little. *They weren't concerned about potential outsiders claiming the bounty? Why no guards?* Reaching behind her black leather coat, she pulled the tiny leather pouch nestled in the small of her back clipped to her sword belt. Opening it, she chose two metal picks of the proper size to defeat the lock.

"Get me first!" Came Er'laya's frenzied whisper.

You don't need to speak to me with your voice. I hear your thoughts. Now shut your mouth. I need to pick the lock. Lil sent.

Kneeling before his chest, Lil quietly slid the picks into the lock and felt for the pins. As Lil worked on the lock, her nimble fingers danced over the mechanism, a symphony of precision. She could hear Er'laya's desperate pleas echoing in her mind, his thoughts a discordance of fear and desperation. And with each click, Er'laya's untaught mind jabbered *yes*! This filthy man plotted and silently cajoled her in secret. Conniving that he didn't think she could hear. He played out every nuance of the conversation they would have. Working every angle to convince her to let them go. In the end, everything he had was already hers. He had nothing with which to pay, even had she been amenable. She was not.

This man tied up all of Lil's problems in one package. *I will lay him alive, at Tara's feet, and beg her forgiveness for taking her father's life. And when Tara is done with us, I will finish this bounty for the coven. If she doesn't kill us both first.*

With the final audible click, She put away her picks and cut the ropes. Lil cautiously lifted the lid of the fat man's sea chest and recoiled with disgust. The stench of sweat and excrement, accumulated from being confined so long, was disgusting.

Er'laya stared up at Lil, struggling to lift his stiff bulk. He said, "So glad you came to save me, my dear. They have kidnapped us." Fear replaced the relief that had filled his eyes while looking over her shoulder.

Lil spun, a deep voice invading her mind, powerful arms enveloping her. *Yes. So glad you came to save him, my dear. Now, you belong to me, too.*

Lil tried to reach out to Ivan. To call to the shadows. But they did not answer. This Vam'Phire's mind was too powerful. While he was touching her, their minds had to agree. His thoughts did not. She felt his fangs puncture her neck. Frantically, Lil struggled physically to break free. All went dark, and the last voice in her mind was his. *I have a choice to either kill you or send you back. But now that I have tasted you, I can do neither.*

Lil was fading in and out. He had drained Lil to the point of unconsciousness. Her mind was sluggish, and she could not move. But she still felt him there. She felt his physical presence, his thoughts crawling through her memories. He lifted her in his arms. Her body lulled. Lil knew they had shadow walked. Feeling the lurching of her physicality moving between two points in space. Unconsciously, her mind felt his thoughts probing hers. He rested her on a hard surface, uncovered and cold.

Yantee, the Pirate Prince, observed her in slumber. His disheveled brown locks cascaded loosely. He wore a knee-length black leather coat and matching trousers. His hand idly rested on a gold-traced, ornate cutlass. Cross-legged on a table before a gilded throne, he kicked up cuffed, worn leather boots. And there, on it, lay Lil. He sought a queen, and in Lil, he found all he desired: mental prowess, physical perfection, scholarly wisdom, and predatory instincts. She had it all. But under the Law of the Coven, he had the choice to kill her or return her. The law prohibits keeping her for his own against her will.

What would he do with her now? He had a choice, according to the Coven Scripts. He could kill her. That was his right, or he could send her home. He had done neither.

Morteave, the Chronicler, stood beside him, watching him gloat. Yantee, his prince, was smitten with her, but her mind was open and in it was Ivan, the prince of Coth'Venter. Lil had chosen Ivan for her partner. Yantee had stolen her, according to the Scripts. Morteave feared Yantee would not let her go. He could press Yantee. That would only result in her death. If Yantee was smitten, maybe that could grant the time he needed to save her and avert a war.

Yantee needed to persuade Lil and, from the strength of her mind, that was going to take a long time.

Morteave, the Chronicler, broke his reveries. "My Lord prince. You are obliged to follow the law. The Coven Scripts are plain. Lil presents a problem. How do you intend to solve the breach of protocol?"

Yantee did not move beyond stroking his mustache and goatee. "I have not yet decided what to do with her. The Scripts grant me time to decide. Do they not?"

"Yes, my Lord, but you must inform the Coth'Venter coven that you killed Lil during her attempt to liberate the subject of both parties' hunt. Namely, the Bishop. Or do you intend to let her go?"

"Aye. Or I could send you to inform her prince that I killed her and I could, at my mercy, decide not to after you have gone. And mayhap she would, when she recovered, decide to stay. There do be many things in my Power to decide. Should yea push me to decide now? Well," He made an offhanded gesture, "Yea, do be aware, I might could decide to kill her? Now what would dat cause?"

Morteave, the Chronicler, nodded. "A war given what her mind has allowed us to glean of her prince, my Lord. Did you know I am required to inform my prince of his responsibilities? You realize that the position of Chronicler is part of the Council of Covens?" Torn between emotions, Morteave struggled. Having sworn himself not just to the prince but to the creed and to report the violations of the Coven Scripts of Law. Beyond that, now he was angry to be placed into a position caught between his desire to remain loyal to his prince and bring order to his coven. He needed a private meeting with Da'Vain to inform him that Lil was to be held against her will at the Island of Far'Mora. Without regard for Yantee, commanding it or not.

Chapter 28 Bed Of Stone

"Choose your poison. What will take your life? Will you walk in valor or crawl in fright? Can you live like there is no tomorrow? In the end, comes your last reward. How do you wish to be remembered? A warrior's resting place is a bed of stone or grave of water. Immortality is born of your deeds. Will your legacy be terror, or will it be courage?"

The water in Far'Mora's harbor sparkled brightly in the heat of the morning sun. Va'Yone's mount trailed after De'Nidra and Tem'Aldar as they rode in a pair. Turning in his saddle, lagging after. He could not help it. The island's harbor, nestled beneath the endless jungle canopy, stole his breath. He cast one last gaze before letting out a weary sigh. "I barely had time to see anything in the city," he complained.

"It is not going anywhere, Va'Yone. We are going to come back." De'Nidra was suppressing a laugh. "I am sure that lovely girl you were working your charms on will still be there."

"Stop teasing me, De'Nidra. That is not it at all. I just wanted to see more of the city."

Tem'Aldar harrumphed, "You might as well give it up, lad. De'Nidra saw you last night after dinner, working your charms on that girl by the bar."

Va'Yone felt his cheeks getting hot. "Oh, my gods! You were watching me? I was just talking to her. She is nice. That was all. Really De'Nidra, that was it." His voice was a mix of protest and pleading.

"Ah, I see," De' said, her voice light with amusement, "You do realize that it always starts out like that, don't you?"

Tem coughed as if he had swallowed a bug while attempting to take a sip from his canteen. "First, you find the girl attractive, and then you convince yourself of her intelligence and wit. That, of course, is how it starts. Then one thing leads to another and you are bouncing a babe on your knee."

De'Nidra gave Tem'Aldar a dangerous look. "Is that how it happens?"

"Not with you, my love," Tem'Aldar replied. "Our love was fate."

"It is lucky for you I am allowing you to work your way into my good graces again. You are going to have to work harder to get yourself out of that one." Her smile was almost wicked. Full of teeth, a bit of a snarl, and squinty eyes.

"Of course, my love. I will begin worming my way back into your good graces immediately." He nodded, with the air of a man to who was just given an appropriate challenge.

De'Nidra left men breathless no matter what she did. "But you and Tem'Aldar are not like that. You love each other." Va'Yone protested. "Your relationship is like something from a dream. You are perfect for each other."

"It's all about effort, Va'Yone," De'Nidra remarked, skillfully steering her mount around a gnarled root, her eyes lingering thoughtfully on the leafy canopy above.

"A lot of work," Tem'Aldar added, ducking under a low-hanging branch.

De' raised an eyebrow at him.

"What De', I agree with you?" Tem said. His arms spread wide in question.

Mercifully, the thick tree cover left the trail filled with shadows mingled with sunlit patches of stony ground. As they ascended, the sea's scent faded into the background, replaced by that of the earthy jungle. They passed remnants of forgotten history, obscured by vines and moss draping the trees. Buildings covered by a world trying to remember how to grow verdant again. Patches of paved streets ran crisscrossing into the jungle, only to disappear behind taller dense trees in a field of moss and vines.

Va'Yone's imagination got the better of him and he had lost track of time and even the tiredness that comes after a long ride. His horse came to an abrupt halt, bringing him out of his daydreams. It was fast approaching night, and the jungle had cooled. Creatures silent during the heat of the day whooped and hooted.

"You okay, lad?" Tem asked. "You've been quiet for hours."

Beneath the canopy, the humidity clung to them like a second skin. Va'Yone wiped his brow, peering at the vine-covered ruins. "This city must have covered the entire island. What cataclysm could have led to its downfall? The Shattering and the Breaking of the Balance, events we describe as the destruction of civilization and reality, don't do justice to the scale of this ruin." Va'Yone swept a hand across the jungle absorbed city. His voice ended in an awed breathlessness.

De'Nidra dismounted. "Yes, it is fascinating. Much study needs doing about that time. The little we know is from our digs and books in a language that few understand anymore."

"But surely there are beings that remember? Like the immortals or gods?" He asked.

"There are rumors, of course. It is said that a great dark Lord named Amorath lived before the Breaking. But I have met him and if he did, he has grown so addled he has forgotten the truth. Al'len said that EL'ALue came into being after and does not remember it. Some say that Sib'Bal was born before and transformed into a goddess in the wave of the Breaking. In the energy of the tearing of reality, she reformed anew. But I will not be the one to ask her. If anyone ever did, they only lived long enough to spread the rumors." De'Nidra winked at him slyly.

They pitch their tents and set the campfire. Tem'Aldar made tea. They had a meal of stewed vegetables and meat and cheese. After the hard day of riding and the heat of the jungle, Va'Yone crawled into his tent, gratefully, and slept, filled with dreams of adventure.

Deep in the heart of the Blackened Lands, the wind howled mercilessly against the fortress, with sand grains pelting the thick glass with tiny, persistent taps. Inside, the air held the chill of ancient stone and a faint, musty odor, a stark contrast to the raging storm outside. Amorath seethed in silence, his once-cherished humor and wicked delights extinguished by a mere boy's actions. Watching Moros gaining Power at such an alarming rate had been more than he could handle.

Time is running out. It might already be too late, Amorath. Mali'Gorthos, his slumbering dark god, had given him a year to ready the child, but it could wait no longer. Idly, he rubbed a graying, flaking hand at his chin, feeling the necrotizing tissue peel away, and promptly ceased.

A knock came at the door, robbing him of his much needed machinations. "What is it? I'm busy!" He snapped. Snapping was his norm, keeping people on edge, wary of speaking needlessly. But of late he had been doing it more oft and with a little maiming mixed in for good measure.

Rem'Mel entered, the heavy black doors groaning shut behind him. Amorath turned, his gaze piercing the dim light. "You called for me, great Lord?" Rem'Mel said, his voice barely concealing his apprehension. It had the sound of a man dipping his toe into hot water to avoid being scalded.

Amorath found Rem'Mel's sniveling tone infuriating. The irony that he had to rely on this nearly worthless piece of biological material for his ascension gnawed at him. He had well-trained and powerful High Mages capable of facilitating the process, but he couldn't trust them. Once separated from his lifeless vessel and cast into the Dark Well, he would be at their mercy. That very notion of '*mercy*'. He uttered the word with disdain, the lingering taste of benevolence souring his parched mouth. No, there was nothing for it. He would have to use this halfwit Rem'Mel, sharing the Dark Well and the technology of the transfer, and that meant teaching him. He could dispose of him after. Amorath couldn't risk leaving that kind of knowledge walking about. "Ah, Rem'Mel, please come in."

Rem'Mel pushed the heavy black doors open and entered. His master's rooms were dark. As he pushed the doors open, the dead fire's coils flared briefly, and melted candles sputtered on a stand, dripping wax onto the table. "The Great Lord Amorath summoned and I obey" he said, giving an elegant swish to ostentatious robes well beyond the worth of some middling mage.

Amorath nearly pulled the words from his mouth as he spoke them with effort. "Good! I have been watching you now for fifty years, Middle Mage, Rem'Mel, and while you have believed me to have no interest in teaching you! That was the furthest thing from the truth!"

"My Lord?" Rem'Mel begun to object, saying some such about loyalty and honor to serve. His normal drivel, but Amorath cut him off with an upraised hand.

"You misapprehend the situation, Rem'Mel. I have been testing your loyalty and with every slight you have endured. You have my trust. As you might imagine, with all the scheming and backstabbing that goes on around here, it was necessary." Amorath gave a yellow teethed smile. "So, with all your long years of service, I have chosen you as my new apprentice!"

Rem'Mel's mouth dropped open. "What my Lord?" He stammered. "I thought you hated me."

Amorath sighed. "You can decline, of course, if you wish to. In either event, your treatment will improve, as will your housing, and monthly stipend is here after doubled. We acknowledge and appreciate your value as a trusted confidant! There will be changes! No further need for you to use the title Great Lord with me unless we are in mixed company, you understand?" Amorath kept his composure and ended with a grin. But it was difficult to maintain the effect. "That was why I called for you, Rem'Mel. You let me know if you decide to accept my offer."

There was a knock at the door.

Amorath's voice remained pleasant. "Come in."

Re'Vano the *Dorm'ata* entered. An old, hunched grey skinned man in black livery who bore the laborious responsibility of managing the household for Great Lord Amorath. Holding the title of Dorm'ata as long as anyone could remember, Re'Vano knew that he was completely loyal to his Lord. An infraction of any kind would always be reported, as would every meeting with friends, and every spoken word, if he could manage it, reported to his master. What the content of your social interactions was. Everything reported and diligently scribed into his logs. Right down to what your favorite foods are and what's purchased and delivered to your domicile.

So, if anything had come out of his change of position, it was that he was now being watched more. Not less, and that could only mean one thing. Amorath had plans. He needed Rem'Mel for something. *But what do I have beyond my relationship with the child?*

Dorm'ata Re'Vano escorted Rem'Mel to his new quarters. The heavy wood doors groaned open. A spacious reception room greeted him off of a dining hall.

Re'Vano bowed low, "Your rooms, my Lord. I took the liberty of having your things brought. To the rear, you will find that your apartment connects to Lord Moros's apartments so that you have access to him, day and night."

Rem'Mel thought, realizing, *So, my relationship with the boy is what he desires. It is the child and the bond we share. Amorath must think me a blind fool.* "Thank you Re'Vano. I will be taking my meals here with Lord Moros if you could be so kind as to send the invitation?" *It made no sense to avoid playing the fool for him.*

"Of course, my Lord. I will send your meal at nightfall. If you wish anything specific, please send word and I will provide it." With that, Re'Vano bowed himself out.

That night, before the second sun slipped below the desolate horizon, Moros entered through the side door. He did not knock. He just walked in and strolled down the connected hall to the dining room. Servants had lit lamps and set a fire on the dark volcanic stone hearth. It crackled, devouring the dry, twisted wood imported from verdant lands. Its lively light played an almost cheerful game with shadows as the Little Sister bled a fading red light through open windows. The sand storm had stopped, leaving a slow breeze that blew in, rustling heavy drapery thrown open, letting in the last remnants of the dying light. Rem'Mel sat at the head of the table. The red robes of the middle mage gave a marked swish as he stood and gave Lord Moros a proper bow. "My lord, thank you for dining with me this evening."

Moros brow was knit, accenting anger, touching blushed cheeks. "Hey, they moved all my stuff without even asking me and then brought me to this place." He folded his arms, crossed his chest. "I mean, it's nice, but no one bothered to ask me. When Re'Vano told me you lived next door, I let it pass. Still, it would have been nice to be asked."

Rem'Mel's eyes took Moros in. He wore his black jacket over grey and black silk with charcoal colored cotton pants and a small, curved silver dagger topped with a ruby at his waist. "I am as surprised as you, Moros. Great Lord Amorath granted these apartments to me today as well." His eyes squinted at Maros, "along with an increase in monthly wages." Rem'Mel raised a quieting finger to his lips. "I am to become his new confidante. Apparently, all of my hard work and loyalty over the years have paid off."

"What!," Moros scowled. "That old wraith does not care about you. He wants something."

Rem'Mel pointed to his ear and winked at Maros. "Now, Moros, you know how hard I have worked, and it is a long overdue recognition. I have worked hard for the opportunity and I intend to accept the offer of an apprenticeship."

Moros cocked his head and nodded. "Well, you have worked for it, and I am glad he is trying to be nice to you now." His head shook with obvious disbelief. "I can't say that I understand the change of heart."

It was at that moment, just as the last light of the second sun slipped away, that the servants brought the meal. Five scantly robed women carried wine and silver platters with a service for two. When seated, these servants placed plates and table wear before them and lifted the lids of the platters, allowing an aroma of expensive meats and spices to fill the room. A blond woman in sheer silk smiled as she poured red wine into glasses. Reality rippled outward for Maros like a stone thrown into a pond. Time slowed and the slashing of the wine into cups slowed to a stop. Everything just stopped moving except for Maros and Rem'Mel.

The boy child's countenance nearly vanished, revealing a deeper and more profound intellect. "Alright Rem'Mel. What is going on?" Moros asked.

Rem'Mel barely got the words out. It could not have been more than a whisper, but Moros listened just the same. "He wants something from me, my Lord. I don't know what it is. But he needs me for something concerning our relationship."

Moro's eyes were a child's, but they burned with deep arcane knowledge. He steepled his fingers under his chin. "Let's play the game for a bit, Rem'Mel, and we will see what he is doing. Once he tells you what it is, we will figure out how to use it." Time rippled back, and the room lurched to life as if nothing had happened.

Chapter 29 Seat Of Pride

"Darkness, the liar and disillusioned stronghold, yields only to humility's embrace. For in the presence of Truth and Love, the purest Light, shadows have no refuge—they flee at its sight."

The wind rippled through High Seat Lord Gan'Vile's thinning hair, revealing the encroaching baldness of his once-hidden crown. Perched at his balcony, he observed High King Mel'Lark and Lord Lars of Haven striding into the courtyard, their retinue of knights and nobles trailing like shadows. Pack animals bore the spoils of the hunt. Boar and deer carcasses draping broad backs, the resounding clatter of horseshoes echoed back at him from battlement walls. "It appears the hunt went well. Tonight's feast promises a hearty meal," he mused to himself.

Gan'Vile's robes billowed, his hands slamming against the double doors of his chambers, creating a thunderous crash. Echoing off the high vaulted ceilings, his voice roared, "Where are my body servants?"

"Here, my Lord." Two monks rushed in to serve him.

"I must dress immediately. The High King and Lars of Haven have returned from the hunt, and I have pressing business with them that cannot wait." Gan'Vile panted, his bulk heaving as if from a run.

Beneath the twin suns' relentless blaze, their clothes clung to them, heavy and damp, silent witnesses to the rigors of their journey. Mel'Lark, the High King, pushed the pace relentlessly all the way back to the shining walls of Haven. Lars found himself drenched in sweat, much like the others. However, he understood the urgency. They had met the Maid of Light. Even in a construct form, she was frightening. Powerful was what you might call a warrior. She is a warrior, but it falls short in description and even in a lesser form, she maintained a godlike presence, tempered with humility, taking an active role in the life of her people. Astonishingly, she had pledged her life vow to Priest Knight Antoff Grant, choosing to love a mortal—an act as profound as it was shocking. The descriptions of her in the hidden archives matched her appearance.

The High Mage Heli'os attempted to unleash a fiery assault upon her. She blazed, engulfed in the energy he threw at her. If she had been a building, he would have turned her to dust. But she shrugged it off, treating it as nothing more than a fleeting discomfort. It left no doubt that she was the construct of EL'ALue, the Maid of Light. Her dreams became a manifest reality to mortal eyes. Lars wanted to swear to her there and then, as did Mel'Lark, but she rejected them as liars. *This harsh truth shadows us: we are no less deceitful than the High Seat, equally shrouded in the same Darkness.* Lars, Like Mel'Lark, sought to set it right, even to the point of laying his kingdom at her feet.

Lars dismounted beside the High King and asked, "What's our first move?"

"A bath, and then we see to a fat prelate." He thumbed his hand toward the High Seats rooms just as a broad smile stretched across the High King's face. "I intend to lull him with a feast and then pack him up and throw him to a goddess when he feels most secure. You and Heli'os will stand ready for the moment and we will deliver him into her hands together."

With that, Mel'Lark and the High Mage strolled purposefully for their rooms and a hot bath. After giving the necessary orders for a feast, Lars hurried to his bath, only to be met by the Holy Seat flouncing down the stairway red-faced and puffing from effort. "Where is the High King?" he clung to the baluster as if he would fall over without it. His brow, powdered with fresh makeup, glistened with perspiration.

"He has gone to his rooms for a bath and then we are having a feast in your honor, Your Eminence. I am about to do the same. The meal will take some hours to cook. I know that the High King is excited to see you then." Lars used the answer as an excuse to bow himself away and trot up the grand stairway to his room. *Little chance that the fat man can run me down.*

That night, the grand dining hall of Haven Castle reverberated with lively music played on strings and pipes. Tables loaded with meat of the hunt and wine stood ready in large clay pitchers that ran with beads of perspiration after being in the chillers. The enormous honey colored doors hung open, and servants in white livery threw every window open to the evening air. Candles and lamps were lit the grand hall, flickering in a breeze that gave relief to the day's heat. Then the doors were closed again to onlookers, all the preparations made.

When the bell tolled, a throng of eager nobles gathered, their hunger palpable. The doors swung open, releasing them into the feast like a river breaking its banks. Taking their places amongst the rows of many tables stacked high with fresh meat from the hunt mixed with the normal fair. The High King and his entourage entered, followed by the Holy Seat and the High Mage Heli'os. The last to enter was Lord Lars of Haven. All stood and waited for the High King Mel'Lark to sit. When he did, the feast began. The staff wheeled in casks of wine packed in ice and tapped them. The pitchers flowed as fast as the guests could empty them.

Like the wine, the feast's music was heady, filling the hall with jubilation. Some sang songs, and younger, less reserved men and women cleared a corner and took up the dance. It was quite an affair. That was, until the High King stood to address the grand hall. Mel'Lark held up a hand, and the music stopped, the noise diminishing to silence. High Seat Lord Gan'Vile had an overloaded fork of wild pork halfway to his mouth when he finally noticed. He sighed with disappointment but forced himself to observe the civilities. A blush colored his cheeks as he realized the High King was waiting for him to finish.

"My apologies, Your Grace," Lord Gan'Vile said, his voice tinged with both disappointment and embarrassment as he lowered the pork.

Mel'Lark laughed and gave an indulgence smile. "Nothing to forgive, Your Eminence. I am glad you are enjoying it." He then turned to address the crowd of Lords and ladies. "I am sure that it has come to your attention that there are some issues regarding the security of both realm and church. As to the defense of the realm, his High Holy Seat Lord Gan'Vile has called a crusade, and we its nobility have answered. However, there yet looms a larger threat. One of faith and right that only his Eminence himself can officiate. Under the guise of a hunt, Lord Haven and I undertook a mission of secrecy on the behalf of the Order of the Light. We went to RavenHoff and the old city of Coth'Venter to see this Maid of Light for ourselves."

There was a gasp from nobles and servants alike at that statement. High Holy Seat, Lord Gan'Vile stood up and shook with indignation. "What is the meaning of this? I commissioned no mission on behalf of the Order of the Light." Flustered and suddenly filled with the realization that he had blurted out an objection before the congregation, he amended. "What were your findings, High King?"

"My findings are that while the woman is indeed impressive, we are not the ultimate judges of such matters, and the accusations against the Order of the Light are grave. The only righteous and fair examiner of such matters is his Holiness, himself, who can confront these vile accusations and put it to rest once and for all."

Gan'Vile looked as if he had swallowed a rotted fig. "What? You want me to go to Coth'Venter and confront this artificer of vile rumor and lies?"

Mel'Lark's face slipped from a grin to disbelief. "But, Your Eminence, that is your place, is it not? Who else could officiate such matters to the satisfaction of the common folk and the nobility?" The nobles stood now and shouted demands that the Holy Seat put down this ruckus.

Lord Gan'Vile's hand lifted, silencing the room. A hush fell over the nobles, their eyes darting amongst each other, a silent language of shared secrets and unspoken truths passing between them. *They simply will pretend ignorance, and they will whisper these objections to the common folk. You have boxed me into a corner, Mel'Lark.* "You say you have met this woman who claims to be the Maid of Light? What say you of her High King?" *That should, if nothing else, put him on the spot as well.* Gan'Vile thought. He returned Mel'Lark's grin petulantly.

Mel'Lark returned the smirk with an equally childish sullenness. "We did, my Lord. The High Mage Heli'os performed the test." Again, the crowd of nobles gasped. "That's right. The test was required within the Holy Articles." He gestured to the High Mage.

Heli'os stood a bit disconcerted, pretending to be placed on the spot. He let out a heavy, reticent sigh. "It is true," he admitted. "She controls reality around herself to the point that the energy that should have vaporized her had no effect. Truth be told, it did not even scorch her shirt. According to the liturgy, she is legitimate from the perspective of the Conclave of the Light. The last true justification or denial must come from the church. You as High Seat are the final voice in this matter. Thus, you must interview her and decide if she has a legitimate claim as the head and founder of the Order of the Light."

"What? You want me to walk into this charlatan's den and proclaim her a lie? Are you insane? If she is half as powerful as you say, she would melt me down!" His High Holiness had indeed lost his cool. If you thought his face was a blush with outrage, it was as red as a beet now. He pointed at Mel'Lark. "You are putting me at risk."

Lord Mel'Lark shook his head. "You put us all at risk if you fail to recognize or deny these claims in person. I, Lars and High Mage Heli'os will be with you and share in your risk. If she destroys you, she will probably kill us all. We can offer no better assurances than that." The Lords and ladies of the court watched the conversation between the two most powerful men bat back and forth until finally Gan'Vile gave in, defeated.

"Very well, I will go with you and put this vile lie down. How soon do we leave?" Gan'Vile asked.

"Tonight!" said the High King. "They have assured me she will receive us."

The purple light of the Mage Gate strobed against the statue of Ram'Del as Lord Mel'Lark, Lars, Gan'Vile and lastly, High Mage Heli'os stepped through. The Gate winked out with a last flash that prickled the High Seats' skin. Like ice water washing over him, the Mage Gate left a bone-deep chill. The smell of the grassy fields and trees mixed with the smooth summer wind. It felt almost wild, a stark contrast to the confines of the Lands of Light. There was a kind of freedom here that Gan'Vile found refreshing. It was elusive, and words did not truly describe the feeling. It was like choice itself lived in the air.

Tara hurried down the long grand stair of the Cathedral of Light with Edward in tow. The guard was at the top of the landing before the doors. Except for a few patrols and carts rolling in and out preparing for war, there were no outward signs that the four men's arrival by Mage Gate was neither unexpected nor unwelcome. She wore black leather thief's armor and knee high riding boots. Twin silver inlay curved short swords belted at her hips and wore a long gray cloak fringed in gold. Upon it was the symbol of Edwards and her union, were a black and white dragon facing a single gauntleted fist holding two crossed lightning bolts.

It would not be correct to say that she dismissed the High King or the Holy Seat. But her attention was for Lars, whom she warmly embraced, her voice whispered a fond "Father!". Lars lifted her up and spun her, eliciting her chiming laughter.

"Put my wife down, sir," Edward mockingly chided his father. Lars did with a grin, and the two men embraced.

"She is a joy, son, that is for sure," Lars said, his eyes twinkling with affection. "But you don't get all of her attention when I am around." He said, while holding out a hand to Tara. She took it with a smile for Edward and Lars. He held out her hand toward Lord Mel'Lark and Gan'Vile. "You have, of course, met The High King my dear. However, this other person is the High Holy Seat of the Order of the Light, His Eminence Lord Gan'Vile."

Tara and Edward gave a bow. A curtsy would have looked funny without the dress. Tara felt the large man's apprehension. "You are here to see Al'en?"

"They are here to see her." Lars said. "I am her to see my daughter."

Tara grabbed Edward's hand with her other and led them toward the cathedrals dining hall.

Gan'Vile gave Mel'Lark a sidelong look and whispered out of the side of his mouth. "That is not the reaction I normally engender from someone the first time." His voice filled with as much injury as disbelief.

Mel'Lark shrugged as they began to follow. He leaned in close, overtopping the height of the plump clergyman. "I am not the High King here, and your position as far as she is concerned is in question. You see, they know that Al'len is the construct of EL'ALue, the Maid of Light. It is you who are unconvinced."

Gan'Vile's glance was sharp. "And you are not unconvinced?"

The High King raised a questioning eyebrow at him. "I am convinced. It is you that are here to certify or deny, not me."

Al'len stood before the fireplace nearest the open balcony doors, Moonlit curtains stirred, allowing the cool breeze to wash over her. She threw her long blonde hair tied with a golden cord over one shoulder and grasped it with her right hand in a tight fist. The fire was not lit, but the Maid of Light burned with anger. Every voice from the square drawn to her. Every word heard. She wore a white cloak embroidered with a white dragon, and her left hand rested on the beautiful two-handed longsword at her hip. *I should be pleased*, she thought. *The High King of the Lands of Light just declared himself for me.* But she was not. Al'len had known that Lars and Mel'Lark were hers before they had left from their last visit. This was an old anger. One that came from her denial and theft of the order that she had started before any of them were born. She was trying to force it down. *It was not this man that did it. It was another mortal and another time.* She told herself. *I must remember that or I will burn him for having the arrogance of wearing these same robes before he can even open his mouth.*

Antoff's voice scolded her from the balcony. "Remember my love, we are here to listen first and then you must decide what to do with this High Seat."

Al'len felt his cautioned words through their bond before he said it. His eyes were on her and she felt that as well. "I know that, Antoff. I also know what this mortal and his ilk have been up to for ages. I am trying to let that go. For the moment, I will hear him out before burning him to ash if he displeases me." She turned and her eyes danced with a blue fire in the candlelit room. They met his ice-blue, and she gave him an easy, but seductive, warrior's smile.

Tara and Edward led the visitors into the room. It shone gold in silver in candlelight and the radiance of the silvery moons. "I have delivered them to you, Al'len," Tara said before turning to go with Edward. She walked out into the dark hall, speaking as she closed the doors. "Be gentle. Mortals rarely know that what they do has long-term effects beyond what they think they can see. They are seeking wisdom and direction. Be kind in your persuasion." With that, the heavy doors banged closed.

Lars bowed in concert with Mel'Lark, the High King of the Lands of Light. "There," he pointed. "There is your Maid of Light."

Gan'Vile's gaze settled on Al'len, her cloak adorned with the golden-threaded symbol of De'Adin, the White dragon, her stance defiant even from behind. None in this age would know the symbology. Only someone who had access to the forbidden archives would see it for what it was. A declaration to the world that she stood here before him. The Maid of Light. His voice quivered and he tried to get out the words, but they refused to come.

Al'len still faced the cold dead fireplace. A shadowy outline of a young Priest Knight stood at the balcony rail, watching her intently as she spoke. It was barely a whisper, but it reached out to him and held him spellbound. Her voice was honey and burning fire. "*What shall I say to you? How can I say it? Shall I recount the frigid ages of my solace? That you shattered a heart of gold, yet not a single tear stained your cheeks. I shall have none of you. Until the day you turn and declare your allegiance to the Maid of Light. My silence shall remain unbroken. Your cries shall echo through the desolate halls of the Darkness that consumed you. But if you turn toward me and acknowledge my presence, I shall turn towards you. Yes, even I, the Maid of Light, shall turn toward you and answer your call. Let all the heavens tremble and the foundations of El'idar roar, and may Darkness flee your sight, for the radiant glory of the Light shall burst forth in a Priest Knight once more!*" Antoff ignited like a paragon of Light.

"I remember those words," Gan'Vile said. His voice trembling near tears at the end.

"I said them then. Just as I have spoken them to you now. You seek me and I have turned." Al'len faced him. "Will you repent and come clean? Will you declare yourself for the Maid of Light?"

The High Seat Lord Gan'Vile swayed and fell to his knees under the weight of her stare.

Chapter 30 Beneath Rocky Dirt

"The luster of gold pales next to love and life. When it is over, all the riches in the world will not purchase you more. Both love and life will suffer if wealth can ever buy more of either."

Prince Yantee sat on his throne, his silver-tooled boots resting on the table where Lil lay. He had sent his Chronicler, Morteave, to Coth'Venter to deliver the news that they had destroyed Lil during her mission to capture the bishop. It was completely untrue, of course. Though, he'd paid gold to be a spider on that wall when Ivan the Prince of Coth'Venter read it.

It was long past nightfall, and Morteave watched the purple strobing of a Mage Gate flickering at the forgotten Cathedral of Light. Or someone should have forgotten it, but that was not what was going on here. It was full of new life and the mortals were thick within it. He knelt beside the broken wall, among the remnants of a tower. His long leather coat flared out, covering him. He projected his thoughts, signaling to Da'Vain that he was awaiting his arrival.

Shadows exploded behind him, materializing as a mix of wispy smoke and dissipating threads. He felt Da'Vain's presence and his mind, along with no small measure of outrage at the breach of protocol.

This is not proper, Da'Vain sent through their mental link. He was agitated, or maybe he was dreading it. There was something else there, too. Hidden in the background, beneath the surface.

Morteave remained calm. *It was necessary. Once I explain, old friend, you'll understand the need to forego formality.* Standing, he turned to Da'Vain and held out a silver cylinder the length of a fresh candle and the thickness of a thumb. *I need not tell you what it says. You already know.*

We lost her then. Da'Vain sounded more like a crushed father than an immortal giving proper respects for the Scripts.

The silver and gold spotted eyes ran over the Coth'Venter Chronicler. *Perhaps that is what I should tell you. It is what the notice says, anyway.* Morteave's flour-white finger pointed at the silver tube. The tip of a long black nail bit at the red wax seal. *But, if I did say that, old friend, one of us would be a liar.*

Are you saying that she lives? Da'Vain asked, hope clearly unmistakable in his thoughts.

Morteave let out a long breath. He had not realized he had been holding. *I would like to tell you a story. Long ago when we were yet...*

No time for tales now, Morteave. Speak plainly, reveal your truths or be gone, demanded Da'Vain. In addition, he did something that he had never done before. He sent the conversation to Ivan live and without editing the context. He felt Ivan questioning first and then go quiet, listening.

But it is such a good story, my friend. Besides, it is the only way I can say this without betraying my prince.

Da'Vain gave a grim nod of assent.

He began again, *Long ago when I was yet in training. I studied the Scripts. In them was Lev'Aion, the fallen Prince of Menorn. Do you remember it?*

Yes, at the time I was Primer of the Council. Lev'Aion kept Aye'Win. The two clans went to war. It almost destroyed us. It is the reason for the rule regarding this. He held up the silver tube.

Morteave inclined his head in affirmation. *Some had rumored that he was so smitten with Aye'Win that he could not bear to let her go. I believe Lil is of Aye' Win's lineage, is she not?*

Hope flared in Da'Vain. *The rumor is she is her niece.*

Well, there it is then, and in any advent, think about that when I deliver this to you tonight. He tapped the silver cylinder with his fingernail.

Da'Vain handed it back.

I will observe the proper respects in one hour. I would suggest that you and prince Ivan stand ready. The shadows reached for him and when enveloped; he was gone. All that remained in the Darkness were wisps of smoke, threads, and the memory of Aye'Win, Lil's irresistible aunt.

An hour later, Ivan sat on his throne, surrounded by his people. Da'Vain, his Chronicler, stood to his right side and a raven-haired beauty stood to his left, a hand resting on his neck, stroking it with loving fingers. Her pheromones, thick in the air, drowning the atmosphere in seduction and allure.

He is coming. Be mindful, he will transfer this to his prince without alteration. He must believe you have thrown her aside. Your behavior will either grant Lil time or guarantee her death. Da'Vain's voice was forceful, like a frightened father trying to be brave and worried that their performance could falter. *Prince Yantee must believe it, Ivan. He must. Put away your rage.*

Shadows pooled in dim corners from the dark hall. They reached towards the center of the open doorway of the throne room. Then exploded into wisps of smoky threads and Morteave, the Chronicler of the Prince of Far'Mora, was there. His black leather overcoat flared at his knees. He wore a single gold dagger at his waist. In his hand, he held a silver cylinder with a red wax seal at the center, bearing the mark of his prince's signet ring.

Morteave bowed low, sweeping his arm out as he held the cylinder. "Yantee, the Prince of Far'Mora, greets Ivan Prince of Coth'Venter." The voice was deep and powerful in mind. It echoed about the hall, carrying no hint of a lie.

Ivan watched Da'Vain, his Chronicler, step forward and reply. "Ivan, the Prince of Coth'Venter doth greet you. He gladly receives the communication of your prince." He took the cylinder from Morteave and walked it back to Ivan, bowing low and holding it out.

Ivan took it. He destroyed the seal, pressing his thumbnail into the center, and the container broke in two, revealing a small roll of parchment inside. Shaking the parchment into one hand, Ivan tossed the parts of the tube to the floor.

They clanged, and Morteave stood to watch. Ivan unrolled the parchment with a careless disregard. The heady scent of pheromones filled the air, drawing his gaze to a dark raven hair beauty's shapely figure at his shoulder. Her skin was milk white and smooth. Her silver and gold spotted eyes met his unashamedly. As far as anyone was concerned, prince Ivan's attentions were hers alone.

So, Lil failed me in her duties. And your coven has claimed the reward? Ivan's voice flowed into all minds, thick with disappointment.

Morteave nodded. *I believe that my Lord has in spirit and deed fulfilled his responsibility to the Scripts. I am sorry for the loss to yourself and your coven, Lord Ivan. Lord Yantee has been moved by your care, and he has decided to grant you an equal share when the bounties are collected. As a recompense for her death, of course.*

Ivan waved a hand. "*That is acceptable. I will mourn Lil's loss. It is a pity, she was—talented.*" A smile touched Ivan's lips. But his hand went to the girl's hand at his neck. *We shall miss her. Please convey our satisfaction with your prince's message and assure him we will hold him harmless in Lil's death. Lil had a habit of overreaching. This time, it caught up with her.*

Yantee allowed Lil's mind to perceive the scene sent by Morteave. Tears leaked from closed eyes down her cheeks. He knew she received the message. Ivan the Prince of Coth'Venter had thrown her aside.

The Elder Brother rose above the treetops, casting shifting shadows and dappling light across the jungle-covered streets. Roots and vines snarled buildings that lay covered in the decay as life struggle to reclaim the space. Va'Yone was in wonder. "Come on De'Nidra. Really, I just want to explore a little. We could finish in an hour."

De' shook her head, "No, not this time Va'Yone, the dig is only a tad further and maybe if we have time, we can explore on the way back." Just then, the trail broke in to a valley and the heavy tree cover fell away into deep sheer cliff walls that ran downward to the dig.

Va'Yone's mouth fell open. "What is it?" he asked, his voice dreamy. Between the two valley walls, a structure shaped like an arrowhead lay partially covered. Below, beneath the huge wedge-shaped structure, they had cleared away the jungle, revealing the tents and diggers working the site.

Wonder filled De'Nidra's voice as she marveled, "Wow! Look at it. It's almost perfect. There's hardly any damage."

Va'Yone's wonder mirrored hers. "Ya, but what is it? I mean, the bottom is round, and it looks like it fell there and came to rest. But that would mean…" His voice froze midway through his thoughts.

"A ship?" Tem'Aldar asked. "It's too far from the sea for that."

"Yes, a ship," De'Nidra said. "But not for the sea." She reached into her saddlebag and removed a book. She opened it. The book was old and made of dark metal. She pulled a chain from around her neck, which held a flickering teardrop crystal. With it poised between her fingers, she closed her eyes. The Intensity of light grew within the crystal and then the thick fixed page of the book scrolled with raised metal text and pictures as she waved the bright pulsing teardrop over it, dragging the script across the page. "This is a copy of fragments of the Third Chronicle of the Shattered Age." De'Nidra tilted it so he could see. A three-dimensional picture of the same shape as the structure that lay between the valley walls. She translated the text. "*We soared through the heavens in great ships.*"

Va'Yone nearly fell from his horse. "Are you saying this flies?" He climbed down, as Tem and De' did. They huddled together, staring at the book.

"No, I am telling you what this book says it is." De'Nidra smiled at him whimsically. "Do you still want to explore the jungle, Va'Yone?"

But Va'Yone did not hear her. He dropped his horse's bridle and started walking towards the dig.

Tem'Aldar's voice drifted to her, tinged with awe as he exclaimed, "There he goes."

She handed him her animal's rains and with a skip in her step caught up to Va'Yone, taking his hand. "We will explore it together, apprentice."

Va'Yone just nodded.

"I am glad you approve." She said. They left Tem'Aldar to tend to the horses.

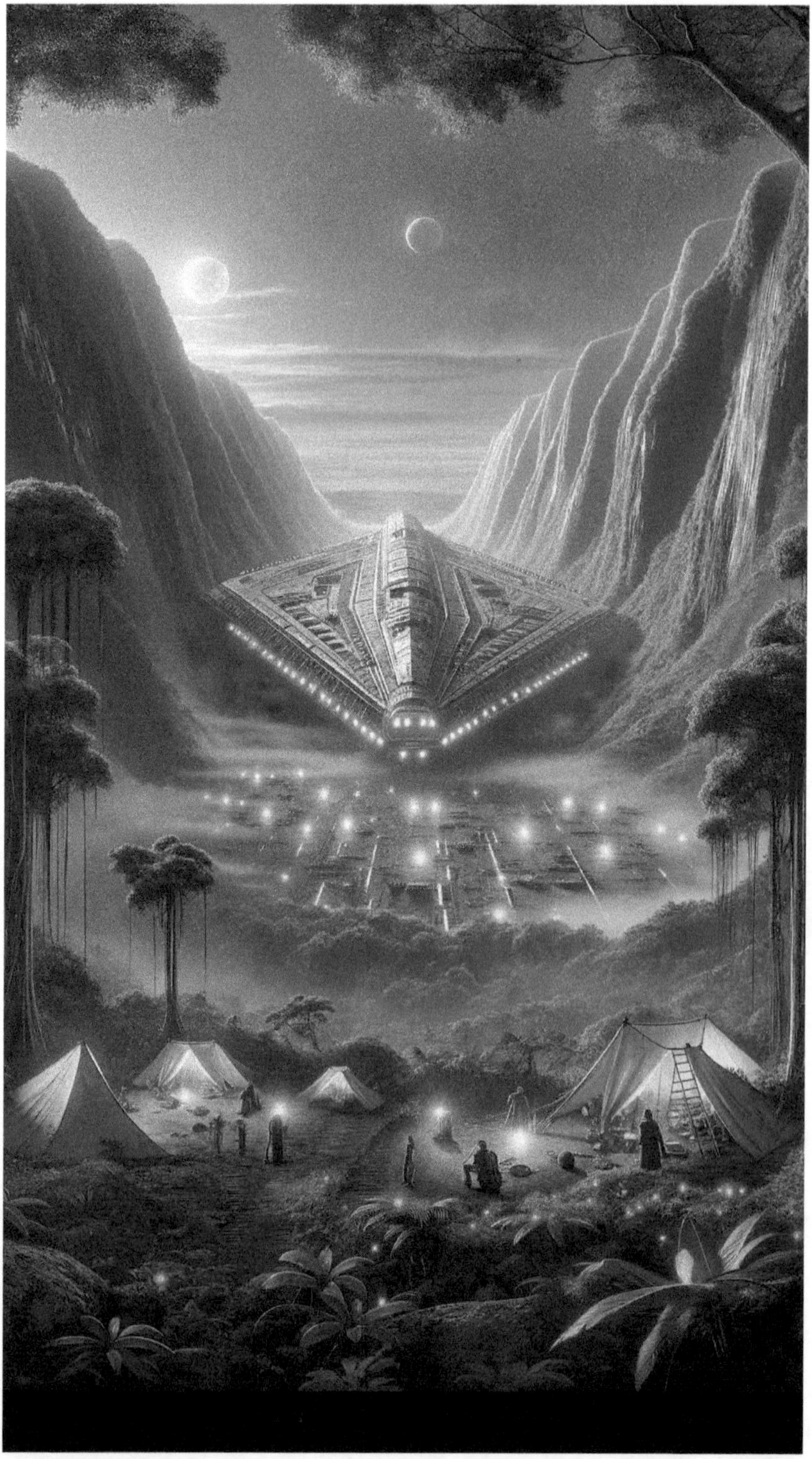

Chapter 31 Fearful Visions

"There is only so much taking you can do before someone, seeing your rules, comes and takes it from you. Justifying it with—You are just getting your due."

※

Golden moonlight piercing through shifting clouds cast a radiant glow over the leafy treetops, climbing the valley sides like a carpet of jungle green. Torchlight and lamps cast dancing shadows on the tent sides, shrouding the valley floor beneath the ship's nose. Artificial lights from the ship illuminated patches of dirt, cleared by workers weeks before their arrival. Countless workers and wagon teams had compacted the red soil, forming rutted paths in the soft dirt.

"It obviously has Power. Can't we just melt our way in, De'Nidra? The real treasures are inside, right?" Va'Yone's voice echoed, a floating orb of light mirroring every cranny of his curiosity.

De'Nidra's voice rebounded back to him amid flashes. Her arcane light reflected off the rounded shape of the lower portion of the ship, nearer to what they had decided was the rear. "This is the treasure Va'Yone. Everything inside is a bonus. There must be a ramp for loading on the bottom. If this is the bottom. It looks that way, but it is hard to be sure. The way in may be higher on the hull between the vertical portion where the wedge's surface starts near the edges." Her voice filled with as much marvel as frustration. "We will figure it out Va'Yone. Besides, we are out of time for tonight."

Va'Yone smiled at the gruff sound of Tem'Aldar's voice in his ear. De'Nidra was getting to him. "For the love of the Light, De', I am starving. Can we get something to eat?" You could tell from his voice that he felt as tired and frustrated as they did. To tell the truth, Tem was carrying all of De'Nidra's gear as well. He trounced along behind her grumbling, a shovel and pick over one shoulder and a leather tool bag and water skin over the other.

"Tem'Aldar! You know very well that I need your help. Beyond that, it is time for a Gate to Coth'Venter, and Tara will want to see the ship. They need to know about it. She is likely to figure something out that we have missed. Anyway, bed time tonight can wait if you are too tired to take part?"

"I said I am hungry, De', not dead." Tem sounded injured.

"Va'Yone, you know Tara will want to see you. Come on. The ship has been here for epochs. It will still be here when she arrives." De'Nidra said indulgently. She pointed with one hand and the other on her hip. "Behind the ship Tem. I don't need one of these superstitious island folk thinking we are calling spirits."

"The rear of the ship is quite a distance. You're really making me work for it, De'," Tem grumbled.

"Call it penance. You are still in trouble for your remarks. And don't say what did I do? You know what you did."

Tara and Edward sat by the three-tiered fountain at the heart of the cathedral's cobbled square. The warmth of the night air mingled with the scent of distant grassy fields. Above them, torchflies danced their silent, luminescent ballet under the street lamps. Around them, the bustle of Coth'Venter continued unabated; wagons laden with supplies rumbled in and out, while the rhythmic steps of patrolling house guards punctuated the night.

Tara's gaze swept over the scene. "Edward, look at the crowds. Where are all these people coming from?" New faces were everywhere, people moving into houses and seeking support to start anew.

Edward's eyes followed her gaze, settling on the bustling section near RavenHof where people were busily restoring the ancient structures. "Everywhere. Most are from the Grey Area. Some are from Haven or even deeper into the Lands of Light. I met a farrier that came from the Darkened Lands claiming escape from a mining camp near the Shadow Lakes."

"What manner of mortal is he?" Tara asked.

Edward chuckled. "*She* is a Zoruk."

"What?" Tara gasped, "A Zoruk?"

"You needn't worry; I've assigned someone to keep an eye on her," Edward reassured. "Unless you are not granting the same rights to them as the others?" He gave a brief grin, knowing her better than that.

Tara thought for a moment and shook her head. "No. She is welcome and has the same rights, remove the watch from her. She is no different from the rest. Make sure she eats at our table at the next meal. Have her seated next to me. I want to get to know her. I would think that she is causing quite the stir and I want everyone to know that I accept her and she is now one of my own." She sighed with conviction in her voice, "Edward, it was wrong of me to hesitate with her, where I have not with others. I will not be someone that racially grants favor. I am Elp'har and we love people for who they are in our lives and not what they look like or for some perceived birthright."

The sound of Ivan jogging down the grey stone stairway of the Cathedral of Light reverberated across the square, drawing Tara's and Edward's attention. He was in a hurry and heading straight for them. Tara addressed him before he made it to the fountain. "Are you okay, Ivan?" Tara inquired, noting the urgency in his stride.

A leather tie at his neck held Ivan's long black hair in a tail. His body covered in scaled armor, also black fringed in red. His black cloak billowed in the night breeze, and his left hand rested on the hilt of his menacing blade. The radiance of the red gem pulsed angrily, its light crimson on white flesh. "Tara, I must accompany you to Far'Mora," Ivan said, resolve lacing his voice. "Someone has taken Lil, and I must rescue her. Da'Vain and the other Chronicler Morteave are calling for a council to investigate the allegations of breach that threaten the peace of the Vam'Phire covens. They could erupt into war."

"War? Slow down, Ivan." Edward said. "What do you mean, someone took her? No one just takes Lil anywhere if she does not want to go." Edward gripped his broadsword at his waist, though neither he nor Tara wore armor.

Tara's voice pitch climbed, and her fist clenched at her sides. "If someone has taken her, I want to help. She is my sister and my teacher, Ivan. Edward, go get our armor and weapons." Tara said, shock and anger in her voice, "Ivan won't be alone. No one takes my sister from me, Ivan! We have lost too many people already. I am tired of people just taking from us. I will help you get her back and punish these people. Who do they think they are? You don't just steal whatever or whoever you want."

Edward started for the rooms at a run. "I will be right back. Hold that Gate."

As Ivan responded, a massive black dire wolf, six feet at the shoulders, followed him down the steps. "He is the Vam'Phire prince of pirates on the island of Far'Mora. And I am going to kill him for stealing my Lil." The wolf nuzzled his hand when he tried to point him back. He was going, and that was the end of that.

Tara patted his head, nearly half the size of her body. "He does not care, Ivan. He loves Lil too. He is going."

A bright light cleaved the darkness before De'Nidra, its shimmer resembling a snake's writhing actions. This light coalesced into an orb of amber, its pulse erratic, suggesting it might vanish at any moment—a gateway formed, teetering between stability and dissolution. Moments later, the eight-foot sphere burst into a brilliant purple strobe. A round layer materialized at the center of the Mage Gate, its appearance shifting from a foggy mirror to a clear, shimmering portal. The event horizon opening onto the cobblestone square. The Coth'Venter Cathedral of Light came into view.

Tara, Edward, and Ivan stepped through a wash of icy energy, followed by the hulking form of the dire wolf, his hair raised along the ridges of his neck, shook off the effect with a fearless shudder. His four large golden eyes taking the scant light that filtered through the canopy. The smell of the decay of the jungle filled the soaking air, bathing faces in the vibrancy of jungle life. The dire wolf lifted his nose to sniff the air, and his ears perked up at the unfamiliar sounds and jungle noises.

The ship reared up before them. Massive circular cone shapes protruded from the rear of the ship, their purpose perplexing. Edward blurted. "What in the name of the gods is that?" He waved a hand at the ship.

"Hello to you too, Edward," De'Nidra replied with a smile, savoring his surprise.

Tara gave De' a wink, "Yes Edward. Don't be rude. How was the journey from the harbor?"

Tem'Aldar piped in, "The journey was fine. It's this thing," he pointed at the ship. "That is wearing me out. De'Nidra has had us hopping about since we arrived, and she is showing no hint of slowing down."

Va'Yone gave a grin, "Hi everyone. Tem'Aldar is just tired and hungry. I see Edward and Ivan too. It's almost like a homecoming. All we need are Antoff and Al'len. Just look at it Tara, it's a ship." He spread his arms toward the stars. "A ship for flying in the heavens."

Tara raised an eyebrow at De'Nidra.

De' confirmed with a nod. "That's right. I checked it and the picture is the same in the copy of the chronicle I brought. Whether it works or not, I don't know? That we will have to see once we get in."

"It's locked?" Ivan asked. "I may help with that, but I will require your help in return."

Tara answered. "Ivan, you are family. You have our help weather you can get in or not. I told you we are coming with you to get Lil."

"To get Lil?" Va'Yone asked, "Where is she? Is Lil lost?" He forgot all about the ship.

Ivan shook his head, his expression grave. "Not lost Va'Yone, Stolen by the Prince of Far'Mora. She was hunting the High Bishop of Haven, who abandoned his post and apparently emptied the church's coffers on the way out. Prince Yantee, also on the job, took both the bounty and Lil. I'm committed to winning her back and getting rid of Yantee. Ivan's fist knotted white knuckled on the hilt of his sword.

Va'Yone stepped close. His hand reached for Ivan's as it trembled on the pommel of his blade. Ivan dominated his height three times over. "I'm going too. Lil is my sister also, and no one gets to keep her where she doesn't want to be."

De'Nidra's mouth was open for just a hair's breadth and she closed it again, clearly revising what she was going to say. "If you go, who will help Tem'Aldar protect me? What about your lessons?" Her dark, beautiful eyes shifted briefly to Tara before returning to Va'Yone.

Tara arched an eyebrow at De' before she addressed Va'Yone. "You have made commitments also to De'Nidra. You can't just duck responsibilities because something new comes up. Besides, if I need you, we can pick out a spot for a Gate before we go and you can jump through and save the day. Okay?"

Va'Yone kicked at a root. "Well, I did make commitments to De' and now that she is pregnant, I hesitate to leave her."

Tara's voice pierced the silence with a joyous shriek, sending a wave of startled tension through the group. As muscles clenched and eyes widened in surprise, a shared ripple of anticipation connected them. "You're pregnant?" Tara's words, laden with a mix of elation and disbelief, hung in the air, drawing everyone closer into a circle of shared joy and concern. The news, a beacon of light amid their fears for Lil, reminded them of life's continual renewal? Her eyes flashed to Tem'Aldar, who gave a roguish smile. Then back to De'Nidra, waiting for confirmation.

De' gave a shy nod, and Tara leaped at her with a hug. "That is wonderful! When did you know?" The two women separated to an arm's length. But Tara did not let go. She just looked into her eyes.

De'Nidra bit her lip, her cheeks warming as all eyes turned to her. "I suspected before we left the Harbor Cities. But it was the daily morning sickness during the trip that confirmed it. I was morning sick every day of the trip and when storms came, I could not stop throwing up. That was when I was sure." She gave Tem'Aldar an accusatory look.

Tem's voice cracked slightly, pretending a hint of hurt underlying his usual bravado. "What did I do?"

Tara arched a questioned eyebrow again, but gave him a loving smile. "If you can't figure that one out, I will leave it to De'Nidra to explain it to you."

"You know what you did. So you can quit asking." De' mused. "Stop pretending you don't."

A grin spread crossed Tem'Aldar's face and when he could no longer contain it, he burst out with laughter, enjoying De'Nidra's furious blush. He thought. *I'm sure I will pay for that, but it was worth it. I love the most beautiful woman in the world.*

***

Floating orbs of light flickered on the ancient hull of the ship. Its surfaces tinged green by moss. Tara touched its wet skin. Cool and moist from the jungle's night air. The humidity blown inland from the sea filled the atmosphere with misty vapor and added to the scent of the jungle's flowering plants and decay. Life had first tried to consume the magnificent vessel and, when that failed, it had buried it in a verdant green. Wedged in between steep hills in a narrow valley, the ship's sides lay partially covered. But beyond that, Tara could detect only minor damage. Constructed of the same metal as the portal arches in Coth'Venter Under City, she pealed the layer of moss from a section hoping to find writing. Something she could translate. "De'Nidra, it's made of the same material as the portal arches," Tara called.

"It is." De'Nidra's voice came, "I have a book and a crystal, but I can't see how to enter it yet. There are no directions that show the opening. There must be one. After all, you have a ship that travels in a sea of stars. The crew still needs food and water. Right?" Frustration laced what was normally a calm voice.

Tara chalked it up to being pregnant and uncomfortable in the wet night air. "Can I see them, the book and the crystal? It may have some information I can puzzle out. The script for the portal room has become familiar to me. I spent so much time with Lil studying it at Coth'Venter." At the end of that thought was a catch. Just the thought of Lil missing from her life was unthinkable. More so after the loss of her mother.

De'Nidra walked closer, passing by Ivan and Va'Yone, who knelt. Va'Yone was describing every detail of the Far'Mora harbor and the layout of the city streets. He drew it with a stick in the hard packed dirt and then transferred it to the parchment. Tara eyed them. It was like a giant watching a child play in the mud.

Holding the book and the crystal, De'Nidra's floating orb of light merged with Tara's, collectively brightening the section of the hull they examined. "Here you are," De'Nidra said, her hand passing her the dark metal book and the chain with a dangling teardrop that pulsed weakly with light.

Tara opened the small metal book. Its texture was cold and smooth. It had only a single thick page that crawled with raised metallic script and a three-dimensional picture of the ship that spun from top view to side and then back to a three point perspective. Tara concentrated on the crystal and it blinked more brightly. Dragging the crystal over the metal page, manipulating and spinning the image that copied the massive derelict that lay silent on the valley floor. "In the Coth'Venter portal room, it connected the metal on the wall and the portal itself somehow. Even though the portal arches floated on a ball that hung in space. I learned the arches existed in both places at once, and size did not matter as long as it was an exact copy of the portal room somewhere else. It was about Power and producing the proper resonance. This technology must all work on the same principle. Virtually, there was no difference between the information on the wall and the arches, so long as you had a crystal to transfer it between devices."

De'Nidra shook her head, "I don't understand Tara. Are you saying our ancestors interconnected everything made of this metal through the crystal?"

"I believe that to be the case. Yes." Tara said. "However, I have never tried a book and an object like this before. If I am right, the crystal will allow an interconnection between what I see in the book and the craft. I am not sure and I don't know how it will work yet, if it works at all. I will try, but if this doesn't work, I will risk Ivan Shadow Walking me in so I can try to open it that way. If it fails, you will need to make a Gate to the outskirts of Far'Mora. It will have to wait until we get Lil back. She knows the language better than I do, and we are going to need her."

"Tara," De'Nidra said, "This can wait. Lil is more important."

Tara whispered so Va'Yone could not hear. "No... Lil would want me to try. There is no guarantee that we are coming back." Ivan turned to look at her. The light from Va'Yone's glowing orb cast eerie shadows, making Ivan's pale skin appear almost ghostly. Turning her eyes back to the book, she aligned the image so that it matched the way it lay between the valley. Just as it did with its bow stretching out above. Then she closed her eyes and concentrated on pushing the image inward. It moved. The superstructure on the image showed only the frame. Like a skinless creature, only the structure remained. Massive main supports ran the length of the hull and smaller ones interconnected them. Doors and rooms formed. But she couldn't locate any opening on the skin.

De'Nidra stood back in wonder. Afraid to speak, as if her voice could somehow break the spell Tara had woven. Her eyes wondered across the page as Tara painstakingly pushed the image around the interior of the vessel. Then she blurted. "Wait! There."

De' pointed to a round room midship. A ball floated in the hull, not touching the structure. It seemed to just hang there in space.

"That's it De'Nidra. That is the way in." Tara said breathlessly. "I just need the address and the resonance frequency and we are in!"

"I can get that," Ivan said. They both turned to look at him. Both he and Va'Yone were on their feet and walking over. Tem'Aldar was not far behind. He had been napping behind a moss-covered boulder. *Waiting for De' to take him to bed, no doubt.* "If I understood what you said about seeing the inside. And so long as I can get a good impression of where that is, I should be able to Shadow Walk to it and get the address. I remember how to get the De'Moggda Lucida off the wall and it should be the same, right?" His eyes met Tara's. "Besides that, Lil would be angry with me if I did not do all that… I could have solved this mystery before we go." His tone was grim.

"I can get you close," Tara whispered.

"Then let us begin so we can be on our way to save Lil," He said.

Chapter 32 Pearls In Shells

"*The beauty of a habitable world is like finding a pearl. We seldom find pearls in every shell. We pry them open only to find emptiness, casting them aside, to be consumed by time like rotting meat. Persistence in our search bears fruit, but at what cost? What is the value of a pearl if our quest lays waste to the beauty of a world?*"

Deep beneath Are'Amadon, distant prisoner cries echoed hauntingly. There was no pity in this place, save perhaps the mercy of a bright sphere of light floating above Amorath's graying hand. The incessant tapping of his staff, synchronized with his crystal's flicker, echoed down the halls, pulsing like an erratic heartbeat. Shadows played a ghostly dance on the rough-hewn volcanic stone, flickering in the uncertain light. The air, thick with torch smoke and the residue of long confinement, stung Moros's eyes in the darkness. Rem'Mel followed closely behind. Moros walked between Amorath and Rem'Mel, forming a tight trio as they ventured deeper into the fortress. Beneath his onyx robes and black leather vest, the childlike form belied the immense Power within.

"How deep do these ancient halls run?" Moros coughed, echoing faintly in the vastness.

Amorath's voice, once a steady ember of command, now flickered with an unusual hesitance, betraying the depth of thought often concealed by his daunting presence. He found particular satisfaction in unsettling small children, relishing their vulnerability. The deep intonations resonated down the hallway, accompanied by dancing shadows as he led them deeper. "Deep indeed. This fortress stands on the ruins of our once-great civilization, fallen during the Breaking of the Balance. I lived before that cataclysm, though my memories of it are but shadows. I was alive before the Breaking, but I remember little of it."

"Why?" Moros asked, his voice threading the line between childlike curiosity and the emerging wisdom of a soul that had glimpsed the unfathomable. Each question marked a step away from innocence, leading into realms where knowledge wasn't just desired but necessary for survival.

In Amorath's mind, the weight of knowledge was a double-edged sword—a source of Power, yet a burden of responsibility. Each secret he held was a piece in a game spanning epochs, his enjoyment of this Power tempered by the gravity of choices made in the ancient past. He loved his torments, holding his knowledge over others. To deny them that Power, but in this case, it mattered not. As they walked, Amorath's voice took on a distant tone. "The birth of the gods twisted reality, erasing ancient memories like dust scattered by the wind. The Shattering of the Balance was not one deity's will, but ten, clashing for dominion. We learned to resist, to remember amidst the chaos."

Moros mused, his thoughts a storm. *Does he underestimate me, or is this a strategic game, each move cloaking his true intentions in shadow, an illusion woven from half-truths to mislead me?* He pondered over Amorath's every word, wrestling with a mix of amusement and a gnawing doubt about the unseen layers in their interaction. *Speaking to me as an adolescent, believing he controls my fate.* "That sounds confusing. How did you know what was real and what was fake? How did you know what to trust? I mean, if people just accepted the change, and it became real for them, even the lie becomes undetectable if you don't know better. You become trapped in the changes, right?"

Amorath halted, the glow from his orb casting eerie reflections on the gold arcane symbols of his coat. Dead eyes glittered back at Moros, cold with malevolence. "Child, you ask too many questions. Questions about things you do not yet need to know."

Moros stepped back, seeking solace in Rem'Mel's shadow. The hisses of his robe, a reminder of their shared past, were a silent anchor in the echoing halls. "But how do you discern reality from illusion? What guides your truth?" Moros's voice wavered, a mix of trepidation and the burgeoning wisdom of one who had glimpsed secrets. Rem'Mel's hand on his shoulder was a silent testament to a bond weathered by shared turmoil. The formality of his touch and the sound of those robes gave him courage. "How did you decide what to do? What was real?" His voice, trembling with nerves, thinly veiled the undercurrent of his fear.

Amorath wagged a finger at Moros. "I shall indulge this inquiry, but let it be your last—for the moment," he said, a cunning smile creeping across his weathered face. "It was not a simple matter, to be sure. I had to decide which god most closely aligned with my desired outcome. It wasn't any of these self-proclaimed gods of Light. They etched their territories across our world's face and retreated, leaving their marks to endure through time. And to answer your next question before you blurt it out, ruining my mood. It has been millennia, and that is more than most mortals know." He turned his back to him and strolled deeper into a slowly sloping hall. Metal doors darkened with age held barred windows.

A man with thick fingers wrapped them around the bars. He screamed an unintelligible sentence. Moros jumped back and then began a laugh as he could see that Rem'Mel had nearly flown out of his own skin. He stood there, holding his heart and panting. "Dam fool has lost his mind! Been down here so long he can't even speak coherently anymore."

Amorath demanded, "Come on, you're wasting time. The Well chamber is this way." He quickened his pace, and the light dimmed as the distance between them lengthened. Moros and Rem'Mel did as well. The idea of being in the dark with these—things was too much to ponder. Rem'Mel made a light of his own and the bright sphere floated before them. His hand rested on Moros' shoulder and Rem'Mel silently urged him forward. Every sound in this dank place was like a ringing bell in his ears declaring danger, but Moros tried... Tried hard to ignore it.

Finally, the hall opened into a room and Amorath's light all but disappeared except for the shadows. They played on the floor stone and vaulted archway that led into a circular room. In the center, a depression held two vast arches larger than a covered wagon in height and could manage two abreast. Awe filled Moros. His question came out breathless. "What is it?"

Amorath replied, tinged with frustration. "Portal architecture, young master. A technology that few know of, let alone understand. Come here, child." He waved Moros closer. His dead gray hand calling to him.

Moros walked nearer to the old mage. As he drew near, Amorath's sphere lifted into the air and grew brighter. The ceiling and walls crawled with Scripts and pictures that he did not understand. His mind bore down on every character of the script... *No, they are equations.* "It's math. The language is math, but I can't quite understand it."

"Indeed, it is," Amorath concurred. "Yet, it transcends mere language, a relic predating the Shattering itself. Most of those that should remember its use cannot, because that information slipped away with the reformation of reality constantly in flux. I preserved some, mind you, just a little, but perhaps together we can learn to use it to its full extent again. However, this is not why I brought you two down here. This way." He swept an arm toward a long, elliptical stairway with a rusty black rail.

The rail was rough and Moros could feel the rust rubbing off on to his skin. Rem'Mel remained close as they followed their limping master lower. At the bottom of the stair, the room opened up and was large as the room above and in the same shape. It must have been a tower foundation before, buried during the cataclysm. All along the walls of the room were metal panels that crawled with a raised script, as above. And beneath them were cabinets with buttons with strange symbols that match the style of the arcane writing. In its center was an enormous ball of crystal supported by a single metallic cylinder. Connected metal beds, spaced evenly with restraints upon them, encircles it. Within the crystal, thousands of lights, akin to torchflies, danced an eternal ballet, each spark seemingly alive, chasing the next in endless pursuit. It was clear there was an awareness. If not of them, then of each other. It was fearful and wondrous at the same time.

"What is it?" Moros asked, even more in awe than before.

As Amorath gestured towards the glowing sphere, his voice softened, "Behold the Dark Well—keeper of souls, not all willingly given, and not all—benign. But all are utterly insane."

"Insane? Why?" Moros voice was little more than a squeak.

"They did not design this for what we have used it for. It was a medical device for temporary transfer, while they provided a new body. Not for its current use. We are going to learn to use it for its proper purpose. To prolong life. First, I need to teach you and Rem'Mel how to use it. There are these four beds, two are for the procedure and one for controlling the transfer. And the last is for the new host." Amorath pointed each out as he named them. "What would you like to learn first, Lord Moros?"

Water dripped rhythmic drops like a timepiece that kept the beat of each moment in the dark depths beneath rock and sea. On'omus looked out at the sleeping form of Er'laya bundled in ragged remains of blankets rotted through. The straw was far from fresh and harbored borfleas, small black creatures with long needle like beaks, that bit and burrowed into his tender skin, now a red angry rash. Their cell was of old dark metal, wet and slimy. The bars of the six-foot by six-foot cell had rusted through in places. But that was not what kept them in there. The scant light of a single candle sputtered, providing a flickering glimpse of the monster on the other side of the bars.

Vam'Phire—they do not need to sleep, and once something has their interest, that fascination does not abate. Blood tinged its eyes with spots of gold and silver. They held an unnaturally hungry light, and it chilled On'omus. *How Er'laya can sleep with that thing out there is beyond me. We are going to die and he has already accepted the inevitable conclusion.* "Coward!" On'omus mouthed the word like the bitter taint of betrayal. *It was not as if Er'laya had left him alone? I was alone the moment this fool gave up. He has condemned us both.*

A menacing grin spread cross his jailor's flour white face. "What say you morsel? My future meal doth speak?" The pirate paced about the room beyond his bars. Only a small table with a feathered hat for decoration and a single stool.

A bright red bloused shirt flared at the cuffs. Gold hoops in his elongated ears swayed with long, black braided hair as he moved. A silver necklace nestled a key that glittered in the weak light of a single candle. It was a promise of release that would only come at death. It stuffed black britches neatly into knee high brown boots, and at his waist was a thick dark leather belt that held a dagger and a cutlass.

"I said I am thirsty and I need something to eat," On'omus responded. But there was no genuine hope behind his words.

"I'm sorry morsel but the meal do be running late. Perhaps if you give me a taste, I might find you something. Otherwise," the seven-foot monster sighed, "It will have to wait."

On'omus swallowed hard and his heart began pounding in his chest, "you were told by Yantee you had to leave us alone." His voice was little more than a breathless squeak. He shivered in the dark even as a cold bead of sweat trickled down his back. The smell of shite and piss lay heavy in the air.

"It could be our secret. What do you say? Just a little nip?" The grin never left the monster's face. Its pale, bloodless lips pealed back, exposing fangs that dimpled it. Glowing eyes shifted in the dancing light and swirled silver, gold mixed with crimson red.

On'omus hesitated, then shook his head shamefully, "Abomination!" He whispered.

A woman's voice echoed from the hall as she drew closer and then entered. She was tall like the monster, but breathtaking in beauty. Her long golden hair fell loose on her back. Golden and silver spotted eyes drew his. On'omus' breath caught as much with relief as desire. She called herself Radean and On'omus had never seen such a lovely creature before he laid eyes on her. Her dress was a white silk, and it flowed down her elegant form, clinging to every luxurious curve like a hot breath. "Am'Brose, quit playing with our—guests." She moved to the bars and slid the tin plates through the trap. "Are you mortals famished?" she asked. She also pushed a bottle of wine in and smiled.

On'omus nodded furiously, "We are my Lady."

Am'Brose sniffed, "Ye sure we oughta give 'em wine, Radean? Won't it sour the meat?" Fangs protruded from a menacing smile.

Radean placed her fists on her curvy hips. "Am'Brose, you are a beast! Leave the bounties alone. They are not to be abused, and if Prince Yantee found out about your little jest? Well," her voice dropped to a purr, "his feelings will be—hurt." She raised a lovely eyebrow at him.

Am'Brose snatched his salt stained black leather feathered hat from the table and gave a sweeping bow as elegant as a courtier. "As you say, lass. I won't be eating em—yet." He winked.

On'omus gave Er'laya a light kick. "Wake up Er'laya, it's time to eat."

Chapter 33 Fallen To Sea

"With each choice we make, a delicate dance between loyalty and principle emerges in a world woven with complexities. Where the heart's bonds get tested against the rigid edges of rules. The echoes of our decisions, they cut like a blade in the silent moments that follow, and whisper to me. Was it, indeed, a test of bond or law, or was it testing me? Whichever you decide, friendship or rule, I hope it was worth it."

Da'Vain and Morteave leaned against the ship's rail, beyond the bowsprit, their eyes transfixed by the marvel of the Shelf. Salt-laden mist sprayed their faces, mingling with the scent of fish. A brisk breeze fitfully played against snapping sails and taut wet lines hummed with tension as the clipper hull rose and fell, cutting a path through the waves. Above, two suns traced their arcs in the sky, Little Sister was at her peak, Elder Brother bowing gracefully towards a cloudless horizon marked by crimson streaks.

The Shelf, a colossal formation of angled stone, emerged starkly from the ocean's depths, its stratified sides painted in a spectrum from fiery red to deep black ash. It whispered of El'idar's ancient upheavals, tales born from the Breaking of the Balance. Below, a secluded cove nestled, its shores caressed by the rhythmic dance of the waves. The Shelf's story, like a vibrant, layered history etched into stone. Time had eroded the upper layer, leaving pale, ghostly streaks across its surface, like waxen tears. The wind lifting the Mer' Gulls that nested along the stone edge, fluttering up to the Rip—a vast, three-league-wide scar in the living rock, a remnant of when continents collided.

Morteave sighed, a deep shudder. His words were a balm to Da'Vain's mind, frightened for Lil. *The Shelf's glory never fades, each viewing a revelation. Our world is so torn and yet filled with its own rugged beauty. This broken crust of El'idar is like a wound that will not heal.*

Nor for me. Some things never heal, my friend, Da'Vain mused silently, his gaze lingering on the expanse of the mainland, as a silent sigh escaped him. Just the thought of Lil being at the mercy of that monster Yantee was too much. It came too close to the unknown histories of Lil's past. In the subtle tension of his brow, an unspoken thought took form - the absurdity to be reduced to such an ordinary arrival when urgency was required. *This law is just a remnant of an age when we warred against one another. Is it truly necessary? When was the last time someone tried to assassinate a member of the council?*

A noise like tapping drew his attention. Turning back, Da'Vain watched the crew. Six-foot Spidrals, with long segmented bodies and eight legs, skittered gracefully across the dark deck. They climbed the two-masted schooner like spiders weaving a web. *Even after ages, I find the appearance of the Spidrals unsettling. Their torsos, like men, augmented with four arms.* Dark, coal-black hair capped their heads, and eight lidless large dark eyes that seem to observe everything at once. Altered mortal clothing revealed glimpses of their skin, which varied in color from milk white to emerald-green. The Spidrals moved with a fluid grace, a tangible echo of their origins—*they are creations left adrift by gods or mages.* In their hesitant movements, one could glimpse their perpetual struggle to find a place in a world not quite their own. *Aliens in a shattered world. Wearing our clothes, trying to look normal. Good luck with that. I don't trust them.*

Morteave cleared his throat, drawing Da'Vain's attention. *Don't stare, old friend. They dislike it. But know this—they are the finest sailors on the Shelf. Post-war, they mastered these waters, and now, despite fears, locals seek them out, though none dare journey as far as Far'Mora.* He paused, then added. *Regarding your question, we travel by ship from North Watch to the Shelf because neither the council nor mortals wish for unnoticed arrivals. The tension between our princes is evidence enough. Our nature leans towards vengeance, and we often succumb to it. It's a short trip—only ten leagues—and I love the view as we enter the harbor.*

Da'Vain let his gaze drift back to the Rip. Mer' Gulls gave shrill cries as they entered the breakwater. Like a dart, their scales, shimmering in multiple colors, plunged after fish into the seawater. Rift' Harbor climbed the split rock like a jagged path upward beyond broken stone as the city rose. Before them, remnants of ancient buildings clung to existence, their rough outlines testament to the sea's relentless claim on history. Most had collapsed into the sea during the Breaking. Fallen block reused for stone docks jutted out into the sea where large ships lay moored, loading and unloading wares. Mortals moved crates and casks in and out of wagons as wooden cranes hoisted cargo hanging from nets.

They rebuilt many structures and warehouses along the streets since I was last here. Da'Vain's gaze traced the streets upward, his thoughts following suit. *Above the break, I see the great spire of Kith'Rondeal.* Grey swirling pinnacles of strange stone, solid and jointless all the way to their hundred meter spiraling sharp tips. No one knew how they were made. If he had to guess, something crafted them using a now-lost material science, a mastery of liquid stone.

Just wait until you see the city. You have been gone too long, old friend. Much has changed. Unfortunately, with the council, much has not. Morteave's tone dripped with foreboding.

Mooring at the discreetly owned council docks constructed of ancient stone, they boarded an unmarked black lacquered coach. Stationed here as a matter of course to transport delegates of council business. They exchanged no words. The driver knew where she was going. The coach rumbled down rough stone streets, angling upward. Dark curtains swayed with the movement of the coach. Da'Vain's long finger pulled them aside for a guarded look. Buildings and warehouses rose around him. It was not the finest of architecture. But then, it did not mean to be. Each structure was a mosaic of blocks from fallen edifices, some etched with artistic lines and swirls, creating a patchwork of history and art. At this level, it was the function that they were after. All manner of mortal moved about and wagons stuffed the street. The air was a mix of boiling fish from vendors pots and the briny scent of the sea.

The wheels of the coach struck the pavement, and the ride smoothed out. Like everything else, the pavement was an old remnant of a shattered past. They could not make it now, and even the repairs were little more than patches of pitch mixed with sand and pounded stone. The great spire of Kith'Rondeal, two mammoth twisting quills, reached for the sky, etching its silhouette against the canvas of heaven.

Morteave interrupted his reveries. *It still takes the breath and lifts the heart, does it not, old friend?*

Da'Vain closed the curtains and leaned back. *It still does. But I feel the press to return. Neither my prince nor yours have any inkling about a trip to the Shelf. What if they discover our absence? Well, let's just say—they will definitely notice our lack of presence.*

Our loyalties lie with the council, Morteave responded. *We are part of the council, and we remind our princes of the Scripts. Documenting the histories of the coven and reporting transgressions. It is a failing of a prince to think otherwise. They've borrowed us as subjects. Our seat is on the council. It is their folly if they forget it.*

Da'Vain's mirth flooded through his thoughts. *You sound like our old Scripts teacher. I remember us seated together during that lecture.*

That was long ago. Morteave mused. *Those rules are necessary and prince Yantee has broken them. This will ruin my seat on the council for another cycle. Yantee betrayed me when he put his own desire for Lil above his duty to the Scripts. The only solace I have is knowing that you, old friend, will ascend once more and put an end to this decadence.*

Ivan stood atop the moss and vine-covered ship. Its hull tinged green, surrounded by the jungle and its creatures. They moved like colored lights in the distance beyond the lit torches and floating, illuminated spheres still held by Tara and De'Nidra. They both burned like the suns filled with arcane Power of the likes of which he could never touch. De'Nidra, formerly known as the mysterious Daughter of Shadows, now served EL'ALue, the Maid of Light. *Can someone truly find redemption from Darkness? Or do they forever lament their past choices? Never truly embracing the forgiveness of the Light?*

Tara held the metal book up to him. With the tear shaped crystals, she moved the image of the ship so that it matched where they stood. "Ivan, we are here." She pointed to the top of the ship and tapped the image with the teardrop. She pushed deeper into the image and it morphed into a view like wires. The interior was visible. Every line was walls and floors. "It's about nine span to the floor of the portal room."

"I see it," Ivan said. He was burning blood and life to do it. Unlike mortals, he could not just eat—food to replace it. Food would stave some effects. But at some point, the only thing that satisfied was life. Fortunately, after this was over, they would hunt Yantee, where he would pay the full price for stealing Lil. "Step back so your Light does not impede me."

Tara and De' stepped away and dimmed their arcane orbs. Ivan gave a roguish smile. His eyes, in the dim light, were bloody swirled gold and a sliver that glowed supernaturally. Shadows pooled around him, snaking out like tendrils of liquid Darkness, enveloping him until he vanished.

Ivan plummeted, the Light above fading into a foggy glow. Enveloped in Darkness, he surrendered to instinct, guiding his descent. At his silent command, the shadows gently deposited him just a foot above the deck, their smoky tendrils cushioning his fall. He landed softly, kneeling on the cold, metallic floor.

The room, lit only by sparse, blinking red lights, felt like the heart of a dormant beast. He drew a candle from his belt, igniting it with a costly fire stick—a luxurious necessity without a mage. The candle's flame battled the encroaching darkness, casting eerie, dancing shadows across the room. *Damned expensive, these fire sticks, yet they're worth every coin. Far better than flint and steel.*

It was overwhelming. As Ivan moved closer to the wall, cryptic texts and symbols swarmed across the surfaces like insect trails. They danced in a relentless flood of arcane knowledge. *How do Tara and Lil make sense of this deluge*? He wondered. Focusing, he searched for the Da'Um, the symbol Lil had shown him, a beacon marking the portal's ephemeral location. If you could even say it actually had a location. It was all so complex. Lil had tried to explain it, but it was too intricate. *My Lil, I am coming for you.* He whispered a silent message to Lil, a futile hope that she might hear his call. All that returned was a chilling void, save for a faint spark—a glimmer of optimism, or merely a trick of memory? Ivan clung to that tiny Light, a beacon in his dark sea of hope.

Tara and De'Nidra waited below the ship, where Ivan said he would appear. De'Nidra clucked, "I don't know if Ivan can find the address. I have studied that language and it would likely take me weeks."

"You underestimate him. Lil has been teaching him. Ivan has a powerful mind, and she said he was an excellent student." Tara gave a girlish smile, remembering the sharing of secrets about their men between herself and Lil. "Yes, Lil is a most demanding teacher."

De'Nidra cocked an interested eyebrow. "Really, perhaps when you bring her home, I will attend class?"

"She will love having you as a student. I know she will say yes." Tara's excitement was confident and De' could not help but meet her smile with a grin of her own. Just then, the shadows pulled like ponding water to a stream in the center. Ivan was spat out. Smoky shadows clung to him, dissipating like mist.

In one hand, he held a roll of parchment. "Tara, here is the Da'Um for the ship's portal. We must be quick now. It will be dangerous soon as my hunger grows." His eyes burned with those bloody swirls of silver and gold. He reached out and handed her the Da'Um.

His gaze was unsettling. Tara swallowed inadvertently before taking it. Ivan was her family, as far as she was concerned, and whatever danger he offered was meant for someone other than her. Yantee, whoever he was, Ivan hated him and it was clear he was saving his hunger for some revenge. "We will do this quickly Ivan, and then we will go after Lil. I promise."

Ivan gave a nod and walked over by Edward and sat down on a large moss covered rock.

Tara turned, and a slash of Light ripped the air before her. It bloomed in to a bright shimmering globe of white radiance before beginning to collapse. Then, just as it was falling in on itself, it exploded into a strobing purple sphere, flooding the surrounding jungle. nearby creatures squawked and roared, dashing away in fear. Their passage through the leafy verge was a brief, rustling torrent, ending as abruptly as it began.

The event horizon on the Mage Gate cleared to the image of the Under Cities Coth'Venter portal room. "Let's get this done, De'Nidra. Ivan won't last too much longer. He will need to feed." De' gave a quick nod. Tara followed her through the gate. The Power washed over them like being drenched in ice water.

The sensation left only the momentary chill when they passed through. Tara let it wink out.

The massive outline of the arches sat silent. Tara allowed her eyes to refocus after the strobing of the purple Gate. A female Vam'Phire was spat out of shadow. "I thought I recognized your mind, Tara. It was the other that drew me." Her marbled gold and silver eyes traced De'Nidra's body.

"Luc'Cinda!" Tara said, happy to see a friend. She often took up calling her Lucie for short. "De'Nidra is with me. I need to use the portal arches. I have to do this and get back to Ivan quickly. He has the hunger." She saw two mages staffs laying on the table, but without Lil to help her translated she dare not use them.

Lucie's eye shifted back to Tara, "The hunger? We will give you something to help him with that." Darkness pulled towards her from every pooled shadow and when they enveloped her. She was gone. Tendrils of smoke shifted and devolved. But Lucie's voice flowed into Tara's mind. *Wait for me, Tara. I will not take long.*

I will wait. Tara sent as she walked to the arches while unrolling the parchment. The Da'Um read $W(d, r) = exp(\hbar \cdot c - i \cdot G \cdot M2) \times [2Gc2(r2+c44G2M2-c22GM)] d$. It was in Ivan's flowing script.

De'Nidra moved closer and peered at the parchment. "Powerful mind indeed." She whispered. "Looking at Ivan, you could miss it and that would be a mistake."

"That is where people make a mistake. They see only the creature and miss the rest." Tara said, clearly puzzling out the Da'Um on the parchment.

It was not long and Luc'Cinda was spat from the shadow once more. She held a silk bag that clicked with the recognizable sound of glass on metal. "Take this to my prince. He will know what to do with it. Take care Tara. I entrust you with our deepest secret."

"I will not look Luc'Cinda, and I will guard your secret. Now we must go. Or at the very least, try to. I have never done this before."

Tara handed the metal book to De'Nidra and held up the tear drop crystal. It pulsed with a weak rhythmic light that dance subdued within the glassy surface. Tara closed her eyes, and the crystal came alive. Time shuddered in a wash around them and a ball of liquid Power grew before her. It writhed like a living thing. Inside a melon-sized silvery sphere, the Power of Darkness and Light clashed, threatening to burst forth. The box before the arch held black sand that lifted from its surface, connected by metallic strands of fine dust. It grew until it to became a ball that slowly spun. Land rose from a molten sea of dark bronze metal.

The glyph pulsed on the land, matching the location of Coth'Venter. The image of planet El'idar spun before them and five thousand six hundred and sixty miles away. A glyph blinked. Tara focused. The view zoomed in and a wedged shaped ship that nested in a valley came into view.

Two tentacles of Power, one black and one white, struck the holes meant to hold the rods of Power. Tara emulated them and fed them with energy. The arches turned slowly at first. Then gaining speed. Faster and faster, they turned until they were a blur. Then they exploded with light. Tara fed them with Power until it match the equation's resonance frequency for the other portal. The energy required to stabilize it was more massive than she had ever used. She pulled on the reservoirs of her dragons and they answered with Power. Tara was only on the edge of her control. The portal, an enormous sphere of spinning energy, erupted in a final radiant flash before stabilizing into a shimmering liquid orb. Its event horizon cleared and a matching room opened to the other side. "De'Nidra, walk through and I will follow." Tara's voice held effort and internal struggle. Moisture beaded on her forehead.

De'Nidra did not wait. She walked through the Gate and shivered with the wash of cold while passing the barrier of the wormhole. Tara followed, not sparing a look for Lucie, but in her mind, she heard Tara's voice. It was a frightening glimpse of a higher reality warring with Power. Tara stepped through, sending—*Gods of Light willing. I will see you soon, Lucie.* The portal collapsed, and the spinning slowed, as did the bright light until it flickered out.

Chapter 34 Dance Of Shadows

"In the dance between light and shadow, one must choose: lead with courage or follow in fear. For every step taken in this waltz holds the weight of kingdoms and the whispers of the fallen. Decide now your standard. Will you crawl in weakness or stride like monsters?"

Beyond the Darkened Gate, twin suns scorched the Twisted Lands as winds danced over the desert peaks. Below, the valley bustled atop the Torn Flowage bridge. Zoruks and mortals swarmed its battlements, bristling with anticipation of the storm. This was no ordinary desert tempest but the herald of a constructed god and her Army of Light. During the cold, hollow hours of the watch, Zoruks and mortals whispered stories in fear and looked out into the night.

Lying beside Antoff, Al'len traced the battle-scarred edges of the bridge with her looking-glass. As she passed it to him, a silent echo of past affections flickered in her gaze. She had been here before, but not with Antoff. It was with Ram'Del. A thousand years had passed, yet the sting of his loss remained untouched.

Antoff peered through, murmuring, "A dozen fists command the bridge, fifteen at most. Tara's dragons at the gate must have caught the Lords of the Night's eye. They are preparing for war." He returned the glass, his stare lingering briefly on Al'len's.

She held his gaze. "Amorath is cunning," Al'len mused. "Sib'Bal's darkness ensnaring Great Lord EL'Keet suggests a trap." Her eyes sought answers from Antoff. "How long before we are ready?"

"The High King has twelve thousand," Antoff replied, "Seven thousand noble knights, the rest foot soldiers. Your Holy Seat speaks of seven thousand Priest Knights and Clerics of the Light. The numbers are meager for an invasion, Al'len. Even with the warriors that have come to Coth'Venter."

Pushing back from the edge of the ridge, they stood hidden from view behind the cliff face. Al'len brushed the soil of the Twisted Lands from her tan leathers and straightened her cream cloak. She tossed the gold fringe of her cloak over her sword, resting her hand on the hilt as she gave Antoff a seductive smile. "What do you think, Antoff? Do I look the part?" Under the twin suns, her golden hair glistened like sunlit hay.

"Are you flirting with me, Al'len, while we are on scout?" Even with those icy blue eyes and a stony face, Antoff barely concealed a smirk. "This force is merely a delay. Mages will summon the real threat by Gate, aiming to trap us between that army and the river."

Her mischievous eyes sparkled, teasing him. "You always know just what to say to charm me," she murmured, leaning closer. "Remember, they aren't the only ones who can summon reinforcements through a Mage Gate."

Beneath the war horses, cobblestones echoed with the clatter of steel-shod hooves. The Coth'Venter Priest Knights patrolled, their presence resonating through the streets. Av'eon leaned nonchalantly against the fountain, observing the Stingers as they pranced by with their riders. He awaited his turn to train the local house guard—a diverse group, including farmers and beggars. He sneered, thinking about how Lord Edward usually handled the training. However, with him gone, someone was bound to be picked and it just so happened that was what he was doing here. Mel'Anor, promoted Proctor, had been rotating the trainers regularly. He gave his reasons. *"To more readily disperse the Warriors of the Light's martial knowledge to the volunteers."*

The guard grouped around his two brothers, teaching sword forms while sparring together. Like him, they wore practice jerkins to avoid injury from an errant swing. The binary suns stitched into their clothing identified trainers from students. *Minor risk of that from the looks of it. Most of this bunch can barely swing the sword.* He mused. While that was not strictly true, they had made significant progress since joining the muster. *True enough if they faced a real foe.* He thought. His primary focus was observing and eliminating targets, reflecting on his own nature as a product of demonic conditioning. A realization that stirred silent panic within. *When they find out, there will be no merriment at my return, only fear and rejection. They will destroy me.*

"Av'eon! You are up, brother. I need a break." The thick shouldered cleric called. His brown hair showed a brow that had barely broken a sweat.

"Right!" He called back as he stood. "Seems like you just started." Av'eon said as he replaced him in the training circle.

"Hardly, Av'eon. You have been daydreaming for an hour." He affectionately slapped his leather training gloves against his chest. "Take it slow. They have only just reached the point they are not cutting off their own foot. Better, yet my foot by accident." Par'Ran chuckled.

Av 'eon's reflexes snapped into action, snatching the gloves from mid-air. He ducked under the training rope, his movements a fluid dance of agility. "Who's next?" he called out, his voice carrying over the murmur of volunteers. His fingers found an Ironwood training sword in the burlap bag, lifting it with a practiced ease. He gave it a test swing, the air whistling around the blade, gauging its balance.

A lass stepped forward and held a training sword up. "Can't say that for this one. It's got nicks everywhere. I can get a new one if you are worried." She gave it a practiced swish.

"What's your name, lass?" Av'eon asked. She was not a small girl by any means. In fact, well-muscled and tall, overtopping the other students a foot or more and her skin was the color of milk. Likely a farmer from the local Vale Lands. She was strange but pretty, with short red-gold hair that framed her face and a willing smile that said she was not letting him out of the training easily, if she had her way about it.

"Millie is what I go by, Priest Knight. My full name is... unimportant. And yours, if I may have it?" She bowed low, spreading her hands in a courtly smile. Not mocking, but in good fun as introductions go.

"Av'eon." He gave an equally pleasant bow and a smile that matched her readiness. "And I am not worried. If it is still serviceable, you may keep it. I am not foreseeing getting hit by it, Millie. Shall we begin?" He stepped to the ring and the other students surrounded them in a circle so they could watch. As Millie stepped forward, Av'eon measured the full extent of her towering stature, a good head and shoulders above him, possibly touching seven feet. His eyes traced her form. Now that he had a better look at her in the ill-fitting practice, jerkin for her outfit did not hide her ample curves and even this close, the scent of her drew him.

Millie raised an eyebrow, her full lips parting slightly to reveal the faint indent of her fangs. "Are you ready, Av'eon, or do you need more... time?" She smiled at him, knowing he was looking her over.

Av'eon squinted at her, his stare intent. "You are a Vam'Phire?" His voice held a tinge of surprise, but his posture remained unshaken. It was a shock, to be sure. They had hunted these creatures once. *I better be careful they hear thoughts. I have secrets I do not wish shared.*

"Al'len assured me of my place among you, sanctioned by Ivan himself. If it's an issue, I can step out, and you can choose another." She tapped the wooden sword in her hand. "I'd hate to make you uneasy?" Her gold and silver spotted eyes focused on him. Judging him. Testing his mettle.

"No, no Millie, I just was unprepared for it. It is only recently that our order has admitted to wrongly judging your—ah... kind. I hope you will let any offence pass because of my ignorance?"

She bowed again elegantly. "None taken. Please allow me to assure you of that, Av'eon. It is difficult for all of us to start again. Shall we begin?" she lifted her sword into a two-handed practice position.

He eyed her and raised his sword to match hers. *A single kiss from her, and I'd willingly concede defeat. Damm it, I need to focus. Can't let Millie's strength or my thoughts give me away.* The scent of her kept filling him.

Her deep, seductive smile drew him closer. "Worry not, Priest Knight, the first time I am always gentle." Millie's eyes took on a slight tinge of blood.

She can hear my thoughts. By all the gods, I must have sounded like an idiot. His face was feverish. *Gods of Light, I'm blushing like a boy at his first dance.* He lunged forward for a strike.

Millie slapped his blade aside and countered so fast he nearly did not get his sword back into position to parry. Av'eon took a step back. *I am going to have to advance my style a bit or this girl is going to have me for lunch.* He raised his sword above his head in a guarded stance.

"I may indeed, Priest Knight, if you are lucky." Hungry eyes and unspoken temptation filled Millie's grin.

His dark eyes met hers, and he sensed her growing interest—a mix of exhilaration and fear. *I like you Millie*, Av'eon thought, *and I don't care if you know it.*

She brought her blade up to match his stance. Her eyes glided over him. She smiled, feeling his next move before it happened and met his sword with hers. Clack! *Despite his mind being as open as a child's, Av 'eon's training as a Priest Knight is unmistakable in his skill. My prince was right. They need to be taught mental discipline if they are going to survive an encounter with an immortal.* "You need not take it easy. In fact, I suggest you bring it. But remember to guard mind and body. The body speaks and when you become predictable, I can see it. The same is true of your thoughts. So, learn to keep them to yourself." Her mind whisper to his, as sweet as nectar, *Or I will hear it.*

"Who is teaching whom here, Millie?" Av'eon asked politely. A little frustration plain in his tone.

She looked him over with more interest. *He is clever.* "As for that question, Priest Knight, the answer is both. Those who teach must also learn." She purred and batted her eyes at him. This time, she lunged. Her blows quickened, a rhythmic clack echoing with each strike, pushing Av'eon until sweat beaded on his brow and his mind stilled in focused combat.

A ribbon of brilliant light tore through the air, its crack echoing like thunder as it cleaved the sky. It was a warning that Al'len gave before her Mage Gate opened. Then it bloomed into a bright ball of golden light on the verge of collapse before bursting into a tall purple sphere of strobing Power. Al'len and Antoff rode Stingers out.

Av'eon stepped back from Millie. He nodded at her. "I need a break. Shall we call it a draw?"

She gracefully inclined head and bowed. "Of course Priest Knight. Perhaps later if you seek me out we can have a private session? If you wish it?"

Sweat dripped on the cobblestone as Av'eon returned her bow. He inclined his head. *If I call, will you hear it?* His dark eyes lifted to hers.

Millie gave a curt nod. *I would relish that.*

The room was round and dark. A large crystal ball sparkled with the light of many souls that danced like torchflies in lamplight. The giant sphere surmounted a metal pedestal that looked like a cylinder. The medical beds attached to it held the still forms of Great Lord Amorath, Lord Moros and the middle mage Rem'Mel, who lay as still as the one operating the controller's bed.

Modred walked a slow circuit around the device. The Dark Well. It contained all the souls of the lost and demons. Disembodied. Eternally abandoned. A place of madness. And he should know, as he was sure that they had drawn him from a similar device used by the Light during the last war. A lost hero of the light thrown to darkness. Anger rose with in him. But he stamped it down. *I am not that person any longer. I am better off.*

Lord Amorath wanted him here just in case something went wrong. *The real question is, how will I know? I am not a mage. Though I can say I would recognize Amorath regardless of what shell he wares. I know him better than most.* The technology used here. Indeed, this whole device was a product of a different world before the time of the Breaking. Whatever it is, the mages and gods had misused it to create terrors. *Horrors like me.* He thought.

The globe strobed quietly now, and the lights within picked up speed. Modred had seen it all before. *It all looks normal to me. Be'elota has a need for the dramatic and loves his torments. He uses a containment device to hold the soul and then releases its hunger on an unsuspecting host. This is how it was supposed to be done.*

The bodies within the beds began to twitch and shake. Modred remembered that as normal and continued to pass and watch. *How easy it would be just to kill them all here and now. I would just take over. Who would know?*

Rem'Mel's focus was razor sharp, his body quivering at the brink of his magical limit. Training with slaves and prisoners under Amorath's tutelage was one thing, but this task was entirely different. His mission seemed deceptively simple: to extract both souls from their living hosts. Amorath's own vessel, now devoid of life, would crumble without the sustaining dark magic. Conversely, Moros' younger body was more resilient, a suitable host for what was to come. The plan was to transfer Amorath's essence into Moros, consigning the young Lord's soul to the eerie suspension of the Dark Well.

Rem'Mel found himself tormented by a grim predicament. Reviving Amorath in a new body might lead to his own demise. Survival could mean a demotion to servitude, stripped of rank and knowledge. Alternatively, preserving Moros would entomb a wealth of wisdom in the Dark Well. This would be an incalculable loss of time for its relearning. Rem'Mel convinced himself that there had to be a more viable strategy.

Resolute, Rem'Mel settled on the only practical course of action. He would fuse Amorath's soul with Moros. The youthful vessel was robust, more likely to endure the process. If disaster ensued, he could feign an inability to isolate the child's soul from Amorath's, a believable failure. Should Moros prevail, a singular entity would contain Amorath's extensive knowledge. Then Moros would discard him to the Well.

Gathering his will, Rem'Mel coaxed Amorath's spirit into his influence. It was not his Power but that of the Dark Well, demanding precise visualization for control. Unless complexity warranted it, he allowed the essence of simplicity to guide his actions. Amorath's soul drifted towards him, initially compliant. Resistance flared as it neared the boy amidst the chaotic chorus of other souls. They cried in despair, pleading for release or possession. Rem'Mel, undeterred by their wails, focused on his purpose. He pushed Amorath's disembodied spirit towards the form occupied by Moros. And thus, the struggle intensified. For the first time, Rem'Mel was the master, and Great Lord Amorath was not in control of his own fate.

Amorath floated disembodied in a fog. A world of mist. His eyes opened, and he was in the room with the Dark Well. It was a fuzzy representation. Like he was drunk and only remotely in control. He sat up on the bed beneath the crystal sphere where Moros had lain. He looked to the right and the empty husk of his previous body remained desiccated within his old ancient robes. Amorath raised his hands, young and vibrant with life, not the old dead grey of his former self! "The transfer was successful." He whispered. He looked left. Rem'Mel was there. His eyes closed, breathing slowly. Obviously, having used all his strength to control the transfer, he had not yet awaken. "Nor will you. Now that you have performed this service, your services are no longer needed. Middle Mage Rem'Mel, I believe it is time for you to be retired."

Amorath raised his youthful hands before him. A powerful ball of energy burst into reality. Liquid and hot, like silvery metal. Dark-blue lighting crawled its surface. Tentacles of energy exploded from its face and struck Rem'Mel. His body smoldered where the Power touched his chest, and he shook violently until Amorath released him. His form went limp, and he ceased to breathe. Amorath let the globe of Power wink out of existence.

Modred's voice came from a dark corner. "A just reward, my Lord?"

Amorath turned to acknowledge him. "Just for the likes of him." He raised his hands and admired them. "The one last thing he could do that would give me pleasure. He was nearly worthless as a mage. That is why I chose him. Besides, he got his reward. He learned a secret."

"Yes, and he took it to his grave. I wonder sometimes how long it will be until I get my reward?" Lord Modred asked.

"No, Modred. So long as you continue to make yourself necessary, you will continue to serve." He walked to his remains. His staff lay propped beside the bed. Taking it in his hand, it felt odd. He reached and slowly mastered the staff again. The Power it held was different somehow. "Strange? The staff feels unfamiliar. I must admit, this child had access to enormous Power. He would have squashed me like a grain rat, eventually. He had much to learn."

"I never held it." Modred said.

Amorath turned his gaze on him. "Never held what?"

"The staff. So I would not know how it felt." Modred said while walking toward his Lord.

Amorath gave a chuckle. It sounded weird in the voice of Moros. "Nor will you ever touch this staff. It is not for the likes of you." He eyed him speculatively. "Why did you say that?"

Modred's body shifted and his form shrunk as it morphed into the mirror image of his new form. "Because I never held it before. I was not sure how it felt for you to hold it. But now I know, thank you."

Amorath felt the staff settle into its normal pulsing rhythm of Power. He watched the illusion of the room fade. His staff melted away into chains that slithered like a legless reptile that wrapped his arms and legs. "No!" His body reformed into his old, discarded self."

Approaching closer, Moros observed the old, gnarled staff pulsing with power as the crystal flickered to life. "Thanks for showing me how it works. Perhaps if you please me, I will allow you to wear something else."

The room went dark.

***

Moros held Amorath's staff. "Leave us Modred. I would speak to the Middle Mage Rem'Mel. Return to your duties and remember, I am still expecting your report."

Modred heard that familiar snap. It was Moros voice, but it came with its normal disapproving ring. The realization that he was speaking to the Great Lord Amorath in the child's flesh was shocking. Just the thought of it drove him to one knee. "As you command. All will be as you say." He then stood and backed away, exiting the room.

Rem'Mel lay still on the control bed. His eyes were closed. After the exchange, he knew Amorath won the internal battle. All he could do was face it and pray the Great Lord was unaware of the plot. He would play ignorant if he could, but failing that, he would face it with dignity. This would be his end.

"I know you are awake, Rem'Mel. Sit up, the time for worry is over. Tell me, who do you serve?"

The sound of the child's voice was ominous. But someone had intended the question to be answered. One way or the other, the being that inhabited that shell knew what he had done and was asking for the truth. "I serve Lord Moros. First and always." Well, that was that.

"Look at me Rem'Mel. You will die for Lord Moros, then?"

Rem'Mel did not have far to go to find the youth's face. He was almost at eye level with him when he sat up. He felt the sweat beading on his forehead. "If I am to die, I do it in the service of Lord Moros and to the seven hells with Amorath, if that is who you are." His voice had a catch in the end. He knew his life was over.

"That is fortunate for you." Moros smiled. "Amorath is screaming his defiance as we speak. We won Rem'Mel. This is the important thing. You must be the only one who knows it."

Chapter 35 Traps Of Time

"Death is not noble nor holy. It is the act that comes before that sets it apart. The moment of sacrifice and laying down life for the living. That is noble and holy. That sets it apart."

The Council chamber rose above them in an elliptical rotunda. Yellowish acrid smoke climbed from burning braziers to the spiraling ceiling, disappearing into the gallery above. Each of the twelve sat in their broad-backed chairs as Da'Vain and Morteave entered. Shadows clung to hooded faces as these tall immortals listened to the presentation on the violations of the sacred law.

Standing beside Morteave on the open stone block, Da'Vain watched as the tall double doors, the only exit, slammed shut, and two hunters guarding them barred any retreat. As the speaker recounted the breach of the Scripts, his deep voice echoed, intimidating and with authority. Any decision made here today will have finality. To the unaware, the room would seem silent if one did not possess the talent to listen. Many did, as the gallery was overflowing with the Chroniclers from other interested coven princes. And though the words flowed with rich authority and knowledge, none but the immortals would hear.

Speak! Commanded the Primer.

As they had agreed, Morteave was the first Chronicler to reply. *It grieves me, but Prince Yantee of the Far'Mora coven has breached the Scripts. Coth'Venter coven duly chose the hunter as the lottery required. No one killed that hunter. And prince Yantee failed to grant death or return her to Prince Ivan of Coth'Venter. I gave Yantee the proper instructions on the Scripts and he ignored that wisdom in order to keep the hunter. Lord Ivan travels there now to destroy Yantee for violating the law and his person by the theft of his mate. Namely, one Lil'Emeran Doe'Minia.*

Primer De'Oblan responded. *The name is familiar to me. She is a scholar, is she not?*

Da'Vain answered, *Yes, Primer. But there is a deeper story here. One you will remember. I shall speak plainly, so you can understand the depth of Prince Yantee's foolishness and why Lord Ivan was so determined to bring her back. He was heading for the Shoal Tower when I last saw him. She is no mere scholar. Some have claimed that Lil is the niece of Aye'Win Doe'Minia, also called the spark and author of Flowers of Wars. Aye'Win was the very reason that prompted the addition of this law.*

The other members stood, and their thoughts crashed down like a waterfall. *She is Dead! Her line has ended.*

Silence! The Primer's thoughts echoed.

But there was another voice that spoke after him. A woman's. *That is why I had requested the destruction of her line. No one should have that Power over another. You!* She pointed at Da'Vain. *You were the Primer of the Council then. Had you but heeded my voice... This issue would never have occurred.*

Da'Vain raised gold and silver spotted eyes to hers. Despite being veiled behind the hood of her robes, the supernatural glow of her eyes met his. *Yes, long have many of you remained on the Council. Indeed, I see only two new members have taken the vow. What has it been now? A millennium? Is it true that in an epoch, only two of you serve as Chroniclers? Only two have laid down the Manacles of*

Power to perform your calling? How can you know the people you yourself refuse to instruct beyond laying down the law and hiding in these chambers? What good are the Scripts if you yourself do not keep the law?

Abomination! Her voice was a vile honey dripping with acid. *You question us? The Council? Is that what you do, Chronicler Da'Vain? You who serve a half-blood prince of questionable lineage? You who housed this line of Doe'Minia whom you refused to destroy when you headed this very body? If anyone is at fault here, it is you, Lord Da'Vain! Let me ask you this former Primer, if you are so wise, why did you not destroy her line and save us all the trouble?*

Da'Vain's voice was a whisper, compelling them to strain their thoughts to listen. *I do not kill indiscriminately. The child bore no guilt. Innocent, she has since repaid us tenfold with her knowledge. The same goes for Aye'Win Doe'Minia.*

Answer the questions! The Primers' thoughts burst out amid the squabble. *You may very well have decided that then and as you held the Manacles of Power, it is irreversible. But, you will answer for it now.*

Without apology, Da'Vain responded, *Lil'Emeran Doe'Minia is my daughter.*

Beneath her shadowy hood, the woman's eyes widened in shock. *What!*

Da'Vain went on, *Aye'Win Doe'Minia was not her ante; she was her mother. I hid her from you. If I was not Primer. I would have killed Lev'Aion, the fallen Prince of Menorn myself. As for who killed Aye'Win—I am still cultivating those rumors.* He looked up at the Councilors. *Be assured, I will find out, and when I do, they, whoever they are, will meet the same fate as Lev'Aion.*

Two moons cast shimmering reflections on the sea as the first one dipped below the horizon. The first moon, red as blood, set as false dawn, would soon rise over Far'Mora harbor. The wind drove white caps beyond the breakwaters. Mer'Gulls cried, riding the winds above as they searched the heaving waves for an easy meal.

In the forest's hushed stillness, broken only by insect chirps and the chilled remnants of an old camp, a ribbon of light cleaved the air, shattering its tranquil repose. It exploded into a sphere of white light. On the edge of collapse, it bloomed into a strobing purple ball larger than a horse and rider. The event horizon clarified and Ivan walked out, followed by Tara. Va'Yone's voice followed, "Tara, you promised the moment you need me you will open the Gate, remember?"

Edward was the last to step through wearing smoked plate armor, with a knight's shield slung over his shoulder. "Va'Yone, Tara promised she would."

"I will." Tara sighed, "Don't I always keep my promises Va'Yone?"

The Gate began closing. "You do. I just don't want you to forget!" Va'Yone called after her.

"I won't. Have I ever told you that you are the best little brother ever? I will see you later Va'Yone." Tara teased.

Exasperation filled his voice. "You better Tara. I will be waiting." The Mage Gate closed on Va'Yone's hollow voice.

Impatience radiated from Tara as she stood beside Ivan, her hands on her hips, near her short swords. Dressed in black thief's armor and knee-high boots, she fixed Edward with a pressing look. "Stop stalling, Edward."

It was almost comical to Edward, had the situation been less deadly and urgent. She looked like a child standing next to Ivan's imposing height. "I'm not stalling, Tara." He waved a piece of parchment at her while giving his best smile. "I'm looking. Here, see? This map that Va'Yone drew for us is fairly accurate, considering he drew it from memory. We should not wait. Sneaking around is going to be hard. Ivan sticks out, if you know what I mean."

His skin, usually as pale as moonlight, had now taken on a ghostly shade of grey. "We won't make it until then. I have the hunger. If I don't leave you soon, someone is going to get hurt and I won't let that be my family."

Tara could see it in his eyes. "You have not been taking care of yourself since Lil left. She and I will speak of it when we get her back."

Ivan's eyes swirled with blood and gold; he struggled for control. She shivered despite herself. A cold bead of sweat trickled down her back. His hunger palpable.

Tara laid a hand on Ivan's black scaled armor. Her voice was only a whisper. "Luc'Cinda has taken care of that." She dug into her bag and pulled out a silk bag that gave the metallic click against the glass. She handed it to him. "Whatever it is, she said its secrets are for you alone. Go, do what you must. We will wait here. You must hide in the city before dawn. If they see you, Ivan, they will kill Lil. Edward and I will find the location with your help. Then I will bring you there and together we will recover my sister."

Ivan took the small bag gratefully and strolled into the jungle. His black cloak billowed in the salt breeze, mingling with the scent of jungle blossoms and animal calls. Hidden among the trees, he removed the red sparkling vial and injector with shaky hands. Pushing the needle through the cork top, he filled it with half the energetic content, saving the rest. He dove it into his arm and squeezed the plunger. Life burst forth and the jungle became vibrant with life sign. Animals hung like lights and moved in fiery streaks of life all about him. It was time to find Lil.

They moved swiftly toward the sleeping Far'Mora harbor. Windows were yet dark, but it would not be long before the diligent shop keepers and waggoners were about the day's work. The streets would team with folks. Sailors heading for the docks and good wives seeking produce for meals or thread for mending.

Below, Tara spotted a dingy inn along the outskirts. "There," She pointed. "That is a good place to hide you, Ivan. Edward and I will get a room and you Shadow Walk up to us. It is a two story. I will rent an upper room and when I come out on the balcony, you come up." Ivan nodded. The light in his eyes was terrifying, as if he were suppressing the monster within.

They moved through alleys filled with the refuse of life: broken crates and barrels brimming with rainwater, and the sweet stench of rotting things lingered in the air. The warm, moist sea air mingled with salt, creating a briny mélange that hung heavy, leaving an aftertaste akin to the flavor of death. Ivan crouched low, and the shadows drew toward him like a blanket of midnight. Not gone, but swaddled in shadow.

Edward, leading Tara by the hand, cautiously surveyed the streets of Far'Mora's dangerous lanes. While not the worst part of the city, as Va'Yone's map shown, it was perilous enough. Close to the docks lay the Dregs, a haven for vagabonds, gangs of thieves, and murderers, shadowing the slave quarters. They entered the inn called the Drowned Sailor. The door of the inn was of old wood. Neglected white wash flaked away as they pushed it open. The common room was heavy with the stench of soured wine and unpalatable food. Lamps dangled from a ship's wheel, suspended by a long rope through a pulley, tied with a sailor's knot to a ring against walls paneled with dark, reclaimed ship wood. A sleeping bully boy lay in the corner with a club nestled at his waist. The common room was full of drunken folk snoring in rickety chairs with their heads on tables.

Tara and Edward's feet dragged a path through sawdust strewn to soak up spills, and occasionally, much grimmer residues. It was a true dive, frequented by rough men and women of the night, a place where plotting shadows spoke more than honest patrons. It was a true bin of scheming and schism.

Behind the bar, the robust mistress busied herself cleaning a grimy cup, dipping it into a wash bin and then wiping it briskly before setting it to dry on a towel spread across the bar. "What do you need? This inn might be a tad lowbrow for your sort. There are better deeper in the city. But I will be taken in your coin if you ask it?"

Tara assessed her—a middle-aged woman with unkempt, dirty blonde hair. Beneath the grime, hints of her once-pretty features lingered. "We will have a room for a day. The less you ask, the more I will pay."

Edward projected his usual nonchalance, a carelessness often attributed to the gentry, effortlessly drawing attention. "Yes, my dear, something above all the smell, if you can manage it." He coughed and pulled his hood and placed it to his nose.

The mistress of the inn gave a disgusted roll of her eyes as she looked at Tara with the expression of, *look around you! What did you expect to get?* "Two for you, lass, and five for his Lordship. That is the best I can do. Your type brings trouble. If there do be that, it will cost yea extra."

Edward dug a gold from his coin purse. "Keep it. There will be one more if your mouth stays shut." He eyed her expectantly.

She gave Edward a key from a ring that hung on a belt at her waist, obscured by a filthy apron. "Room three. Take the stair by the kitchen." She pointed dismissively, "it's none of mine what yea rich folk do. Yea, just be keeping the noise down. Yea, hear me?"

Tara and Edward turned toward the stair and ascended without a reply. The smooth boards of squeaky steps groaned as they climbed. The well-oiled lock gave a satisfying click as they entered. Room three was less than pleasing.

Edward eyed her slyly. "We have to keep it down, Tara."

Tara gazed at the dirty sheets unmade on the bed. "We, Edward, thankfully, are not sleeping in that bed. You need not worry. Noise will not be a problem."

Edward went to the balcony door and threw it open before strolling out. "What do you say we let in some air?" The streets were still dark. The last vestige of the night was slipping away. Already false dawn stained the horizon, melting blood-red to hues of brilliant pink and orange. Clouds were forming out to sea, painted with the grey of rain. Its stormy scent touched the air.

Ivan, shrouded in shadow, watched Edward step onto the balcony. To Ivan's eyes, Edward's body thrummed with a vibrant pulse, each heartbeat weaving like vines through his being. Smoky spiders threads burst from the alley in disappearing tentacles from the pooling darkness. Ivan was spat from pooling corner shadows into the room.

Even knowing he was coming, the cold air of death entered with him. It was unnerving. Tara cleared her throat. "Okay, we are all here. Edward, why don't you close the door? A storm is coming and none need to see it before it is near."

Edward entered and closed the doors.

Chapter 36 God Storm

"Tease not the machinations of the gods. For within them lies a universe. Ask with a compassion for those around you. Cross with care the boundaries of true reality. The world appears quite different from your tiny perspective within the vast halls of divinity's imagination. One whisper from a god can light a world on fire."

The morning was dreary, with subdued light from twin suns struggling against the looming storm. Lightning streaked across the sky, illuminating Far'Mora harbor. Silhouettes of large ships disappeared into the mist beyond the shore's edge. A shipmaster's perennial dilemma lingered in the air: flee before the storm or risk staying moored. A sudden flash of lightning illuminated the docks, revealing the Shoal Tower. It stood in isolation, resembling a limbless tree atop its stone foundation, its lonely beacon light floating, a solemn reminder of the losses from the Breaking's catastrophic tidal wave.

Thunder rolled like war drums through their deep bond, Edward felt Tara's Power ignite, burning with a fierce intensity. "Have you noticed? Storms brew whenever you're stirred with anger, my love?"

Tara's jaw tightened, her words clipped with a frustration that resonated deeper than the thunder. "Then don't make me angry, Edward." She snapped. Her voice betrayed the strain of her focus on the mission.

"Me? What did I do?" Edward asked, spreading his hands wide.

Tara flashed a wicked smile. "You won't melt, Edward. Right now, my focus is only on Lil—getting her back and ensuring her safety. I can't think about storms, war or anything else until then."

The wind howled, and thunder clashed overhead. The gust made them sway as stinging raindrops pelted them. Edward leaned in, his kiss a gentle contrast on her cheek, and whispered. "All I am saying is to be mindful. I remember a time not so long ago when you struggled to affect reality. Now you struggle not to. Don't lose touch Tara, it could be dangerous." Through the threads of their love bond, he could feel her fear. Also, Edward sensed the seething anger within her.

Tara brushed her cheek, savoring the warmth of Edward's kiss, her eyes brimming with unshed tears. "I'll never forget your touch, Edward, and I promise to be mindful of the danger." She paused, taking a deep breath to steady herself, and then gazed back at the storm-tossed sea battering the Shoal Tower. "We need a boat to get there. I could use a Gate, but it would draw too much attention." She nodded towards a dark alley flanked by abandoned warehouses. "Let's head that way. We can bring Ivan and look for a skiff to take us across."

Gusts tugged at their cloaks. Tara stopped struggling against it, allowing hers to stream behind like a torn sail. She led Edward between the tall buildings of thick black stone and grey mortar. The building's roofs lay in disrepair, their broken red tiles scattered across the alley.

Large, heavy drops pelted Edward's armor. He wiped the rain from his eyes, his voice barely carrying above the gale. "Tara, the storm—it's worsening, isn't it?"

"I know—it's my doing," Tara said, a shiver of fear mingling with the icy rain. "We need the cover; only the most desperate or an idiot would be out in this weather," Tara yelled, her voice cutting through the howl of the wind.

"Which one are we?" Edward retorted, his eyes twinkling with the mirth his voice lacked.

Tara gave him a dripping grin. "Shut up Edward. Quit complaining." She closed her eyes. Tara's arcane marks ignited, trailing like hot ash down her face and neck, glowing like molten metal. They writhed like a living thing. "Hold still Edward." Tara opened her eyes and instead of their normal steel grey beauty, they were solid the color of smoke.

Edward felt the fiery maelstrom churning within Tara, a tempest as palpable as the surrounding storm. It was as though he could extend a hand and brush against the raw, blazing edges of her inner tumult. The world closed in around them, pressing down, and tension rose with each passing moment.

Tara whispered, "Um'Ladull Ignos al'Lumannada E'Flecus," as reality rippled around them like a pond responding to a dropped stone. The words seemed to echo from another time, resonating with ancient Power. A fist-sized ball of energy appeared, shimmering like a bubble, mirroring their surroundings on its surface.

Edward felt a surge of energy pass through him, a sensation like a wave of heat crawling across his wet skin. The ball of energy expanded, enveloping them, stretching out to the alley's edges. The sphere inverted in a dizzying whirl, then twisted again, warping the very fabric of their surroundings. It then flipped inside out in another disorienting twist. The outside world vanished, replaced by their distorted reflections on the sphere's surface. Heat enveloped them again as the sphere reached its full size, causing beads of sweat to form on Edward's forehead. It seemed as if they had entered a world apart, with the sounds of the storm being muffled.

"What is it?" Edward asked.

"Inverted light. We are, from the outside view, invisible. It bends light around us and reflects what is behind on its surface." Tara moved back to the very edge of the sphere. "Come on, Edward." She waved him closer. "Quit stalling."

"I'm not stalling, Tara—I just don't know what I'm doing," Edward admitted as he moved closer to her.

He felt the tangible pull of Tara's Power, a force drawing him to her. He let his arms encircle her. A shimmering slash of light cut through the air before them. Like a rip in the fabric of creation, it shimmered and then burst into a sphere of bright light within the mirrored surface, one sphere inside of the other. The effect was so disorienting that he felt the urge to be sick. The seven-foot ball inside the other started to collapse.

Tara channeled raw Power into the strange matter halo, and aligning the other to the image of the room they had rented. Just before it entirely fell in on itself, it bloomed in to a Mage Gate. It strobed in shuddering purple flashes. Its form and color mirroring back on it from the inverted light that encapsulated them. Tara felt Edward shift to one side. He clung to her for support to throw up. She could hear him retch, but dared not break her concentration to look. The event horizon cleared, resembling steam fading from glass. Ivan, ducking low, stepped through. His blood-and-gold eyes swirled, absorbing the pulsating light. Once he was through, Tara let the Gate collapse.

Ivan's eyes traced the interior of the sphere, reflecting their distorted images back. The orb of inverted light shrank, its heat dissipating through them, until it hovered before Tara, small as a piece of fruit. It winked out with one last energetic flash.

"You are going to owe the inn keeper some coin." Ivan said. His unsettling eyes tracing her form.

Edward wiped the rain from his face and wrung out the hood of his cloak. "Why is that? I gave her a gold. That is triple over what she asked for. The room can't be worth more than that, whatever damage may have been done."

Ivan gave a stoic look. "Your Mage Gate, Tara, tore a hole in the floor and consumed a third of the bed when it opened."

"Then Edward will have to pay for it." Tara said. "It's his fault."

A shocked look crossed Edward's face. "Me! Why do I have to pay for it? You are the lady with the estates and money. I have an allowance."

Tara arched an eyebrow at him. "Because it was your comment about sleeping together in the bed that drew my eye when I was memorizing the Mage Gates placement. Anyway, we are doing the next patron a favor. Those sheets were disgusting. I will ask De'Nidra to send her the money." Edward started opening his mouth, but Tara's look shut down any objection. "Time to find a boat."

Edward and Ivan followed Tara out. Beyond the street's edge, the rain lashed the docks in stinging drops. The waves, rising and falling, made the anchored ships bob in the harbor like wine corks, their sails bound tightly around masts and spars. Before the storm, people beached the small fishing boats. The hulls in long rows pointed upward toward the clouds. It was not long before they stood before an upturned boat of considerable size for just the three of them. Someone had applied fresh pitch to the planking and sanded it smooth, brushing on a coat of white paint.

She pointed. "This one I think. It looks recently repaired and is not likely to leak."

Ivan gave a nod and lay hold of the boat. Edward joined him and they flipped it over. It was at least six feet wide and from stem to stern fifteen feet long. Ivan and Edward set the mast into a swivel so they could tip it up. The iron pin pinged, giving notice that it had locked in place. The oars found their spot neatly under seats that stretched the width of the fishing boat. Tara helped them push it in to the sea. They fought to hold it steady as it rose and fell with each wave. Edward got in next, his trepidation obvious in the jerky way he moved. Finally, Ivan pushed them out as he got in. The skiff rocked with his movements until both he and Edward sat side by side in the middle seat. Tara sat at the rudder.

Edward mirrored Ivan's actions and placed his oar in the lock. "I don't know about this, Tara. That water is rough." He pulled in sync with Ivan. He knew that much. Only Ivan was stronger and he was holding back so Edward could keep up.

Feeling the pull, Tara steered them for the open water and the Shoal Tower. "Any other way will alert them, Edward." A heavy wave struck the boat, splashing over the rail. "They are Vam'Phire, and I don't care to announce our coming. It is bad enough with them hearing our thoughts when we get closer."

Ivan shook his grizzled head. "I don't think that will be an issue so long as you think about something other than Lil. If you can't control your thoughts, think about fishing. They would hear that all the time with ships coming and going. But of course, at some point, they will hear you and come for us. We will just have to make it a surprise for them."

Edward gave a grunt. "You hear that Tara? We are going to cross this rough water wearing armor, no less. And when we do, we are going to surprise a tower full of hungry Vam'Phires. Sounds like our plan is shaping up to be about normal."

"Edward Please." Tara gave a forlorn sigh. "Just row the boat."

Chapter 37 Holes Beneath

"Dark places within—these are the abandoned boundaries of mortality. There, true loneliness exists. Detachment from others is our soul's slow slide into the abyss. Reach for the lonely when you see them. Bring Light and love to those dark holes hidden beneath the flesh."

Shoal Tower stabbed into the stormy sky, its stone foundation besieged by waves, swamped in the thrashing saltwater. Tara looked up. Lightning ripped the clouds in long, blinding forks. She guided the fishing boat beside the stone foundation. The craft thumped against the rock, a hollow wooden sound resonating. Ivan reacted swiftly, jumping out to stabilize the boat. Edward reached out, steadying Tara as she struggled for a grip on the slick, weather-beaten stone.

Ivan tapped his temple and then his lips, signaling silence with a hush.

Tara's nod was subtle, her gaze shifting to Edward, one eyebrow arching in a silent query.

Edward spread his arms in a shrug, as if to say, "*What did I do?*" while drawing his broadsword.

Ivan, crouched low, guided them stealthily up the craggy path leading to the tower entrance. Its dark brown stone soared upwards like a giant needle, piercing through the eye of the storm. Above, the wind lashed, and clouds churned. Thunder answered with lightning streaking across the sky, leaving afterimages dancing in their vision. Their hands clung to the uneven stone, slick with muck, as slime dripped from their fingers. Every step closer required an effort not to fall. Finally, they reached the level surface of the foundation. Before them loomed a large double opening. The doors had long since rotted away, leaving only the rusty black remnant of hinges. A golden light pulsed upward towards the beacon high above, illuminating the opening of rotted windows as it rose. Watching the golden light rise, Tara felt a profound sense of insignificance. Towering hundreds of feet into the air, the Shoal Tower stood, blotting out the storm.

Only the upward-strobing light pierced the darkness, its eerie hum stark against the raging storm. When they reached the large door, Ivan held up a fist, and they waited. He then slipped inside. Edward went next, his sword at the ready, and Tara followed him in. The entrance led to a room as big as a grand hall. A round, stone staircase followed the radius of a beam of light that strobed upward to the floors above, while a black metal spiral staircase led lower. Tara followed Edward toward the one climbing up.

Ivan snapped his fingers, getting their attention. The sound reverberating off the interior, then he pointed downwards. Drawing his curved two-handed sword, the blood gem at its hilt flashed with a hungry light. Tara's gaze lingered on Ivan, noting the pallor that clung to him like a stubborn shadow. A twinge of worry knotted in her chest, unspoken yet heavy. *His normal color has not fully returned. He is still weak.*

Ivan's descent sent soft echoes down the metal stairs, their sound a murmur against the storm's roar and the tower's pulsing hum. Below, the thoughts of two mortals railed against captivity, and something else familiar pulled at him. *Lil*, Ivans mind whispered. But she did not answer. Hope burned within his heart. *She is alive!*

Are'Amadon was like a monument to Darkness. Its towering walls appeared to drain the very Light from the world, leaching the life from the fields surrounding it. At least to Moros, it looked that way. He released the dark drape, its heavy fabric swallowing moonlight. How he loathed Amorath's quarters. They were like an external reminder of the madness shouting within. He even wore his grey silks under the leather coat that had flared at his knees. On him it dragged on the ground. Its arcane marking surrounding the hem glittered back at him, gold in the mirror from across the room. He wanted to throw something heavy at it.

Let me out! Amorath wailed.

Moros' smile reflected back at him. *Teach me something new,* he mused, *and perhaps I'll craft you a construct as a temporary vessel. I tire of your tidbits, Amorath. I crave something more substantial. But... if you have nothing left to teach, maybe the Dark Well is a better place for you? Hmm?*

No! Amorath yelled. *They want to rip me apart. I banished so many there.*

They are spirits they can't touch you. Nor you them any longer. Moros prodded at him, mocking his disembodied state.

Amorath sounded hollow, like an empty echo. *I didn't know what you were. If you let me out. If you give me form again, I can serve you.*

A knock came at the dark wood door. Moros blocked Amorath out. "Come," he commanded.

Rem'Mel entered with a flourish. He bowed low with a swish of his arm. "We live to serve Great Lord Amorath."

"Relax *High Mage* Rem'Mel," Moros emphasized his new title. "We are alone. Well, as alone as I can be with this lunatic in my head. How goes the preparations for the war?"

Rem'Mel straightened, "As well as can be expected with Great Lord EL'Keet dolling out to us the dregs of his forces. I mean Zoruks with first and second-year training and pit fighters. Five fists of troopers! He knows the attack is coming here and yet he holds back forces from us. It is like he is trying to rub putrid dirt on an infected wound. He must really loath Amorath!"

Oh, he excels at that, Amorath said snidely. Moros tried to block him out again. "Inform EL'Keet that if he holds back forces, we may take up residence with him next when the Maid of Light comes. That should help him release some troops."

"Have you learned anything useful lately, my Lord?" It was a shameless request, but Rem'Mel was always looking to learn those secrets. Amorath had withheld knowledge from him for so long.

Moros eyed the mage. He did not withhold—much from Rem'Mel and when he did; it was because he was more likely to hurt himself or others around him than master the new Power. The knowledge had been like a leaver Amorath had used to get what he wanted out of Rem'Mel and while he would not do that to him, the feeling of that Power over him had somehow transferred. "You need not worry, my friend, the moment I learn something—useful. I will share it." Moros walked to the raised stone hearth of the fireplace and held up his hands. The warmth penetrated his flesh, and he felt Amorath squirm. *You would have loved to have felt alive again, would you not? The heat on your own living flesh?*

Amorath shivered. *Yes, my Lord, I want that.*

Then find something to teach worthy of that reward. Moros offered.

Rem'Mel watched Moros lost in the flames. By now, his hands must be burning. "Are you well, my Lord?"

Moros pulled his hands away, making fists. "I'm fine. Hire mercenaries, if you must. I will not leave our walls light in the defense. Pay whatever you have to, Rem'Mel." *I must see to our defenses and if needs be... deal with EL'Keet myself.*

Amorath's laugh echoed in his mind. *That's the spirit, my boy! We will make a proper god of you yet.*

"Yes, My Lord. At once." Rem'Mel the High Mage started for the door.

"And Rem'Mel... As soon as I have something new. You will be the first to learn of it." Moros offered. *No sense wasting loyalty. He deserves my respect.*

"Of course, Great Lord." Rem'Mel bowed and exited.

As soon as the doors closed, Moros strolled to the corner next to the bed, where the staff lay propped. Its dark metal twisted and deformed from years of use. Dark energy had warped it from its original straight form. The arcane writings and markings crisscrossed its length and atop the crystal pulsed with a weak light. Moros took it in hand and the Power that was within became available. The strange thing was it also pulled at his Power, drinking it in. Like a half full rain barrow, it filled slowly as he held it in his hand. *This is going to take some getting used to.*

Amorath writhed within. His own desire to hold it overwhelming him. *Give it back! Give back what is mine!*

Perhaps... When you have something to teach, I may even give your construct some magic. Would you like that, Amorath? Moros asked.

Yes, my Lord, something alive to feel with. Something with which to taste life. He quivered hungrily.

Moros walked toward the door and then out into the hall. The tap of the staff was heavy in his child's hand. Servants bowed, and he nodded his head in recognition. That was something he had changed for the better. Acknowledging people for their service. Letting them know they had value. Amorath whined about ruling with fear, but Moros shut him out. The walk to his old room was not far and the depression in the center of the floor had been a mystery to him. It had been a place to play and learn.

It was a place for play no longer. He felt for Little Modred. The tiny demon flew at the edge of the walled battlement, sneaking in murder holes to pilfer food from the guard.. *There you are Little Modred. Now fly down into the open and give me a look.* The little demon gave a small chirp of irritation, but he followed the instructions. Seeing through the eye of the construct, his wings carried him before the walls. Close to the metal gate. The Zoruk tents lay behind it in the vast divisions of their tribes. Banners flapping in the hot wind.

I cannot let them see me as a child any longer. I must be Amorath himself. Before Moros, a dark slash ripped the air above the floor's depression. It then enlarged black and round like a tunnel boring into Darkness itself. Spinning like a whirlpool, it spilled out on to the black soil before the Dark Gate. It was a portal of a kind. Where Amorath had learned it, he did not know. At any rate, it was an older knowledge than the Mage Gate the others used, and that gave a sense of awe and Power to the onlooker. Something only Amorath would know, and dispelling any doubt that the transfer had been successful. With the connection made, the tunnel of darkness shrank until it was just a mere step through. Every eye that stood on the wall was on Moros when he walked out.

Mist sat next to Mel'Temdel on the beast cart. Its worn bench left her backside tender. Not to mention a tail that was made for maneuvering while flying and not for sitting on a bench. "What is this place? Better yet, what was it?" Mist asked, awe filled her voice as she scanned her surroundings. The remains of a marble structure rose out of the darkness. Its fluted columns holding up the weight of the massive roof structure.

"Black Stone." Mel'Temdel mused. His eyes traced the destroyed buildings with hers. The remains of a forgotten highway ran through the middle of melted stone structures. "It was a place of the sciences before the Breaking of the Balance. EL'ALue destroyed it on the day Ram'Del, the Hero of the Light, died. Or so, the story goes. Come, my apprentice, we best get inside." Mel'Temdel put his hand on Mist's shoulder. He snapped the reins and clucked to the beast. Its hairy bulk shifted, tossing its horned head, before it began moving again.

Mist whistled quietly to herself. "Everything burned and melted." She pinched her nose as if she could still smell it. "Look there. That entire building is lying sideways. It fell like a tree before it broke. Some of them must have been many stories tall from the amount of rubble. All destroyed, except for that one." Mist pointed at the tall marble structure that seemed to defy the destruction. "Mostly anyway… It's burned too, but the structure still looks solid. Is that where we are going?"

"You are quite the inquisitive creature." Mel'Temdel said with a warm smile. "To answer your deluge of questions. Yes, and yes and yes again." He laughed at her.

Mist flared a wing in a fanned stretch. "Oh, come on, master, please," she spread her hands. "I just want to know." Her dark complexion taking on warmth as she returned his with a toothy smile.

"Oh, very well." Mel'Temdel gave his best impression of being put out. Mist saw through him and knew he was teasing. "Yes, they fell like trees in the explosion. It had once been called a thermal detonation. Because of the heat, you understand?" Mist nodded as he eyed her. "Larger than anything you might imagine." He went on, "Yes, this structure was the library. And yes, it is where we are going to be living for a time. We are not likely to be bothered, as it is supposed to be haunted." His old leathery, bearded face took on a serious look until his eyes sparkled with amusement and he shook his eyebrows for effect. Mist burst out in laughter, hugging her middle.

The wagon clattered up to the library, its facade of chipped white marble veined with black. The stairs ascended in two sets, twenty steps to the first landing, then ten more to the portico. Fluted columns set upon a large pedestal carried Mist's eyes upward. They supported large horizontal blocks and a prominent gable that jutted out over the step like a porch. The face of the gable featured carvings of mortals in congress. But discussing what? "Mel'Temdel, do you think this place had a purpose beyond storing books?"

Mel'Temdel strolled alongside her. His breath labored as they climbed. With each step, his staff tapped out his rhythmic strides, matching his pace. "Hmm? More questions from you apprentice? A most curious girl, indeed. Yes, it was not just a library. It was a kind of forum for the sciences. A place for postulation and argument. People made advancements in science during that time. We soared through the heavens on great ships."

Mist stopped at that, and Mel'Temdel stopped with her. "What? We traveled stars in ships? How can that be? They are so far away."

Mel'Temdel placed an arm on her shoulder to lead her on. "You have already seen and used some of that technology and yet you do not believe?"

"You mean the portal arches?" Mist answered. "But is that not just magic also?"

Mel'Temdel harrumphed, "Everything that is technologically advanced seems like magic until you understand it." He shook his mage staff before her. "Take this, for instance. You believe it is magic, right?"

"It is?" she agreed with a nod.

Mel'Temdel smiled down at her. "That is because you do not understand it. The writing on it is unreadable by most people. But I can read it. Well, truth be told, I can read some of it. They translated it as the Rod of Power." He emphasized the words in a grandiose manner. Waving a hand with a flourish. "I studied it and the word is Power rod modulator. Meaning it stores and modulates Power. Now we have learned to use it for storage energies that we consider magical. But are they really magic? That is the question."

Reaching the top of the stairs, Mist stopped again and stared up at him. "Are you saying there is no magic?"

"I'm saying we call what we do not understand magic. The mage that had this staff before me believed in magic and he worked his long life to prefect it before teaching me. I have learned much of the lost language that he refused to see. When I am gone, this staff will be yours. I will teach you what I have learned and you will explore, learn and then pass all the knowledge on."

"It seems a lonely life." Mist said. She looked into his eyes, then hers turned down toward the steps. "So sad." She kicked a stone off the edge.

"It is an investment of lifetimes that I hand down to you. Choosing an apprentice is a most serious thing. The question is, do you accept the responsibility of all those lifetimes of knowledge? Will you commit?" Mel'Temdel cupped her chin in hand, drawing her eyes back to his. "Hmm?"

Chapter 38 Lost Sister

"Be aware, your skin is just a wrapper, a covering. Rarely does it show what lies beneath. Even more importantly, how do others see you? The reality of your person lies within their hearts. You are not the crude matter that encases you."

Descending ever deeper, they moved with the light pulsing at the spiral stair's heart, its golden glow lending the metal a ghostly translucence. Each pulse sent a shiver along Tara's spine, the thrill of the unknown beckoning. Their steps echoed, a muffled symphony against the metal, growing fainter as they delved beneath the sea's embrace. The walls were darkened by sleeved metal, encasing the stone and deepening the tower's enigma. Echoes boomed above them, reminiscent of distant war drums, while lightning pulsed in harmony with

Tara's heartbeat—a resonant declaration of her stormy essence, the stormy sky above El'idar, the depths of the ocean embodied—*I am the storm, the sky above El'idar, I am the ocean deep.* She felt it all. Every part of its fabric.

Ivan led, his sword raised, its bloodstone pulsing red, casting stark shadows across his determined face. Tara, following, felt Edward's presence at her back was as unmistakable as her connection to her dragons. Tara's breath caught. *Is he attuned, just like the dragons, since we made our life's vows? They had mistaken me for Edward's bond holder. They said they could locate him as easily as they could me. Edward has access to my channel, but can he use that access? Does he truly understand its purpose?*

The descent felt endless, each step taking them deeper into the unknown. At the stairway's end lay a dome, a nexus where energies converged. Here, Liquid Power swirled in circular motions within the translucent metal. With each surge, a sphere of energy burst upward, tracing the light beam towards the Shoal Tower beacon, suspended as if by invisible threads. The stairway spiraled down to the dome's base, where eight hallways branched out, aligning with the cardinal directions.

Walking down the dome was disconcerting. Beneath them, the material turned opaque as the liquid energy flowed over it. An eerie paradox—the tangible sensation of the material beneath, then seeing it vanish under the flowing Power. Tara tested it with a stomp; solid, yet invisible under the Power's passage.

When Ivan reached the bottom, he lingered for a moment. His eyes swept the room, taking in the direction the halls went. He pointed with his blade and then begin to move. Tara and Edward fell in behind. It was difficult to determine the direction they were heading with all the spinning around on the spiral staircase during the descent. Whoever had designed this place had made the entire structure of metal. Then the structure groaned. Tara and Edward froze. The weight of the sea pressing down. It had been here for millennia. The question was—*would it hold?*

Lamplight flickered over Yantee's features, casting a rogue's dance of shadows across his face. Gold and silver flecks in his eyes gleamed under tousled hair, a pirate's gaze sharp and calculating. Draped in his knee-length black leather, the Vam'Phire Pirate Prince reclined with a predator's casual grace, his authority unchallenged. His fingers, adorned with rings of plunder, toyed with the gold-inlaid hilt of his cutlass, an extension of his will. Lounging cross-legged on a table before his throne, leather boots cuffed and battle-worn, he surveyed his domain. His eyes rested on the sleeping Lil, a prize beyond measure. *She's perfect,* his thoughts a possessive caress. *And she's mine. To the abyss with the Scripts, and that half-dead Ivan from Coth'Venter.*

Radean's silky voice touched his mind. *My Lord, we are not alone. There are one, maybe two mortals entering the corridors. One reacted to the structure's groaning.*

Yantee's smile turned sly, a glint of mischief in his eye. *Just one or two mortals, ye say? Bah, they be mere flies buzzing about a feast. Treasure hunters, lookin' for their glories, I'd wager.* His eyes wandered over Lil's body. With a sigh, he answered, *Still such things no be trivial, Radean. Keep an eye on our guests. Send Am'Brose and the others to sweep 'em up. They be coming down, but they'll not be going back up. Their lives be the bounty of the coven now. Throw 'em in the cage wit the others.*

Wait here. Ivan's mind whispered. Nearly silent, Tara and Edward almost did not hear. Only the contact of his crimson-gold swirled eyes with theirs confirmed the silent transmission of his thought. Darkness washed over Ivan. Like waves crashing in on him from all sides and then exploded into wisps of dissipating smoky threads.

Beating like a massive heart, only the light emanating from the static beam and the pulsating balls of energy granted sight. The halls beyond were dark. Tara and Edward found themselves in solitude. Edward attempted to speak, but Tara swiftly silenced him with a finger to his lips. She shook her head.

Her strands of white-gray bangs swaying in contrast to her long black hair. The molten ash scrollwork ran from her eyebrows to cheeks, flowed below, tracing the delicate curves of her neck. Tara's steel-gray eyes held Edward in place, her gaze piercing. Through their bond, a hammering sense of caution echoed, resonating with silent warnings.

Edward raise an eyebrow at her, and spread his hands, pointing his broadsword to the huge room and the darkened halls. And then he spread them questionably. As if to say, *In the middle of all this? Suddenly Ivan needs to go?*

She tapped his head once more. That was Tara speak for... *Shut up Edward and pay attention.*

A tall man with a feathered leather hat stepped out into the darkened hall before them. He elegantly pulled it from his head and swept a bow. Bright red bloused shirt flared at the cuffs. Gold hoops in his elongated ears swayed with long, black braided hair as he moved. A silver necklace nestled a key that glittered in the weak light. He straightened and placed his hands behind his back and walked slowly in, not bothering to mask the sound. If anything, he accented it deliberately in some fainted form of politeness. Besides that, Edward noticed the dagger shoved into his cutlass belt right off.

Shielding Tara, Edward raised his sword with both hands, his voice firm. "That's close enough, friend."

The pale white skinned named him a Vam'Phire. But his demeanor named him a rogue. His gold and silver spotted eyes swirled with blood. "Oh, did ye whisper a word, little morsel? Quiet as ye are, skulking about where ye don't belong. Deep in the sea's bowels, no less." He strolled forward. "Me name be Am'Brose."

"Stop where you are," Edward said. "Or this gets messy."

Cold death and foreboding shed from Am'Brose, permeating the atmosphere. "And ye no, be afraid of Vam'Phire? By now, most do be given a scream and run. Ye, minds no be open like dat of mortals. Ye been taught to hide the mind, however poorly. By the looks of it, mages, the both of ye. Or be ye somethin' else?"

Tara and Edward, encircled by ethereal flames, stood united—a living, pulsing conduit of Power. A fiery thread wove around them, binding their fates. Tara's voice reverberated like thunder, a warning etched in every syllable, the very atmosphere tingling with the promise of impending danger. "Give my sister, Lil back, and you might yet live," she declared, stepping forward from Edward's shadow. Her Torrent arcane markings glowed like fiery ash, trails of molten metal etched across her skin. In her mind, she sent a warning to Am'Brose, a whisper of imminent peril. *I am not a mage. I am something else. Give my sister back if you wish to see another day.* With a commanding gesture, she summoned a sphere of liquid Power, its surface crawling with blue lightning, a tumultuous dance of Darkness and Light.

"Well then," Am'Brose said. "It do be fortunate for me dat I no be alone."

In a blur of supernatural speed, Am'Brose lunged. His cutlass and dagger appeared in a flash, catching Edward just as he raised his sword in defense. That crucial stance, a technique drilled into him by Ivan and Millie, the female Vam'Phire, saved him from being cleaved in two. Edward's blade sliced through the air with precision, a whirlwind of calculated strikes and swift maneuvers, a testament to years of rigorous training, each move a reflex. Their swords clashed, casting a shower of sparks in the dim light. They moved in a deadly dance, the pulsating beam casting their elongated shadows across the floor, accentuating Am'Brose's towering form.

Tara's steel-gray eyes remained locked on the duel before her, her fingers clenched, a silent spectator to Edward's fierce battle. Edward's chest heaved with each labored breath, his sword arm trembling as he parried Am'Brose's relentless attacks. Am'Brose was only playing with him. Testing his skill. Edward was doing his best, but soon he would tire and the fight would be over. That's when seven more Vam'Phire were spat out of the darkness of the other halls. This was the trap that Edward had joked about. Edward fought on and if she did not do something, it would end as fast as it had started.

Reality rippled out from Tara. She was like a disturbance in a pond. Time slowed to the point of shattering everything and nearly stopped. Pushing Power toward Edward down the thread of their bond. "Edward, take it!" She yelled as Tara solidified the image of Edward. As she saw him in her heart.

Power thundered through the bond, and time itself seemed to shudder, halting between heartbeats. In this slowed reality, Edward felt a heavy resistance, like moving through syrup. Tara's voice, resonant and omnipresent, echoed in his mind, *'Edward, take it!'* In that frozen moment, he surrendered to the unknown, placing his fate in Tara's hands. He trusted her implicitly, whether it led to his salvation or demise. *If I am to fall, let it be through Tara's will. Not at the cold mercy of an immortal,* he thought.

The bond between them was open to the onrush of Tara's Power surging down their tether. It was knocking at the door, waiting. Then it came. Edward surrendered. The Power ran across him like black and white fire that fought for dominance. Then, just as it seemed to fail. Energy was, for a moment, consumed inwardly, and Edward ignited like a paragon of shifting radiance. Darkness and Light flailed at war, the discharge between the battle immense. Black and white fire slowly ran down his sword, from the handle to the tip. Time shook as if rung and reverberated, lurching to normal.

Edward had been in battles where Tara had affected time before. But now, when it bounced back to normal, he was part of it. Not just caught up in the reality of an ascending god. But truly mixed together with her. Joined to Tara in a deeper way. The world in this moment was only a shallow illusion of what Tara was in the higher reality. Her physical form, an embolism on a greater consciousness.

Am'Brose's agile form gracefully retreated, distancing himself from the fray, a sly grin curling on his bloodless lips as he planned his next move, his hand holding the dagger, shading his blood-gold eyes. "Ye no be mortals." Edward, his opponent, blazed with God Fire. "Priest Knight." He spat the words like a curse. Am'Brose eyes, lit with angry light, spoke of recognition. They flicked to Tara and back to Edward. "That do make her a…"

Edward cut him off, his voice resonating with a thunderous, divine Power. "Definitely not a normal girl. I am no Priest Knight." Glowing sea-green eyes took in his own condition. "I am… something else."

Shadows swirled and congregated at the room's heart, forming an ominous, inky vortex that seemed to hunger for darkness. It cloaked something big. Wisps of smokey threads hung in the air. Am'Brose roguish smile crossed bloodless lips. "Mayhap, that be true. But as I say. I no be alone." Then superiority slid from his face. His eyes drifted to the center of the room.

Out of the blackness of shadow came Ivan's voice and a deep, predatory growl. "Neither are they." The curtain of shadow drew back. And there was Ivan, the Dire and her little brother, Va'Yone.

Chapter 39 Gods Enamored

"The Enamored, drawn by duty or love, chosen for destiny's path. Reshaped and reborn, in their devotion to a god's purpose, they find their Light. Standing as warriors in celestial battles, reality transforms around these few. With no path back to their past, they look only forward, epitomes of a deity's fervor. The trumpets sound, and the Priest Knights cry out: Forward, the drums of war!"

In gleaming armor, the Warriors of the Light, hooves ringing, shattered the night's tranquility. They rode astride broad-backed Stingers, lances held aloft. Formidable rows, four abreast, thousands deep, poured forth from RavenHof's gates. The beat of rhythmic drums guided them, while footmen and archers, in their dense, rigid formations, followed in their wake.

Al'len and Antoff led the cavalcade, their armor aglow in the ethereal light of twin moons. Above the Twisted lands, volcanic ash mingled with murky clouds. Approaching at a gallop, Mel'Lark, High King of the Lands of Light, and Lord Lars of Haven joined their formation, crossing the field with regal urgency. Around them, the meadow's tall grass swayed gently, encircling a unit of Heavy horse patiently awaiting their Lords' return.

Their Stingers slowed to a stop in a gallant spray of debris, and quickly dismounted. "We have prepared, Al'len," High King Mel'Lark answered before she asked the question. Their white warhorses pranced beside them. "High Mage

Heli'os, and his Holy Seat, Lord Gan'Vile, oversees the baggage. Together, we've rallied a battalion of heavy lancers. Heli'os is prepared to open the gate upon your signal to the designated location."

Al'len nodded in agreement, then asked, "And the other?" Her voice carried a tone of inquiry. *I know the answer,* her mind whispered. *I just need him to say it.*

Mel'Lark cleared his throat, with the moon glinting off of his golden plate. "Yesterday morning, in the name of EL'ALue, the Maid of Light, Lord Gan'Vile and I ordered the Holy Archives opened. We included our signed confessions in the affair, posted now in every state building and the city square."

Lars added dryly, "Heli'os reported a tumultuous riot in Alum 'Tai's capital tonight. The High King has only sufficient troops remaining to protect the castle. They have not yet restored order."

"They'll come around," Antoff said, with a barely contained aggression. "The people have every right to be infuriated. We broke their trust. I nearly throttled his Holiness myself upon hearing the news. Al'len's intervention alone stayed my hand." He offered Al'len a wry smile, acknowledging her tempering influence. "Once again, she was the voice of reason."

Allen's eyes danced to Antoff's. "Was I, truly?" She mused, her smile soft yet radiant, mirroring the warmth in her heart. She then focused, her gaze encompassing Lars and Mel'Lark. Her blonde hair, tied back in a braid beneath her helm of white and gold, shimmered in the moonlight. "Lord Gan'Vile and I will make an appearance tonight to address the crowds. Do make sure he is ready. Being prim and proper won't serve the people's needs. I intend to strip him of all vanity. He can respect them by showing the proper amount of shame. They need the truth and the freedom to choose for themselves what they want to believe. What they need is our assurances that we will make it right. That they are not helpless and the Maid of Light will not abandon them again to greedy mortals."

Lars gave a chuckle. "No problem there. He is biting his nails, wondering what you intend to do with him. Will you keep his service or throw him to the faithful?" Some seriousness had leaked back into the question by the end.

"That rests upon him," Al'len declared. "My mission is justice for all our people, and he is no exception. Yet, I hope to temper them with reason. Without mercy, there can be no true justice. Ultimately, it is the people who shall decide, not I." She swept her cloak aside, revealing a belted sword, her hand resting upon its hilt. "I am just the instrument, ensuring the reckoning."

My prince. Am'Brose sent. *These be no mere mortals. Prince Ivan do be here to claim Lil. He be no alone! If we stay to fight them, we do be undone.*

What! Lamplight cast a dancing glow on Yantee's face as he stood abruptly. His dagger was out in his hand and he did not even remember pulling it. Nor did he remember standing or with supernatural speed, drawing to Lil's unconscious throat. His hand shook. But something within made him stop. Lil's blood trailed beneath his blade. A slight cut on intention, but halted by desire. It was all that had saved her. *I can't do it*, he thought.

Am'Brose was growing frantic within his mind. *My Lord, what be ye orders? There be a beast, and mortal child. But that be no the worst of it…*

"You can't handle a single Vam'Phire, a beast and a child?" Outrage filled Yantee's mind, and it came through.

No. There be more. There do be a flaming Priest Knight. Tis wit a goddess, she is. She's angry, and do be screaming to give her back her sister Lil.

Am'Brose. Yantee sent. *Ye be getting back. We be handling it for what it be. An incursion.* Yantee's eyes transformed into a mesmerizing whirlpool of silver and bloody-gold, a reflection of his inner turmoil. He brandished the dagger, striking swiftly, just as shadows enveloped him. When he was gone, all that remained was disquieting smoky thread clinging to the shadows in the dark corners of the room. That and a vibrating dagger next to Lils sleeping head.

Am'Brose stepped back further and spread his hands in a bow. The shadows reached for him at the same time it did the others. It was like a sea of shadow washed out of the darkened halls. And then they were gone.

Ivan walked toward Tara and Edward. Tiredly, he raised a hand shielding his eyes. Looking them up and down. "Edward, what happened to you?" He rasped.

Edward thumbed over his shoulder towards her smoldering form. "Tara." He said, as if that explained everything. Power thrummed within him. He was as bright as direct sunlight.

"Better turn it down a bit, Tara." Ivan said. "They will see us coming a league away."

Va'Yone was right behind and the dire came straight to Tara, acting aloof to Edwards' condition entirely.

"Whoa! That's new." Va'Yone exclaimed.

Tara reached down and hugged him. "What are you doing here Va'Yone? You were safe at camp."

He tried to fight her off. Well, maybe only a bit anyway, before giving in and returning her embrace. Va'Yone did his best to sound angry. "You were supposed to send a Gate when you got in trouble. When Ivan showed up bursting out of the dark. It startled me half to death. He said it was getting interesting. He said you needed help. I wouldn't let him go without taking me, regardless of the danger involved in Shadow Walking me here." He pushed back from her. "You promised to send a Mage Gate." He stomped his foot. "I waited."

Tara cupped his chin. "I would have. If I realized how much danger we were in. It happened suddenly and Ivan was already gone." But Va'Yone would not lift his eyes. She gave him a little shake. "Look at me."

He slowly lifted his eyes to hers. Fear and a sense of deep hurt overwhelmed him at the thought of losing her.

Tara looked at him. Into him. Beyond the trappings of mortal flesh. There was love for her in Va'Yone's heart, a fine thread that tied his heart to hers. "I promise, I will call on you when I have need."

Va'Yone pulled her close and hugged Tara hard. "Don't you ever do that again." It was not a cry, but it was close.

"Okay Va'Yone. I won't," Tara said. "I am surprised De'Nidra let you come at all."

Va'Yone stepped back from her. His wild hair was a messy mop when he shook his head. "She does not know. And before you say it, Tara. Ivan said he had no time. So I went. Besides, I am a grown man."

Tara sucked in a breath. "Oh, Gods of Light, Va'Yone, De'Nidra knows you are a grown man. She has taken on responsibility for teaching you and this will worry her sick. Likely, she and Tem'Aldar are looking for you now. If this rescue doesn't kill you, she will." She arched an eyebrow at him. "I should send you back."

"No!" Va'Yone exclaimed. "I am staying Tara. You need me. I can see nearly as well as Ivan in the dark. If there is a price to pay with De'. I will pay it." Tara opened her mouth to object, but Ivan saved him.

"Let's move," Ivan pressed. "Every second we delay, Lil's danger grows, and our adversaries bolster their defenses." He gestured towards the shadowed path ahead, his sword emanating a muted, ominous glow from the pulsing bloodstone. "They're aware of our intent. If Yantee senses his position threatened, he will not hesitate to eliminate Lil."

Ivan chose the hall where Am'Brose had materialized. A thoughtless act on his part, he was sure Ambrose had hunted these halls many times. The idea of him adjusting a strategy that worked did not add up. "This way and keep your minds quiet." He strolled on ahead.

Edward was last. Though Tara had adjusted the glow a bit, he still stuck out. *Great*, he thought, *I am now a beacon for monsters. May as well hang a sign around my neck that says eat me.*

Tara pulled Va'Yone near, "Stay close, I am not losing you in here. I could not stand that and besides, I would never hear the end of it." She turned her gaze on Edward. Even dimmed, he smoldered with Power. "Edward! Stop stalling and come closer."

Edward spread his hands in exasperation. "Look at me! I'm a beacon, Tara. Staying close puts everyone at risk."

Tara pointed just behind Va'Yone. "Closer Edward. It does not work like that. Vam'Phires see heat and life. It is how they hunt. You blind them as if looking into the suns."

Edward caught up. "I was just trying to keep you safe." He grumbled.

Tara huffed, "Stop arguing, Edward!" She took a breath. "We're all in this together," Her hand ruffling Va'Yone's hair. She eyed Edward grinning with a mix of frustration and affection. "You're so annoying Edward, but cute when angry." Tara allowed her mind to recede from the sea and storm above. It was taking a toll on her, becoming too much to manage. *Stop that!* She told herself. *You are snapping at Edward for no good reason. He is down here in all this danger because he loves me.* All she wanted to do was save Lil and then get everyone back out.

They hurried to catch up with Ivan. The Dire had moved close and nuzzled her back, nearly knocking her over. His four yellow eyes drank the flickering Light radiating from Edward. Tara grabbed a hand full of hair to steady herself and gave him a pat of recognition before letting him run for Ivan. His mind whispered to hers. *Keeper.*

Edward's flames bathed the dark corridor in a haunting luminescence, their shadows elongating into dancing specters that frolicked before them. The Dire ghosted ahead. Ivan walked with his sword readied. Little doubt in anyone's mind the danger was coming. The question was when?

Chapter 40 Blood and Sisters

In shadowed halls, mist and luminescence danced at the edge of Darkness and Light. Vam'Phire moved with predatory grace. Here, reality blended the two realms, creating an eerie, shifting landscape. A massive wolf stalked ahead, its form ghostly in the dim light. Prince Ivan, a silhouette in the darkness, moved with a cold, ethereal presence. Trailing him was the vivid aura of a Priest Knight, a divine sentinel, his radiance engulfing the corridor in a blinding light.

Ambrose and his Vam'Phire paused at a corridor junction. Down the hall, a Priest Knight's glow casts a dense, obscuring mist within the shadow space between reality. *Ye let the wolf and the prince take the lead*, Am'Brose sent, his thoughts sounding like a ship captain on rolling rough seas. *Then we be ambushin' the Priest Knight from the shadows. Severs his ties to dat god first. If he fallen, the rest be easy prey 'fore the prince can lend aid.*

A woman's voice, as sharp and quiet as a shadow, chimed in, *And what of Ivan of Coth'Venter?*

Prince Yantee be handlin' em, himself, Am'Brose replied, his voice a low growl. *Quiet your minds now, they be nearing.*

The massive Dire prowled ahead, its snout skimming the ground, inhaling deeply the scent trail. It snorted abruptly, the ridge hairs bristling as it detected Lil's scent. With a low growl at Ivan, it surged forward. Ivan, quick to react, hastened past the T-intersection, his pace urgent. *Quickly, the wolf's onto Lil's trail; we can't lose it now.* He sent.

Tara quickened her pace, and Va'Yone did his best to keep up. He did not have armor like the others. Just the adventurer's outfit De'Nidra had gotten him. Dark green with brown pants and a long cloak. His only possessions were his sword, the dagger Tem'Aldar had given him, and a full purse, which was of little use here. He was not great with hand weapons. And there was no buying his way out of this one. But he did have his magic. He decided on that and prepared the tools of his trade. One he knew and could use without preparation. But the others he had learned from De'Nidra. Those required some setup and half of his pool. *Nevertheless, I chose to come and now, for the safety of all; I am committed.* He whispered the incantation to himself and prepared the last words that would activate the device.

Behind them, Edward moved with cautious determination, his blade as light as a feather yet ready to strike. His gaze swept the corridor, sensing, almost precognitive, a rift in the worlds drawing near. "We're not alone, Tara. Something's near," he whispered urgently.

"I don't sense it," Tara replied, her hands drawing twin short swords in a swift, fluid motion. She would have elaborated, but the moment for words was gone. Before them, as if conjured from the very essence of shadow, emerged Am'Brose, shrouded in smoky tendrils, his cutlass gleaming, already falling in a stroke towards Edward.

Instinct overtook thought for Edward, his body reacting with a speed that bypassed conscious decision. Time seemed to stretch, dilating around him as he tapped into an otherworldly speed. His broadsword, alive with crawling electrical discharge, like wild vines, glowed with a stark contrast of black and white Light emanating from his skin. As he parried a vicious strike, a monstrous clash of sparks lit the dim corridor. Though he couldn't grasp the intricacies of his Powers, their effectiveness was undeniable. The towering Vam'Phire, a full foot taller, struck with such force that it staggered Edward.

Am'Brose's cutlass danced furiously against Edward, the Priest Knight, each matching the other's ferocious speed and strength. The lethal ballet was so intense that one successful strike from either could be fatal. Am'Brose presented a chilling, bone-deep terror, fought with relentless aggression. Meanwhile, his coven descended upon the unsuspecting goddess and child.

Surrounded by an explosion of shadow, Tara and Va'Yone faced the towering Vam'Phire. An oppressive dread filled the air, gripping Tara's heart in a vise of ice. Despite their efforts, they were too slow. A striking Vam'Phire woman lunged, her thin daggers like nails piercing Tara's leather armor and pinning her to the wall. A scream escaped Tara as one of her swords clattered to the ground. With a desperate grasp, she drove her remaining sword into the Vam'Phire's midsection—a feeble thrust, but miraculously effective.

Edward instantly sensed Tara's fear and anger as if they were his own. "Get off me, you bitch!" Tara's shout, raw with emotion, echoed through the chaos, a fierce reflection of her fury. He knew Tara better than anyone else. Now, while her speech was not exactly eloquent, Edward could tell she meant every word, and it had come from her heart. Most important of all, she was not dead. Tara was furious. For a fleeting moment, Edward thought of a line from a story he'd once heard, something about "the blade provoked to deeds of violence." It seemed fitting here, in this dance of death.

The Vam'Phire retracted its taloned claws, sliding back in a fluid motion. It dragged a claw along the fresh wound, tasting the blood with a sinister hiss. "God or no, dat's gonna cost ye, lass," the creature spat with venomous spite.

Va'Yone's words came fast as a crossbow trigger, "En'Surcum, Em'Persona Flam'Meer." The female Vam'Phire skin blistered and erupted in fire. "No one hurts my sister!" Va'Yone said as a static ball of blue fire formed crackling between his fingers. She took one look at his next attack coming and ran back down the hall, screaming and beating at her body.

The first sign of peril came from Tara. Her steel-gray eyes suddenly widened, shifting to a smoky, ghostly white as she detected something malevolent creeping up behind Va'Yone. The arcane marks etched across her skin sparked to life, glowing like embers from her brows to her neck. Time itself seemed to warp around her as she sprang into action, her hand shooting out to grab Va'Yone's shirt and pull him close. In her other hand, a blade, slick with blood, ignited with flames that licked its edge. She thrust it with precision over his shoulder, narrowly missing his head, and struck with a fiery roar. Va'Yone found himself pulled tightly against her, her body shielding him as she engaged his unseen assailant.

Am'Brose wielded his cutlass with a relentless, savage speed, each strike a deadly blur. He poured more of his life's essence into each movement, pushing his limits. Against him, Edward, the Priest Knight, was an unstoppable force, a living myth far surpassing the whispered rumors. This battle was beyond anything Am'Brose had ever faced; Edward matched him in speed, his movements a mirror to his own lethal dance. Am'Brose's usual advantage, reading his opponent's mind, was useless here. Edward's thoughts were a fortified citadel, impervious to his mental probes. Fear racked his mind. *He do be no Priest Knight. He do be a Vam'Phire Slayer!*

Blood wept from Am'Brose's eyes, staining his pale cheeks as he expended his vitality in a bid to overpower Edward. Edward, too, felt the strain, his body screaming, on the brink of collapse. The words of his father echoed in his mind: "*Every choice has its cost.*" The weight of his impending fate bore down on him, but his resolve only hardened. If death was inevitable, *let it be for Tara, not a hollow crown.* He redoubled his efforts.

In a frenzied onslaught, Am'Brose attacked with wild abandon. His cutlass aimed for Edward's throat, a desperate, lethal jab. However, Edward, trained by Ivan, moved with a deadly grace, allowing the blade to miss and graze his cheek. Edward spun, a dance of death, his broadsword arcing with his movement. As Am'Brose lunged forward, Edward's sword, gripped in both hands, struck true. With a searing hiss of black and white fire, the blade cleaved through flesh and bone. Am'Brose's head fell, and a crimson cloud burst forth, filling the air with the stench of death as his body crumpled to the floor.

In the blink of an eye, Edward's warrior instincts took in the dire scene. Chaos reigned; the air was thick with the sounds of struggle, the distinct cadence of Va'Yone's incantations in a foreign tongue, and the acrid smell of seared flesh. A figure, engulfed in flames, fled down the corridor, screaming, chased by a six foot Dire Wolf—a testament to Va'Yone's deadly magic. Closer, Tara fought fiercely, her blade a fiery arc as she struck at a Vam'Phire threatening Va'Yone. But danger lurked just behind her, another Vam'Phire poised to strike with a blade she couldn't see. Edward's heart raced; even with his supernatural speed, the distance was too great. He could not reach her in time.

Ivan's warrior reflexes kicked in as the attack descended. His body, honed by a past life as a sword master, reacted instinctively. He shifted aside, narrowly avoiding a blade that whooshed past his back. Spinning left, he feigned a powerful two-handed strike. The Vam'Phire, seizing what seemed like a vulnerable moment, lunged for a killing stab. Ivan's mind raced—*Is this the end?*—but his body moved on its own accord, like a puppet master controlling his every reflex. The world around him muted into silence, leaving only him and his assailants in a deadly ballet.

As the enemy's blade neared, Ivan recoiled just enough, allowing it to miss. Swiftly, his elbow rocketed up, striking the ambusher's face. The satisfying crunch of shattered bone under his scaled arm resonated as he crushed the Vam'Phire's nose in a spray of blood. Ivan's blade, guided by instinct more than thought, followed through in a lethal arc, cleaving through and disemboweling his opponent.

In the periphery, shadows danced and recoiled as Ivan's gaze fell on Tara and Va'Yone. Outnumbered, fighting three Vam'Phire with valiant but grim determination. Feeling the weight of the moment, Ivan embraced the encroaching Darkness, letting it envelop him, surrendering to its icy embrace. He called, and it claimed him.

Edward's shout pierced the chaos, "Tara!" She whirled around, trying to deflect the twin daggers descending from a Vam'Phire. Her heart sank; this felt like the end. Desperately, she pulled Va'Yone close, hoping to shield him with her body. With a deep breath, Tara closed her eyes, resigning herself to her fate. Ascending god or not, this was the end.

In that dire moment, Edward sensed a shift like a tide. From a swirling void of Darkness, Ivan emerged like a specter. With a swift, predatory movement, he grabbed the Vam'Phire by its mail, yanking it backward while driving his blade ruthlessly through its back. The blood stone at Ivan's hilt throbbed ominously, absorbing the life force of his foe.

Tara's eyes fluttered open in disbelief. She was alive, against all odds. In the distance, Edward charged forward, enveloped in Power, his blade a deadly arc above his head. Turning, Tara saw Ivan, now kneeling victoriously over the fallen enemy. The blood stone on his weapon cast a sinister red glow, contrasting starkly against his blood-splattered, alabaster face. Behind her at a blue flash of Va'Yone's Mage Strike and slash of Edward's blade. Another body hit the floor.

Lil lay defenseless and unable to move. Blood trickled down her neck. The wound was not deep, but she had only a little life left to lose. Deep within, she pulled on all the will she had left. *Ivan!* She called, and he answered.

Chapter 41 Blood For Blood

"To fall for a friend is better than learning to live with their loss in order to kill your bitterest enemy."

Ivan's mind pierced the void as he sought Lil's consciousness. His mind's voice echoed in the silence, a desperate, wordless call that stretched out for her presence. "We need to hurry. Lil is fading fast."

Edward's hands moved with practiced care as he tended to Tara's wounds. Nearby, Va'Yone crouched, pausing for a moment before retrieving a bloody key from the remains of Am'Brose's neck. "Gross!"

"What did you think it was going to look like, Va'Yone?" Edward shoved two torn rags from his shirt beneath Tara's armor to staunch the bleeding. Then he tightened the belts for pressure. "That is all I can do here, my love. You need rest if you're going to heal."

At the mention of healing, Tara's eyes clouded over as the scars of loss briefly resurfaced. Memories of Cur'Ra, her mother and mentor in the healing arts, flickered like a snuffed-out candle, reigniting her ache at the loss. Her mother, Cur'Ra, had guided her in mending others, but in her own affliction, she felt powerless. She steadied herself on Edward as she picked up her fallen sword. "We are coming, Ivan," Tara called. "I will heal later. Right now, Edward, we need to save my sister."

They followed Ivan, leaving the bloody remnants of battle behind. They turned right at the next junction and there sat the Dire next to a seven foot tall smoking corpse, acting completely aloof. His singed fur and the bloody gash on his side, the marks of her nails, served as the sole evidence of his role in her demise. He stood with a quick backward glance, placed his nose to the floor, gave a sniff and a growl before padding off into the blackness. Other than Edward's glow, there was nothing to illuminate the hall.

Cold wisps of still air clung to them like icy tentacles, and thoughts veered to the depths of the sea and the monstrous pressure with each deep groan of the metal structure. Ivan sensed the minds of the other Vam'Phire as he closed on a metal hatch at the end of the hall. It was secure. Fastened by a lever that he pulled, giving a creak of rusted hinges as he pushed it open. There on a table lay Lil before an empty throne. Recklessly, Ivan held his sword under one arm, while he fumbled at his belt, removing the half full syringe of crimson liquid, with its sharp needle tip protected by cork.

Lamp light played on Lil's perfect face. He could see nothing but her. Everything else in the world had fallen away. His eyes ran over her and he saw the dagger driven in to the table next to her head and the blood slowly dripping from the cut at her neck. He firmly gripped Lil's arm, poised to inject the life-restoring liquid.

Before the needle could pierce skin, reality flickered, and in that dimming light, Yantee watched, his intentions as dark as the shadows that cloaked him. When both of Ivan's hands were engaged, Yantee seized the opportunity and launched an attack. Ivan sensed Yantee, the Prince of Far'Mora, emerging from the shadows. Yet Ivan wanted to save Lil more than life itself.

Yantee was more monster than Vam'Phire when he burst from the shadows, its wispy smoke clinging as his cutlass stabbed. Ivan did move, but not fast enough. Ivan felt a surge within, a swordsman's instincts not his own, commanding his body with an authority that transcended thought. He slid a step to the side, instinctively covering Lil to protect her. The blade, originally intended to sever his spine, instead plunged deep into his side. Ivan let out an animal scream, and the needle flew from his hand.

Yantee's malevolent thoughts seeped into Ivan's mind, twisting through his consciousness like dark tendrils of smoke, echoing his possessiveness. *I tell ye for true, Prince Ivan. If I cannot have her, neither will you.*

As Yantee's sword twisted in his gut, Ivan, wincing, clutched the hilt of his own blade, a steadfast anchor amidst a sea of pain. Before he knew what was happening, he had stepped back against Yantee, not allowing his blade to clear. He felt the cut go deep as his body slammed hard against him, throwing Yantee back. Ivan got an elbow to Yantee's face for his trouble before his sword tore free. Blood oozed from the wound. Had his sword not fed him life from the earlier fight, Ivan would have been dead. As it was, if he kept losing blood. Ivan would not last long.

Tara, close on the Dire's heels, watched in a blur as Yantee's blade found Ivan's back. Battling in a whirlwind of supernatural speed was impossible to follow. The needle spun end over end, crossed the room, shattering against the dark metal wall. The Dire, a silent yet imposing presence, advanced with bristling fur, its eyes scanning the chaotic scene with predatory precision, waiting for the perfect moment to unleash its fury.

"I have to save Lil." Tara cried, staying clear of the tussle between Ivan and Yantee. She ran for Lil. Va'Yone ran behind her, a blue ball of fire rolling between his hands. He protected Tara while she did what she could for Lil.

Edward ran past the throne, his broadsword blazing to secure the other door. As he reached for the handle, it began to slide back. He grabbed it and put his back into it. Edward grunted through his teeth as he struggled against monstrous strength. "Tara, this is not going to keep them out. They will use the shadows."

"I will do it." Va'Yone said. "I can stop them from getting in." Now, after saying he could do it, he wished he had not. The fact was, he didn't really know if he could. Va'Yone had already prepared Mage Strike and rolled it from hand to hand, waiting to use it. He'd had problems doing more than one thing at once since he started learning magic. De'Nidra said it was a block that he would have to get past if he wanted to be proficient. The problem was, his magic did not work like Tara's. She could imagine it in every detail and overwrite reality. He could not. He had to divide his mind every time he did something new. And therein lay the crucial problem. He had never done it before. Va'Yone had only gotten close.

Tara sheathed her swords while climbing onto the table next to Lil. Her voice, a strained whisper, rose barely above the cacophony of the battle raging in the corner, a maelstrom of Ivan, the Dire, and the Vam'Phire Lord. "You will have to, Va'Yone." Tara yelled amid the battle. "I learned to heal from a mortal, and I need all of my concentration. Never having tried it on an immortal before, I don't know how it works. I am counting on you. I will be defenseless. Va'Yone, this is the moment I would send the Mage Gate for you." Tara placed her hand on Lil's chest, closed her eyes, and delved.

"Va'Yone, hurry up!" Edward roared. "Shut the fucking door!"

A sinking sensation gripped Va'Yone's stomach as he whirled around, his eyes widening at the sight of the open door. He had left it open. A lamp's dim light spilled like a beacon into the oppressive darkness of the hall. "Oh, shit!" He said, as he ran for the door. Sparing a short look for Ivan and the Dire struggling against the Vam'Phire that was getting the better of them.

Ivan's two-handed sword whirled, locked in battle with Yantee's cutlass. It came faster and faster until it was a blur. Ivan struggle to catch the blows. His physical condition worsened as blood poured from his wound. If not for the Dire creating diversions, leaping and biting at legs and arms, this fight would have already been over. As it was, Yantee must have had eyes in the back of his head to keep up.

The Vam'Phire Prince of Far'Mora, a pure blood. Ivan a Half Dead construct of mages. A cross between the Vam'Phire Lord De'von and a demon from another world called a Demonian. Yantee was faster and had Ivan been whole, he the stronger. And while Yantee was clearly old and experienced. Ivan had two things he did not. Ivan had the soul of a dead hero and a six foot dire wolf. What's more, Ivan was willing to trade his life to save Lil from this monster. This fight had now reached supernatural speeds to where Va'Yone was a slow blur running for the open door.

When Va'Yone reached the door, it took all his might to slam it shut. Its hinges creaked with rust. *Apparently, Vam'Phire need not use doors much.* He thought. The metal door hammered an echo down the long hall as he locked the squeaking lever in place. Va'Yone closed his eyes and began dividing his mind in two. It is not a simple thing dividing yourself in two. You must start with the core of who you are and work outward from there. It is not a copy. Your mind must literally become two in a single body. Va'Yone strained at the very edges of ability and being. At the cellular level, he was going to have to use a portion of his life storage, and then he would never again be the same. *No wonder mages are insane.* He could simply drop the Mage Strike and then create a bright Light, but Tara was defenseless and so was Va'Yone if they opened his door. He loved all of them, but Tara, more than anything in the world, including himself.

Tara delved deep into Lil. Her spark fluttered on the verge of going out. She could not heal her. There was no life left for that. Her pool was dry, and she had no lifeline or future to draw on. If she tried to heal her wound, Lil would die. Tara dug deep within and her life spark became a furnace. Where her hand touched, Lil's graying flesh, blue light burst forth in a slow pulse. Tara had to decide. She was going to break the promise she gave her mother. Threads of Tara's life wound like a coil down her arm, and into Lil. Ever so gently, she fed Lil's dying spark with her own life, like kindling to a fire. Slowly. Tenderly she fanned until Lil's life caught flame. Lil's needs seemed bottomless. Not only did she receive what Tara gave her. Lil drew it forth, and as she did, awareness flooded in. The awareness of Tara. Of Ivan. Of everyone. Tara felt herself waver.

Lil's eyes opened. *Stop! You will kill yourself.*

Tara was on the edge of slipping away. *I don't care. You're my sister.*

Lil's voice, weak yet firm, broke the silence. "I do. That's enough, Tara. You've saved me. Now, please stop." Tara stopped, her eyes closed. She went as limp as a fish and started to fall. But Lil caught her while sitting up and cradled her weakly like a child in her arms. With Lil's blood pool nearly depleted, she felt the pulse of Tara's blood resonating within her, its rhythm pounding in her ears as she rocked her like a child.

Edward yelled out, "I can feel it! They are coming!" He struggled to hold his latch shut. But then raw balls of Light bloomed in the center of the room and in every corner. It was not the pure Light, but warm and so bright that it eliminated all the shadows. "That's It Va'Yone they can't do it!"

The handle behind Va'Yone creaked, and the door was flung open. The Vam'Phire shielded his blood-gold eyes with an upraised hand. A flash of blue streaked the hall as Va'Yone's Mage Strike struck his imposing chest. Flesh sizzled, and blue lightning crawled across his form. Va'Yone's high pitch voice rang down the hall. "If you step in front of the door, you will get the same thing he did. Courtesy of Va'Yone the Magnificent!"

Va'Yone's blinding lights left Yantee in a state of disorientation, causing him to flail with his cutlass, his vision obscured. Nor could he withdraw. There were no shadows to call to. Ivan did not need to see. Closing his eyes, Ivan surrendered to his deeper senses. His blade master instincts roared to life, steering each movement with lethal precision. Yantee's cutlass flashed and Ivan's blade turned it at the same time his wolf got a healthy portion of Yantee's calf, hamstringing him. On a faltering downward stroke, Ivan bashed his blade aside, slamming Yantee into the wall with a shouldered under blow. He reared back his head and Ivan sunk fangs into Yantee's neck. Dropping his sword, Ivan pinned his arms to the metal wall. He drank deeply of Yantee's life as they struggled. Ivan could feel the great dire wolf pulling in jerks at Yantee's leg while he held his arms.

Please let us come to an accord. Yantee begged. His body was growing weak and his struggle feeble.

Ivan was tempted to take his last drop and end him there and then. He decided on a different course, feeling Lil hungry and awake. *No, I have a better fate for you. The one you deserve.* Ivan stopped as Yantee slipped into the very edge of Darkness. His cutlass tumbled weakly from sleeping fingers.

Ivan watched as Yantee crumpled to the floor, a puppet with its strings cut. Gritting his teeth, he pressed a hand against his side, staunching the flow of blood with a grimace. Looking down at the Dire, he said. "Release."

The Dire's four eyes turned upwards to him as if to say. "*You got to be kidding me.*" He gave another provincial tug.

"No. Release." The Dire released with a snort. But sat down before Yantee, waiting for any excuse to bite.

Ivan turned to Lil. He saw her their weakly rocking Tara in her arms.

She whispered hungrily. Ivan's eyes met hers. Gold-silver blood swirled, drew him in. *Ivan.* He felt himself being pulled to her as if in a dream. Ivan reached out and pulled Lil and Tara close.

He felt the gentle pierce of her fangs on his neck. *Drink, my love*, his mind whispered. *Take all you need from me.*

Lil did drink, and as she did, she could feel the essence of so many within Ivan. And as she had tasted him many times before, she knew that it had come from Yantee. Ivan mixed with herself and so many others. It was an intoxicating blend; But she stopped when Ivan's heart became a little labored. Her fangs withdrew and her eyes found his, and she kissed him gently. *Thank you. I will require not so much as that, my Lord prince.*

There was a familiarity there in her tone that told Ivan that his reward would come later.

Lil handed Tara's sleeping body to Ivan like passing a precious child. Edward had stopped struggling at the door. There was no one pulling at the handle. Lil sat up, her perfect unclothed form swayed with a seduction going from gray to milk white before his eyes. It made his mouth go dry. He averted his gaze and his cheeks flushed hot with one look at sleeping Tara. He left the door and took her from Ivan.

"It's Okay my friend. Lil can't help it and neither can you." Ivan gave a pained smile. He leaned heavily against the table.

"What about them?" Edward motioned to the door with his chin. Edward's glow had faded to nothing as Tara had drifted to sleep. He was as weak as Ivan, and his muscles felt shredded. Ivan's eyes, now their normal gold and silver spots, moved over him. Edward felt weighed and judged. Yet he also found a fond acceptance in them if that was possible. "I thought we were dead."

"We were." Ivan rasped. "But we were saved courtesy of *Va'Yone the Magnificent.*" Ivan spared a grinning bow of his head, and a flourished hand towards Va'Yone, who was rocking on his heels with a satisfied smile. "I am conversing with this coven now. They know it is over. Yantee no longer rules here." Ivan said. "They will not disturb us any longer."

Va'Yone took a bow, letting the lights and Mage Strike go out as he did.

Lil bent down before Yantee. Her hand found purchase in the great wolfs thick fur. She stroked him lovingly as she eyed Yantee.

His mind whispered to hers. *I saved you. By all rights and the Scripts, you should be dead.*

No. Lil Said. *You had another choice. You should have returned me. But the rules did not apply to you. You have gotten so used to taking whatever you want. You stepped too far. You are worse than a rabid animal. And unlike this wolf, he listens! He has rules! You have none!* Lil looked at the Dire and planted a kiss on his head and then stood up. She let her fingers slide from his fur. Her voice was without feeling as she spoke. "He is beyond mercy. Finish him."

The wolf's quartet of eyes locked onto Lil's, its irises narrowing into intense golden flames, mirroring the lamplight's flicker. Hair raised up on his back and down the ridges of his neck. The Dire's mind sent Yantee a message as he growled deeply. *No one hurts my pack...* He lunged forward. Va'Yone threw up and Edward looked away from the carnage.

Chapter 42 Lies Between Sisters

"Things that lie between sisters can be an unbearable weight that is needlessly borne for years. It kills joy and wastes a lifetime of sharing. Be rid of it, carry it no further. It is a vile poison! It is killing you as well as her."

It was the deep hollow groaning of the structure that woke Tara. The Shoal Tower was an ancient construction built before the Breaking of the Balance, and held out the enormous weight of the sea. Now, just cold remains were left after the Shattering had occurred. An empty tower basement full of lost memories, and a forgotten people.

A sudden spike of fear, followed by the comfort of being in Edward's sleeping arms, made her feel safe and at home in the oneness of their bond. She untangled herself from him and sat up, only to discover that Edward had undressed her, cleaned her wounds, and bound them. A sharp pain stabbed into her shoulders, jolting her awake and flooding her mind with memories of yesterday's injuries. "Lil." Tara whispered before her eyes had focused. Edward stirred but did not wake.

Tara's hand on Edward's chest offered solace, her touch a balm to his wounds—visible tokens of his sacrifice. Through their bond, she wove a comforting vitality, easing his pain. Using this connection, she coaxed healing into his body. It required very fine control, manipulating minuscule threads just enough to ease the bruises. Tara looked around. Fashioned from the same dark metal as the rest of the structure, the room echoed starkly, its utilitarian air amplified by the metal shelving and spartan furnishings. Someone had placed two pallets together for Edward and her to sleep on. The room had clearly been for storage at one time or the other, as empty metal shelving lined the walls that held their clothes and armor. There was also a door, complete with the familiar lever as before.

There was a soft knock. "Just a minute," Tara called. Covering her chest and arranging Edward's blankets. "Okay, come in."

When the door pulled back, the hinges creaked, and there was Lil. "You are looking better. I heard your call."

Tara threw the blankets off and ran to her. "Sister." It was more of a collision than a hug. But Lil, laughing with delight, held her close. Tears ran down Tara's face and her voice was breathless. "I was so worried for you and for Ivan. We were both so lost, Lil. I don't know what I would ever do without you." Lil's size so overtopped hers, she had to lean down to fully embrace her.

"Sisters." Lil said the word as if it had much more meaning to her now. "Well, thanks to you all, I am safe and whole again."

Lil's tone held a hidden pain, something left unspoken. Something that was causing her shame. Lil's feelings opened to Tara. "But what is wrong?"

Edward sat up, the blanket sliding off his chest, and joked, "The problem is, I have two beautiful women in my room, and the one who belongs to me should be asleep."

"Edward!" Tara turned, hands resting on her unclothed hips, and said, "You belong to me! The dragons said so. And another thing: Why am I wearing no clothes? Answer me that?"

Edward gave her his best smile. "Well... because I had to clean your wounds and dress them."

Tara huffed, "My wounds are on my shoulders, Edward." But there was a curl of a smile. Edward started to answer, but Tara raised an eyebrow and held up a finger. That shut him down. Tara went to a shelf holding her rumpled clothes and armor. "Edward." She said, pulling on her britches. "You didn't even fold them."

"What, Tara? Are you kidding?" Edward winced as he spread his arms. "I could hardly move my arms."

Tara pulled on her shirt with obvious effort. Lil helped her finish.

"Men are at best housebroken, Tara. We are lucky to get them to that point." She regarded Edward with a smile.

"What did I do?" Edward asked.

Tara eyed Edward with Lil appraisingly. "You're right Lil. But they do have their uses. I think I will keep him. Training another would be too difficult."

Edward sighed. "I am in the room, you know?"

Tara batted her eyes at him. "We know Edward. Now Lil and I have things to talk about. You get dressed. And no stalling." She tugged on her boots, giving them a stamp. The weapons and armor she left.

Edward's mouth hung open, words trapped in the space between thought and voice. Both women left the room with him sitting there, befuddled.

Lil whispered, "Sister, that was deftly done, but he deserves a reward for his bravery."

"Oh, he will get his reward many times over. I spoil him, and he knows it." Tara said. "Now, enough of that. I know you have something to say, Lil. So, just say it."

Lil started as if it was being dragged out of her. "I have something to show you. Actually, two somethings. I will leave it to you if you want to call them people." Lil led Tara to a room with an open metal door and wooden table and chair. On it a candle that flickered on the rust eaten bars of a cell. A foul odor, a mix of unwashed flesh and excrement, pervaded the room.

A thin man clung to the bars, and a fat man slept. "Let us out, child. You cannot leave us here with these monsters. In the name of EL'ALue, let us out!" He shook the bars.

Disgusted, Lil's voice stabbed at the men behind the bars. "The thin one serves the fat one. I don't know him. I have known the fat one for many years." Lil shook her head as if deciding how to start.

Tara's steel-gray eyes met her sister's silver-gold ones. "Lil... you know I love you. So, whatever it is. No matter how bad it is. You can say it."

Lil dropped her eyes in shame. "Mortals, they hire us. Our wages are sustenance. They hire us to rid themselves of people that cause them problems. We are told they are criminals or murderers. Sometimes, even old clerics." Lil studied Tara's face.

Tara shook her head. "I don't understand."

Lil went on. "We have a lottery. I got chosen to do the job. We don't know for what until after selection and then we are bound by the Law of the Scripts to carry it out. No matter how long it takes."

"Lil please." Tara said. "Just say it." There was some deep hidden thing that Lil was not saying and she needed Tara to hear it. She was just having a hard time getting it out.

Lil steeled herself. She normally could control her emotions, but they were leaking out of her. "The fat one is High Bishop Er'laya of the Order of the Light and the thin is Diocesan On'omus. High Bishop Er'laya hired us to kill your father, Master Duncan, because he was researching things that were considered by the bishopric to be heretical."

Tara's gaze turned hard as she looked at the cell as On'omus backed away from the bars.

"I had nothing to do with that." On'omus pleaded. He pointed to Er'laya. "It was him who ordered it. Not me."

Tara walked to the bars, feeling her anger rising once more, like a furious tide within her. Fists clenched at her sides as she spoke. "That is the man that killed my father?" She eyed On'omus. All he did was nod. Tara raised her hands. A ball of molten Power crackled, illuminating his sleeping form. He wheezed with each labored breath, covered in a red rash.

Lil's voice, rich with unspoken sorrow, pierced the veil of Tara's fury, hinting at the depth of her own pain. *I said he ordered it. But it was I that killed your father. I did not know you then. And if I could change it now, even at the cost of my life, I would.* She knelt before Tara. Her hand reaching. *If knowing I killed him serves your pain and grants justice. Then I offer my life as well... Sister.*

Tara turned and look down at Lil kneeling. "And are they your bounty? Were you assigned to kill them as well?"

Tears welled in Lil's eyes as the words rushed out. "I was chosen. The bounty required them to be returned alive with enough essence to survive a trial and no more. It is how we endure, Tara. It is why we are not hunted outright. Though they claim we are."

"And if I kill him, what of your bounty?" Tara asked. Her voice was hard as stone.

Lil shook her head. "I will have failed and must be... removed from the coven by Law of the Scripts. It is death to fail."

The ball of Power in Tara's hand extinguished in a furious flash. "If I kill him. You die. Willingly you offer yourself to me to make amends for the death of my father, knowing the price? You would rather die at my hands than your covens?"

Lil held her eyes with her own. "Yes. You are my sister. You offered your life to save mine. If it would please you, I give it back."

The pause was long. It seemed to stretch out in time, as if Tara was between decisions. Between a higher and lower reality of thought. "Your life is mine?" It was a divine echo that filled the entire room and all of Lil's being. It hung there waiting for an answer.

Lil nodded. "It is."

Tara's eyes turned white as she leaned forward. Driven by a force from a higher reality, she pressed her thumb against Lil's forehead. Beneath Tara's thumb, it thrummed with Power glowing brightly. Tara's voice thundered in her mind. *Lil'Emeran Doe'Minia I receive you. I accept your life in trade. I forgive you. Dispose of your bounties as you will. Destroying them will not bring back my father. Remain as you are and fulfill the Scripts. I grant you service... Sister.* When Tara removed her hand, a glyph in the shape of intertwined black and white dragons rose on Lil's forehead.

Lil felt the Power flow through her. Felt it intertwine with her being. She was now connected to Tara, and she knew it was an unbreakable bond. It was a choice she didn't regret. When Tara pulled her hand away, Lil raised her fingers to her forehead and felt the raised ridges of dragons.

The jungle teems with life. Its moss-covered trees struggle against a lost metropolis. Roots sink deep into broken streets. Its canopy keeping secrets only verdant growth could conceal.

De'Nidra walked the ancient streets, avoiding the tangle of vines and roots tugging at her boots. Behind her, Tem'Aldar called. "Va'Yone! Answer me, boy. Call out if you need help. For the love of the gods of Light, call out if you don't. De'Nidra wants to kill you."

De'Nidra turned and narrowed her eyes at him. "That is not going to help Tem'Aldar. He can find out that part after I get my hands on him." She huffed. "He is just as likely done picking through the rubble in this jungle somewhere and maybe back to camp already. If some jungle predator hasn't eaten him first."

Tem gave her a roguish grin. "Fat chance of that. The boy is too slick to get trapped by a predator. But you're right De', eventually he will get hungry and drag his tired carcass back to eat and you can finish his job the adventure did not."

De'Nidra's hands reached for Tem, and he drew her into a hug. "I'm going to throttle him, Tem'Aldar, for scaring me half to death. If anything happened to him, I don't know what I would do."

He patted her back. "You are going to be a wonderful mother, De'."

"You think so?" She asked tenderly.

Tem'Aldar nodded and whispered into her ear. "Yes, you will. If you don't kill me first."

She fisted him hard in the gut, extracting a grunt. "Believe me Tem'Aldar. You won't get off that easy."

Ivan and Lil waited in the large room below the spiraling staircase. Power pulsed up the long beam of light, turning the dark metal translucent. Tara, Edward and Va'Yone stood near the center as a slash of Light ripped the air. A golden sphere taller than the grew blossomed and fell in on itself before a purple globe in strobing radiance took its place. The event horizon cleared, giving a view of the jungle and the rear of the forgotten starship.

Lil's voice drifted to them as she slipped into Ivan's arms. *I will see you again soon. Thank you for my life. Go with our love. You are family... always.*

Va'Yone ran to Lil and hugged her. "When I study. It is your voice that I hear. Your translation of the book helped me grow. In that way, you are the real hero Lil. You saved us all." He gave her and Ivan one last squeeze and then ran through the Gate. Edward was next.

Tara held them in her sight for memory's sake. *I will see you both soon, brother and sister, when we are all home and safe together.* Ivan bowed his head in acknowledgement, and Lil felt the ridged surface of the glyph on her forehead with her fingertips. Tara walked through the Mage Gate and it winked out.

De'Nidra greeted them with her angry voice. "Where in the seven hells have you been, Va'Yone?" She fell on her knees before him and hugged him. "I could strangle you. Tem'Aldar and I were worried sick."

Tears ran down her cheeks, making Va'Yone's neck wet. "Tara needed my help, and there wasn't any time. I'm sorry De'Nidra. If I would have known, I would have left a note or something."

Edward stepped up. "If Va'Yone had not come, we would be dead. I am sure of that. He saved us De'Nidra. He saved us all."

Tara nodded her support.

"You're still in trouble, Va'Yone. Go to your tent and tend to your books. We have lessons and you are already late. You have an hour to get ready. I have a pop test. Now get!"

"Yes, master." Va'Yone said as he ran for his tent, sparing Tara a smile. She gave him a wink.

"Don't punish him too greatly, De'Nidra." Tara said, pleading on Va'Yone's behalf. "He saved us and, as a result, he has grown. I think you will find out to what extent during your test. Besides, that is my little brother. So take it easy. Okay?"

De'Nidra smiled at her. "You are ever the protective sister. However, we have a lot of work to do to figure out this ship. It has been killing me to wait. I promised Va'Yone we would explore it together. And I need to teach him a few things before he is ready. Thank you for bringing him home." There was something motherly in De'Nidra's tone. Something that said that as long as she lived, she would see Va'Yone trained and safe.

The other Gate collapsed as a new thread of Light ripped the atmosphere next to it. Tara did not need to look to see it blossom into a Mage Gate. "I will check on your progress soon. I hope to help you figure it out. But for now, I have other things I must do." Tara turned to Edward. "Time to go home, my love." With that, Tara and Edward walked through. Beyond lay the cobblestone square of Coth'Venter Cathedral of Light and the three-tiered fountain with Ram'Del.

Chapter 43 Weary Trumpet's Call

"Owed to all those who go to war for their people. That great branch of a heroic limb that sacrifices self for the tree of liberty. They give away their futures so that ours may unfold. In their honor, we live; in our memories, they endure. We hand down to our children the seeds of their sacrifice, in memory of all that is due. We salute you."

As the suns climbed toward first midday, the sky brightened, with clouds drifting lazily, puffy and white. A warm summer breeze carried the scents of the tall grass in Dan'Nor's Field thick with flowers. Past the grand cathedral, a grey horizon loomed, where smoky ash billowed from Forge 'Wrath's Peak, nestled deep in the Twisted Lands.

Edward and Tara climbed the vast approach, ascending the grand stair. Two House Guards flanked the massive doors opening for them as they went inside. Normally, these halls bustled with knights and clerics. But today they were hollow. Save but for families that had not yet found homes or those in service, it was silent.

But that did not last long. Mic'Ieal, the First of Her Guard, stood waiting by the great dining hall.

Mic'Ieal bowed low. "My Lady Tara, and my Lord Edward, I have a message given to me by Al'len and Lord Commander Antoff." He held out a roll of parchment sealed with gold wax, impressed with a white dragon.

Tara took it, "Thank you Mic'Ieal." She broke the seal with a thumbnail and read it.

"What is it?" Edward asked. Tara handed him the letter.

Edward's words hung in the air, each one heavier than the last. "They've started the campaign? Without us?" His eyebrows knit together, a storm brewing in his eyes as he released a sigh heavy with the weight of unspoken fears and frustrations.

"No, '*Edward*', because we were busy, and they needed to set up the troops," Tara said. "Life does not stop happening everywhere, just because we are not there in the middle of it.".."

Edward's gaze lingered on Tara, a storm of unvoiced feelings swirling in his eyes. "I just... I imagined us riding out with them, you know? Together, as one. Like the stories."

Tara shook her head. "It will not be like heroes in the stories. People will be dying for us, Edward. Some needlessly if we are not there to save them. So let's have something to eat and clean up. Then we will do our best to get there before the fight begins. Shall we? We can't fight on an empty stomach."

"I'm just saying it would have been nice if they waited. That's all." Edward growled.

"Edward!" Tara jabbed him with a finger. He winced from bruised flesh and strained muscles. "Quit complaining. Let's have something to eat and get ready."

Edward spread his arms. "What did I do?"

"You know what you did, Edward," Tara said. "Now come along."

Mic'Ieal held the door, raising his eyebrow, whispering out of the side of his mouth. "I fear you are in trouble again, my Lord."

"I know," Edward scowled. "My mouth does that sometimes." He followed Tara into the dining hall.

Freshly bathed and dressed, Tara reflected on sharing a bath with Edward—a bit of indulgence she occasionally allowed. After all, he had been injured for her. It was a practical decision, she reasoned; someone needed to tend to her wounds. *That was the fine excuse she allowed him to justify it with.* Yet, there lingered a question in her mind about Edward's recent change, a transformation. Al'len, she knew, would have insights into what Edward had become.

After a bath—which took much longer than expected—Tara donned her thief's armor. Mic'Ieal had it cleaned and tended during the bathing. They headed down the long flights of stone stairs from the rectory and into the stable yard. The suns had declined passed second midday, and the breeze had picked up the aroma of horses and the forge fire mixed with the tall grass. The doors to the stable stood open. Grooms came out to meet them. The smith and his apprentice, a girl with a ready smile, bowed deep in heavy leather aprons before returning to the ringing of the hammer and pumping the bellows.

The grooms bowed as well. "Will my Lady Tara and Lord Edward be requiring their horses?" The boys snickered.

One boy had brown hair, and the other had reddish blonde. Tara looked at them and smiled. "You look like sturdy lads. Are you new?"

"No, my Lady Tara. I am Mens'vil." The redhead said.

"I am Nate. Father is the smith. Dad sometimes brings us to work. When the others need a day off."

Mens'vil was clearly shy. "The girl is my sister. She wants to be a lady like you... I mean, my Lady." He blushed.

Tara bent down, digging in her purse, and held out three silver coins. Her eyes sparkled with amusement. "I will have to take an interest in her then. Give these coins to your father. He can decide if you have earned them later. We won't be needing our horses." She smiled, knowing the boy had snickered because the horses were missing. Tara nodded, "Now, off with you." At that, the boys ducked a bow and ran back to their father.

Tara walked to the gate. Edward lifted the latch. It moved freely and smelled of oil. He pulled open the small gate and waited for Tara to walk through. The Field of Dan'Nor waved in the wind, grass rippling outward toward the trees that bordered the Lost Kings Highway. Above, Edward felt it before he could even see them in the sky.

"Oh, no you don't Tara. I don't mind the Mage Gate anymore. But, I am going to draw the line at riding dragons."

Tara paused, tilting her head slightly as she regarded him, her eyebrow arching in surprise. "You sense their presence?" Her voice was soft yet laced with intrigue, reflecting the ever-deepening layers of their connection and the mysteries that still lay between them. How profound was his change? *What have I done to you, Edward?*

"I do." Edward said. He looked up and pointed to the sky above the Leaf Water. The dragons were little more than speckles in the sky. "Look at that Tara. There are so many of them now."

From a distance, they looked like a small flock of birds. But as they grew closer, the detail became clearer. A black and white dragon much larger than the others flew towards them. Tara closed her eyes and let the sensations flood her. Hearts pounding deep as kettledrums. The wind coursed over her wings that beat in mighty strokes. Comfort and oneness flooded their bond. Voices of others questioned. Feelings reached out for hers. The Black silenced them with a thought. He did it kindly. There was a need for introduction first and the little ones were getting ahead of themselves. They reached their zenith above the field. Tara felt her stomach drop when they rolled, tucking their wings in, and fell like darts from the air. Inhaling sharply, Edward took her hand.

Falling, falling, the wind roared in her ears louder than thunder. The ground came faster and faster. They blazed below like life, like liquid fire. And just as it seemed too late, surely they would hit the ground. Mighty wing snapped open with a pop, like wind filling a sail. The bulk of the dragons passed only meters above their heads. *You have grown again.* Tara's mind whispered to them.

Edward ducked, feeling the force ripple through the trees and grass. "Take it Easy there!" he shouted. In response, the Black let out a roar of satisfaction, scattering a cloud of bloodbats from the cathedral's tower.

Tara sighed, "They are just greeting us, Edward. It is their way."

"Showing off is more like it," Edward snorted. "Tara, you can't expect me to ride." He pointed. "That."

With majestic grace, the dragons carved arcs in the sky, a ballet of Power and precision. The White descended first, its massive form cutting through the air with the ease of a leaf on the breeze, only to arrest its motion just above the ground with a display of strength that sent waves through the grass. His bulk belied his elegance. Powerful wings beat in a stall above, kicking up grass and dirt. Coating Edwards mail.

"Great." Edward said, wiping the dirt and grass from his face and hair. "We just bathed."

The White only snorted his reply as the Black came in. Powerfully, he suspended his bulk above the grass that rippled as if in a hurricane. Seventeen meter wings held his mass. He bellowed as his talons tore into the dirt. Last of all were the twelve Dragon Hounds of every color. The Black sent: *These are Dragon Hounds no longer. They are in their place. Servants and guardians of Dragon Lords, You're bonded.*

They landed one at a time. The Black and White towered over them. Tara made as if she might approach, and even at twice the size of a warhorse, they skittered back. She named them Dragon Horses.

Tara halted mid-step, the realization dawning in her eyes before it ever touched her lips. "They're afraid," she whispered to the wind, her heart sinking as the distance between them felt more than just physical.

They fear you. Said the White.

The Black sniffed at her, *With good reason. You have history with one of them.* He said. *They feared us as well before we received them into our hold.* He snorted. Slowly, the Dragon Horses advanced, drool dripped from the maws, and it smoked in the grass. The largest was first with red scales edged in black. *We are Are'Nok, if it pleases the bond holder. I know you from the cave where I scouted you for the Dark Lords.*

Tara's mind murmured. She slowly advanced, holding out her hand. *I remember. I sent you a wind to confuse our trail. You were too smart to fall for it.* Edward was going to move closer. But Tara motioned with her other hand, warding him off. Are'Nok breathed her scent in, filling his lungs and his mind with her. Her mind whispered to him through the bond. *We are enemies no more. You are a family now. Not servants, friends. That is my command.*

Tara knelt down and the Dragon Horses lurched forward, looking as if they would swarm her. Edward was going to draw his sword but warning shot through the bond and he left his hand to rest white knuckled on the pommel. They all breathed her in. Like, through her scent, they could absorb her being.

Tara touched each of every color. They bowed their heads and backed away as she stood. She walked over to the White and he leaned his head down for her to mount.

The Black lumber toward Edward. "No Tara. I said I draw the line at riding dragons." She had already settled above on the White's shoulders. To Edward's eyes, she truly looked like a goddess.

Tara raised an eyebrow at him. "Did you enjoy our long bath together, Edward?"

Edward nodded. "I did, my love. It was quite refreshing."

Tara gripped large scales along the ridges. "Well, if you want to enjoy another one with me, Edward. I would suggest you get your ass on that dragon." She gave him a brilliant smile.

The Black nudged him with his snout, almost toppling him over. *You better heed your bond holder's command if you wish to mate.* He leaned his neck lower. *Females of our species often assert dominance, and we males typically yield. I suggest you do the same.*

"Gods above, that's an image I could've lived without," Edward grimaced, assaulted by vivid, unsolicited visions.

Tara burst out with laughter, then covered it with batting her eyes at him. "It's how they communicate, Edward. They can't help it."

Edward looked up at Tara, grabbed a fist full of scale and climbed up. His armor clanked as it hit the hard ridges of the Black's neck. The Black bellowed a roar once Edward settled. It reverberated through his body. Edward nearly shite his armor as it spread its wings. With a powerful beat, he rose from the ground. *Hold tight Gray Knight, I would be... irritated if you fell.* The image of him tumbling from the dragon's back made him swallow hard.

"Oh... shit!" Edward cried as they rattled rocking trees, flying over the road, the Black's mass gaining speed and altitude.

Tara giggled with joy as the White leaped into the sky to follow.

Chapter 44 Fealty Or Murder

Justice is not a debate. It either is, or it is not.

Al'len, the construct of slumbering EL'ALue, the Maid of Light, stepped onto the balcony of the temple, her gaze sweeping over the capital city of Alum'Tai in the Lands of Light. The largest sun, known as the Elder Brother, slid slowly towards the horizon, painting the clouds above the square in an angry red. Smoke wafted up from the streets, littered with paper and smoldering debris. City folk were still destroying everything not nailed down.

Torches held high, they were threatening to burn the church. Old clerics and knights struggled not to hurt them, just to keep them away. A man screamed, "Liars!" while a woman clutching a babe in her arms cried out, "Frauds and thieves."

They had not yet seen Al'len. But they would. Lightning forked across the sky, a lattice of light preceding the thunderous roar that echoed the moment a man struck a cleric. "Shame!" boomed Al'len, her divine voice louder than the thunder rumbling above. It shook the square in a quake that threatened to knock mortals from their feet. Al'len ignited and drew every eye. "Shame and sorrow!" Her voice touched everyone in a whisper.

Al'len's arms swept the crowd. "Is this what comes from greedy mortals and sleeping gods?" She shook her head. Sadness permeated the square, emanating from Al'len with the visceral pain of a fresh wound, as profound as the loss of Ram'Del. "Is it?" She boomed as lightning blew stone from the fountain, toppling a Priest Knight statue above. It fell on the cobble street, shattering. "Is this what you want?"

The man that struck the cleric yelled while pointing at the clerics. "They are liars!"

"Thieves!' the woman roared, her voice echoed by the crowd's unanimous agreement.

"Yes!" answered Al'len. "Thieves and liars! Not just for you, but for me as well. They stole truth and freedom! And what shall their punishment be?" Antoff pushed Gan'Vile out onto the balcony. He wore a simple cleric's robe. But they knew who he was.

The crowd's anger crescendoed, voices uniting in a chant, "Thief! Liar! Give him to us."

Al'len's gaze smoldered as it fell upon Gan'Vile. As he attempted to retreat, Antoff propelled him forward with a rough shove. "Time to face your people, Your Eminence." The Holy Seat rested heavily on the rail.

"Wait," he stood, lifting his hands to quiet them. But the crowd roared.

The storm abruptly cleared, and the night stilled. "Is this what you want?" Al'len's whisper carried, pointing at Gan'Vile. "Is this truly your desire?" Al'len's whisper spanned the square, a soft murmur with the force of a decree. Threads of light spiraled from her fingertips, encircling Lord Gan'Vile in a luminous embrace, casting ethereal shadows that danced like torchflies beneath the starlit sky.

"No, no, no!" Gan'Vile's voice cracked, the desperation palpable as he fought against his constraints. "You swore fairness!" He yelled while being lifted from the balcony like a beacon high into the air, encased in the fiery grip of an angry goddess.

Al'len's voice vibrated through the square, and the ground shook. "Will this satisfy your lust for blood? Will this pay the price?"

They cried. "Yes! Give him to us."

"So be it," Al'len said. Sadness and sorrow filled the square. "Here is your justice." Gan'Vile slowly lowered toward the masses that swarmed in, waiting like rabid predators.

"Justice!" the crowd bellowed.

"Justice then," Al'len said, nodding her head. She lowered him further, just out of reach. "Justice." The Maid of Light tested the word. "Can there be justice without mercy? Or mercy without forgiveness? Is this what you have become? You who were to be a Light unto the *Lands of El'idar*. The shining city where love and Light never sleep. And what can I say to you now? You break the heart of gold and still not one tear?" But Al'len wept and her tears were of a goddess and her pity flooded the streets. "I pity you. Is that how you would have me judge you? Without love? Without Light? No mercy? No forgiveness... Is that the justice you seek? If it is, then you are in the wrong land. I suggest you move out." Al'len lowered Gan'Vile to the cobble of the square and the people moved away in fear.

The crowd reached for Al'len. Some fell to their knees. "No... Let us stay."

"Very well then." Al'len nodded. "I grant you parole. Extend the mercy to Gan'Vile, that you would have me extend to you." They made way for him to leave the square. "Before you go Gan'Vile. There's no need for me to tell you that you are being removed. However, mercy requires I grant you a boon. You will from this day forth until your ending receive one gold monthly, which you will live off of in service of the poor. I recommend you spend it wisely. I will be watching and so will they. Your titles and all that goes with it is forfeit. You will spend the balance of your life distributing your wealth and lands to the poor. Be diligent, you have made many."

One of the old Priest Knights grabbed him roughly by the collar and gathered him into the church. The people were done with him and they did not protest. It was as if Gan'Vile did not exist. "Go home. Tomorrow, you clean the streets. You will spend your own labor and money on repairing it. When I return, and it will be soon. Our capital, Alum 'Tai, a beacon of Light, shall once again radiate with love and mercy."

Al'len and Antoff stepped off of the balcony. From below, the crowd watched as the Light from a Mage Gate blossomed, strobed, and then vanished. EL'ALue, the Maid of Light and her Hero were gone.

Modred looked out over the Darkened Gates, the doorway to the Blackened Lands bulged with troops. Most were Zoruks. Behind the battlements, their camps teemed with war tents, a recklessly assembled hodgepodge to match the writhing masses. Between each tribe, banners with symbols declaring their line and lusty nature. Startled, Modred turned and then knelt on one knee. His wings were powerful, cloak like, swept back as he bowed his head, still overshadowing his Lord. "Forgive me, Great Lord, since your exchange, I can no longer detect you."

"Pity that. No more undead chill?" Moros said, "I am sure you enjoyed having the warning." Moros turned. "Walk with me Modred."

Modred, the legendary Great Black Demon, trailed behind. Previously towering over Amorath, who now inhabiting the child's form, could easily overpower him. His master's new form did not fool him. If anything, Amorath was stronger than ever. He took slow strides, an irritating mixture of waiting and moving. The heavy tap of Amorath's staff in the child's hand was grating. Indeed, among the captains of other Dark Lords of the Council, he and his brothers were a laughingstock. *We will see who is laughing when war kicks off. I have survived many. You pretenders, the replaced of fallen captains and warlords, don't even have a memory of it. We will see how far you make it with your Dark Lords, when a goddess of Light appears and bodies start hitting the ground. Amorath has proven himself a survivor. The oldest of the Lords to survive the Breaking of the Balance and the God Wars both. The final aftermath will reveal who is laughing in the end!*

Moros climbed the stone stair that led up the tower and then above the gate. The Twisted Land stretched out. The perfect killing ground. Half a league between the gates. Further, the walls of the cliff sides revealed a gorge. It was as if some gods, with blade and beast, had plowed through it. Straight and narrow all the way to the dusty cliff sides. Moros pulled an eyeglass from his robes and sighted down it. The Torn Flowage and the bridge battlements were black with troops. "I gave you a chore, and you can tell me, Lord Modred, of your successes. Tell me you have found all the grain rats in our bin. Tell me you know were De'Nidra, the Daughter of shadows is and you have discovered her plans?"

A shiver ran down Mordred's spine. That was Amorath all right, child's body or not. That was him. It came out in a rush, like a dam opening. He had failed. "I cannot tell you any of that, Great Lord. I sent a possessed to question the mayor of RavenHof. Afterword, the poor fool was so scared that he ran. Discarding his dead butler in the alley behind his house. In a word, my Lord. De'Nidra is gone. She has not surfaced. Thus, there is nothing to find. Yet, the war will draw her out. Ever was she a spinner of webs and shadows, my Lord? Twisting her webs in the dark."

"Modred, De'Nidra is wiser than most know." Moros replied. "It is why I pushed for her seat on the Dark Counsil." Moros said. "I saw this coming, Modred, and it was an epic failure. As the war is here, you and your brothers shall lead the defense. Remove yourself from my presence and go to the bridge. Perhaps if you do what you do best, I can let you live a little longer. Watch yourself Modred. If the Maid of Light does not kill you, De'Nidra will. She hates you."

Modred's deep voice trembled. "As you command, Great Lord," he thought, his mind a whirlwind of fear and resolve as he spread his bat-like wings and took flight for the bridge over the Torn Flowage. *That was Amorath, for sure.*

Within Moros, Amorath whispered. *Have I not served well, my Lord? Surely Modred cannot believe you are the child now?*

You have done well. Moros offered. He held out his arm and Little Modred landed on it with a chirp. *I told you Amorath, if you pleased me, I would give you the use of a construct, did I not? Something with which to feel and move about?*

Yes, my Lord, I want that. Amorath's voice shook with anticipation.

Moros opened a channel to Little Modred.

Life's sensations flooded through him—a cascade of smells, the caress of wind, and the renewed awareness of muscle and physical form. The channel opened wider and some of Amorath's consciousness flooded in. He was not fully in the little beast. But he had control of a kind.

Moros lifted his arm and Amorath flew off. It was a child's giggling following him. However, deep within the higher reality, his laughter would shake worlds.

⁂

A wind rose out of the Twisted Lands. Over the mountains, beyond the smoking summit of Forge 'Wrath, spilling into the star filled night sky of the Vale Lands. Below, in the grassy fields amidst the Lost Road, the Army of the Light made camp.

It smelled of cooked meat and hot buttered bread, mixed with the scent of Stingers, dragons and warriors in need of a bath. For Tara, it was the smell of home. It was the place that she belonged. Her House Guard had pitched a tent for them in the middle of the formation, not separated from the Priest Knights and Clerics of the Light, near Al'len's and Antoff's tent. As usual, they had her surrounded. Edward was off getting something to eat. That was as good an excuse as any to be rid of him for an hour. Tara wanted to speak with Al'len alone.

Throwing back the flap of their tent, the banner of a fist and two bolts faced by two dragons rippled overhead. It snapped in the wind that smelled of the meadow and the traces of the dust of the twisted Lands. Two of her warriors slammed a fisted spear into chest armor. She inclined her head as she passed by. Then she picked her way through the din to Al'len. The tent flap was open, and within, Al'len examined a map and scouting reports.

Tara cleared her throat. "If you are busy, Al'len, I can come back later?" Al'len's armor was a white plate with gold edges, a tan cloak in matching trim, and a white dragon in flight. Her helmet was on the table, holding down the papers that ruffled in the wind beneath it.

"No, not at all. Welcome." Al'len reached for Tara, and with smiles, they hugged each other. "What is it, child? She raised an eyebrow at her with a kind of motherly interest. I said you could always come with your questions, did I not?"

Tara nodded. But her gut felt tight. She didn't want to ask. *There is nowhere else to get the answers about what I have done to Edward.*

Tara winced as Al'len held her out by the shoulders to have a look at her. Al'len cocked her head in a half smile. Beneath her hands, green-blue light pulsed cold like ice and hot as boiling water as it threaded through her. Then it stopped, as suddenly as it came, and the pain was gone. "I am sure you did not come for a healing. Let's call it a bonus." Al'len gave her shoulders a squeeze before letting go. "Now. Out with it, child, what has your tongue?"

Tara tried to sound normal, but it ran out of her as fluttery as the Hornbees in her stomach. "I have done something to Edward again." Tears welled up. "It just happened, Al'len, and I don't know why."

Al'len raised an eyebrow at her. "That does not tell me what you have done, Tara. Can you narrow it down a bit, or do I need to have a look at him?"

"Ivan was gone, and it was just Edward and I, Vam'Phire surrounded us. I knew he had access to my channel. It was desperate, Al'len. So I sent him Power, and he took it. I don't know what I have done." A tear ran down her cheek. "I just keep changing everything. Why can't I stop?"

"I see," Al'len grumbled under her breath. Something about children playing with fire sometimes get burned. "Edward has become your Knight. But what is he and at what cost? You provided the Power to change his reality. But it was Edward that made the choice of what he would become. In that moment, Tara, he embodied what you needed most. And that need was a construct of your shared experience."

Tara covered her mouth in fear, but Al'len went on. "My clerics and elders train Priest Knights throughout their entire lives to understand what it means to be a Priest Knight and, more importantly, what it does not mean. What they embody and how it works. When I bond with them, they are ready for it, molded and shaped into the same image. Edward had the training he knew and your need at the moment. That was all. It was a wonder his body could even undergo the transformation. He should be dead. That means you have been teaching him, Tara, whether you are aware of it or not." Al'len shook her head and tapped her on the tip of the nose with a finger. "And you are not supposed to be doing that yet. You are unique, Tara. That makes you dangerous to the others like me."

"What do you mean?" Tara asked.

"You have not ascended. Not yet. This will scare the other gods. So don't speak of it. Also, think long and hard about what you want Edward to become. I recommend you watch him closely because he is the mold that all the rest of your knights will come from."

"No, no more knights, Al'len," Tara's voice broke, a mix of defiance and despair. "I want none of this."

Al'len's face was sad. "Neither did I. Yet it still comes."

Antoff came in carrying their dinner. "What comes?"

"Men, at all the wrong moments." Al'len mused.

"I could leave. If you two require privacy?" Antoff said. His icy blue eyes flicked between their faces.

"No." Al'len took the plate. "You are here and I am hungry. Tara, have you eaten yet?"

The deluge that Al'len had dropped on her still dazed Tara. "No. I sent Edward ahead. I told him I would join him."

I see. Al'len said. "Antoff and I have missed you. Now, sit with me and share my plate and tell us all about your adventure with the Vam'Phires."

"The what!" Antoff said. "I can't let you out of my sight. You are always in to stuff way over your head."

"Hush Antoff. She is going to tell the story, and this one is going to be good, I can tell." Al'len pushed the plate toward Tara and rubbed her hands together. "Now, sit down."

They all took a seat, and Tara told the story.

Chapter 45 Feast For Gods

"The gods eat lives and devour souls, but it is you who choose what they eat."

Beneath the arid dust of the Twisted Lands, in the Bastion of Light, Sib'Bal, the Veil of Darkness, channeled Power into the arches' inset holes. Not clumsily like that old fool Mel'Temdel, but with the full knowledge of how it worked. The device, using nanomachines no larger than grains of sand, crafted a three-dimensional world before her eyes. A world resurrected from a technology long dead. The globe spun before her, glyphs shimmering to life across its surface, blinking like ancient stars. It spun and stopped at the address. She waited for the sequence to complete and then zoomed in.

The arches whirled until the resonance frequency matched. It became a blur of Power erupting into a brilliant ball. Finally, like a giant eye opening after sleep, the event horizon cleared, revealing a mirror image of the room she was in, except for the fifteen-foot Dominion that stepped through.

Behind him, an endless mass of hellish warriors waited. His red eyes, gleaming with demonic cunning, surveyed the room. With a spread of his vast wings, he bellowed a command in the ancient demon tongue.

Sib'Bal let the portal collapse behind his bulk. She felt his eyes brush over her as he hungrily licked his lips. Her beads clicked and flashed in the torch lit room as he traced her breast and hips through transparent silks. "Mind your filthy tongue, demon, and keep your eyes in your head. Unless you want me to pull them out. You are not my type." The strange thing was, he could not tell whether he was speaking her language or she was speaking his.

The Dominion, a king in his own right, bristled at the woman's insolence. Mage or not, she would learn her place and have proper respect. "Open that blasted portal and let my warriors through. Where are my servants, Mel'Temdel and Mist? If you have hurt them, you will answer to me." He reached for her as if to take her by the waist.

His palm, as broad as a saddle, lunged at her, its fingers thick as saplings, tipped with nails sharp as spears, but it did not get the chance. Around Sib'Bal, reality itself seemed to warp and ripple, distorting time and space. Chains with thick links like golden fire reached up from blocks of metal within the box forming on the floor beside him, wrapping his body, legs, and arms. When he was dealt with, time rang like a bell and lurched back to normal.

The Dominion, king of Demons in his world, was a slave once more. He struggled against the glowing bonds, but they did not give way. He spat his hate at her. All of his fury. Sib'Bal felt a flicker of amusement at the Dominion's bravado, her heart steady as the ancient rhythms of her Power.

Sib'Bal tapped her plump red lips with a red lacquered nail. She wrapped his face in a golden gag. "Good puppy. There you see. You are hardly worth the trifle." Then Sib'Bal clicked her tongue as she examined her nails. Distracted by a chip in her nail, she fixed it first, of course, before going on. "First things first, demon, and perhaps your biggest mistake. I am not by any stretch of your tiny, tiny imagination, a mage."

He struggled, and she raised a pensive brow at him; the bonds constricted like snakes driving the air from massive lungs.

Sib'Bal placed her hands behind her back and paced a little like a girl on a fresh spring day. She kicked at the hem of her silks as the room filled with the scent of trees, flowers, and the salt sea of her garden. She said as she watched him struggle for air. "Oh, I'm sorry. Let me loosen those bonds so you can breathe. Remember now." She smiled like he was a handsome prince and she was his conquest. "If you displease me, I will not loosen them again, and you will die. Do you understand the rules?"

He nodded and when his chains eased; he sucked air raggedly into his lungs, but he remained still and did not speak. *This is not a mage? Then what is she?* He listened with interest.

"My name is Sib'Bal, the Vail of Darkness, the oldest of the Elder gods and mortal before the Breaking. Do not think to bargain with me. You will either do my bidding as a king, or as a mindless slave. That is the deal. Take it or leave it. It matters none to me." She raised an eyebrow questioningly. "Now, what will it be? Lobotomized or whole?" A seductive smile played on her lips as the gag left his bleeding mouth. Her eyes glowed as if the irises were on fire. For the first time, the Dominion an eater of worlds felt something he had never felt before. Small and filled with fear.

Dawn's first light broke, the morning mist hugging the vale as the Elder Brother crested the mountaintops, its rays casting long, bladed shadows across the swaying grass. A league from the Torn Flowage's bridge, Al'len and Tara conjured Mage Gates. Their magic tearing through the fabric of reality. Above, startled Crag Lions scattered as mammoth spheres of light, pulsing at the brink of collapse, transformed the tainted terrain into blooming spheres of strobing purple haze, clearing like fog from a lens. Tara and Edward, followed by the House Guard in one, and Al'len, her hero Antoff and the Warriors of Light, poured out like a flood twelve abreast.

Atop the bridge, Modred unfurled his wings and brandished his sword, its blood gem throbbing with life energy. His command, "Mages Spells!" echoed, igniting the battlements with the glow of Mage staffs. A protective dome shimmered into existence, lightning skittering across its surface in anticipation of the onslaught. Crossbows rose in unison, their bearers' cries mingling with fear and determination. Amidst them, EL'ALue's voice summoned the anger of lightning from the heavens, a tempest of fury.

Blinding it flashed, falling in ropes of twisting Power as the sky turned to blood, leaving the air charged with the smell of ozone. Once, twice again and again until the shield threatened to fall. As if on cue, on the ridges above, Mage Gates opened and Zoruks poured out like black oil, firing a hail of bolts from above and running down ridges. Falling before the charge, Zoruk bodies tumbling like hay beneath a scythe as Stingers swung bladed tails splitting flesh in concert with the Priest Knights lowered heavy lances.

Tara looked up as fear crossed her face, and time rippled out. She was the center. A single stone tossed into a pond. The world slowed near to breaking. Reaching up, Darkness and Light spread out like a sheet burning the deadly thorns to ash. But she did not get them all. Slowly, they came. The tips penetrating armor and flesh in long, low screams as warriors fell like leaves in hail. Time rang vibrating before shuttering forward.

First the Warriors of the Light and then beside her, Edward ignited. Paragons of Light, they destroyed all that stood before them.

Tara's Dragons plummeted from the clouds like darts towards rivers aflame. They executed their roles flawlessly: a single incendiary sweep before withdrawing out of range, awaiting her next summons. Angels of death breathed out as wings popped like sails. Living fire devoured two strips five spans wide from the horde on the ridge above. Acrid smoke rolled into the valley, choking lungs. Dragon Horses reached with talons, ripping Zoruks from ledges, soring high before letting them fall. Zoruks screamed as they plummeted towards the ground, rushing towards their deaths.

Was the tide turning? In all the confusion, Tara did not know. She still had hope that they would destroy the enemy and she would make the world safe. She could avenge Cur'Ra's death.

That hope turned to despair when the Black sent her an image of a massive portal opening above Forge 'Wrath Keep. He blinked, and the second lens dropped into place, and his irises constricted. They watched in fear as it cleared and an endless stream of demons vomited out. One larger than all the rest black as his scales drank the light of the morning suns. He glowed, and with a roar of hunger, his skin ignited.

Sparkling, the Steps of glass shimmered majestically. Within her stasis chamber, she slept. The window above her face was frosted, showing only an outline of the being within. Her view drifted beyond the peaks of glass where the river flowed from rents in an ancient cistern. Low along the water, her mind followed, then climbing above the Smoking Plains where she had destroyed the army that had killed Ram'Del. She followed all the way to Forge 'Wrath Keep. Above it, she watched a river from hell spilling out. Creatures from a destroyed world ready to eat another. Some flew toward the Lands of Light, But a writhing mass headed for Antoff and the Army of Light. *Never again*!

Within the temple, the lid of her chamber slid open. After an epoch of sleep, EL'ALue, the Maid of Light, sat up.

End Book

Epilogue

"The Gray Walker strides between Darkness and Light. In her hands are stars and glory. Worlds will shatter like breaking glass and melt like wax in the fires of her wrath. In covenant with the Maid of Light, they shall mend torn fabric and make crooked ways straight. And woe unto you who dwell in Darkness, for together, they are as a furious fire. Who can abide them? Not the wicked. And who shall witness their sun's rise? None but the righteous. Let all the heavens tremble and the foundations of El'idar roar; let the Darkness flee your sight, for the radiant glory of the Light shall burst forth in their Knights once more!"

Prophecy of the Gray Walker. From the lost author's Third Chronicle of the Shattered Age.

Afterword

Thank you for reading Between The Darkness And The Light, Chronicles Of The Night Book Two. The third book will be released soon and if you want to preorder, please check it out at https://www.glhouser.com/where links will be available to your favorite vendors as soon as it is ready. If you join the newsletter, I will email you updates and answer your author's questions.

If you enjoyed this book, please leave a review at the place of purchase. I cannot begin to tell you how thankful I am for your support and patronage. Thank you so much for reading Between The Darkness And The Light: Chronicles Of The Night Book Two and I can't wait to get you the next book in this exciting epic fantasy/sci-fi hybrid series.

Milton Keynes UK
Ingram Content Group UK Ltd.
UKHW050638010524
441987UK00020B/627